THE EXPANSE
AND PHILOSOPHY

SO FAR OUT INTO
THE DARKNESS

The Blackwell Philosophy and Pop Culture Series
Series editor: William Irwin

A spoonful of sugar helps the medicine go down, and a healthy helping of popular culture clears the cobwebs from Kant. Philosophy has had a public relations problem for a few centuries now. This series aims to change that, showing that philosophy is relevant to your life—and not just for answering the big questions like "To be or not to be?" but for answering the little questions: "To watch or not to watch *South Park*?" Thinking deeply about TV, movies, and music doesn't make you a "complete idiot." In fact it might make you a philosopher, someone who believes the unexamined life is not worth living and the unexamined cartoon is not worth watching.

THE EXPANSE AND PHILOSOPHY

SO FAR OUT INTO THE DARKNESS

Edited by

Jeffery L. Nicholas

WILEY Blackwell

Registered Office
John Wiley & Sons, Inc., 111 River Street, Hoboken, NJ 07030, USA

Editorial Office
111 River Street, Hoboken, NJ 07030, USA

For details of our global editorial offices, customer services, and more information about Wiley products visit us at www.wiley.com.

Wiley also publishes its books in a variety of electronic formats and by print-on-demand. Some content that appears in standard print versions of this book may not be available in other formats.

Library of Congress Cataloging-in-Publication Data

Names: Nicholas, Jeffery, 1969- editor.
Title: The Expanse and philosophy : so far out into the darkness / edited
    by Jeffery L. Nicholas.
Description: First edition. | Hoboken, NJ : Wiley-Blackwell, 2022. |
    Series: The Blackwell philosophy and pop culture series | Includes
    bibliographical references and index.
Identifiers: LCCN 2021042942 (print) | LCCN 2021042943 (ebook) | ISBN
    9781119755609 (paperback) | ISBN 9781119755616 (adobe pdf) | ISBN
    9781119755623 (epub)
Subjects: LCSH: Expanse (Television program) | Corey, James S. A. Expanse.
    | Philosophy on television. | Philosophy in literature.
Classification: LCC PN1992.77.E97 E97 2022 (print) | LCC PN1992.77.E97
    (ebook) | DDC 791.45/72–dc23
LC record available at https://lccn.loc.gov/2021042942
LC ebook record available at https://lccn.loc.gov/2021042943

Cover Design: Wiley
Cover Image: © Expanding Universe Productions

Set in 10/12pt Sabon by Straive, Pondicherry, India

SKY10032211_122821

To all those involved in *The Expanse* world. Thank you!

Contents

Contributors:
Expanded *Rocinante* Crew List

Matthew D. Atkinson is an Associate Professor in the History and Political Science Department at Long Beach City College. He teaches classes on democratic theory, social movements, and global studies. The *Expanse* inspired him to find ways of incorporating science fiction into the global studies curriculum—a development that has met with a great deal of student enthusiasm.

Lisa Wenger Bro is a Professor of English at Middle Georgia State University who specializes in postmodernism and speculative fiction. Prioritizing, she's managed to frame and hang an "Evolution of the Cylon" poster in her office but not her actual degree. She's written and published a lot of essays and articles with semicolons in the titles and also co-edited *Monsters of Film, Fiction, and Fable: The Cultural Links between the Human and Inhuman*. Her current work explores class, capitalism, and biopolitics in science fiction. She's also exactly like Amos—she likes peaches, doesn't mind long hikes through nature, and is never quite sure which way's right.

Eric Chelstrom is Associate Professor of Philosophy at St. Mary's University in San Antonio, Texas. His research is primarily in social philosophy and phenomenology. A specific focus in recent years in his research is on the relationship between forms of collective agency as it relates to issues of oppression. He is the author of *Social Phenomenology*. Like Holden, he finds joy in a quality cup of coffee.

Diletta De Cristofaro is a Research Fellow in the Humanities based between Northumbria University, UK, and Politecnico di Milano, Italy. She is the author of *The Contemporary Post-Apocalyptic Novel: Critical Temporalities and the End Times* and the co-editor of *The Literature of the Anthropocene* (a special issue of *C21 Literature: Journal of 21st-Century Writings*, 2018). Her writings on contemporary culture, crises, and the politics of time have been published in venues like *Salon, The Conversation,*

RTÉ, b2o, *ASAP/J,* and *Critique.* She used to have a Milleresque haircut but lacked his cool (and pet nuke).

Darin DeWitt is an Associate Professor of Political Science at California State University, Long Beach, where he teaches courses in positive political theory. He studies American politics with a focus on institutions, celebrity, and conspiracy theory politics. Thanks to *The Expanse,* he'll pack a few portable lamps and water bottles on his maiden voyage to outer space.

Claire Field is a postdoctoral research fellow on the research project Varieties of Risk, based at the University of Stirling, in Scotland. The project is funded by the Arts and Humanities Research Council, and her current research focuses on what makes risks reckless. She has also published on the epistemology of incoherence. In her spare time, she is compiling the system's first comprehensive rule book for the game *Golgo*—a recklessly ambitious project that is most likely doomed.

Max Gemeinhardt is a PhD candidate in chemistry at Southern Illinois University Carbondale (SIUC). Since an early age, the philosophy of science has been an interest to him when he began his academic journey many orbits ago. His research primarily deals with the devolvement of MRI contrast agents and new methodologies to improve MRI utility for medical imaging. He has been published in several papers and book chapters on topics within the field of Nuclear Magnetic Resonance. When not busy with research or work, he is at home with his wife, three cats, carnivorous plants, and tarantula. Proudly displayed on his desk sits a model of the *Roci* next to the other great spaceships of the imagined future.

Margarida Hermida has a PhD in biology and is currently a PhD student in philosophy at the University of Bristol, UK. She works in philosophy of biology and has received a scholarship from the British Society for the Philosophy of Science for her project on the life and death of animals. She'd love to see more of the solar system, but with no Epstein drive, she's probably stuck on Earth for the time being. Which is not such a bad thing, because Earth really is the best. And she's not just saying that because she's an Earther.

Caleb McGee Husmann is an Assistant Professor of Political Science at William Peace University in Raleigh, North Carolina. His research interests include fiction and political theory, borderlands, Darwinian interventions in the social sciences, and policy narratives. In addition to his academic writing he has published two novels under the pseudonym C. McGee. He is 45 percent certain that he can beat Amos in an arm-wrestling contest.

Leonard Kahn is an Associate Dean of the College of Arts and Sciences and Associate Professor of Philosophy at Loyola University New Orleans. He works on moral theory and applied ethics and often wishes he could swear as well as Chrisjen Avasarala.

Elizabeth Kusko is an Associate Professor of Political Science at William Peace University in Raleigh, North Carolina. Although her research generally focuses upon the Narrative Policy Framework, she most recently co-edited a volume entitled *Exploring the Macabre, Malevolent, and Mysterious: Multidisciplinary Perspectives* and co-authored a chapter in that volume addressing Hannah Arendt's banality of evil in Shirley Jackson's "The Lottery." She believes that Camina Drummer is the best character in all of science fiction and has fully embraced Drummer's signature eyeliner look.

Tiago Cerqueira Lazier investigates the dynamics of human action and embedded meaning guiding people's political behavior, particularly focusing on Hannah Arendt's thought. He currently teaches at Leuphana Universität Lüneburg, Germany. As a good millennial, he also works on various projects at the intersection of philosophy, politics, literature, and technology. He is the co-founder of *Engajados* Institute of Collaborative Technologies and an associate of the Research Institute for the Defense of Democracy of Piracicaba (IPEDD), Brazil. Together with the crew of the *Rocinante*, he has been learning over the last seasons that one can act but not defeat uncertainty.

R. S. Leiby is a PhD candidate in philosophy at Boston University. Her work deals primarily with the intersection of political and moral philosophy, with a particular emphasis upon issues of transitional justice. Like James Holden, her first order of business after a near-death experience (and, to be honest, experiences more generally) is to locate the nearest coffee machine.

Stefano Lo Re earned his PhD in philosophy in 2019 from the University of St. Andrews and the University of Stirling, Scotland, and is presently a fellow of the Centre for Ethics, Philosophy and Public Affairs of the University of St Andrews (CEPPA). His research focuses on German philosopher Immanuel Kant, and currently he is working on applying the principles of Kant's political philosophy to outer space. He is an avid *Misko and Marisko* merch collector.

Andrew Magrath is the Academic Support Services Manager at Hillsborough Community College, Brandon Campus, where he occasionally still moonlights as a philosophy instructor. His interests include tutoring centers, analytic philosophy, Eastern thought, and listening to radio free slow zone. His office is easily recognizable by the *Deep Space Nine* poster on the door, and he secretly wishes he was as cool as Bobbie Draper.

Trip McCrossin teaches in the Philosophy Department at Rutgers University, where he works on the nature, history, and legacy of the Enlightenment, in philosophy and popular culture. Whenever a class goes well, he thinks of the last line on the plaque just inside the *Roci*: "A Legitimate Salvage."

Jeffery L. Nicholas edited *Dune and Philosophy* and is author of *Love and Politics: Persistent Human Desires as a Foundation for a Politics of Liberation*. He is an associate professor at Providence College, mainly because Michael O'Neill (see below) didn't quite tell the truth about how much snow Rhode Island gets. While he'd much rather be Joe Miller and is known as "the Fedora Guy" on campus, he's more likely to be the angel on Holden's shoulder acting as his conscience.

Michael J. O'Neill is Associate Professor of Philosophy at Providence College in Providence, RI. His teaching and research interests include the philosophy of history, political philosophy, and philosophical aesthetics. He is not sure if "drinking like my enemy helps me think like my enemy," but figures it is worth a try.

James S.J. Schwartz is an Assistant Professor of Philosophy at Wichita State University where they specialize in the philosophy and ethics of space exploration. They are author of *The Value of Science in Space Exploration*, co-editor with Linda Billings and Erika Nesvold of *Reclaiming Space: Progressive and Multicultural Visions of Space Exploration* (in preparation), and co-editor with Tony Milligan of *The Ethics of Space Exploration*. You can learn more about their research at www.thespacephilosopher.space. In what the UNN now describes as an unfortunate accident, James was exposed to the protomolecule at an early age, and the work continues.

Sid Simpson is Perry-Williams Postdoctoral Fellow in Philosophy and Political Science at the College of Wooster. His research focuses on late modern and contemporary political thought, continental philosophy, and critical theory. He's published research on things like Nietzsche, the Frankfurt School, international relations theory, punishment, Frankenstein, and *Black Mirror*. While he generally thinks that throwing rocks at people is rude, he's willing to make a few exceptions.

Pankaj Singh is an Assistant Professor at the University of Petroleum and Energy Studies (UPES), Dehradun, India. Although his formal research interests include philosophy of mind and existentialism, he also loves to write about pop culture and philosophy. He authored "Affordance-based Framework of Object Perception in Children's Pretend Play: A Nonrepresentational Alternative" in the *International Journal of Play*. He has submitted the final accepted draft of a chapter on India in *Indiana Jones* for the Blackwell Philosophy and Pop Culture series. He is also working on the paper "Hasan Minhaj as Philosopher: Navigating the Struggles of Identity" for *The Palgrave Handbook of Popular Culture as Philosophy*. He often fancies being part of *Roci*'s crew someday to travel to all the rings connecting to different worlds.

Diana Sofronieva is the editor of a Bulgarian short fiction zine, and an assistant professor at the University of Economics, Varna. She often mistakenly submits her short stories to academic journals and her philosophy papers to fiction zines. She just wants to know everything about ethics and about what Avasarala is wearing.

S.W. Sondheimer holds an MTS from Harvard Divinity School, the acquisition of which seemed like a really good idea at the time. She then earned a BSN from UMass Boston because she decided that being able to buy groceries and sleeping under a roof seemed like even better ideas and also, helping people is cool. She now writes social media copy for the food and shelter part and yells about books, comics, and sci-fi/fantasy/anime on ye olde inter webs. She lives in Pittsburgh with her spouse, two smaller beings with whom she shares DNA, two geriatric cats who have suddenly decided they're allowed on the table to eat leftovers, and four plants named Tanaka, Kirishima, Asta, and Yuno. At least, she thinks she does. There's always the possibility she's a protomolecule construct without a hat.

Guilel Treiber is a postdoctoral researcher at the Institute of Philosophy, KU Leuven, Belgium. He specializes in contemporary social and political thought, specifically French poststructuralism and critical theory. He has published articles on Foucault, Althusser, and Clausewitz and is currently working on his first book manuscript. He is confident that only Chrisjen Avasarala can solve the covid-19 global crisis and what will ensue. In any case, he has rented a room on Luna just to be on the safe side.

Acknowledgements

I want to thank all the contributors to this volume. They made the work significantly easier than it could have been and put up with my delays without comment. I also wish to thank Marissa Koors at Blackwell for her support of this project. Great thanks to Bill Irwin, series editor. He was much more involved than I expected, for which I am truly grateful. He probably should have made me work harder, but I won't complain.

My thanks go especially to Daniel Abraham and Ty Franck, obviously for the joy that they brought to me and the world with the book series and the TV series, but also for their agreeing so readily and being so supportive for of a book on *The Expanse and Philosophy*. I relished reading the foreword they wrote for this volume and am especially thankful for it. I also wish to thank Nick Merchant at Alcon for help with securing permission for the cover photo—how wonderful! And let me also thank the wonderful actors who have brought the series to life for us on TV. To get to relive the novels through their interpretation is a wonderful experience.

I'd like to thank my wife, Janet, for letting me buy a bigger TV to watch the show on.

Foreword

Science fiction, like philosophy, is an act of critical imagination.

The heart of philosophy is how to think meaningfully about issues that defy measurement. Great questions of philosophy—what is the universe made from, how does the natural world function, what is life and how did it begin—give way over time to science as measurement and data collection provide evidence, answers, and definition. The elements are revealed not to be earth, air, fire, and water, but atoms and the things that make up atoms. The origin of life becomes a question of chemistry producing amino acids and evolution selecting for stable replicating structures. Philosophy moves forward into the realms where data and its interpretation don't yet exist.

Science fiction is also a way to think about what we don't yet know, but can imagine. Over time, even the most rigorously meant speculations of science fiction are shown to be inaccurate or else proven true and cease to be speculative. What was once Science Fiction becomes Fantasy, and the next generation of writers and artists, actors and game designers move on to places where the truth isn't yet established.

And so, slowly, between the imagination of the artists and philosophers, and the discoveries of the scientists and engineers, the universe becomes better understood, the breadth of human knowledge is increased, and nature of culture is changed.

The Expanse is at its heart a collaborative project. As a series of novels, it began with two of us. As television show, it grew to include the efforts of literally hundreds of talented, engaged artists with specialties in set design, visual effects, acting, sound and lighting design, editing, and dozens more.

It also grew as an instance of popular culture through the efforts of fans and critics, marketing departments and online Lang Belta teachers, and the shared enthusiasm of people who came to the project and then brought other people in.

But it also began with the books that we read when we were growing up—Alfred Bester, Larry Niven, Arthur C. Clarke, C. J. Cherryh, Harry Harrison. And with the historical figures and events back to pre-classical times that we used as models for the events we imagined in our collective future. The taxonomy of what *The Expanse* is—where it begins, where it ends, what its boundaries are—is, like so many taxonomies, only clear at a distance. The border becomes much less defined as it is examined more closely.

And just as history—both the documented acts of real people and the literary and genre conversations that came before us—gave us a lens to make sense of our project, The Expanse is going on to provide a lens for other people to engage with their own stories, their own analyses, and their own contributions to the ever-wider acts of cultural and intellectual creation.

This is not a book we wrote, but one we helped to inspire. In it, you will find arguments, observations, and opinions on a wide variety of philosophical subjects with *The Expanse* acting as a kind of touchstone for the conversation. It is gratifying in a way that's hard to put in words to see the conversation we took from the generations before us carry through beyond the work we've done. It will challenge you, reframe some of your ideas, and—hopefully—leave you a little more awed, a little wiser, and a step or two further along your own intellectual journey.

Because philosophy, like science fiction, is an act of critical imagination.

James S. A. Corey

Introduction

Jeffery L. Nicholas

"I am that book!"

So declared *Leviathan Wakes* in 2011 when James S. A. Corey published it. And, to quote Chrisjen Avasarala, they weren't bullshitting. *The Expanse* series is a phenomenal science fiction read that delves into the greatest questions of human life, a part of the "literature of progress" that challenges our everyday world by thrusting human life out to Mars, the outer planets, and worlds beyond the Ring Gates.

And when *The Expanse* premiered on the SyFy channel, it declared with equal strength: "I am that show!" You know the one, the one we've been searching for that is better than any other sci-fi series out there. *The Expanse* TV series has wonderful characters, cast, and filming, and dialogue that pulls us in and doesn't let go.

The TV series is particularly phenomenal for me. See, I suffer from aphantasia—pictures don't populate my brain like they do most people, and it's not from some transcranial magnetic stimulation. I feel empathy just fine, and when reading books, I lose myself in the characters. But I don't see the *Roci* searching the stars for a safe harbor or picture Jules-Pierre Mao kneeling at the feet of Avasarala. Watching the *Rocinante* on screen, seeing the torture that Naomi goes through to save people's lives, only makes me love the books and the characters more.

You are here, reading this book, because you love the books, the series, or both. And we too, the authors of the chapters you hold in your hands like Joe Miller holds Julie's necklace, we love *The Expanse*. These chapters sing our love to you. They sail through this shared world, both books and TV series. We look at the challenges of flying our Epstein drive into space, explore the challenges of populating different worlds around Sol and out beyond the Ring Gate. Like Avasarala we interrogate our characters: Miller, Holden, Amos, Bobbie, Naomi, and, of course, Avasarala herself. I've seen online people wondering who would win a fight, Amos or Bobbie, but we're interested in who's more evil, Amos or Avasarala, and who might be good, Naomi or maybe Holden? We examine the costs of interstellar migration and wonder if it's worth the cost or whether we even have a choice.

The chapters in this book cover the first five seasons of *The Expanse* TV series, with hints and suggestions of what we might expect in the sixth by looking at *Babylon's Ashes*. We offer these to you so we can enjoy the books and TV series even more.

Taki taki. Yam seng!

First Orbit
FROM EARTH TO THE STARS

The Infinite and the Sublime in *The Expanse*

Michael J. O'Neill

It made a damning comment as it looked over Fred Johnson's actions against the Anderson Station civilians ("Back to the Butcher"). It stood over Holden's shoulder as he talked with his mother by the campfire and she gifted him a copy of *Don Quixote* ("New Terra"). And it strolled alongside every character that has donned a suit and ventured out of their craft to walk in space. One of the most important characters in *The Expanse* is not named in the credits. It cannot compete for our attention with Avasarala's Machiavellian cleverness, with Naomi's resourcefulness or even with Holden's dreamy hazel eyes. But this character is onscreen almost constantly. The fact is, it is on camera more than any character in the credits. It is the infinite.[1]

Chiaroscuro

The aesthetic techniques used in *The Expanse* are indicative of the infinite space that is an essential and ever-present character in the show. Even the claustrophobic condition of the Belters on Ceres, Ganymede, and Eros points to the infinite space outside. The design of the show keeps infinite space always present.

In the opening credits, the directors and art designers of *The Expanse* give us the setting of the story in a context of infinite space. Views of several planets—Earth, Mars, Saturn—are framed by black spaces that communicate that these huge objects are mere specks of activity in an endless darkness. The opening shot of Saturn might be the best example. The planet is offset in the camera frame—set to the left side as we look out over the famous rings of the planet. What then is the center of the camera's focus? The darkness beyond Saturn. The cinematography and set design of *The Expanse* make extensive use of *chiaroscuro* (ke-ah-ro-skoor-o)—a

The Expanse and Philosophy: So Far Out Into the Darkness, First Edition. Edited by Jeffery L. Nicholas.
© 2022 John Wiley & Sons, Inc. Published 2022 by John Wiley & Sons, Inc.

famous artistic technique in the history of painting. The use of dark shadow, and the contrast of light and dark, create the illusion of volume in three dimensions on a canvas. If you have seen a painting (that is, not one of his many portraits) by Rembrandt or by Caravaggio, you have likely seen *chiaroscuro* used.

Of course, the aesthetics of the show are not an accident. *Chiaroscuro* was a technique developed in the seventeenth century. The many references to *Don Quixote* in *The Expanse* point to the same century. Season one, episode one is named "Dulcinea." Dulcinea is the love interest that the delusional Don Quixote de la Mancha idolizes in the story. Season one, episode seven is named "Windmills"—the monsters that the delusional Don Quixote fights on horseback. *Rocinante* is the name of Don Quixote's horse. And, if that were not enough, Holden's mother gifts him a copy of the novel in season four. All of these references bring our attention to the idea that Holden may be a deluded hero on a quest in a universe he does not understand.

However, they also link the show to a time when the human race first confronted the idea of infinite space—the seventeenth century.

Artistic techniques, like technology, forms of language or music, are expressive of the mind of the age from which they arise. The use of *chiaroscuro* in the show is compelling visually and situates the viewer in two times—the twenty-fourth century of *The Expanse* and seventeenth-century Europe. The technique was born of a time when the idea of the infinite space of the universe was working its way into the human imagination. *The Expanse* plays with the idea of infinity and makes it a theme and element in the thoughts and actions of the characters. A quick detour to the seventeenth century will help us understand this theme of the show better.

A New, Infinite (And Wonderful?) Universe

The first time the human race confronted the infinite spaces of the universe, it found itself at a loss to understand its place in that infinity. Galileo (1564–1642) had demonstrated the truth of the heliocentric model of the solar system. (Fun fact—Galileo also discovered one of the Belters' future homes, Ganymede.) The idea that points of light in the night sky were stars, like our sun, which were moving through massive spaces and were far, far away was discussed in the salons of France and the academies of England. In 1687, Isaac Newton (1642–1727) published the first unified mathematical model of the motions of all bodies moving through space. All of the scientific world celebrated. Newton had done it—found the mathematical key to everything! It would be more than 200 years before relativity theory would throw the Newtonian model into question.

Like the presence of the Ring System in *The Expanse*, Newton's model inspired enthusiasm about human possibilities and human enlightenment. Alexander Pope (1688–1744) caught the mood of the late seventeenth century well when he wrote, "Nature and nature's laws lay hid in night: God said, 'Let Newton be!' and all was light."[2] But did this new understanding of the universe have a dark side? Were we on a promontory looking at the beauty of nature newly understood and looking toward a human future full of wonderful possibility? Or were we on a precipice over an empty abyss into which we would fall?

The Abyss Looks Back (Nietzsche Warned You . . .)

What do you see when you look over *The Expanse*? Holden sees hope and the need to struggle for justice. Miller sees a quest to find the real Julie Mao. Avasarala sees nothing but the coming of an eventual existential threat to human life. Fred Johnson sees the possibility of redemption. The Mormons, the need for a journey to find God.

For Blaise Pascal (1623–1662), the infinite space discovered by the new physics of the seventeenth century was a terrifying emptiness—proof of the insignificance of human life and the need for faith in God. (He is in both Avasarala's camp and the Mormons, perhaps.) He writes, "For, after all, what is man in nature? A nothing compared to the infinite, a whole compared to the nothing, a middle point between all and nothing, infinitely remote from an understanding of the extremes; the end of things and their principles are unattainably hidden from him in impenetrable secrecy."[3] When you think about something infinitely large, like the universe, are human beings not a "nothing compared to the infinite"? And, when you think about the fact that the molecular, atomic, and subatomic world is infinitely small, are human beings not "a whole compared to the nothing, a middle point between all and nothing"?

Our place as rational creatures would seem to put us in a position of distinction in all of this infinity. But, "the end of things and their principles are unattainably hidden from [us] in impenetrable secrecy." Pascal believes that, despite our scientific achievements, reason cannot seem to see what the goal of life is, what the principles that govern human behavior are, or what the ultimate point of our actions is. For Pascal, science gave us power over the "middle" of things but no insight into the meaning of infinity. It is strange to think that we spend our lives reasoning about what is to be done, how we will prosper, how we will serve the community and our fellow human beings, but do not have rationally justified ends to order our actions.

Put another way, practical reasoning (the thinking we do when we are deciding to act) is both extremely difficult to do well and the most commonly successful activity engaged in by human beings. While the details of the context in which we reason can be excruciating to master, and our own desires, prejudices, vanity, and other flaws can obscure the thing that we should do—somehow much practical reasoning gets done successfully.

For philosophers, the general formula is relatively simple. We analyze thinking, character, context, the moral ideas applied (rules, duties or virtues, for instance), the end pursued, and then we evaluate any consequences. What is startling to think about for the characters in *The Expanse* is that the formula is truncated, decapitated really—or at least missing a limb. "The end of things and their principles are unattainably hidden from [us] in impenetrable secrecy." In other words, despite our new scientific achievement, knowing whether our actions are right, wrong, foolish, or wise in this new universe of the seventeenth and twenty-fourth centuries is impossible.

Avasarala understands this problem. She is nobody's fool and wants to be wise. Her argument with Nancy Gao over the issue of whether to allow "a new gold rush" of humans into the Ring System shows her concern for the lack of knowledge and information surrounding any decision about the Ring. During their tense exchange, Avasarala warns that, like the Yukon before it, this gold rush will result in piles of body bags with "more fools ready to line up and take their place" ("New Terra"). This issue will eventually cost her the election to United Nations Secretary General— Gao's hopeful view of the possibilities inherent in the Ring will sway voters. The tragedy of Avasarala's political fortunes is that she will never know enough to make an informed decision on the meaning of the Ring System for human beings. She tries to be wise; yet, even as she recruits Holden to make the trip to New Terra, we can see Pascal shaking his head at the futility of it all. "*The ends are hidden in impenetrable secrecy . . .*"

What had changed in the universe for Pascal? Before Galileo and Newton, the prevailing understanding of the universe was that its purpose, the point of why anything existed at all, was so that human beings could live as rational beings who could find their way to God. We were the point. The universe was a small place centered on the earth and human life. It was a stage on which the drama of human life played out. God was understood to intervene directly at times in that drama. What is the point of life in Newton's universe? Pascal writes, "When I consider the short span of my life absorbed into the preceding and subsequent eternity, *memoria hospitis unius diei praetereuntis* [like the memory of a one-day guest (Wisdom 5:15)], the small space which I fill and even can see, swallowed up in the infinite immensity of spaces of which I know nothing and which knows nothing of me, I am terrified, and surprised to find myself here rather than there, for there is no reason why it should be here rather than there, why now rather than then. Who put me here? On whose orders and on whose decision have this place and this time been allotted to me?"[4] For Pascal, this new sense of infinity makes everything we do and are seem random and capricious.

What is the point of an infinitely small human life in this infinitely large *Expanse*?

Is It *Large* Out Here? Or Is It Me?

Pascal's concerns can be seen as a kind of existential agoraphobia—a crisis of meaning brought on by infinitely wide-open spaces. In fairness to him, the problem is a deep and serious one—philosophically speaking. Miller, a child of the claustrophobic Ceres, has this agoraphobia written into his bones. It is not abstract, or philosophical, it is a concrete affliction that he feels. Yet, he still is able to overcome it to continue his quest to find the meaning of Julie's life and her death. This is one reason why he, like Holden, is a quest-hero in the series.

Miller's quest really begins when he is fired by Captain Shaddid ("Rock Bottom"). Before that moment he had been doing (in a somewhat shoddy way) his job. He then became intrigued by the mystery of Julie's disappearance, fell in love with the idea of her, and eventually found the object of his quest. Once he is fired, his decision to follow the investigation is his own. After searching Julie's apartment, he hangs up his hat—a symbolic removal of the superficial Earth culture he emulates and a return to his authentic Belter self—and he commits to his quest to find the real Julie. Before leaving, he brings Julie's necklace as a token with him (like a good quest-hero). Then, the show gives us the irony of a Belter who hates space buying a ticket for a voyage into the infinity outside.

On the transport to Eros, Miller has a conversation with a Mormon missionary who has joined the 100-year expedition on the ship that Fred Johnson is building for them (soon to be renamed the *Behemoth*). Miller asks him, "Nobody really knows what's out there . . . Doesn't that scare the shit out of you?" The missionary tells Miller that his faith is what sustains him in the face of the infinite unknown that he will confront on his journey. Miller responds, "You guys are gonna get on this big ship, ride out into the great beyond for 100 years. What happens when you get out there and there's nothing?" ("Salvage"). Pascal's confrontation with infinity occurs in his imagination. Miller has to literally step into it.

Miller's courage in overcoming his fear of space is a good metaphor for the way the characters of *The Expanse* address their situation in the void. Some sci-fi treats science as a kind of alchemy that can always be called on to decipher the unknown—problems are solved by mixing together just the right kind of particle and, like the fabled magical art that could turn lead into gold, return all that had been radically changed during the episode back to normal. (I'm looking at you, *Star Trek*.) *The Expanse* is different. It does not allow for neatly wrapped-up solutions. How could it? When the ends of things are hidden in impenetrable secrecy?

Problems in *The Expanse* are solved by negotiating with the unknown. We see this idea in Holden's series of negotiations with the mental projection of Miller. Holden is deliberating with an interstellar being that is itself unaware of the meaning of its own purpose, through a proxy that is generated by his own brain. That situation is, to say the least, complicated.

Before Miller is liberated from the protomolecule, he is driven by the purpose inscribed in it. Like the Katoa hybrid in the lab on Io who cries out to
Jules-Pierre Mao that he "must finish the work" ("Triple Point"), Miller
too feels driven to complete the protomolecule's work—"the case," as he
calls it. He is focused on the protomolecule's immediate goal—a goal given
to it (and him) by an extinct civilization and situated within an overall plan
that he does not know or understand. Holden could be forgiven for thinking that this endeavor is pointless and inconceivable.

However, Holden and the characters of *The Expanse*, even though they
are adrift in the infinity of space, do not give up or lay down and die in the
face of a universe in which their lives are so small as to be insignificant.
Why do they struggle against injustice? Against an alien threat? Against
each other? Where do they find the source of motivation for their actions?
Are they simply unaware that their lives and goals are insignificant in the
way Pascal understands the universe? It is not simply that they stoically
endure this sense of their smallness in the scheme of things. They do something else; they assert themselves. They stand up and demand that they be
heard and recognized as dignified. Perhaps Captain Camina Drummer said
it best on the bridge of the OPA's *Behemoth* as the ship entered the Gate,
"We are Belters, nothing in the void is foreign to us. The place we go is the
place we belong!" ("Intransigence").

Freedom and the Sublime in *The Expanse*

For some reason, the infinity of *The Expanse* attracts us. The confrontation with infinity brings us a certain kind of pleasure. We feel awe, wonder.
What is it about this experience that draws us to it? The look and design
of the show indulges us in an experience of the *sublime*.

Immanuel Kant (1724–1804) understood the power and importance of
this experience. For Kant, the experience of the sublime is the experience
of something formless, something without limit. It is the experience of
reason's ability to understand being completely overwhelmed.[5] The design
of *The Expanse* returns to *chiaroscuro* again and again as a way of tapping
into this experience for the viewer. The cinematography attempts to take
the inconceivable and represent it artistically.

Consider Holden's conversation on Earth with his mother in "New
Terra." They sit together by a fire. She gifts him a copy of *Don Quixote*.
During the entire scene, the fire lights the faces of both characters. However,
the shot is framed so that the darkness behind each of them is prominent.
We are left with the understanding that this conversation is unique and
individual but situated in infinite space.

A particularly clever example of this technique is the use of the exterior
on Ilus/New Terra (I do not want to take sides in that naming debate!).
When you watch the characters move across the landscape, notice what

the director has done with the sky on Ilus (ok, I took sides). With few exceptions, the sky is an uninterrupted white—a white that is unbroken and infinite. It is a photonegative of *chiaroscuro* and produces the same effect. We are pointed back to the fact of infinity.

Kant ruminated on the significance of infinity, and the infinite space of the universe, for the meaning of human life. He understood Pascal's concerns well. Kant took the measure of human beings situated in infinite space and came up with a different account of its meaning. Where Pascal saw insignificance except for our capacity for belief in God, Kant saw a creature that had the capacity to confront the infinite and immeasurable power of nature and, rather than being overwhelmed by it, find in itself something larger, more profoundly powerful and dignified than all of the power of nature combined.

Kant spoke of two kinds of sublime experiences, the mathematically sublime and the dynamically sublime. In each experience, reason is overwhelmed by something so enormous and formless that it cannot be conceptualized. This experience of having our reason overwhelmed throws us into a new understanding of ourselves.

For Kant, the mathematically sublime experience is an experience of reason being overwhelmed in the presence of something infinite in size. You lie on your back looking up at the night sky, seeing the infinite space and uncountable number of stars; the mind spins and cannot grasp what it is experiencing. We feel wonder and awe—that is the mathematically sublime. Taking a spacewalk outside the *Rocinante* is mathematically sublime. The view of the *Behemoth*, as its own massive size is dwarfed by the infinity around it, is mathematically sublime. The battlefield of the UN Marines and the MCRN Marines against the first protomolecule hybrids on the surface of Ganymede is mathematically sublime set as it is, without an atmosphere, against an infinite sky. A sublime setting in which to die, but of course, Bobbie Draper refuses to go gently into that good night—you get the idea.

Dynamically Sublime

The dynamically sublime is an experience of infinite power, but not where our survival is threatened by it (that part is important). You are in your living room looking out at the hurricane howling outside, filled with awe at the infinite power of nature outside your window. The mind spins again and cannot gather this experience into a concept—that is the dynamically sublime. It is important that you have this experience while at a slight distance from it, as an observer.

If you were ever to actually confront the sublime directly, two issues would emerge. First, because of the danger to your life involved in a direct experience of the dynamically sublime, you might have other things to think about rather than the meaning of the event. It is hard to be reflectively aware of an experience you are having while you are fighting for your life! Second, and this is definitely related to the first problem, infinitely large natural forces have a good chance of killing you. As far as we know, the dead do not experience the sublime.

The fate of the civilian survey ship *Arboghast* illustrates the need for some distance from the dynamically sublime. On its mission to Venus to monitor the activity of the protomolecule, the research ship descends into the atmosphere and, in a stunning visual, is completely disassembled in an instant. We see the shock and terror of the experience frozen on the faces of Colonel Janus and Dr. Iturbi ("Abaddon's Gate"). The confrontation with the sublime in this case is a direct one and it is horrifying. Before descending into Venus' atmosphere, Colonel Janus and Dr. Iturbi have a brief discussion about whether to bring the ship closer to the surface to get a better idea of what the protomolecule was up to. We see the wry smiles on their faces and the twinkle in their eyes as they both understand that their "debate" is just a formality. They are pulled toward the event below them. It is not just about their mission. They are drawn to it by a kind of primal curiosity.

As the decision is made and the *Arboghast* begins its descent, we can almost see Pascal shake his head in pity.

As shocking as the fate of the *Arboghast* is, Marco Inaros' attack on Earth using stealth-tech cloaked asteroids is more horrifying ("Mother"). It is the first time in the show we see the weaponization of the infinite. We are given the image of a man on the beach (ironically throwing pebbles into the sea) as the asteroid hits Earth. We see the man's skin begin to blister as the shockwave annihilates him—his experience is one of horror, not sublimity. As we watch the scene unfold, we are confronted with the added challenge that this infinite horror is a *human creation*. That the attack is intentional, deliberate, adds an element of dread and repugnance to our evaluation of it.

After Inaros' attack on Earth, Avasarala is told that there has been a report of a "200–300 kiloton explosion" at the impact site. (To put that number in some perspective, the combined power of the atomic bombs dropped on Hiroshima and Nagasaki in 1945 was 40 kilotons.) The quantification of the event seems to reduce the scope of it. But "200–300 kilotons" is not a number that is very informative—like a blood pressure, a test score or a speed limit. What is the point of this report? How is it supposed to influence our thinking about this event?

Such attempts at description and explanation of sublime events are a way that our psyche tries to assert power over our dread of the infinite. Having a number to measure a phenomenon seems to make it accessible, understandable. It is as if we are telling ourselves, "No need for existential dread here—there is nothing beyond our understanding!" But attempts at explanation cannot contain an infinite moral horror nor can they explain away a sublime experience. Our dread of ourselves and reason's inability to capture the infinite remain. The infinite and the sublime cannot be explained. But they can be experienced.

No one experience can be *more* sublime than another. By definition, the sublime is an experience of the infinite and formless. An experience is simply sublime or not. To be clear, only those safely removed from an event can view it as sublime. Attacks of the kind imagined by Marco Inaros are unfathomable moral horrors—they are not strictly speaking sublime. Kant's view of the sublime is rooted in an experience of nature—either of its infinite size or infinite power. Kant, like many of the Romantic thinkers of his day, saw the sublime in nature as an opportunity for spiritual growth.

Despite its overwhelming power and size, the experience of the sublime can be inspiring—standing on the edge of the Grand Canyon, the Hoover Dam, or the bow of a ship looking at the night sky, being out in the woods while the thunderstorm rolls in, or anywhere when an earthquake shakes your surroundings. If we were pressed, we might admit that we enjoyed them all at some level. Why? Yes, the experiences evoke emotions of wonder and awe at the power and infinity around us. Kant wants to say, however, that something else is going on inside us during these experiences, something that shows us our true value as beings in the cosmos.

Howl at the Moon If You Want To

When we confront the infinite in the form of the dynamically sublime, we could be forgiven for thinking that a good hiding place is the best response. What can an animal do during a big storm or during an earthquake? Only obey instinct. The forest is intensely silent just before a thunderstorm— every creature alive in the vicinity goes to its home. Except human beings, we just might want to hang around and feel what happens. However, if you wanted to, you could stand out in a field during that thunderstorm. You could dance a jig in the middle of the street during an earthquake, if the impulse so moved you.

That option, of staying around and feeling what happens, is an experience of our own freedom in direct contrast to our instincts. All of the animals have gone to ground because that is what their programming demands. We can face the infinitely powerful, defy our instincts, and in the confrontation with the sublime, experience a pure intuition of our own freedom. Yes, we feel wonder and awe. These are the emotions that arise, not from the challenge of the infinite and infinitely powerful, but from the recognition that we are free. For Kant, because we are free, we are greater than the whole of the power of nature.

Holden, as he descends alone in his space suit to the Ring station, discusses why he is doing what he is doing with Miller. Miller says with a smile, "You are following your program, just like me." Holden replies, "I always had this crazy notion about free will." Miller replies, "Then how come it is that every time there is some clusterfuck shitstorm situation in the universe—there's James Holden?! Shrugging his shoulders, saying, 'How the hell did I end up here?'" ("Dandelion Sky"). Holden has the correct intuition of his own freedom. He just does not have Kant around to tutor him on what to say to Miller. But Holden has had the experience of the sublime—repeatedly. Ironically, his conversation with Miller is set within the mathematically sublime experience of space.

You are free and responsible for that freedom. The experience of the sublime is one proof of your freedom. Because you are free, you are different from the rest of creation. You are significant. The absence of your ability to know the significance of what you do in the context of the infinite does not diminish the significance of what you do. The characters of *The Expanse* know this. They act because they know they must, and they have faith that what they do matters.

It may seem strange to end with a quote from Amos, whose amorality is more on display in the show than his morality. But the truth is, Amos spends the show looking for guidance and slowly, but clearly, articulates the moral situation the characters are in. In a heated exchange with Alex, he says, "Do you want me to say this is some weird shit? Yeah, it's some weird shit!" Alex replies, "Thank you! We are playing way out of our league here!" Amos finishes, "That's been true ever since we've been sharpening sticks and going after lions, but we're still here" ("Dandelion Sky").

Look again at *The Expanse*. You will find the cinematography, the art direction, and the film direction, all try to bring the sublime into artistic representation. That feeling you have when you see infinite space represented on screen that tickles you at the back of your psyche may be an intuition of your own freedom.

It may be proof that you are more than the infinity that is the setting of *The Expanse*.

Notes

1. By "infinite" in this chapter we don't necessarily mean literally without end. Instead, we mean inconceivably large or great.
2. Alexander Pope, "Epitaph on Sir Isaac Newton," in James L. Ford and Mary K. Ford, eds., *Every Day in the Year: A Poetical Epitome of History* (New York: Dodd, Mead & Co., 1902). Online https://www.bartleby.com/297/154.html.
3. Blaise Pascal, *Pensées and Other Writings* (Oxford: Oxford University Press, 2008), §199.
4. Pascal, §102.
5. Immanuel Kant, *The Critique of Judgment* (Cambridge: Hackett Publishing, 1987), §§23–24 and 28.

2

Interplanetary Expansion and the Deep Future

Margarida Hermida

"Platinum, iron, and titanium from the Belt. Water from Saturn, vegetables and beef from the big mirror-fed greenhouses on Ganymede and Europa, organics from Earth and Mars. Power cells from Io, Helium-3 from the refineries on Rhea and Iapetus."[1] At the start of *The Expanse*, human beings live all across the solar system; on Earth, Mars, in space stations in the asteroid belt, on the moons of Jupiter, and beyond. A vast interplanetary commercial exchange is in place.

While the details might differ, our solar system is indeed full of resources that could support a much larger human population than Earth.[2] Contemporary philosopher John Leslie, author of *The End of the World: The Science and Ethics of Human Extinction*, argues that we have basically two options: either humanity has a long and prosperous future, expanding beyond Earth, and possibly even spreading across the galaxy; or else it is likely to go extinct within the next few centuries.[3]

So, which is it going to be? We can't answer that question without considering the challenges facing humanity.

Does Humanity Have a Future?

In *The Expanse*, the future of humanity is constantly at stake. Danger comes from the protomolecule, with its uncanny capacity not only to turn every human in its path into a contagious vomit zombie, but maybe even to terraform Earth under unknown alien instructions. After Eros crashes on Venus, the protomolecule's inscrutable activities continue, suggesting the possibility that it could destroy the entire solar system. Additionally, humanity faces the threat that the alien civilization that built the protomolecule might return. Even more worrying is the threat from whoever or whatever killed the original protomolecule makers. Most of all, though, a constant threat to humanity is all-out war between Earth, Mars, and the

The Expanse and Philosophy: So Far Out Into the Darkness, First Edition. Edited by Jeffery L. Nicholas.
© 2022 John Wiley & Sons, Inc. Published 2022 by John Wiley & Sons, Inc.

Belt, culminating in the catastrophe of the Free Navy asteroid attack against Earth, killing billions of people.

Although the death of billions of people is immensely tragic, it pales in comparison to the threat to the very existence of humanity. The philosopher Derek Parfit (1942–2017) devised a thought experiment that asks us to consider three alternative scenarios:

(a) Peace
(b) A nuclear war that kills 99 percent of the human population
(c) A nuclear war that kills 100 percent of the human population[4]

Everyone agrees that (b) and (c) are both much worse than (a), but Parfit's point is that (c) is much worse than (b). In fact, he believes the greater difference lies there—the extinction of humanity is a much worse outcome than most people think.[5] Extinction is not the worst just because it would mean the non-existence of a great number of people in the future, which—assuming their lives would be worth living—would be a great loss. The loss of possible happiness of future people pales in comparison with the loss of our entire species. Human extinction would entail the loss of all possible future achievements of our species, for instance in the arts, the sciences, and in "the continued advance towards a wholly just world-wide community."[6]

Contemporary philosopher Samuel Scheffler argues that not only should we care about the future of our species, but we already do, more than we realize.[7] The reason we don't realize it is because we simply take the "collective afterlife" for granted. In fact, many of the things that we dedicate our lives to now, in the present, only make sense under the assumption that humanity will continue to exist in the future. Most of our goals and purposes in life would lose their meaning if we were to find out that we were the last generation of human beings. Scheffler believes this means that we have a deep concern for humanity, something we might even call love, which coexists with our baser impulses.

We see these conflicting motives time and again in *The Expanse*. Greed, selfishness, and blatant disregard for other people's suffering are exhibited by Dresden and the Protogen corporation (in *Leviathan Wakes*), by Adolphus Murtry (in *Cibola Burn*), by Marco Inaros (in *Nemesis Games*), and by Admiral Winston Duarte, later High Consul of Laconia (in *Persepolis Rising* and *Tiamat's Wrath*). Meanwhile we witness the fundamental goodness of common people, such as the crew of the *Rocinante*, who repeatedly risk their lives for the future of humanity.

The Value of Humanity

We might ask ourselves whether the existence of humankind is valuable in itself. Perhaps surprisingly, some people believe that our extinction would be no great loss.[8] We hear echoes of this profoundly pessimistic worldview in Miller's comment "Stars are better off without us," after the *Nauvoo* is repurposed from a generation ship into a missile to drive Eros into the Sun.[9]

People who hold this pessimistic view seem to think that most human lives are not worth living.

In contrast, Parfit argues that this view might have been plausible in earlier centuries when many people lived lives filled with suffering and with little hope of improvement, but it is certainly wrong today. Notwithstanding the amount of poverty, suffering, and inequality that still exists today, we have come a long way toward reducing human suffering. Consider medical advancements, such as the discovery of anesthetics and painkillers; and consider improvements in living conditions and gains in freedom for all, and not just for a privileged few. It seems likely that in the future we would be able to prevent most human suffering.

Unfortunately, it doesn't necessarily follow that we will. Many people in *The Expanse* live miserable and wretched lives. For sick Belters with no access to medicine to forestall the effects of living in low-gravity, high-radiation environments, trafficked women and children forced into prostitution on Ceres, and the victims of organized crime and corrupt biotech corporations, life might not be worth living. But all this suffering is not a necessary part of human life. Rather, it is a consequence of poverty, poor living conditions, lack of freedom, inequality, social injustice, and political ineffectiveness. Human life can be wonderful. The existence of human beings is definitely a good thing provided we as a species make every possible effort to ensure that most people live lives worth living, and that we strive to achieve the "wholly just world-wide community" Parfit talks about. It certainly seems worth trying, rather than throwing our hands in the air and complaining about how terrible human life is.

Philosopher James Lenman points out that, since all species will eventually become extinct, the question is not whether our extinction is a bad thing, but whether it matters how soon that moment comes.[10]

One way to answer this question is to appeal to the intrinsic value of biodiversity. Suppose it is intrinsically good that many different species exist. This idea is highly plausible and generally accepted. However, the problem is that human beings are not having a particularly good effect on biodiversity; quite the opposite, in fact. We are in the process of causing the Earth's sixth mass extinction, which is definitely a bad thing. In *The Expanse*, things are only getting worse, with overpopulation, pollution, and habitat destruction on Earth decreasing biodiversity to pitiful remnants. Even Amos, in *Nemesis Games*, is somewhat surprised that despite humanity's pressure on ecosystems, wildlife on Earth still exists. Human beings might still, in the future, go on to have a positive effect on biodiversity overall (more on this below).

To be clear, biodiversity is not just the number of species that exist. It includes functional diversity, an ecological concept that is related to the particular niche an organism occupies in an ecosystem. For example, we could say the rhinoceros occupies a relatively similar ecological niche that the triceratops once occupied. From the perspective of functional biodiversity, the extinction of all flying animals is far worse than the extinction of any particular flying species, because it means the complete loss of this particular way of life. Looking at humans from the perspective of functional biodiversity, no other species has ever occupied the particular ecological niche that humans occupy. Although other species have culture (for example chimpanzees and whales), no other species on Earth has civilization.

In *The Expanse* vestiges of an ancient alien civilization with incredibly advanced technology have been found—which eventually permits human interstellar expansion through the gates. But in our reality, we have no evidence for the existence of any civilization other than human. Considering the sheer size of the universe and the number of stars and galaxies, though, it is likely that other intelligent life exists somewhere. Nevertheless, we might never find out for sure.[11] What we know for sure is that we, *Homo sapiens*, are, in the words of Parfit, "a part of the Universe that is starting to understand itself."[12] By doing the best we can to guarantee a future for our species, we can also make the universe a better and more meaningful place. We should therefore take the possibility of our extinction seriously indeed.

Life and Biodiversity

Lenman argues that, even if we agree that biodiversity is a good thing, it only means that it's good that there should be natural diversity while life exists on Earth. It doesn't mean, however, that it's worse if life on Earth goes extinct sooner rather than later.[13] Just because biodiversity is good does not mean that life is good.

I don't find this view plausible; actually, it seems rather parochial. Why should biodiversity matter only on Earth? If we are trying to view things from an objective perspective, biodiversity in the universe is what should matter. While we have no way of finding out how much biodiversity the universe contains, Earth is the only inhabited planet in the solar system, as far as we know. As things stand, if all life on Earth were to go extinct, then the biodiversity in the whole solar system would drop to zero. In the future depicted in *The Expanse*, with self-sustaining habitats established in various locations, extinction of life on Earth would not end biodiversity in the universe—although it's true that no other habitat comes even close to Earth in terms of biodiversity.

Comparing existence in time with existence in space, Lenman argues that it makes sense to lament the extinction of the white rhino, but it makes no sense to lament its nonexistence in northern Scotland. Nor does it make sense to argue that it would be better if white rhinos lasted for 1 billion years rather than, say, 1 million. But that is because other living beings exist in Scotland and, we hope, other living beings will be around 1 billion years from now. On the contrary, since Earth is, as far as we know, the only planet in the solar system with a biosphere, if life on Earth were to disappear, no other life would exist anywhere in the solar system, possibly ever again. That would be an incredible loss. If we could prevent this extinction by spreading life to currently lifeless planets, that would be a good outcome.

Suppose humans were to colonize Mars (at first). Not only would humans be on Mars, but we would also need to take plants and microbes along with us, at the very least, since we would need to create a new ecosystem to sustain human life. Consider the Ganymede greenhouses in *The Expanse*, the ever-necessary photosynthetic plants to produce oxygen in the Belt colonies, or even the ferns that humans end up carrying with them to another solar system.[14] In fact, self-sustainable ecosystems that would allow long-term human survival probably require a high degree of biodiversity, upwards of 4,000 different species.[15] The expansion of humans beyond Earth would also be the expansion of Earth life beyond its native planet. And that would certainly be a good thing.

It matters that those planets are lifeless, however.

If we found life on Mars, for example, we would face a moral dilemma. We might decide that we would still have overwhelming reasons to colonize Mars, but we would at the very least also have a strong reason to preserve any native Martian life. The alien protomolecule makers seem to have had no such qualms. They produced a technology capable of destroying all life on a planet, just to build a galaxy wormhole superhighway for themselves. We don't know their motivations, but it's possible that the alien civilization that created the protomolecule just didn't care about any species other than themselves. Or they might have been under the impression that most life in the universe is simple and unicellular. Yet, this should not be a reason to disregard it or consider it without value. Imagine if the protomolecule had arrived on Earth instead of getting stuck in the outer planets. Complex life on Earth might never have evolved.

The difference between the careless destruction of other life forms by the protomolecule makers and the prospect of humans (along with other Earth life) expanding to lifeless planets is the difference between morally objectionable colonization, where a particular people (or, in this case, alien species) takes some territory or resources for themselves, without regard for its original inhabitants, and the positively desirable biological colonization of new habitats, which arguably increases the amount of value in the universe.[16]

Unfortunately, in *Cibola Burn*, the first planet outside the solar system that humans colonize is already teeming with native life. The colonization is morally objectionable, not only from the point of view of the preservation of biodiversity, but also because it is dangerous for the colonists themselves.

Hedging Our Bets Against Extinction Risk

While we might not be facing interplanetary war or the unpredictable consequences of ancient alien technology, many serious dangers face the human species today. We are quite resilient and have survived numerous disasters in the past, including floods, earthquakes, famine, pandemics, and wars.[17] However, we have never faced a real threat to our existence as a species. Most disasters are localized and kill many people, but within a geographically restricted area. Even highly contagious diseases with high mortality rates never kill the entire population; some individuals tend to be immune. However, some disasters might affect the entire human population or even all complex life on Earth.

Although it seems to have somewhat faded from public consciousness, the possibility of nuclear war remains a major danger. Some authors argue that, even though the probability of deliberate use of nuclear weapons might have declined (and that itself is arguable), the probability of accidentally triggered nuclear war has actually increased over time, due to obsolete automated systems and a faulty logic of "preventive" and retaliatory strikes.[18] A scenario of runaway climate change is even more likely, in which a moderate increase in greenhouse gases generated by human activity raises temperature sufficiently to initiate permafrost thaw, releasing large amounts of methane and carbon dioxide. This in turn increases the greenhouse effect, leading to more thaw, triggering an unstoppable feedback loop. Other possible threats to human existence include uncontrollable biological weapons or nano-machines (think of a human-made protomolecule), a large meteor strike, artificial intelligence gone wrong, or even unforeseen effects of high-energy physics experiments in future supercolliders.[19]

Small population size and restricted distribution range are factors that increase a species' extinction risk. For instance, animals or plants that occur only in one small oceanic island are at high risk of extinction. Humans might seem to be relatively protected from that risk, although our enormous population size is in itself cause for concern, due to the depletion of resources. However, any terrestrial species is powerless against threats to all life on Earth. A planet is much like an island. As astrobiologist and philosopher Milan M. Ćirković puts it, "the terrestrial biosphere is (. . .) a single system—and uniqueness is always more fragile than multiplicity."[20] In this context, human expansion beyond Earth seems like a prudent move, which would certainly increase our chances of survival in the long run. That is, if we don't end up killing each other, because, as amply demonstrated throughout *The Expanse*, warfare is one extinction risk that might follow us into space.

Colonizing other planets will not be easy. The most obvious candidate is Mars, due to its proximity, the existence of an atmosphere, water ice, relatively similar day/night cycles, and other features.[21] Making it habitable, however, will be arduous. In *The Expanse*, the terraforming of Mars is an ongoing process, one which, incidentally, brings the Martian people together under a common cause. The truth is that no other planet in the solar system is as hospitable as Earth. Even in *The Expanse*, when humanity is already spread out across the entire solar system (but before interstellar expansion), Mars and the Belt are still dependent on Earth. When Holden is contemplating the possibility that Eros might crash into the Earth, causing the protomolecule to terraform the entire planet, he muses that "Mars would survive, for a while. Pockets of the Belt would hold out even longer, probably. They had a culture of making do, surviving on scraps, living on the bleeding edge of their resources. But in the end, without Earth, everything would eventually die."[22]

Dependence on Earth might seem to contradict the idea that human expansion would function as a "backup" in case of disaster on Earth. We must bear in mind, though, that expansion to other planets is a long-term plan. Colonization does not avoid our having to take measures to prevent runaway climate change, unfettered population growth, and resource depletion. You can't build a self-sustaining ecosystem on a desert planet overnight. Terraforming a planet can take between 1,000 and 100,000 years. Still, that is a lot quicker than the 1.5 billion years evolution took to get from the beginning of life on Earth to an oxygen-rich atmosphere.

Pessimists will say it can't be done; that it's a waste of resources. The obstacles are indeed tremendous, but we should not give up before we start. Air travel and landing on the moon were once thought to be impossible. Furthermore, space exploration promises us a better understanding of our own planet in the context of other planets. This advance in knowledge deflates the argument about the waste of resources. Some people will argue that we should invest more in the protection of our own planet instead—in the prevention of climate change, biodiversity loss, and so on.[23] But we must do both, if we are to hedge our bets against extinction. Interplanetary expansion is a very long-term prospect; it is not a replacement for having to solve the problems we have here *now*.

Astrobiologist Charles S. Cockell argues that, in fact, the goals of environmental conservation on Earth and space exploration, far from being incompatible, are actually beneficial to one another.[24] As an example, he asks us to consider solar panels. We are going to need solar panels on Mars, and they had better be highly efficient, since sunlight is less available. Yet the development of efficient solar panels would certainly benefit the Earth environment right now.

Future Humans

Interplanetary expansion could potentially bring about speciation, which means the separation of *Homo sapiens* into different species. *The Expanse* includes some signs that this might be starting to happen; Belters are well adapted to low-gravity environments but unable to survive on Earth anymore. Certainly, the changes are merely environmental, but it's possible that, in the long run, they might become genetic as well. Speciation might not happen if there's enough genetic exchange between the two populations. As Holden explains to his racist Earther mom prior to bringing Naomi to meet her, "Earthers and Belters can have kids just fine. We're not a different species."[25] In a scenario of prolonged isolation, though, it might happen. This can be problematic because humans are not at their best when dealing with difference. Our species has a low rate of genetic diversity; yet people still find a way to discriminate based on outdated concepts of "race" which do not even adequately track actual biological ancestry.

In *Leviathan Wakes*, Havelock criticizes Miller for espousing racist propaganda that "the difference in environment has changed the Belters so much that (. . .) they aren't really human anymore."[26] Obviously the Belters still belong to the same species as Earthers. But the phrasing "not even human anymore" betrays how much we're used to being the only human species in existence. As paleontologist Clive Finlayson explains, we are so used to being alone on this planet that we imagine that it was always this way.[27] But actually, for most of human evolution, several human species existed simultaneously. Neanderthals, for example, were a separate human species with which *Homo sapiens* coexisted, and recent evidence shows they were quite intelligent. Actually, their brains were slightly larger than those of modern humans. They had language, cared for the sick, and buried their dead. Other species, such as *Homo ergaster*, *Homo erectus* (who discovered fire), and *Homo heidelbergensis*, were human too.[28] While it's true that Neanderthals eventually went extinct and modern humans survived, this was not simply a matter of modern humans killing them off.[29] Even if it had been, it stands to reason that competition for resources on the same land by prehistoric hunter-gatherer bands is not representative of what a future scenario of human speciation on different planets would look like.

Does the diversification of humans lead to unique dangers and, if so, should the project of interplanetary expansion be dropped? Phil Torres, who writes about existential risk, believes that it would inevitably lead to a constant state of war, which would greatly increase human suffering.[30] We, therefore, should abandon the idea of expanding beyond Earth. But this reasoning has several problems. First of all, it's unclear that diversity *per se* is what drives aggression and warfare. After all, it's not as though humans don't engage in war with other humans who are exactly like themselves. Religious, political, and ideological differences, as well as territorial disputes, are much more powerful forces of conflict than genetic or morphological differences.

While some sources of conflict in *The Expanse* stem from the racist or xenophobic attitudes of Belters, Martians, and Earthers, human diversification is not the main factor. Politics, lack of trust between governments, and people's dissatisfaction with living conditions seem to be the main factors in generating conflict. For instance, although the attack on Earth in *Nemesis Games* is carried out by Belters, it is not the OPA, but the Free Navy, that causes it. The Free Navy is an extremist faction of the OPA and does not speak for all Belters despite Marco Inaros' attempts to do so; many Belters, including Naomi, would be appalled at the attack. The Laconian Empire also stems from a disaffected faction of the OPA. Ultimately, the UN, MCR, and OPA manage to come together despite their differences to form a special task force against the Free Navy. Moreover, many people from different places do get along well, as is the case with the diverse crew of the *Rocinante*, which includes Earthers, Martians, and Belters. When Filip accuses Naomi of betraying her own kind, her reply is illuminating: "Let me tell you about my own kind. There are two sides in this, but they aren't inner planets and outer ones. Belters and everyone else. It's not like that. It's the people who want more violence and the ones who want less."[31]

Ćirković argues that not only is "the whole tradition of liberalism and the Enlightenment" based on the assumption that "free choice, as a source of all diversity, is of an intrinsic value," but diversity itself is not a source of conflict.[32] On the contrary, the attempted suppression of diversity and the imposition of uniformity on the part of repressive regimes has brought on the most horrific episodes of human history. Ćirković also points out that not expanding to other planets is no guarantee of non-differentiation. Speciation can occur even in the absence of isolation, and all the more so if we consider the possibilities afforded by various "post-human" enhancements.

In fact, while autocratic political regimes see human diversity in all its forms as a threat which must be suppressed, democratic societies value the diversity of people, of cultural practices and ways of life, which enrich the human experience. Attempting to prevent conflict by preventing the diversification of humans through authoritarian means would more likely lead to a Laconian Empire-style regime, an abhorrent outcome which people who value their personal freedoms are prepared to fight against, even at the cost of their lives.[33] Arguably, the Laconian Empire poses a much more significant threat to the human future in the solar system and beyond than the existence of people with different morphologies because they grew up under more or less gravity.

Yes, parts of our nature are worse than others. We are smart enough to recognize that, and even to want to do better. Our nature is not immutable; we are also what we make of ourselves. We among all the animals are the only ones who can have preferences about how we'd like to be, who can form second-order preferences about our own preferences. Why should we not want to do better? When Ganymede station is collapsing, we are introduced to a couple of Earth-born missionaries from the Church of Humanity Ascendant, a naturalist religion whose theology is basically "Humans can be better than they are, so let's do that."[34] Honestly, sign me up!

What Really Matters

Even if humans manage to expand to other habitats in the solar system, the human species we are now—*Homo sapiens*—might eventually be replaced by other human species. Does this defeat the point of expansion, which was to avoid extinction in the long run? I don't think so. The survival of humanity matters to us not because it is important that our particular species survives forever (which is not possible in any case). Rather, we are deeply invested in the existence of beings who can contemplate and attempt to understand the universe, as well as themselves. The existence of such beings certainly seems to be a good thing in itself. At the end of the second volume of his magnum opus *On What Matters*, Derek Parfit claims that "What now matters most is that we avoid ending human history. If there are no rational beings elsewhere, it may depend on us and our successors whether it will all be worth it, because the existence of the universe will have been on the whole good."[35]

Human interplanetary expansion offers not only the prospect of human survival, but also the continuation of human history into the far future, the long-term prospect of the continued existence of rational beings, and of life itself, in the solar system, for as long as that existence is sustainable. If that life is composed of descendants of Earth life, and those rational beings are the descendants of *Homo sapiens*, so much the better. I don't know what greater legacy into the deep future we could possibly hope for.

Notes

1. James S. A. Corey, *Leviathan Wakes* (London: Orbit, 2011), 19.
2. Estimates based on the amount of carbon, water, phosphorus, and nitrogen on carbonaceous asteroids suggest that the solar system could theoretically support a human population 100,000 times that of the present Earth population. See Michael N. Mautner, "Life-centered Ethics, and the Human Future in Space," *Bioethics* 23 (2009), 433–440.
3. John Leslie, "The Risk that Humans Will Soon Be Extinct," *Philosophy* 85 (2010), 447–463.
4. Derek Parfit, *Reasons and Persons* (Oxford: Clarendon Press, 1984), 452.

5. A recent study confirms that most people do not at first sight seem to think that human extinction would be much worse than near-extinction, which allows for recovery, but the reason might be that they focus too much on the immediate death and suffering. When prompted to think about long-term consequences, they tend to agree that extinction is worse. However, the quality of the alternative future is relevant—people consider extinction much worse if the alternative future would be very good. See Stefan Schubert, Lucius Caviola, and Nadira S. Faber, "The Psychology of Existential Risk: Moral Judgments About Human Extinction," *Scientific Reports* 9 (2019), 1–8.
6. Parfit, *Reasons and Persons*, 453.
7. Samuel Scheffler, *Death and the Afterlife* (Oxford: Oxford University Press, 2013); Samuel Scheffler, *Why Worry About Future Generations?* (Oxford: Oxford University Press, 2018).
8. For example, David Benatar, *Better Never to Have Been: The Harm of Coming into Existence* (Oxford: Oxford University Press, 2008).
9. *Leviathan Wakes*, 465.
10. James Lenman, "On Becoming Extinct," *Pacific Philosophical Quarterly* 83 (2002), 254.
11. A recent estimate is that there might be around 36 civilizations in our galaxy and that it might take over 6,000 years of SETI efforts to achieve communication. Tom Westby and Christopher J. Conselice, "The Astrobiological Copernican Weak and Strong Limits for Intelligent Life," *The Astrophysical Journal* 896 (2020), 58.
12. Derek Parfit, *On What Matters*, volume 2 (Oxford: Oxford University Press, 2011), 620.
13. Lenman, "On Becoming Extinct," 257.
14. James S. A. Corey, *Cibola Burn* (London: Orbit, 2014), 44.
15. Alan R. Johnson, "Biodiversity Requirements for Self-sustaining Space Colonies," *Futures* 110 (2019), 24–27.
16. For an interesting discussion of this topic, see the talk by philosopher Gwen Bradford, "Is There a Moral Obligation to Go to Mars?", especially the Q&A, in which colonization is discussed. Lone Star College-Kingwood (Nov. 1, 2019). "Curious Minds: Is There a Moral Obligation to Go to Mars?" Presented by Gwen Bradford [Video]. YouTube. https://www.youtube.com/watch?v=w4iaAONU7u4.
17. P. A. Carpenter and P. C. Bishop, "A Review of Previous Mass Extinctions and Historic Catastrophic Events," *Futures* 41 (2009), 676–682.
18. Dennis Ray Morgan, "World on Fire: Two Scenarios of the Destruction of Human Civilization and Possible Extinction of the Human Race," *Futures* 41 (2009), 683–693.
19. Leslie, "The Risk."
20. Milan M. Ćirković, "Space Colonization Remains the Only Long-term Option for Humanity: A Reply to Torres," *Futures* 105 (2019), 166–173, 169.
21. Joseph Gottlieb, "Space Colonization and Existential Risk," *Journal of the American Philosophical Association* 5 (2019), 306–320.
22. *Leviathan Wakes*, 512.
23. That is a specious argument—like begrudging money spent in biodiversity protection "when there are people dying of hunger." We cannot wait until there are no immediate needs before starting to tackle other long-term problems.

24. Charles S. Cockell, *Space on Earth: Saving Our World by Seeking Others* (New York: Palgrave Macmillan, 2006).
25. James S. A. Corey, *Caliban's War* (London: Orbit, 2012), 578.
26. *Leviathan Wakes*, 62.
27. Clive Finlayson, *The Humans Who Went Extinct: Why Neanderthals Died Out and We Survived* (Oxford: Oxford University Press, 2009), 44.
28. See, for example, the following books, all of which consider other *Homo* species as human: G. Philip Rightmire, *The Evolution of* Homo Erectus: *Comparative Anatomical Studies of an Extinct Human Species* (Cambridge: Cambridge University Press, 1993); Finlayson, *The Humans Who Went Extinct*; Chris Stringer, *Lone Survivors: How We Came to Be the Only Humans on Earth* (New York: Henry Holt and Company/Times Books, 2012).
29. Finlayson, *The Humans Who Went Extinct*.
30. Phil Torres, "Space Colonization and Suffering Risks: Reassessing the 'Maxipok Rule,'" *Futures* 100 (2018), 74–85.
31. James S. A. Corey, *Nemesis Games* (London: Orbit, 2015), 410.
32. Ćirković, "Space Colonization," 171.
33. As shown in James S. A. Corey, *Persepolis Rising* (London: Orbit, 2018) and *Tiamat's Wrath* (London: Orbit, 2020).
34. *Caliban's War*, p. 111.
35. Parfit, *On What Matters*, vol. 2, 620.

3

Humanity's Dilemma before Abaddon's Gate

Leonard Kahn

James Holden manages to convince an alien technology—Abaddon's Gate, created by the protomolecule—that human beings are not a threat. It opens up 1,300 Einstein-Rosen bridges, providing humanity access to at least as many habitable worlds. Humanity faces a dilemma at the start of the fourth season of *The Expanse*. How should we proceed? Should we use the Ring System to explore and colonize the galaxy, even though trying to do so might kill us all?

Throughout the season, UN Secretary General Chrisjen Avasarala and her political rival, Nancy Gao, debate this question. While Avasarala advocates a slow, cautious approach, Gao champions immediate and aggressive exploration and colonization.

NANCY GAO:	"Whatever is out there, we'll deal with it because that is the history of our species."
CHRISJEN AVASARALA:	"Right up to the moment that our species ceases to exist." ("Subduction")

By the end of the season, Gao has won the debate. She replaces Avasarala as Secretary General and appears poised to begin what James Holden fears will be a "blood-soaked gold rush" ("Abaddon's Gate").

But we can ask, who should have won the debate?

Gao's reasons for favoring a rapid and forceful approach to colonization are rooted in Earth's dire circumstances. Centuries before the series begins, humans have damaged Earth's ecosystem. As a result, about half of its 30 billion inhabitants live on Basic Assistance, a welfare program that provides just the minimum needed to survive. The only way to break free from Basic Assistance is to get a job or training, and competition for these escape routes is so fierce that only 1 in 6,000 people manages to do so. Nico (a man whom we briefly meet in "Cascade") admits to Bobbie Draper

The Expanse and Philosophy: So Far Out Into the Darkness, First Edition. Edited by Jeffery L. Nicholas.

that he has been waiting for a spot on the vocational training list for 35 years. Gao herself was able to escape Basic Assistance only because a well-connected family friend interceded, a fact that Avasarala gleefully threw in her face. As Gao put it, "the system is broken," and the way to fix it is to allow Earth's inhabitants to use the Ring System to explore the hundreds of new worlds available to them ("Oppressor").

Yet the alien technology, the protomolecule, responsible for opening Abaddon's Gate is dangerous. Experimentation with it caused the Eros Incident, which almost killed everyone on Earth. Even after the opening of Abaddon's Gate, the protomolecule was on the verge of wiping out the entire solar system because it saw humanity as a threat. The protomolecule is dangerous, so we need to consider both the benefits and the costs of using the Ring System.

How effective is this response to Gao's reasoning?

The answer depends. In part, we have to know whether Gao counted the benefits correctly. Providing better opportunities for 15 billion people would be wonderful, of course. Yet doing so pales in comparison with other benefits that utilizing the Ring System could have. Gao's reasoning becomes much stronger if we consider the future, rather than just the present, effects of using the Ring System.

Looking at the other advantages means imagining the ends of our potential as a species.

Colonizing the System

The very first words of *The Expanse* appear on a title card: In the twenty-third century, humans have colonized the solar system. In addition to the 30 billion humans on Earth, 1 billion people inhabit its moon, and another 10 billion live on its former colony, Mars. Furthermore, tens of millions of humans live among the Outer Planets, comprising asteroids between Mars and Jupiter and a number of the moons, like Ganymede, of the outer giant planets.

Human colonization of the solar system is a shopworn trope in science fiction—so much so that we might not give it a second thought. Yet, that would be a mistake. Understating the overwhelming importance of expanding beyond our home planet is easy.

Start by considering Derek Parfit's (1942–2017) famous thought experiment:

Compare three outcomes:

1. Peace.
2. A nuclear war that kills 99 percent of the world's existing population.
3. A nuclear war that kills 100 percent.

Obviously, (1) is the best outcome, and (3) is the worst outcome, with (2) sitting between them. However, as great philosophers often do, Parfit pushes past the obvious truth and discovers insights hiding just out of view.

"Most people believe that the greater difference is between (1) and (2), but I believe that the difference between (2) and (3) is much greater. The Earth will remain habitable for at least another billion years. Civilization began only a few thousand years ago. If we do not destroy humankind, these few thousand years may be only a tiny fraction of the whole of civilized human history. The difference between (2) and (3) may thus be the difference between this tiny fraction and all of the rest of this history. If we compare this possible history to a day, what has occurred so far is only a fraction of a second."[1] One of Parfit's main insights is that the future has the potential to contain vastly more value than the present. (We'll return to Parfit's other main insight later in this chapter.)

Toby Ord, a philosopher at Oxford, expands on Parfit's thinking. "If all goes well, human history is just beginning. Humanity is about two-hundred-thousand years old. But the Earth will remain habitable for hundreds of millions more—enough time for millions of future generations; enough to end disease, poverty, and injustice forever; enough to create heights of flourishing unimaginable today."[2] On this quite reasonable assumption about the habitability of Earth, our planet could support an upper bound of 10^{16} human lives of normal duration over a billion years. More than 1 million times as many humans as exist today could exist in the future, and at least ten thousand times as many humans as have ever existed.

Nevertheless, as good as this earthbound possible future would be, humanity has another possible future that is many, many orders of magnitude better. This possible future is one in which we expand far beyond the bounds of our solar system. Ord gives us a glimpse of this possible future: "if we could learn to reach out further into the cosmos, we could have more time yet: trillions of years, to explore billions of worlds. Such a lifespan places present-day humanity in its earliest infancy. A vast and extraordinary adulthood awaits."[3] Expanding beyond our solar system could allow humanity and its descendants somewhere between 10^{34} and 10^{71} lives of normal duration.[4]

In other words, failing to colonize our solar system, the Milky Way galaxy, and perhaps even the Virgo Supercluster could cost the future between 10^{18} and 10^{55} human lives.

These numbers are so immense as to defy understanding. Here is one provocative way of thinking about the matter. The worst disaster in human history so far has been World War II, which cost about 50 million human lives over six years. Sticking to conservative estimates, failing to colonize the Milky Way would be worse—one hundred trillion times worse. Put somewhat differently, the loss would be approximately equivalent to one

World War II every second from 1200 BCE (at the time of the Late Bronze-Age Collapse, the writing of the *Rigveda*, and the zenith of the Shang Dynasty) to our own present day.

A moment ago, we noted that it is easy to understate the importance of humanity's ability in *The Expanse* to travel across and colonize the solar system. Now we can see why. Moving beyond the confines of the Earth is the first step toward achieving humanity's interstellar potential, what Max Tegmark, a physicist at MIT, has called our "unlimited cosmic endowment."[5]

Colonizing at the Speed of Light

Yet, once it becomes evident just how much is at stake, another point comes into view. It matters greatly, not only that humanity expands, but how quickly. On one self-consciously conservative estimate, every second that we delay colonization of the Virgo Supercluster is "a loss of potential equal to about 10^{14} potential human lives."[6] That is one thousand times as many human lives as have existed until now.

The opening of the Ring System is even more important than it might seem. About 130 years prior to the beginning of the series, humanity had barely begun to colonize our solar system. The settlement on Mars was dependent for resources on Earth, a planet that was struggling to provide its own inhabitants with the wherewithal for survival. The invention of the Epstein drive changed this situation radically. By allowing humans to move much more quickly throughout the solar system, the inhabitants of both Earth and Mars could begin to extract and utilize the resources of the asteroid belt and the moons of the giant planets beyond. The Epstein drive's importance is made clear by the fact that during the first four seasons, the only substantial flashback we see is to Solomon Epstein's invention of the drive named after him ("Paradigm Shift"). Improvements in the Epstein drive continued for more than a century, and the results rightly impress. As the series begins, the construction of the LDSS *Nauvoo*, a generation ship with the most sophisticated Epstein drive ever created, the G4000, is close to completion. The G4000 is so powerful that eight of them can accelerate a ship that is 2 kilometers long and half a kilometer wide to over 10 percent of the speed of light. By way of contrast, the tallest building as of this writing, the Burj Khalifa in Dubai, is not even half the size of the *Nauvoo*. Moreover, the fastest humans have managed to travel in space is 0.0037 percent of the speed of light, just 1/27th of the speed of this generation ship.

Even so, the *Nauvoo* would have taken about 100 years to reach its goal, the Tau Ceti system, a mere 12 light years away. The journey of the *Nauvoo* would have exposed its crew to a century's worth of extrasolar risks, all of which it would have to endure without any possibility of help. Moreover, even if the inhabitants of the *Nauvoo* were lucky enough to avoid 100 years of extreme danger, Tau Ceti might not have a world habitable by human beings. The journey could easily have been a literal dead end for everyone involved. Now, consider the fact that the Milky Way's diameter is between 170,000 and 200,000 light years. Hence, relying on Epstein drives to explore and colonize the galaxy would take hundreds of million—if not billions—of years and cost an unimaginable amount of future human lives.

In contrast, the Ring System presents humanity with over 1,300 portals to worlds that they know to be habitable. The system allows journeys that would take unnumbered generations millions or billions of years to be reduced to a matter of months. For example, a mundane research vessel like the *Edward Israel* traveled from Ceres Station, just beyond Mars, to the planet Ilus in a mere 18 months. Though we are not told how far Ilus is from our solar system, it could easily be tens of thousands of light years. Furthermore, though the Belter settlers on Ilus, such as Felicia, Jakob, and Lucia Mazur, were clearly on the bleeding edge of human expansion, the Ring System allowed them to remain connected with the rest of humanity. They arrived on Ilus with limited supplies, but they planned to extract lithium from the planet so that some of them could return through the ring to our solar system. Unlike the would-be colonists on the *Nauvoo*, these settlers didn't have to do the impossible and plan for every contingency. To be sure, the Belters faced great dangers on Ilus—and not only from Royal Charter Energy's goons. But colonizing the rest of the Milky Way galaxy via the rings would be many orders of magnitude less risky for individual settlers than doing so while relying on Epstein drives. More importantly, it would also be many orders of magnitude faster.

Unimaginable Opportunities

We can now return to the debate between Gao and Avasarala. Clearly, Gao underestimated the potential benefits of rapid expansion by means of the Ring System. Not only could doing so provide better opportunities for billions of humans today, it could make possible orders of magnitude more human lives in the future.

But the debate is not over. We have only looked at one side of the ledger.

The risks involved with using the Ring System are clear from the Eros Incident. Gao acknowledges this, but she maintains that, given the "unimaginable opportunities" provided by the Ring System, the "real danger of Eros is that we only react to it in fear." Always ready with the pithy rejoinder, Avasarala retorts that the real danger of the Eros Incident was "that it was about to kill everybody on Earth" ("Oppressor"). She is concerned with the fates of the 40 or so billion human beings alive at the time of *The Expanse*. In order for her response to Gao to convince us, Avasarala needs to expand her circle of moral concern beyond those alive today to those who will live in the future. Risking the lives of 4×10^{10} humans for the sake of the lives of as many as 10^{71} humans seems more than reasonable. At that level, the population of the solar system is a rounding error at more than 50 decimal places.

However, this line of thought is flawed. It involves comparing the gains for all humans who will ever live if we successfully colonize the galaxy with the losses for all humans who exist right now if we go extinct as a result of using the Ring System. This calculation ignores all the humans who would have existed if we either did not use the Ring System or were more cautious in its use, as Avasarala suggests. In other words, Avasarala's response to Gao is most convincing when we think of using the Ring System as what philosophers call an "existential risk."

Ord defines existential risk as "a risk that threatens the destruction of humanity's long-term potential."[7] If use of the Ring System kills the current generation of humans, 40 billion people die. As bad as that is, the result is actually much worse. It also prevents the existence of all future human beings.

Recall Parfit's point: even if we remain earthbound, we might live here for another billion years during which time about 10^{16} humans can live sustainably. Yet, our comparison is not the number of humans on Earth, but the number in *The Expanse*. Humans have already begun interstellar travel and colonizing the galaxy. Even at radically subluminal speeds that will delay colonization of the galaxy by tens or hundreds of millions of years, the potential number of human lives could come within several orders of magnitude of the potential number of humans if we did successfully use the Ring System.

Here, then, is Parfit's second main insight (promised earlier): the value of preventing human extinction and thereby making the fulfillment of humanity's long-term potential more likely is much, much higher than it might seem. Given what is at stake, Avasarala's response to Gao seems strongest when it is framed in terms of existential risk. As noted, the proto-molecule has already come close to driving our species to extinction. More importantly, use of the Ring System is closely related to whatever killed its mysterious creators 2 billion years before the events of the series. Those creators were destroyed despite having advanced their technology to something indistinguishable from magic. It might not be possible to say with any precision just how hazardous use of the Ring System is, and we do not want to minimize the difficulty of making rational choices under conditions of ignorance. Despite the benefits the Ring System might offer, it does not seem like an existential risk worth taking. Our future, flawed as it is, is too good to endanger.

Therefore, Avasarala should have won the debate with Gao, and humanity should say "Thanks but no thanks" to using the Ring System—or at least use the system with far more caution than Gao advocates.

Or so says this philosopher.

Unfortunately, history has witnessed a long, sad tradition of philosophers playing the role of Cassandra, the mythological priestess of Apollo who was cursed to utter true prophecies that no one believed until it was too late. This tradition goes back at least as far as Socrates, who argued (correctly!), though to no avail, against the execution of the generals of the Battle of Arginusae and later of Leon of Salamis. Eventually execution came for Socrates too.

We have to wonder whether Avasarala and her cautious approach ever had a chance. The colonists on Ilus arrived by running the blockade maintained by the truce between Earth, Mars, and the Belt. That truce could not last forever; eventually one of the three powers in the solar system would break with the others and attempt to use the Ring System. Avasarala goes so far as to leak classified video from Ilus in order to frighten the electorate enough to side with her ("The One-Eyed Man"). Yet scare tactics like these will only work in the short run, if at all. Hundreds of ships from Earth waited outside Abaddon's Gate as the season began. With pirates like Marco Inaros picking them off, it seems likely that many of the would-be colonists would eventually prefer to take their chances running the blockade. While UN ships were willing to destroy Belters who tried to run the blockade, they probably wouldn't have done so if the ships were full of their fellow citizens. Gao was likely more right than she knew when she said, "Colonization of the Ring systems is inevitable" ("Subduction").

While philosophers might imagine that truth will always win in the marketplace of ideas, Avasarala had no such illusions after losing the election. She left the incoming Secretary General a remarkable message: "As for policy and the direction you're taking Earth and all her peoples, well, we disagree. One of us is wrong. I think it's you. But I hope it's me" ("Cibola Burn").

Actual Threats to Our Existence

Of course, *The Expanse* is a work of science fiction, and its success or failure rests primarily on whether it entertains us, not whether it tells us something significant about our own world. And we certainly do not face the threat of extinction because of accidental exposure to alien technology! However, we would do well to recognize the actual threats to our existence. One survey of risk experts concluded that there is a 19 percent chance of human extinction by the year 2100.[8] Ord's estimate is closer to 17 percent.[9] Some of that risk is the result of familiar nightmares such as nuclear war and engineered pandemics, and some of that risk is a function of technology that is, for the moment, only the stuff of science fiction, such as molecular nanotech weapons and runaway artificial general intelligence. These technologies present humanity with a dilemma that is similar to the one presented by Abaddon's Gate. Should we develop these technologies quickly, even though they pose a significant risk of killing us all and extinguishing forever our vast potential? Can we resist developing them even if we recognize it is a manifestly bad idea to do so? We may soon see for ourselves. Like Avasarala, we can only hope that the pessimists are wrong.

Notes

1. Derek Parfit, *Reasons and Persons* (Oxford: Clarendon Press), 453.
2. Toby Ord, *The Precipice: Existential Risk and the Future of Humanity* (New York: Hachette Books), 3.
3. Ibid.
4. Nick Bostrom, "Existential Risk Prevention as Global Priority," *Global Policy* 4 (2013), 15–31.
5. Max Tegmark, *Life 3.0: Being Human in the Age of Artificial Intelligence* (New York: Knopf), 221.
6. Nick Bostrom, "Astronomical Waste: The Opportunity Cost of Delayed Technological Development," *Utilitas* 15 (2003), 308–314.
7. Ord, *The Precipice*, 37.
8. Anders Sandberg and Nick Bostrom, "Global Catastrophic Risks Survey," Technical Report #2008-1, Future of Humanity Institute (2008), Oxford University, 1–5.
9. Ord, *The Precipice*, 167.

4

Hate Expectations
Politics and Gender Roles in *The Expanse*

S. W. Sondheimer

"Everyone gets a pony and a blow job" sounds like a can't-lose campaign platform for any politician running for any office she desired.

I'm being facetious of course: this sharp, ironic turn of phrase is a favorite example of Chrisjen Avasarala's cutting, sarcastic wit, not an actual proposal to her constituents. Instead, she offers the citizens of Earth a far more practical, if a bit more mundane, promise: experience, intelligence, political savvy, a willingness to take on the less savory tasks of governance, and a proven track record of having saved humanity from its own ego several times over.

Yet, when the election results are tallied, Avasarala discovers she has lost to the younger, inexperienced, untested Nancy Gao.

How could such a thing happen? Would it? Would such a large percentage of the population disregard logic and rationality when the specter of war and the promise of future crisis loom on the horizon? Surely an experienced leader is the best foundation for a stable government. One need only examine the conversation between Gao and Avasarala regarding the name of the colony planet on the other side of the Ring System to see who the more careful, steady leader would be.

GAO: It's New Terra. That's what our citizens call it unless you forgot.
AVASARALA: Does its name change what's happening there?

Gao expounds on the ways in which sending settlers through the Ring System will solve all of Earth's problems easily and essentially without conflict. Avasarala asks her what she plans to do when those settlers face inevitable challenges and, possibly, resistance from other species that the protomolecule has proven exist—or at the very least, existed at one time. Gao claims, "We'll deal with it because that is the history of our species."

The Expanse and Philosophy: So Far Out Into the Darkness, First Edition. Edited by Jeffery L. Nicholas.
© 2022 John Wiley & Sons, Inc. Published 2022 by John Wiley & Sons, Inc.

Avasarala, who's seen far more of that history, responds, "Right up until our species ceases to exist."

If you were one of the settlers, which of these women would you want making policy? Which of them would you want as a rear guard? In control of the supply chain?

Avasarala, no question.

She's a bit abrasive though, isn't she? Tells people to "get the fuck" out of her office a lot. Not to "stick their dick in it." Flaunts her intelligence. And why didn't her husband go to Luna with her? Do you think she had that Belter tortured? And Gao wasn't wrong when she called Avasarala a member of the "political aristocracy." Does she know what it's like to work for something? She probably does think she's better than everyone else.

The mold of what a woman should be was cast millennia ago, and, while we like to think we've progressed as a people and as a larger society, even a superficial survey of the Western world's view of ideal femininity and a woman's place in the larger whole, and especially in politics, shows we haven't evolved much since Adam crunched into that pomegranate. Avasarala knew that and still dared to be herself, still dared to demand the respect due her intelligence, wit, and experience despite being well aware that, even if equines and oral sex had been on offer, she would still have lost the position of General Secretary. That she refused to be anything else is a sign of her bravery; that her loss was inevitable under the circumstances is a travesty. This travesty has roots so far back in the annals of human history, so deeply embedded, that we saw their influence in the real-world election of 2016 and are forced to acknowledge that it's unlikely an election in 2350 would be any different.

For the sake of clarity and brevity, this chapter will use binary language as regards gender. Female should be understood to include anyone who considers her/themself female/femme.

The Male is By Nature More Expert at Leading and Other Complete Drivel: Aristotle Tries to Find his Ass With Two Hands and a Fakós

If it were up to Avasarala, she would continue to operate as she always has: honestly, bluntly, directly. Of course, when men do this, they're "assertive." When women do it, they're "nasty or bitchy." Her husband, however, insists that she hire a campaign manager. (Interesting that he wants her "managed" then, considering that he never has before and that this is when he starts to "manage" her body, directing her posture, speech cadence, and facial expression.) She does as he asks to please him, and one of the first things her new team does is recommend that she shift her manner from regal head of state to "nurturing, caring family matriarch" ("Oppressor"). On the policy side, they instruct her to focus on domestic issues such as grain allotments rather than the very real threats of renewed war and alien invasion.

Avasarala's team is shoving her back into the modern equivalent of the role Aristotle (384–322 BCE) established for women. You can almost hear them, how dare Avasarala be confident enough to stand up in front of everyone and discuss matters affecting the planet and solar system when there's food to distribute and the constituency doesn't like it when she yells, and goodness she's using big words again. I mean honestly, you have a uterus, act like a mother or you'll scare them off.

Aristotle tried to explain why women could not be good politicians. Women were in a subservient position because, at least according to Aristotle, they were, rare to medium. Men were well done, which meant that the "courage of men lies in commanding, a woman's lies in obeying."[1]

In case you were wondering, no, that's not a metaphor. Aristotle's philosophy was built on the foundation that all material substances were a combination of "form" and "matter" with matter defined as a thing's potential and form as its reality. Everything needs both matter and form to exist. However, it's important to note that in Aristotelian philosophy, matter cannot exist without form to embody it. Ultimately, then, form determines what a thing is. "Matter," he posited, "yearns for form as the female for the male and the ugly for the beautiful."[2] Simply put as applied to gender: women need men to complete them while men enjoy, but do not require, the presence of women.

How does this belief apply to politics? Humans, Aristotle continues, bond in pairs for sex and stay together to make certain at least some of their offspring survive to adulthood (if we are to have men, we must perpetuate the species after all), to divide chores (80/20-ish women/men), and because it's pleasant to spend time with someone you "like and respect" (read: dominate and can force to do what you want). The man is, of course, in charge but not, as many assume, because women are ruled by their emotions. No, men are in charge because they are form, while women are matter. It's all about chemistry, you see.

Women's contribution to the perpetuation of the species is blood. Men's contribution, sperm, is "cooked blood." That means they, and any offspring who produce sperm, are "better cooked." They are more complete beings.[3] This difference in cold and hot blood, Aristotle argues, is why the females are larger, softer, slower, and more likely to stay with the young in most species. Males, on the other hand, are smaller, more active, more aggressive, and more likely to have tusks and horns. (Aristotle, apparently, never met a lion.) Additional proof of this theory lies in the fact women have "fewer teeth than men," and are thus, incomplete and deformed males.[4] Unfortunately for men, you cannot complete a recipe without all of the ingredients and, thus, they must tolerate the presence of their less complete and subservient selves.

Aristotle didn't chide women for this; if half of humanity wasn't under-cooked, there would be no species and who would do the women's work? The woman defers in marriage, in society, in politics because someone must be the mature party and it cannot possibly be the underdone female.[5] Athenian law forbade women from owning property or accounts, though they could hold them in trust for their sons until they married again (which they were compelled to do) because their incomplete minds couldn't com-prehend the intricacies of money or land ownership. For this same reason, women could not be citizens. Minds so lacking could not be counted upon to vote wisely. And if they could not be counted upon to weigh options, they certainly couldn't be counted upon to make policy. Thus, Aristotle concluded, it was safer for all to release women from the burden of leadership.

For their own protection of course.

Living in a more modern world, Avasarala is a citizen and politics is more than her job; it's her milieu. She grew up immersed in it and her adult life has been consumed by participation while her husband, Arjun, took the quieter, academic path and seems to perform the majority of domestic duties. We don't know who was primary parent when the couple's children were young. Aristotle would, no doubt, have been shocked to see his neatly arranged society not only violated but violated and functioning just fine, thank you very much.

Would her team want her to play the father figure if she were a man? The caring patriarch? Doubtful. Because if Avasarala had been a man, her true self would have been the expectation, not the exception. Stern. Authoritative if not authoritarian. Decisive. Powerful. Bold. All of the things Avasarala is would be virtues if she had a penis and facial hair. Because those are lacking, because she can, and has, given birth, the citi-zens of Earth look past her record, past her successes, past the fact she saved all of their lives and demand she fit herself into a mold that will never suit her, one made for ancient, fictitious, gelatinous, half-baked protoplasm, rather than actual human people.

Gao, in contrast, is calm. She has nurtured the futures of those who allowed her to succeed. She has a rosy vision of the future where no one dies in the void of space and everyone has enough to eat, an Earth mother distributing plenty. She, as Aaron Burr says in *Hamilton*, "talks less and smiles more." While she may be out in the world doing things political, she is, insofar as 2350 is concerned, a homebody. She hasn't been collaborating with the traitorous Martians or filthy Belters like her opponent. If the Aristotelian woman had a future self, she'd look a lot like Nancy Gao. She's familiar. She's comfortable. She isn't going to rock anyone's boat or anyone's world. And let's be honest: world rocking isn't what anyone is looking for in a Secretary General. The folk who found nations get parental monikers for a reason.

Me and My Husband and My Byronic Hero are Taking Our Giant Helmet and Going Home

As we continue our journey through time and space, we discover not only that men insist on viewing the stuff from which women are made as inferior and our demands to be treated as equals worthy of scorn and (literal) curses, but that they see very little worth in women as individuals in any capacity other than mothers, maids, and sex toys. David Hume (1711–1776) went so far as to insist that women are unable to appreciate the truly sublime because we don't have a brain capable of synthesizing a subjective opinion.[6]

In "An Enquiry Concerning the Humean Woman," Christine Battersby points out that, while Hume didn't write a single work exploring the vapid female, one can draw a portrait by gathering tidbits from his various works into a composite. In *The History of England*, for example, Hume posits male readers might find it difficult to take Queen Elizabeth seriously as a leader because they "find it difficult to reconcile our fancy for her as a wife or mistress."[7] An interesting take considering Elizabeth was a leader, and no man's wife, for forty-five years and Hume was king for zero years.

Women, Hume contended, might be superior at social artifice and politeness (a.k.a.: the fake stuff), but only because, if they weren't created better than men at something, they might as well be slaves.[8] In his *Second Enquiry*, Hume doubles down, comparing women to "livestock" and "barbarous Indians." Essentially, women are an entirely different species, considered human only because their "wiles" are pleasing to men.[9]

Men, he continues, in contrast might pretend and perhaps even defer to the ladies from time to time. Appeasing the fairer sex proves man a benevolent dictator after all and demonstrates male superiority. It also allows him to go about his business unburdened and unhindered by women's emotions and carryings on, which grow extreme when untended. In "unrelated" news, Hume's argument against polygamy had nothing to do with Christianity or morality. Rather, he believed that appeasing so many women would take up too much of one man's time, preventing him from getting the real work done.

Men, however, may also be as "venereal"[10] (not a typo) as they please with no fear for their reputation because boys will be boys. Despite expectations of perfect restraint, "chastity, fidelity, and modesty," on the part of women, men may run amok without fear of reprisal. Women are the ones lacking in the judgment and bravery necessary for them to take on the duties of household, let alone political, leadership.[11] Women are, alas, naturally submissive, bashful, timid, gallant, pathological liars, and have the tendency to fall deeply and ardently in love which divests them of all reason. Men, despite being venereal, can somehow maintain the mental and moral faculties necessary to guide humanity through the present and into the future.

In an interesting twist, Hume has argued himself into a little bit of a dilemma: if men are responsible for guiding society, they're the ones in charge of women's education which, according to the philosopher, is inferior. This inferior education is, in large part, responsible for the deficits in female character, which implies that, with a better education, women would be improved on all counts. All it would take to implement such a plan is for men to decide it should be so.

In "Displacement," Avasarala dares to take command of a military situation (you know, because she's Commander-in-Chief and all), throwing female timidity (*snort*) to the wind, deciding to send United Nations Marines to board a Belter ship and capture terrorist Marco Inaros rather than destroy the ship and the civilian crew. The mission goes badly, the Marines and the civilians are lost, and Inaros gets away.

In the next episode, Avasarala delivers a speech written by her staff in which she says ordering the action was a mistake and that, going forward, she will reorder her priorities. After her mea culpas, she berates herself for abasing herself in the public eye. Arjun asks her why she's so upset.

AVASARALA:	They just made me admit I was weak.
ARJUN:	All you admitted is that you're not infallible.
AVASARALA:	In an election, they're the same thing.
ARJUN:	You got out in front of it and you told the truth.
AVASARALA:	It's better not to say anything . . . I should have trusted my judgment.

Men in politics have the luxury of error, of "venereality," as Hume would have phrased it. Thomas Jefferson raped his slaves. Nixon resigned, but it wasn't over the travesty that was Vietnam because democracy! Kennedy snuck Marilyn Monroe into the White House and, I mean, who wouldn't have? Clinton was impeached by the House but not by the Senate over the Monica Lewinsky episode which, while not illegal, was surely real gross, and Donald Trump was elected president despite recorded evidence of him having sexually assaulted several women, bankrupted several businesses, screamed about immigration but used undocumented labor for his construction projects, and allegedly cheated on his taxes.

Meanwhile, the press hammered Michelle Obama for trying to improve school lunches and hounded Hillary Clinton about email, her hairdo, and the fact that she was photosensitive for a few days after a concussion. Neither of them held actual public offices at the time.

Are we seeing the dichotomy? Men in positions of power get away with (figurative but maybe also sometimes literal) murder. If Errinwright had ordered the attack on the Belter ship and it had gone wrong, would it have been a mistake? Unlikely. The fallen Marines would have been heroes killed in action attempting to apprehend a dangerous terrorist and awarded posthumous medals while Errinwright sent condolences and the next platoon. But because Avasarala is a woman, because she stepped outside of her purview and made a decision firmly and resolutely, without deferring to any of her military advisors (all men, mind you), her decision became a lapse for which she is expected to apologize. From which she is expected to shrink, after which she is expected to "rewrite her narrative." From that point forward, every decision she makes is scrutinized, assumed to be flawed. Staff whispers behind her back. Her husband storms out of the room when she says something he doesn't like. Generals resign.

Hume would be overjoyed.

Paint Me Like One of Your Manic Pixie Dream Girls

Surely the women of the Romantic Era, immortalized so strikingly in paintings such as Frederic Leighton's *Flaming June*, Edmund Blair Leighton's *The Accolade*, and Sir John Everett Millais' *Ophelia* had the respect of the men who painted them, who chose such august legends into which to insert them, such vaunted figures in which to incarnate their likenesses?

Meh.

Lasting from approximately 1800 to 1890, the Romantic Era was, if anything, more restrictive for women than the period during which Hume was spinning in his hamster wheel vis-à-vis the origin of female deficits. The women of Gothic literature were, at the very least, permitted their wanderings of forest and moor or the occasional late-night flight from an accursed castle, suggesting it wasn't untoward for their real-life counterparts to, say, take a walk once in a while, even if it wasn't through the halls of Parliament.

Mary Wollstonecraft (1759–1797) and others suggested equality in all realms was "a logical extension" of the much lauded "Lady Liberty" and tried valiantly to use Hume's logic loop to argue "if it's our lack of education that makes us inferior then spend less time focusing on our bodies and more on our minds!" Lawmakers responded by tightening legislation that regulated women's bodies. Doctors, rather than midwives, began to attend births. Society increased focus on birth control and which parties could regulate it, instituting stricter laws with higher financial penalty for "hiding" pregnancies.

At a couple of points, Romantic-Era philosophy intersects with Avasarala's treatment in *The Expanse*. The first is the way Arjun responds when she mentions the death of their son during the memorial for the aforementioned Marines. He accused Avasarala of using "our son's death for political gain," of lying when she spoke of her feelings for Charanpal, the ways in which she mourned him, and how much she loved him. When she tells Arjun everything she said about Charanpal was true, he storms out rather than discussing it with her further. By leaving at that moment, Arjun takes control of Avasarala's narrative of motherhood, just as doctors and lawmakers did during the Romantic Era with new practices and regulations. By refusing to listen to what Avasarala has to say, Arjun maintains control over her part of the story, making their shared experience of parenthood, and their son's death, his rather than theirs and discounting the parts of it that are Avasarala's alone.

In the Romantic Era, social mores went from lauding general male superiority to denigrating the female body in addition to the female psyche, insisting the only good woman was an idle one. While early feminists like Mary Wollstonecraft protested, philosophers like Jean-Jacques Rousseau (1712–1778) agreed that the proper activities for ladies were those that did not require exertion: painting, music, and needlework, for example. During at least the first half of the period, fashion was designed specifically to restrain movement with corseting, layering, and hoops that made the basic movements of walking and breathing difficult. Excessive, fragile decoration was added to make women reluctant to exert themselves even if they had been able. Mobility did not improve when fashion shifted the skirt's volume to the bustle because supporting the heavy accessory required additional corseting. Only at the tail end of the nineteenth century, when the suffrage movement gained momentum and women moved (back) into the workforce, did fashion change. Women's factory and secretarial jobs made bustles and corsets impossible; men conceded physical freedom, though the concessions came at the price of intellectual gains.

Just after this period, in 1916, Jeannette Rankin was elected to the US House of Representatives, though she couldn't vote for herself (women weren't granted the right to vote in the US until 1920). Hattie Wyatt Cattaway, the first female Senator, was seated in 1932, replacing her husband who died in office, though she later won reelection on her own. One hundred and twenty-seven years, and one hundred forty-three years, respectively, after one of the newest nations in the world was born.

Another issue is stillness, an often-sought-after quality, though in the case of *The Expanse* "idleness" is more symbolic than literal. In the show's fourth season, we only ever see Gao inside of the UN building or at debate locations. She is never outside, never in orbit; we never even see her at home. She is confined, constrained, and, by virtue of this constraint, one of the people—most of whom will never leave Earth unless there is a fundamental change in Earther society. It's a change Gao is offering that Avasarala is not.

Avasarala, however, has been a great many places: we've seen her in space (and heard tell of how much she hates it) aboard Jules-Pierre Mao's ship, then the *Razorback*, and then the *Rocinante*. She has worked directly and discretely with Martians, Belters, and chronic pains in the ass (looking at you, Holden). She leaves the UN building to meet with Bobby by the ocean. She and Arjun have a home away from the General Secretaries' apartments. She goes to Mars (wearing my favorite of her many saris). She goes to Luna.

Avasarala has never been confined. She has never been constrained. How then, Gao might ask, can she be trusted to understand what life is like for the majority? Has she, like those wandering women who went to work outside the home during the nineteenth century, who didn't wear corsets and bustles, who took walks, been corrupted? Is she a, god forbid, free thinker? A feminist? What is she going to want next? To be able to vote for herself?

Hyperbole, of course, but you can see where the populace might be more likely to trust Gao because she has always, like the idle ladies of yore, been in sight. They know what she's done, and they can predict what she might do in the future. Avasarala, by contrast, is a wild card who dared wander against all rules of decency and cannot, therefore, be predicted. That which cannot be predicted cannot be trusted.

Who's the Nasty One Now? Fear Mongering and the Fragile Male Ego

Victoria Woodhall, a stockbroker and newspaper publisher, was the first woman to make a bid for the US Presidency in 1872 despite being four years too young to meet the requirement set by the founding documents and, like Jeanette Rankin, unable to vote for herself. Due to her radical ideas on divorce (everyone who wanted one should be able to get one) and her embrace of Spiritualism (remember, Mary Todd Lincoln was having seances in the White House not ten years prior, so not really out of bounds), Elizabeth Cady Stanton and Susan B. Anthony, noted suffragettes and feminists, decided not to endorse her. It's unlikely, though, that their refusal to endorse was the nail in the coffin of her campaign. In 1964, Margaret Chase Smith was the first woman to have her name entered into contention at a major party's convention (Republican—surprise!). In 1972, Shirley Chisholm was the first Black woman to seek her party's nomination. When Pat Schroder sought the Democratic nomination in 1988, someone asked her how she could be both a mother and the President, to which she responded, "I have a brain and a uterus, and I use both."

I know, guys, color you shocked.

Men in politics certainly don't want to believe women can multitask so efficiently. They want their constituents to believe that women are 100 percent defined by their uterus. Okay, maybe 90 percent by their uterus and 10 percent by their hair. They want society to believe having a uterus means we've been unworthy to be queens, to be equal partners, to be complete beings, to be capable of rational thought, to literally be worthy of walking the planet.

Admit it. You believe it. We're born believing it. We're bred to believe it.

Think I'm exaggerating? Let's look at the 2016 Presidential election.

One candidate is an experienced politician. She's an accomplished lawyer. She spent eight years learning how to navigate White House life. She served as Secretary of State. She was a Senator. She's run charitable foundations. She can debate anyone. She is intelligent, witty, and well-nigh unfazable. Is her record spotless? No. Some potential financial discrepancies and a questionable decision regarding an email server are in her past. Like Avasarala, though, she makes solid decisions based on up-to-date intelligence information and takes the hit when people accuse her of mishandling situations that only she had complete information on. Perhaps she is a member of the political aristocracy, but she has always taken that responsibility seriously and done what she thinks is right for the planet and its people. She is excellent at sorting priorities and taking the long view.

The other candidate is a business magnate of questionable efficacy. He's never held political office, even at the local level. He doesn't know the law. He has fits of temper. He yells rather than debates. He doesn't seem to understand the difference between humor and insult. Is his record spotless? No. Credible accusations of sexual harassment and rape have been leveled against him. Credible accusations of treason have been made against him. He has used undocumented workers in construction projects. He refused to disclose his tax returns as Presidents are not required, but traditionally offer, to do. He did not divest himself of his business interests while campaigning (which, may I point out, even Lex Luthor did).

In fairness, Nancy Gao is a better candidate than that guy. She is at least intelligent and well-meaning. She did, however, use personal connections to help her queue jump the Apprentice Lottery, giving her immediate opportunity others wait decades for. When called out, Gao justifies the advantage by explaining she hired the people who were skipped in her favor—except the one who died of a drug overdose before she could find him. Rather than address the root of the accusation, she turns the lens back on her opponent. She's good at picking up on buzz words and using them to garner attention, but she makes promises without knowing whether or not she'll be able to keep them. She has no idea how to project and plan, which has a good chance of leading not only to financial difficulty, but also to political upheaval and quite possibly loss of life.

Who do you vote for?

Logic says you vote for the first candidate. The one with experience. The one who knows the law. The one who didn't collude with foreign nations, who isn't a sex offender, who isn't currently breaking an unknown number of laws.

The one who can prioritize. Who knows how to plan, who can take the long view. Who understands that slow and steady isn't always satisfying but it does work.

The one who understands how the law works and how people work. Who can prioritize and predict.

And yet, it's the second candidate who's using the Oval Office. When he isn't out golfing.

The second candidate who is going to lead the people out among the stars.

How? Why?

Because Donald Trump's campaign figured out how to play the Aristotle angle, the Hume angle, the angle that's been perpetuated through human history and on to today.

Because Nancy Gao fits the mold Avasarala refuses to be forced in to.

The angle that paints any woman who dares try to use her brain, to show her intelligence, to say, "I am worthy of being your leader," or, "I can do a better job than this man," as power hungry and vicious and nasty. Our society has such deeply embedded fear of powerful women, women who don't fit the demure, soft, pliable mold after millennia of being told "this is the way," that it's an easy thing for demagogues to tug on the thread that connects them to demons and whores, to strum it and have us humming an ancient tune.

Tell her to smile more; she says no. Insult her; she responds with sarcasm. Try to menace her physically; she'll stab you with the sharpest verbal knife you've ever experienced. She doesn't care what you think of her because she knows she's your equal. She is the Queen Elizabeth who was, not the distracting mistress Hume saw. And rare is the man seeking power whose ego will take such an attack. Rare is the man who won't use the oldest weapon men have against women to win that battle. And rare is the Western-educated individual who can avoid a knee-jerk fear response when they see the winged demon coming for them.

Conclusion: Whatever I Goddamn Like

I'd like to think that by 2350, we'd have managed some progress on the nasty woman thing but, alas, we've held on to it this long. Is it rational to think a couple more centuries will make a difference? Humans aren't great at self-reflection; we tend to get uncomfortable when taking long, honest looks at our gooey insides and admitting that we've internalized something we've been pretending doesn't exist anymore. That's not going to be any kind of party.

The truth is, Avasarala probably would have lost that election to Nancy Gao. She may be the Secretary General people need, but, unless some bomb explodes revelation glitter all over the Western Hemisphere and the glitter has nanites and the nanites rewrite our programming, Nancy Gao is the Secretary General they want. Bread and circus promises in a pretty, polite, sweet, pulled-herself-up-by-her-reasonable-pumps package. Doesn't drink or swear, at least not where anyone can see or hear her. Doesn't challenge the military complex, smiles for the camera, isn't messy or complicated, and doesn't eat pistachios while she's interrogating OPA suspects.

Will Gao be a good Secretary General? I've read the books, but out of respect for those who are going the show-only route, I won't spoil things by giving you an answer. Besides, that's not really the question, is it? The question is why she's measuring for new drapes when Avasarala, who has served long and well, is advising the transition team before going into retirement. I think our journey through time and space has answered our questions. As to when we, and the denizens of *The Expanse* universe, will finally dig this garbage philosophy out of our shared consciousness and set it on fire, how about now?

I'm free right now.

Notes

1. Charlotte Witt and Lisa Shapiro, "Feminist History of Philosophy," *The Stanford Encyclopedia of Philosophy* (Spring 2021 Edition), ed. Edward N. Zalta, https://plato.stanford.edu/archives/spr2021/entries/feminism-femhist/.
2. Ibid.
3. Francis Sparshott, "Aristotle on Women," *The Society for Ancient Greek Philosophy Newsletter*, 107 (1983), https://orb.binghamton.edu/cgi/viewcontent.cgi?article=1106&context=sagp.
4. Witt and Shapiro, "Feminist History of Philosophy."
5. Sparshott, "Aristotle on Women."
6. Theodore Gracyk, "Hume's Aesthetics," *The Stanford Encyclopedia of Philosophy* (Summer 2020 Edition), ed. Edward N. Zalta, https://plato.stanford.edu/archives/sum2020/entries/hume-aesthetics/.
7. David Hume, *The History of England*, volume 4 (Edinburgh: Edinburgh University Press, 2013).
8. Christine Battersby, "An Enquiry Concerning the Humean Woman," *Philosophy* 56, no. 217 (1981), 303–312, http://www.jstor.org/stable/3750274.
9. Ibid.
10. Ibid.
11. Ibid.

Second Orbit

IS IT THE PROTOMOLECULE, OR JUST HUMAN NATURE?

5

The Banality of Evil
Hannah Arendt
and Jules-Pierre Mao

R. S. Leiby

Imagine attending the judicial event of the century: the trial of Jules-Pierre Mao. There he sits in the defendant dock, cuffed, and flanked on each side by blue-helmeted UN MPs. Well-dressed, Mao still exudes an air of power and wealth; yet there is a new sense of sincerity and contrition about him. Mao's legal team has been working hard to convince the judges and the people of the System that he is a well-meaning, long-suffering, much-maligned hero of humanity. Imagine the uproar from the gallery when he enters his plea: not guilty.

In what way does Mao mean that he is not guilty? Does he mean that he himself had not signed off on or directed the entire, blood-soaked protomolecule project, from the destruction of the *Canterbury* to the genocide on Eros to the human experimentation on Ganymede and Io? Well, clearly not. After all, his involvement is crystal clear based on the evidence that has been entered into the court's records. In that case, perhaps he means *not guilty in the sense of the indictment*—a phrase familiar from history.

As it happens, the eminent philosopher and political theorist Hannah Arendt (1906–1975) once attended a similar trial with a similar plea: the 1961 trial of the mid-level Nazi official Adolf Eichmann. For eight months, Arendt observed, reported on, and theorized about Eichmann's testimony, his reaction to witnesses, and (ultimately) the pronouncement of his guilt and subsequent execution. Arendt, herself an internment camp survivor and victim of Nazi anti-Semitic aggression, painted a surprisingly nuanced portrait of the doomed Eichmann. She refused to disregard him as pure evil, a moral monster. Instead, she portrayed him as an exemplar of what she termed the banality of evil.

The Expanse and Philosophy: So Far Out Into the Darkness, First Edition. Edited by Jeffery L. Nicholas.

How Can Evil Be Banal?

Adolf Eichmann had been an SS officer at the time of the Holocaust. During the early years of World War II, he was tasked with managing the logistics of mass deportation and emigration of the Jewish residents of the Reich. As the years went on and the Nazi leadership moved away from the program of forced emigration and toward a program of extermination, Eichmann became one of the go-to "experts" on "the Jewish question." In this role, he and his staff facilitated the transport of Jews to concentration and extermination camps, sending millions to terrible deaths.

After his capture in 1960, Eichmann was tried on charges including war crimes and crimes against humanity. Just as Mao could not reasonably deny his involvement in the genocide on Eros and subsequent violence, Eichmann never denied that the Holocaust occurred nor his involvement in its implementation. Instead, he pled "not guilty in the sense of the indictment." Supposedly, he saw himself as guilty perhaps morally, but not guilty in the eyes of the law.[1] He had, after all, only been following orders. When, in our imagined scenario, Mao invokes this plea of not guilty in the sense of the indictment, he seems to mean something similar: not necessarily that he had been following orders (because he, after all, was the one giving orders), but that he was simply doing what anyone would have done in his situation. Perhaps, in this capacity, we might be persuaded to see Mao's evil as merely banal, dull, and unoriginal.

When Arendt referred to Eichmann's evil as banal, she wasn't trying to imply that the things he had done in the service of the Nazi Reich weren't morally reprehensible, that they didn't themselves constitute evil acts. Remember, she had suffered firsthand as a result of Nazi policies of anti-Semitic aggression. What she meant, at least in part, was that Eichmann didn't cut the figure of a sadist or a fanatic; shockingly, he appeared at his trial to be the blandest, most vapid bureaucrat imaginable. He was no raving Hitler, just as Mao is no starry-eyed Dresden or deadpan Cortázar. Eichmann was, she wrote, simply a joiner who enjoyed the idea of being part of something bigger than himself. He relied heavily upon clichés and "official language" when he spoke in his own defense. He showed no deep convictions because, as Arendt noted, he seemed to have no deep thoughts. He was, in short, small and unremarkable: a man more concerned with the trajectory of his own career (and annoyed by the petty and grand turns of fortune that derailed it at points) than with the morality of what he was doing. Even the psychiatrists who examined him before the trial found him troublingly normal. Arendt reports: "'More normal, at any rate, than I am after having examined him,' one of them was said to exclaim, while another had found that his whole psychological outlook, his attitude towards his wife and children, mother and father, brothers, sisters, and friends, was 'not only normal but most desirable.'"[2]

The million-dollar question, for Arendt, was, can someone commit great evil without actually being evil themselves?

Arendt seemed to think that they could. Eichmann was an exemplary case of the thoughtlessness and lack of self-reflection that goes into setting unthinkable atrocities into motion. In place of his own moral code, Eichmann had adopted the moral code of the Nazi regime; in place of his own conscience, Eichmann had (apparently) blithely adhered to the lack of conscience demonstrated by his superiors. At his trial, he repeated again and again that he had never personally killed anyone, nor had he ever given a direct order to kill anyone. In this matter, his conscience was clean. This avoidance of one's own moral duties when faced with the moral commands (or lack thereof) of one's society or regime presented a curious problem for Arendt. After all, it's not just the architects of great atrocity that are required for evil to be done. It is also the many men and women— maybe even hundreds or thousands of men and women—who obey without thinking, without questioning their own grounds for action.

At a first glance, Jules-Pierre Mao bears little resemblance to Adolf Eichmann. Most pressingly, he is the primary architect of the protomolecule project that leads to the genocide of Belters on Eros. He's the one pulling the strings. He's the one who gives Dr. Dresden—and, later, Dr. Strickland—the go-ahead to continue projects of human experimentation and destruction. Surely, we can call him plainly evil—right?

Not so fast. As it turns out, even though Mao might be who Eichmann dreamed of becoming, the case of Jules-Pierre Mao is a bit more complicated than meets the eye.

A Moral Monster?

We're introduced to Mao in a message that Detective Joe Miller finds in Julie Mao's apartment. Mao is chastising his wayward daughter, Julie. "Since you have no intention of returning home, I'm forced to consider selling the Razorback. You're naïve, sweetheart. It's time to come home. Please. I'll make everything right again" ("The Big Empty"). In the space of fifteen seconds, Mao uses every weapon in his fatherly arsenal (from outright threat to condescending paternalism to begging and promising) to get Julie to come home. Even if we're suspicious of his motivations here, he appears to genuinely care for her wellbeing. If nothing else, he hires Star Helix and, by extension, Miller, for the kidnap job that's supposed to get his daughter out of the crossfire of the coming war and back to the inner planets where she'll be safe.

After Julie dies on Eros (or becomes subsumed by the protomolecule), Mao has what we would tend to think of as a reasonably emotional reaction. When Dresden calls him with the news from that tiny nightmare of a bathroom at the Blue Falcon and shows him Julie's corpse on the video feed, tears run down Mao's face ("Critical Mass"). He mourns the death of his daughter even as he argues with Sadavir Errinwright over the importance of the protomolecule project, placing fresh-cut flowers at the base of her favorite tree, and his admiration and love are palpable.

> This was Julie's spot. Far from the house, where no one could find her. Where she could find her adventures. She taught herself to shoot a bow and arrow at this tree. Nine years old. Just woke up one morning and taught herself. My Julie. ("Safe")

Much later, when Mao temporarily takes Mei Meng under his wing, we are led to suspect that he does so because she reminds him so much of Julie at that age ("Assured Destruction").

Mao is, in short, clearly a man who cares about his daughter. He seems to take no pleasure in her death, not even in an overbearing, I told you so fashion. What are we to make of this? Well, for starters, we should entertain the notion that Mao is not a simple moral monster, a soulless man with no degree of care for those near and dear to him. Like Eichmann, he clearly has some capacity for emotion, some recognizably normal attachments to those for whom he cares. Importantly, these attachments don't seem to be limited to his own flesh and blood.

On Io, while Dr. Strickland heads up the project of infecting children with protomolecule, Mao seems to have what we might think of as the correct reaction to Strickland's scientific emotionlessness. Watching the children play together via video feed, Mao comments with a smile that "It's good the children get to play together." When Strickland responds with no apparent regard for the emotional and mental health of the children themselves—"Oh, absolutely. It keeps their cortisol levels low, which enhances protomolecule uptake"— Mao turns to look at him with no small amount of judgment ("Assured Destruction"). Later, when Mei's friend, Katoa, starts to become violently ill as a result of his intentional infection with the protomolecule, Mao puts his foot down. "Stop what you're doing to the children." When Strickland protests about the value of the project, Mao responds with emotion in his voice: "We're torturing children."

At this juncture, it seems as though Mao is in danger of developing a genuine conscience with regard to his facilitation of the protomolecule project. Like Eichmann, he doesn't seem to be a full-fledged moral monster. Unfortunately, also like Eichmann (whose calls to conscience were short-lived and half-hearted at best), he chooses not to let his capacity for conscience get the better of him. By the time Mao sees Katoa's connection to the protomolecule in action, he's back on board with the project, even at the expense of the wellbeing and survival of the other children whom he seemed determined to spare ("Reload").

Making Sense of Fanaticism

Like Eichmann, Mao doesn't cut the figure of a hardline fanatic, blinded by ideology. Occasionally at least, he exhibits a capacity for critical and moral reflection. These should indicate to us that he's not quite the same as some of his subordinates, who are genuine fanatics.

On one hand, Dr. Dresden enthusiastically attempts to justify the genocide on Eros in terms of the benefits it will bring. Cornered on Thoth Station by the OPA and the crew of the *Rocinante*, he doesn't apologize or beg. Instead, he opines on the value of what can be achieved if the project is allowed to continue.

> "Then *everything*. Belters who can work outside a ship without wearing a suit. Humans capable of sleeping for hundreds of years at a time flying colony ships to the stars. No longer being bound to the millions of years of evolution inside one atmosphere of pressure at one g, slaves to oxygen and water. We decide what we want to be, and we reprogram ourselves to be that. That's what the protomolecule gives us."
>
> Dresden had stood back up as he'd delivered this speech, his face shining with the zeal of a prophet.[3]

Dresden is what we might call a *true believer*, someone taken over entirely by the rhetoric of the project and completely indifferent to the cost of achieving his dream. In "Doors & Corners," he even offers to work under the OPA's patronage as opposed to Mao's, avowing that he doesn't care who controls the project as long as the work is allowed to continue. If Dresden were on trial, we might come to different conclusions about the applicability of the banality of evil; his fanaticism is too clear to mistake.

But Mao himself never seems to approach this level of fanaticism. He doesn't just want the work to continue at all costs, he wants the work to continue in his name. He never seems to lose sight of the fact that this project can and should only proceed with his blessing. He must remain at the center of everything, no matter the cost. Mao's unwillingness to place the cause ahead of his own desires should indicate that he isn't wholly blinded by fanaticism, as Dresden is. Mao makes clear, rational, self-interested choices at every stage of the game, and it's difficult as a result to imagine that he would have made the same offer as Dresden makes to the OPA, to have the protomolecule project continued no matter what. The same disconnect between fanaticism and self-interest plays out in Mao's relationship with Strickland as well. Strickland stubbornly refuses to abandon the human experimentation project on Io even after he is directly ordered to do so. Like Dresden, he cuts a compelling figure of the true believer ("Reload").

On the other hand, Dr. Cortázar is physically altered so that he can no longer consider any life other than his own to be meaningful. Cortázar presents a troubling and unhinged character that bears little resemblance to Mao's cool and collected command. While Cortázar takes evident delight in hearing about the evolution of the protomolecule on Eros ("Static"), Mao is clearly troubled by the experimentation on Io once he witnesses it in action.

This dynamic should give us some pause. Because figures like Dresden and Cortázar are so committed to the cause, appeals to morality are incapable of making a dent in their myopic worldview. Mao, though, doesn't seem to have the stomach for casual cruelty once he is confronted with it face to face. Hannah Arendt noted a similar lack of fanaticism in Adolf Eichmann. He was happy to complete the paperwork and hold the meetings that sent millions to their deaths, but he couldn't bear to watch the killing in action. What the case of Eichmann shows us, according to Arendt, is an extraordinary ability to disengage his actions from the devastation and destruction that he caused.

Mao appears to have the same ability.

Lack of Imagination

In her characterizations of Eichmann, Arendt noted his odd lack of imagination, his inability, in other words, "to think from the standpoint of someone else."[4] Partly for this reason, she argued that Eichmann was content to carry out his work unplagued by the pangs of conscience. He was incapable of thinking critically and reflectively about the experiences of others.

Jules-Pierre Mao appears to have a similar lack of imagination. This judgment may seem odd, considering that Mao chides Errinwright precisely for such a lack of imagination. "You're witnessing a discovery that could rewrite the story of humankind and your imagination takes you as far as putting the boot heel to your former colleague" ("Safe"). Clearly Mao has some capacity for imagination. Presumably he's spent a good deal of time imagining all of the things about which Dresden spoke so earnestly: the ability for humans, adequately transformed by the protomolecule, to live and work in the vacuum of space, to hibernate long enough for colony voyages beyond the reaches of the solar system, to rewrite evolutionary biology as we see fit.

Eichmann, too, was capable of some imagination: he had professional aspirations and projects (promotion through the ranks of the SS, recognition by his political and social superiors, the early goal of a Jewish homeland outside of the Reich to which émigrés could be shipped) that, while doomed, help us to make sense of some of his motivations.

Yet Mao can't imagine the experience of anyone other than himself. He doesn't imagine the plight of the infected people on Eros. He doesn't imagine the experiences of the killed Marines, both UN and Martian, on

Ganymede or of the killed sailors on the MCRN *Donnager* or of the killed ice-haulers on the *Canterbury*. He doesn't imagine the pain and suffering that the war he sets in motion will inflict upon every inhabitant of the System. Instead, he imagines a weapon that he can sell to the highest bidder. If Errinwright's imagination takes him as far as the trajectory of his own career, Mao's takes him as far as the trajectory of his own enrichment and glory.

Mao's lack of empathetic imagination is born out in his reaction to the misadventures of his own daughter. He seems incapable of understanding (at least in any significant way) Julie's motivations for joining the resistance in the Belt. Though he admires her resolve and spirit—as he implies to Clarissa in "Intransigence"—it seems that what he admires about her is precisely that which reminds him of himself. As Julie claims in "The Big Empty," perhaps that is also what he hates.

Granted, Mao doesn't seem to be completely and utterly unimaginative. As we saw, on Io he briefly breaks out of his own self-absorption to sympathize with Mei and the other children being experimented upon. This flicker of empathetic conscience is brief, however. By the time he sees Katoa's disassembly of the nurse in action, Mao is jolted back into being unable to imagine things from a viewpoint not his own: not the terror of Mei, nor the visceral fear and self-repulsion that Katoa must be experiencing in his moments of lucidity. Perhaps if he had had a more robust capacity for just such a kind of imagination, he would have been a better man, and ultimately, a better father.

Anyone Can Do It! (Or Can They?)

When both Eichmann and Mao plead *not guilty in the sense of the indictment*, part of what they seem to be trying to get at is the notion that anyone would have done the same in their shoes. Throughout his trial, Eichmann declared repeatedly that his refusal to deport and transport Jews during the Holocaust would have resulted simply in his being replaced by someone willing to do so. It would not have forestalled the subsequent atrocities.

When Mao, in our imagined scenario, pleads not guilty in the sense of the indictment, he seems in part to be suggesting that he shouldn't be held accountable for what anyone else would have done in his position. He just so happened to have the particular combination of wealth and resources that would make him the ideal head of a project designed to study an extra-solar biological weapon. Faced with the same stakes, anyone would have done the same. In the face of the extinction of the entire human race, one hundred thousand Belters on Eros and a handful of Ganymede children are no large sacrifice.

Let's call this defense the "anyone would do it." The notion behind the defense is that Eichmann and Mao aren't unique moral monsters; they're simply acting as anyone else in their position would. The "anyone would do it" defense goes something like this:

1. In my shoes, most people would do the same as I did.
2. If most people would do it, it's not morally wrong (or not morally wrong in a way that makes me blameworthy).
3. Therefore, what I did is not morally wrong (or not morally wrong in a way that makes me blameworthy).

One way the "anyone would do it" defense is acted out in the real world is through obedience to orders. After all, most people would follow orders under the right conditions.

Consider, for instance, Stanley Milgram's (1933–1984) famous obedience experiment. This so-called "Milgram experiment," or "Milgram shock experiment," was motivated, in part, by a desire to explain the psychology of those who, like Eichmann, perpetuated genocide. Milgram wondered: is following orders a strong enough motivator for people to act against their own consciences? Milgram's hypothesis was that following orders was not a strong enough motivator, and he put that hypothesis to the test.

Participants in the experiment were ordered to give what they believed to be painful electric shocks to someone they could not see in order to "teach" them certain memory tasks through negative reinforcement. The people being "shocked" were actors—no one was harmed in the making of this experiment. Well at least no one was harmed physically: the participants themselves, those who were doing the shocking, generally protested mightily and even suffered physical symptoms at the thought of injuring the learner. The experimenter in each case, however, ordered them to continue. In no uncertain terms, participants were told that they could not stop shocking the learner without fundamentally and irreparably damaging the experiment. More often as not, participants obeyed, albeit frequently with great reluctance. Milgram was astonished; most people were so susceptible to authority, so deeply inclined to obey, that they followed orders even when it profoundly violated their ethical sense of self to do so.

Let's revisit the "anyone would do it" defense in terms of following orders.

1. In my shoes, most people would follow orders (this seems true, based on the Milgram experiment).
2. If most people would follow orders, it's not morally wrong (or not morally wrong in a way that makes me blameworthy).
3. Therefore, following orders is not morally wrong (or not morally wrong in a way that makes me blameworthy).

This kind of argument was the core of much of Eichmann's defense during his trial: anyone else in his position would have followed orders and, therefore, he shouldn't be held wholly morally culpable.

While Mao doesn't have the defensive luxury of following orders, he still has the ability to fall back on the "anyone would do it" defense. Anyone would make a reasonably small sacrifice, in terms of human life, to save the entire human race—wouldn't they? Isn't this exactly the sort of thing that the crew of the *Rocinante* were prepared to do when they nearly died chasing Eros sunward? If anyone would make a reasonably small sacrifice, in terms of human life, to save the entire human race, then it starts to look as if our ability to judge Mao as plainly evil is on shaky ground.

The Milgram experiment shows that we human beings are highly susceptible to doing bad things if we think we have sufficient reason for them (or can reasonably justify them to ourselves). Even the "good guys" aren't exempt from this rule.

When Miller shoots Dresden on Thoth Station, Holden and Johnson are furious with him. But Miller's reasons for killing Dresden go beyond mere revenge for Julie; he's afraid of just how susceptible human beings are to the siren song of making moral tradeoffs. When he and Johnson speak on Tycho Station after Dresden's killing, Miller says, "I know and you know, Dresden was going to get away with it. But I didn't kill him because he was crazy. I killed him because he was making sense" ("Static"). Miller is highlighting the seductive nature of the sorts of moral tradeoffs made by people like Eichmann and Mao. He's pinpointing, in other words, the deep and apparently boundless capacity of otherwise well-meaning people to do wrong if they think they have sufficient reasons, just like the participants in the Milgram experiment. For Holden and Johnson, those reasons look a lot like potentially saving humanity from an extra-solar biological weapon, and those reasons may have been sufficient for them to allow Dresden to live if Miller hadn't acted. For Mao, those reasons look like potentially saving humanity and getting rich in the process, which seem, upon reflection, to be very compelling reasons indeed.

Let's return for a moment to the million-dollar question: can someone commit great evil without actually being evil themselves? Based on Miller's reaction to Dresden's diatribe—"he was starting to make sense"—the answer seems more affirmative than we would like.

Should Mao Be Pardoned?

Mao, like Eichmann, does not fit our preconceived notions about someone who is plainly evil. He cares about his daughter, and even, for a brief moment, about the children experimented on at Ganymede. He doesn't seem to approach Dresden's or Cortázar's levels of fanaticism. Like Eichmann, he seems self-interested, lacking in the kind of moral imagination and reflection necessary to confront critically his own participation in the dehumanization and destruction of others.

We might imagine Eichmann's claim, that he never personally killed anyone nor gave a direct order to do so, mirrored in Mao's own defense: for what the latter ordered was an experiment, not a genocide. Genocide just happened to be an unfortunate outcome of the experiment. Mao's legal counsel might argue that Protogen's soldiers and scientists, not Mao, should be the ones held accountable for the loss of human life in the proto-molecule experiments.

Here the judgment at Eichmann's trial seems salient:

> For these crimes were committed en masse, not only in regard to the number of victims, but also in regard to the numbers of those who perpetrated the crime, and the extent to which any one of the many criminals was close to or remote from the actual killer of the victim means nothing, as far as the measure of his responsibility is concerned. On the contrary, in general, the degree of responsibility increases as we draw further away from the man who uses the fatal instrument with his own hands.[5]

Arendt's final word on the subject is not even that Eichmann—that small, thoughtless, vaguely ridiculous bureaucrat—should be pardoned. He committed crimes for which no satisfactory moral or legal excuse is available. Her ultimate claim was not that he was guiltless, but that he should act as a warning concerning the ability of a totalitarian regime to alienate us from our moral choices; to rewrite, as it were, the laws not only of the land but of our consciences. If Eichmann should be doomed to pay with his life for his transgressions—even operating as he was under the skewed morality of totalitarianism—then Mao, as a free and autonomous agent, should be doomed doubly. Unlike Eichmann, who had some leeway to appeal to the authority that shaped him, Mao has no such excuses. Not only, we might think, should Mao not be pardoned, but his guilty verdict should render a lesson all the more chilling: that one does not need the apparatus of a totalitarian regime to engage in atrocities or cause harm to others (as the Milgram experiment well demonstrates). Even the most affluent and free among us can commit crimes beyond comprehension if only the conditions are right.

Notes

1. Hannah Arendt, *Eichmann in Jerusalem: A Report on the Banality of Evil* (New York: Penguin Books, 2006), 21.
2. Ibid., 26.
3. James S. A. Corey, *Leviathan Wakes* (New York: Orbit Books, 2011), 419.
4. Arendt, *Eichmann in Jerusalem*, 49.
5. Ibid., 247.

6

Amos Meets Nietzsche

Pankaj Singh

A constant threat of violence, Amos is always ready to let punches and bullets fly. Miller refers to him as a "200-pound homicidal kid." Is that description fair? No doubt, "Amos is different. Okay, very different." Clearly, he can be your worst possible enemy, but he can also be a valuable ally. How can we make sense of this guy? Intensely loyal, practical, straightforward, almost fearless, with a wry sense of humor, Amos is also analytical, a quick thinker, and exceedingly aware of his surroundings. He likes to take action, but is he good or evil?

People of Three Kinds

Amos philosophically (yes, sometimes he does sound philosophical) says to Alex, "The way I see it, there's only three kinds of people in this world, bad ones, ones you follow, and ones you need to protect" ("Paradigm Shift"). He determines who the bad ones are by looking to the people he follows and considering who he needs to protect. At first, he follows the lead of Naomi, "kind of like his Guide star." Detained in an MCRN ship, under attack by the stealth ship, and on the verge of death, he says to Naomi, "I want to say thank you. You know, for helping me all those times you did. You're a good person" ("CQB"). In "The Big Empty," Holden questions Amos about his relationship with Naomi. Amos replies, "You must think I am pretty stupid, don't you? I mean, you're right. I can take a core apart and put it back together with my eyes closed. But ask me whether or not I should rip your helmet off and kick you off this bucket, and I couldn't give a reason why I should or shouldn't. Except Naomi wouldn't like it." Clearly, Amos prefers outsourcing decisions concerning matters of right and wrong.

The Expanse and Philosophy: So Far Out Into the Darkness, First Edition. Edited by Jeffery L. Nicholas.
© 2022 John Wiley & Sons, Inc. Published 2022 by John Wiley & Sons, Inc.

In "Caliban's War," he talks to Naomi about his perplexity, "I've been trying to make choices of my own lately, and I don't seem to make the right ones." In "Cascade," he tells Prax, "Holden and Naomi, they are not like me. They are better." Amos trusts Holden and Naomi in moral matters, but his trust is not blind. Due to his rough past, he is quick to assess people intuitively. He allows people to guide him as long as he thinks they are picking better alternatives. In "Back to the Butcher," running to save their lives, the *Rocinante* crew needs to settle the issue of going to Ceres or Tycho. Despite Tycho being the reasonable option, Naomi votes "No" and looks at Amos, who reluctantly nods, "I'm with you, boss." Later, he confronts Naomi. "I always back your play because you always do the right thing. But usually, I can figure out why." Eventually, he talks Naomi into going to Tycho.

Amos wasn't always fond of Holden. After spending tough and adventurous times together, Amos changes his attitude toward Holden and regards him as a good person. At one point, the protomolecule monster pins Holden to a wall with a cargo container. Amos comes up with a plan that could kill Holden, but he takes time to express appreciation for his goodness: "You were always trying to be a good man. Not everyone does. Thank you. It was nice not having to worry about being on the right team" ("Caliban's War"). Amos also adjusts his view of Naomi. Alex asks Amos what he thinks about Naomi when she gave the protomolecule sample to the Butcher (Fred Johnson). "She's not the person I thought she was," he responds ("Fight or Flight"). The point is that Amos is a man of action; he simply wants to exercise his skills to do something rather than worrying about being on a right or wrong team. However, he can figure out others' reasons for doing things, and he is capable of making his own decisions based on gut feelings.

His words of assurance tell us about the people Amos believes need protection. He assures Prax, "Doc, no matter what happens down there, I got your back" ("Triple Point"), and to Anna he says, "I am not gonna let anyone hurt you" ("Abaddon's Gate"). Amos is a man of his word. If he says he's going to protect someone, he'll sacrifice his life, or a few fingers, to do it. When the *Roci* is severely damaged by the stealth ship and needs patchwork, he goes to patch it even though Naomi warns that one hard maneuver would kill him ("Doors & Corners"). Indeed, Amos embodies Friedrich Nietzsche's (1844–1900) famous slogan, "live dangerously!"[1]

"Good and Bad" or "Good and Evil"

Nietzsche argued that the concepts good and bad have their origin in the aristocratic noble class. "The judgment 'good' did not originate with those to whom 'goodness' was shown! Rather it was 'the good' themselves, that is to say, the noble, powerful, high-stationed and high-minded, who felt and established themselves and their actions as good."[2] Their concept of good involved war, adventure, hunting, dancing, and in general vigorous, free, and joyful activities. Nietzsche found that the concept of bad was originally associated with the "common," "plebeian," and "low" class, whose action was considered as worthless, vile, wretched, cowardly, mean, and ugly. This conception of good and bad based on noble class is what Nietzsche calls "master morality."[3]

Nietzsche argues that values were re-valued at a certain point along the lines of Christianity. The wretched, poor, impotent, and lowly became good. The deprived, sick, and ugly became pious, blessed by God. What was powerful or noble became "evil"—the cruel, the lustful, the insatiable. Nietzsche calls this newer demarcation of good and evil "slave morality."[4] In the first of these pairings (good and bad), good refers to a spontaneous act. Good is primary and bad is secondary—bad is derived from good. In the second pairing (good and evil), evil is primary and good secondary—we judge some actions as evil, and whatever is not evil must be good.

Amos embodies characteristics of the Nietzschean noble. He is a fighter—free, healthy, aggressive, violent, and sarcastic. Nietzsche says, "when your soul grows big it becomes mischievous, and there is sarcasm in your sublimity."[5] Amos makes various mischievous and sarcastic remarks throughout the show: "I bet those pretty tin suits bind up something awful in the crotch" ("Remember the Cant"); "You know, for a badass Mickie Navy boy, you are a pretty whiny little bitch" ("CQB"); "How come I am the one who always gets shot?" ("Here There Be Dragons"); "Let me know if you want your face to look a little different" ("Back to the Butcher").

Nietzsche writes, "According to slave morality, those who are 'evil' thus inspire fear; according to master morality it is precisely those who are 'good' that inspire, and wish to inspire, fear, while the 'bad' are felt to be contemptible."[6] Although Amos hasn't felt fear since he was five, he certainly arouses fear in his friends and enemies alike. Amos wanted to learn why Naomi didn't tell him about Holden logging the call on the *Canterbury*. "I don't know," says Naomi. Amos responds, "You were afraid of me" ("Rock Bottom"). In "Windmills," Holden, seeing Amos ready to kill some more Martians, shouts, "Naomi was right to be afraid of you."

What does Amos think of himself? In "Cascade," Prax asks how many people he's killed. Amos responds, "Well, I'm not a homicidal maniac." While his enthusiasm for violence can seem malevolent, those who know Amos better understand who he is and how he became that way. Naomi explains to Miller why Amos killed Sematimba, Miller's friend: "Caught in a terrible moment, and he did what he thought he had to do . . . Amos is different. Okay, very different. But he is not crazy and he is not evil." Actually, in Nietzschean terms, Amos would be evil according to slave morality, but good according to master morality. So how do we decide?

Ressentiment

Although Amos is always ready to wage war, he doesn't seek, or encourage others to seek, revenge. Alex, frustrated with what happened to the Belters on Eros, says, "I'm gonna feel better when I watch those assholes burn." Amos tries to make Alex realize the futility of revenge. "Look, I'm for killing whoever needs killing. But it's not gonna make you feel better" ("Doors & Corners"). When Prax thanks Amos for taking care of him, Amos says, "You can thank me if we get your little girl back." Prax adds, "Or get even" ("Triple Point"). Eventually, Prax reaches the moment where he is ready to shoot Dr. Strickland, but Amos stops him, saying, "You're not that guy." After Prax leaves, Amos utters perhaps the most quoted line of the show, "I am that guy," and kills Strickland ("Immolation"). Amos is the guy who will kill, but he doesn't do it for revenge.

Had Prax shot the doctor, the killing would have been out of *ressentiment*, the spirit of revenge. *Ressentiment* is a French word that is roughly equivalent to the English word resentment. As one scholar explains it, "*Ressentiment*, for Nietzsche, involved the repeated experience and reliving of a negative emotional state felt by some individual, group, or category of persons seen as having inflicted an injury, or otherwise made one suffer, together with hostility, frustration, and a thirst for revenge which cannot be directly expressed."[7]

Nietzsche traced the beginning of slave morality to a creative reversal of values fueled by *ressentiment*. "The slave revolt in morality begins when *ressentiment* itself becomes creative and gives birth to values: the *ressentiment* of natures that are denied the true reaction, that of deeds, and compensate themselves with an imaginary revenge."[8] The low or common people bottle up their grudges so that they can take revenge at a convenient time. They are clever, understand how to keep silent, how not to forget, how to wait, how to be provisionally self-deprecating and humble. Their revenge ultimately takes the form of labeling powerful people as evil.

When labeled evil, the powerful suppress their instincts, and the result is bad conscience, "All instincts that do not discharge themselves outwardly turn inward—this is what I call the internalization of man . . . Hostility, cruelty, joy in persecuting, in attacking, in change, in destruction—all this turned against the possessors of such instincts: is the origin of the 'bad conscience.'"[9] Amos seems beyond the reach of the slave morality with its resentful demands to suppress instincts. His outward discharge of instincts is not motivated by revenge or bad conscience; instead, it results from spontaneity and impulsiveness. Amos rarely bottles up his feelings, but instead goes on the offensive with words, fists, and guns, as the circumstances require.

In "Safe," Amos senses Miller's *ressentiment*. "If you and I have something we need to get sorted out, we should get to that. Your pal Semi? You're upset about that, right? I had nothing against him. I thought he was a decent guy . . . If you need to square up, you know where I am. Otherwise, you should move on." Miller punches Amos. Then Amos floors Miller with one punch and says, "Stay down, Miller." When Miller attacks again, Amos starts choking him until Naomi stops him. To his credit, Miller gets over his *ressentiment*. In their next meeting, Amos indicates for Miller to sit next to him at the dinner table and passes him the "Kamal family recipe" lasagna. Miller narrates a funny story about "cheese thieves" and seems to have put his conflict with Amos behind him. This is good. In Nietzsche's eyes, "To be incapable of taking one's enemies, one's accidents; even one's misdeeds seriously for very long—that is the sign of strong, full natures in whom there is an excess of the power to form, to mold, to recuperate and to forget."[10] The scuffle was an outward action that allowed Miller and Amos to clear the air of anger and move on without *ressentiment*.

Spontaneity and power saturate Amos' interactions with Adolphus Murtry, chief of security for Royal Charter Energy, on Ilus. In "Jetsam," after Murtry shoots someone in cold blood, Amos meets him in the canteen. Murtry says, "Someday, I think you and I are going to end up bloody." Amos responds, "How about now? I'm free right now." Murtry puts off his violence until later. Yet, the moment of spontaneity is always there for Amos. At the end of Season 4, aboard the *Rocinante* and on their way home from Ilus, Amos visits Murtry in his quarters. He has just regrown the fingers that Murtry shot off, and he tells Alex, "I'm going to test them out now." When Murtry takes the first swing, Amos says, "Thank you" and dishes out the violence he'd come to serve.

After Miller kills Dresden, Holden kicks him off the *Roci*. Amos takes some of his stuff back to him. He tells Miller, "Captain doesn't want you around anymore. We don't want you around neither. For what it's worth, I get it. He killed your girl, and you shot him." Miller replies, "No. Just a guy who needed to go down." Amos explains, "The captain always gets a little jumpy when you kill people without talking it over first." Miller laughs and responds, "Yeah, I'm sure you would've asked for permission too." Amos replies, "Well, here's the thing. You and me, we're a lot alike. We've been around" ("Static").

One might argue that Miller killed Dresden out of *ressentiment*, but if so, Miller's *ressentiment* is different from bottled up *ressentiment*. Nietzsche clarifies, "*Ressentiment* itself, if it should appear in the noble man, consummates and exhausts itself in an immediate reaction, and therefore does not poison."[11] Spontaneity, strength, and lack of *ressentiment* make Amos and Miller alike. They are sarcastic and do not hold grudges; they vent their instincts outward.

In "Pyre," Alex notices that Amos isn't interested in helping others and he accuses him of being selfish. Amos counters, "Isn't that most people's problem, if they are being honest?" From Amos' point of view, everyone wants to act according to their selfish motives, but they hide their true intentions because they have become calculative and clever. Nietzsche writes, "Whoever makes no secret of himself outrages others."[12] We see this when Amos reminds Alex of his hypocrisy—he doesn't even help his family on Mars. Enraged by the mention of his family, Alex pushes Amos. Grabbing Alex in response, Amos diffuses the tension with his quirky, sarcastic remark, "I don't wanna fight you, Alex. Please don't make me. Cause if we do, who's going to fly the ship?" The quarrel does not create a wedge between the two but a stronger bond.

What kind of friendship is this where Amos is also ready to attack the people he claims to protect? An unusual one, but in Nietzsche's view, friendship can afford a healthy outlet for releasing emotions and impulses that would otherwise transform into *ressentiment*.[13] Amos not only acts out his feelings quickly, but also motivates others to discharge any poisonous enmity they are holding back. When Holden struggles with hallucinations of Miller, Amos advises, "Look, if there is anything that you need to get off your chest, I'm not much help, but I also don't judge. Vent away. Break some shit if you have to. I don't care" ("It Reaches Out"). Amos is strong enough to help, but he does it out of strength rather than pity. As Nietzsche says, "the noble human being, too, helps the unfortunate, but not, or almost not, from pity, but prompted more by an urge begotten by excess of power."[14]

Will to Power

According to Nietzsche, our fundamental drive is the desire to gain and express power. He calls this the will to power, and he believes it is even more basic than the will to survive. As Nietzsche writes, "Your will and your values you set upon the river of becoming; what the people believe to be good and evil reveals to me an ancient will to power . . . The river is not your danger and the end of your good and evil, you wisest ones; but this will itself, the will to power—the unexhausted begetting will of life."[15]

Amos oozes with the will to power. When he catches an onboard spy, Kenzo, messing with the comms on the *Roci*, Amos tells him, "Either way this plays out, you're dead. And I am the one that's gonna bring you the good news. You're a loose end. It's nothing personal. Like water's wet. Sky's up" ("Windmills"). Amos understands that the will to power is a simple fact of life: "It has nothing to do with me. We're just caught up in a churn, is all."

Amos further illustrates the churn, saying, "The only game. Survival. When the jungle tears itself down, and builds itself into something new. Guys like you and me, we end up dead. It doesn't mean anything. Or if we happen to live through it, and well, that doesn't mean anything either." Here Amos seems to recognize the futility of finding meaning in mere survival. But when the *Canterbury* is destroyed, Amos ends the crew's discussion by demanding a focus on survival, "Who gives a shit? Let's focus on staying alive. We'll worry about Mars later" ("The Big Empty"). In "Doors & Corners," Alex regrets that they could have saved more people from Eros, if they cared for the poor Belters. Amos reminds him, "We saved us. Crew comes first. If we'd have went back for strays, we'd end up dead like them."

Survival is not the whole picture. One wants to survive in order to continue gaining and expressing power. The will to power takes precedence over self-preservation. Nietzsche writes, "A living thing seeks above all to discharge its strength—life itself is will to power; self-preservation is only one of the indirect and most frequent results."[16] Fittingly, in many other scenarios, Amos doesn't care about survival. In "Fight or Flight," stuck between hard choices, Naomi persuades others that "Tycho is how we survive." Amos doesn't like the idea of going to Tycho, but he agrees with Naomi at first. "We should go to Tycho. It's the only way to keep the crew breathing." Holden then proposes a new plan in which they can go to Io and search for Prax's daughter. Amidst the ongoing discussion, Amos shouts, "Io. Fuck it, I'm in." He chooses Holden's risky option of going to Io over survival. In "Critical Mass," seeing innocent people being kicked by mercenary security people, Alex asks, "Are we just gonna stand here?" Naomi replies, "We can't just charge in and start shooting." Amos doesn't agree. "Pretty sure we can." He starts shooting mercenaries. In "Dandelion Sky," on the directions of a simulated Miller, Holden proceeds to go to the alien station, ordering Alex and Amos not to follow for their own safety. A Martian skiff starts following Holden. Alex warns Amos that going after Holden would be a suicide mission against a Martian Marine fire team. "It's better to go down swinging than rolling over," he says. When Alex states that they're playing out of their league, Amos responds, "That's been true since we have been sharpening sticks and going after lions, but we are still here."

Amos Is No Superman

Looking at Amos through a Nietzschean lens makes us reluctant to judge the character as good or evil. After all, it depends on what one means by the terms. The slave morality would classify him as evil, but the master morality would classify him as good. Amos gives spontaneous expression to the will to power and is free from resentment. For all that, though, he is a loose cannon. Amos has not channeled or sublimated his will to power. He has not overcome himself and humanity. Ultimately, he is far from becoming Nietzsche's ideal figure, the *Übermensch*. Amos is no superman, but, then again, who is?

Notes

1. Friedrich Nietzsche, *The Gay Science: With a Prelude in Rhymes and an Appendix of Songs*, trans. Walter Kaufmann (New York: Vintage Books, 1974), 283.
2. Friedrich Nietzsche, *On the Genealogy of Morals and Ecce Homo*, trans. Walter Kaufmann and R. J. Hollingdale (New York: Vintage Books, 1989), 25–26.
3. Friedrich Nietzsche, *Beyond Good and Evil: Prelude to a Philosophy of the Future*, trans. Walter Kaufmann (New York: Vintage Books, 1966), 204.
4. Ibid.
5. Friedrich Nietzsche, *Thus Spoke Zarathustra*, ed. Robert Pippin, trans. Adrian Del Caro (Cambridge: Cambridge University Press, 2006), 33.
6. Nietzsche, *Beyond Good and Evil*, 207.
7. Warren D. TenHouten, "From Ressentiment to Resentment as a Tertiary Emotion," *Review of European Studies* 10 (2018), 50.
8. Nietzsche, *On the Genealogy of Morals*, 36.
9. Ibid., 84–85.
10. Ibid., 39.
11. Ibid.
12. Nietzsche, *Thus Spoke Zarathustra*, 41.
13. If you are interested in exploring a comparative Nietzschean view on friendship with a pop culture topic, see Jeffery L. Nicholas, "Of Gods and Buggers: Friendship in Ender's Game," in *Ender's Game and Philosophy: The Logic Gate Is Down*, ed. Kevin S. Decker (Oxford: Wiley Blackwell, 2013), 124–135.
14. Nietzsche, *Beyond Good and Evil*, 205.
15. Nietzsche, *Thus Spoke Zarathustra*, 88.
16. Nietzsche, *Beyond Good and Evil*, 21.

7

Is Amos Evil?

Diana Sofronieva

Pointing a gun at Clarissa Mao, Amos says, "It'd be easier if I put her down." When Anna Volovodov says, "You're not going to shoot her," Amos misunderstands. "Well, what if I override the auto-doc to do an overdose?"

Amos is always ready to kill. His line of victims is long. Even Wei, a friend Amos likes, isn't spared the bullet when she gets in his way. Amos doesn't think twice before pulling the trigger, and he experiences no regrets after doing so. He doesn't feel compassion and appears to place little value on human life. At first glance it seems almost impossible to square these facts with the idea that Amos could be anything but a bad, perhaps even evil, person. As we'll see, though, Amos is actually a better person than most.

"I am that guy"

Amos' enemies are afraid of him for a good reason. The indifference with which Amos can pull the trigger sends a chill down the spine. But Amos doesn't feel that chill. He doesn't feel the fear the person across from him feels. He doesn't connect emotionally with that person. Amos shoots Dr. Strickland without a moment's hesitation. The contrast between Prax and Amos is apparent. Prax is shaking and sweating, unsuccessfully trying to muster up courage to pull the trigger. Amos does it quickly, without any emotion or second thoughts. It's just something that needs doing. For Amos killing people isn't much different from moving undesirable objects around. In this sense Amos places little value on human life and seems to lack morality.

Amos doesn't connect emotionally with others, and emotional connection seems important for morality. Empirical studies suggest that feeling what another person is going through—"emotional empathy"—is

The Expanse and Philosophy: So Far Out Into the Darkness, First Edition. Edited by Jeffery L. Nicholas.
© 2022 John Wiley & Sons, Inc. Published 2022 by John Wiley & Sons, Inc.

positively correlated with prosocial behavior. Charities know and exploit this fact; they know people are more likely to donate if they are presented with the plight of a single individual than with statistics. In fact, people are even more likely to donate if they know that their donation is going to help one person rather than two![1] This is known as the "identifiable victim effect." Arguably this effect occurs because we can emotionally connect with an individual in ways we can't connect with a group of people. We aren't able to fully empathize with more than one person at a time.

Another reason why emotionally connecting with others is important is that it helps to keep us from harming them. Prax can't pull the trigger to kill Strickland, despite his determination to seek revenge. Prax feels emotionally connected to this person kneeling in front of him; killing Strickland would haunt Prax for the rest of his days. It takes something to be different, to be "that guy." Most of us are like Prax. We have a natural response of emotional empathy that prevents us from causing harm to others. Even the thought of doing so distresses us.

In the grim and sobering should-be-compulsory-reading-in-school book *Humanity: A Moral History of the Twentieth Century*, Jonathan Glover speaks of this emotional connection with others as one of our "moral resources" that can prevent us from harming others.[2] The reason the twentieth century has seen so many atrocities, Glover argues, is that the conditions of war often depleted and eroded our moral resources. For example, soldiers would dehumanize the enemy, speaking of them in derogatory, impersonal ways, in order to side-step the natural barrier to killing them. In Amos this natural barrier has already eroded. The contrast is apparent between him and other people in this respect. When Clarissa Mao murders her colleague and mentor Ren Hazuki, she is so distressed she nearly crashes the K-47 into the *Thomas Prince*. When Octavia Muss shoots the two siblings who are about to murder Miller on Ceres, she is devastated, and gets physically sick. Despite having done the right thing on this occasion—saving Miller from certain death—Octavia is haunted by what she has done. Most people would react the same way in her situation.

Not Amos.

Amos experiences emotions differently than other people, and emotions help us make the distinction between moral and conventional transgressions. A moral transgression is a child hitting another child. A conventional transgression is a child talking in class. A much-discussed set of experiments conducted by R. J. R. Blair showed that psychopaths were less likely than non-psychopathic controls to be able to differentiate between moral and conventional transgressions.[3] Jim Baxter, a contemporary philosopher, argues that psychopaths' lack of full-blooded emotional experience interferes with their ability to see other people as valuable.[4] Psychopaths simply can't feel the emotional force of moral transgressions as opposed to conventional ones. That is why for them the wrongness of hitting another child is no worse than that of talking in class.[5]

Amos is not a psychopath.[6] Yet, he shares with psychopaths an emotional absence and an inability to connect with others emotionally. This goes some way toward explaining why he treats other people the way he does and why he isn't always able to make a distinction between the moral and the conventional. After their fight on the *Roci*, Amos nearly kills Miller simply because he stands up after being told to stay down. When Naomi stops Amos, he explains, "I told him to stay down" ("Safe"). In a different situation, Amos asks Alex not to fight him, aware of the risk he might kill Alex. "Cause if we do, who's gonna fly the ship?" ("Pyre"). Amos isn't threatening Alex here. He genuinely doesn't understand how chilling his request is.

For Amos, eliminating people who pose a threat doesn't feel much different than throwing away the trash. Amos' antisocial behavior shows that he doesn't have a spontaneous emotional recognition of the value of others.

What Happened to Amos?

As we've seen, Amos is different—he doesn't connect with others emotionally. The link with his emotional side was partially severed as a result of his traumatic past. Amos grew up in Baltimore, a place where selling children for sex slavery was the norm, where "getting by was getting even" as he tells Prax ("Assured Destruction"). Amos lived in a world with no moral order. He has seen the worst side of human nature and consequently he doesn't think too highly of people and doesn't value human life highly. Amos grew up seeing so much horror, abuse, and death that he became desensitized to them. He doesn't feel anything when witnessing, or causing, harm to others.

Amos' inability to feel what the person across from him feels, his general mistrust of people, and his difficulty in bonding emotionally with others— these are all due to his past. It would have been simply inhuman to feel connected to others while witnessing all the horror and suffering in Baltimore. The only way Amos could have escaped Baltimore sane or even alive was by cauterizing his emotional side.

Amos finds making certain choices difficult. He tells Naomi: "It's just that I've been trying to make choices of my own lately, and I can't seem to make the right ones" ("Caliban's War"). Arguably, a lack of emotional engagement is what makes it hard for Amos to make decisions. Often you need to feel what the person across from you is feeling in order to figure out what the best thing for them is. It's not only the difficulty of understanding others' emotions, however, that influences Amos' actions. It's also his general lack of emotional experience that makes it hard for him to make decisions.

Antonio Damasio's pioneering work on neuroscience and the emotions has shown that emotions are indispensable for decision-making. Damasio studied people with a particular kind of brain damage that shut down their emotional center but left their cognitive area intact. Despite their perfectly good ability to perform cost/benefit analysis, these patients found making certain mundane choices particularly hard. On one occasion a patient spent nearly twenty minutes deciding whether their next appointment should be on Tuesday or Wednesday. Another patient spent an incredibly long time choosing a restaurant. These people lacked an emotional "push" that would attract them to one option and repel them from another. Damasio hypothesized that in order to make choices, cognitive reasoning alone is not enough. We also need "somatic markers." These are feelings that we might or might not be aware of, that mark things as good, bad, or indifferent, and sway us in the direction of one choice or the other.[7] We rely on emotions in order to make decisions far more than we might have realized.

Amos, however, can't rely on his emotions to the same extent many of us do. He doesn't connect emotionally with others, so he finds choices that have to do with other people hard. Amos has to process such choices in a purely cognitive, "cold-blooded" manner, relying mostly on logic and experience to navigate the world. So it's no wonder that despite his clear thinking, he sometimes finds it hard to make decisions.

Amos is well aware that he doesn't have the internal tools for making some moral decisions. "Ask me if I should rip your helmet off and throw you off this rock, and I can't give you a reason why I should or shouldn't" ("The Big Empty"). Fortunately for Holden on this occasion, Amos looks to someone else to guide him. "Naomi wouldn't like it." Amos latches on to other people to be his moral compass: Naomi, Anna, later Holden himself. He looks up to them because he is not always able to tell what is good or even socially acceptable.

Amos wants to reconnect with the world. In this regard, he is the opposite of Paolo Cortázar, the Protogen scientist who chose to cauterize his emotional center with a brain procedure. In other ways, Amos and Cortázar are a lot alike. Neither of them feels empathy or experiences full-blooded emotions. However, Amos has only vague recollections of a life with emotions and with empathy; he was too young when his emotional side was cauterized. Cortázar, by contrast, has been in both worlds and has made the conscious decision to live in the one without emotions. When he experienced "the calm" of not having emotions, he decided "on that first day, within five minutes" not to go back ("The Seventh Man"). Amos, however, remains unconvinced that he is better off now than he was before the world broke him. He wants to know if his condition is reversible. He wants to reconnect with the world, and he seems to suffer from his difficulty in doing so.

Is Amos Really "That" Guy?

Amos doesn't connect emotionally with others and sometimes doesn't know how to make decisions that will result in the least harm to other people. But to conclude that he is evil would just be a projection of our own fear, an emotion which Amos has only vague recollections of.

Amos isn't evil in any conventional sense of the word. He lacks many of the attributes that we usually associate with evil people. He isn't malicious, greedy, or narcissistic. Amos hasn't felt fear since he was five, but also, he seems to feel no spite, no envy, no resentment. He is most certainly, as he tells Prax, not a homicidal maniac ("Cascade"). His violence is sterile. It's just about doing what needs to be done. In fact, it's much more sterile than that of other, presumably more normal members of the crew. Alex, the lasagna guy who wouldn't hurt a fly, fantasizes about revenge for the genocide on Eros. "I'm gonna feel better when I watch those assholes burn." Perhaps ironically, it's Amos who warns him, "Look, I'm for killing whoever needs killing, but it's not gonna make you feel better" ("Doors & Corners"). Amos doesn't get satisfaction from killing people. In this regard he's the opposite of Murtry, who always looks for excuses to kill. Amos diagnoses Murtry accurately when he confronts him. "You have all these excuses that make you seem right. But the truth is your dick got hard from smoking that guy in front of everybody, and you can't wait to do it again" ("Subduction"). Murtry is a bloodthirsty killer. Amos isn't.

Still, there is another kind of evil. A less emotional and more "banal" kind, to use the famous phrase coined by Hannah Arendt.[8] This evil results from a lack of concern with effects on others. This evil may occur without one's explicit intention, but one's shallowness and thoughtlessness still make one culpable. The person who fired a weapon tells herself she is not the one responsible for the murder; she was simply following orders. The person who gave the order tells herself she is not the one responsible for the murder; she didn't fire the bullet. These two otherwise ordinary people aren't evil in the more conventional sense of the word, for they lack malice or hatred. They might not even want the murder to happen. But they are nevertheless evil. Their "terrifyingly normal" thoughtlessness and lack of concern with the bigger picture are just as bad as, if not worse than, the malicious kind of evil we often read about in stories.[9]

Could Amos be evil in this cold-blooded, thoughtless way? No, Amos is far from thoughtless. On the contrary, Amos cares deeply about doing the right thing. He is not a "joiner," as are many of the people who commit thoughtless deeds. He has an inner moral code that he doesn't compromise. Family—in his case *Roci*'s crew—comes first, even if it comes at the cost of other people's lives. Amos shoots Wei because she protects Murtry who is about to kill Holden. Amos is loyal to Holden and goes out of his way to protect him. Amos also hates bullies, and he takes it upon himself to punish them. Nobody else stepped in to do it, but Amos teaches the chicken guy on Ganymede a lesson.

Amos doesn't compromise with his inner moral code, so he can't be accused of thoughtlessness. Speaking about Fred Johnson, Naomi says, "I've known guys like him. Guys with causes. Causes that get people killed" ("Back to the Butcher"). Amos couldn't be more different from that. He isn't about ideology. His allegiance isn't with Earth, Mars, or the Belt. It's solely with his family.

Amos latches on to other people to be his moral compass, and that might make him seem insufficiently concerned with morality. After all, not taking moral decisions upon oneself but following what others say seems lazy at best and deeply troubling at worst. The infamous Milgram experiments are a terrifying illustration of how wrong things can get when we defer moral decisions to others instead of taking them upon ourselves. Yet, Amos doesn't follow others blindly. He has to be able to follow their plans logically. He backs Naomi in her decision to not go to Tycho station, but it's not easy for him to do so. Immediately after the vote he tells her, "I always back your play because you always do the right thing. But usually, I can figure out why" ("Back to the Butcher"). For Amos, knowing why the decision was made is important, because he wants to make sure he is doing the right thing. Further, if Amos was lazy or unconcerned with morality, he wouldn't have bothered finding an external moral compass in the first place. He most certainly wouldn't have taken so much care in selecting the few people he follows.

Amos is concerned with doing what is actually right, not just what the tribe thinks is right. It's not a coincidence that Amos follows Naomi—he believes she's a good person. Likewise he quickly sees the goodness in Anna and becomes protective of her: "I'm not gonna let anyone hurt you" ("Abaddon's Gate"). Amos doesn't think much of Holden at first, but once he figures out he's a good person, he follows him too. Amos thanks Holden in a way that says plenty about how important morality is to him. "It was nice not having to worry about being on the right team" ("Caliban's War"). An evil person wouldn't say such a thing. Amos has an almost canine sense of differentiating between good and bad people, of immediately figuring out who is to be trusted, and who isn't.

This acute sense must have helped Amos survive the churn in Baltimore. He senses danger before anyone else on the *Roci*, and it is nearly impossible to take him by surprise. For example, it is Amos who figures out they are set up for an ambush in the hotel on Eros. Always well aware of the sort of person he is dealing with, Amos picks up instantly that Murtry is a bully, seeing right through him. "The others don't get it yet, but I know what you are" ("Subduction").

Despite his acute sense about others, Amos is perhaps wrong about one person. Himself. Amos knows his own limitations, and he thinks of himself as a bad person. Naomi and Holden are not like him, he tells Prax: "They are better" ("Cascade"). He tells Miller that Holden is "as close to righteous as it gets out here" ("Static"). Amos is aware that it's his having "been around" that has broken him. He sees himself as "that" guy, the one different from the others, the person who gets his hands dirty. Perhaps too quickly, Amos has resigned himself to the fact that he can't be as moral as the others. But he is far from complacent. It's important to him that the people he follows are good. A truly bad person wouldn't care. So it seems Amos underestimates himself.

The Upsides of Amos

In some ways Amos is actually a better person than most. His lack of emotion has upsides. Amos is not subject to panic or fear, and he's by far the most cool-headed person on the *Roci*'s crew. His mind is clear and logical, not clouded by overpowering emotions or prejudice even under the most immense pressure.

Amos is non-judgmental and far more open-minded than most. When Holden starts seeing Miller in his mind and appears to be talking to himself, Amos tells him, "Look, if there is anything you need to get off your chest, I'm not much help, but I also don't judge" ("It Reaches Out"). It is indeed, as Holden says, a "great quality." Great and rare.

Amos would not benefit from going to a mindfulness class; he already knows the drill. He lives in the present. He is not divided; his intentions and actions are perfectly aligned. Amos acts without hesitation and lives with no regrets. The past doesn't haunt him. When Alex feels bad about not having saved more people on Eros, Amos replies, "We saved us. Crew comes first. If we'd have went back for strays, we'd end up dead, like them" ("Doors & Corners"). The painful truth is that Amos is right here. He almost always is. His clear, logical thinking might be hard for others to swallow at times, but it is often correct. Amos is much better than others at giving up on things outside of his control. Giving up control is one of the hardest things to do, and trying to keep things in control is one of the biggest causes of unhappiness.

Notably, Amos is the most honest person among the *Roci*'s crew. He rarely lies or misleads anyone. People are not always happy about his brutal honesty, but that says more about them than it does about him. On Tycho, Alex doesn't want to face up to the reason he's mad at Amos. The truth is that Amos defended Alex against a guy in the bar who attacked him, making Alex appear weak. "Is that what you think?" Alex asks. The fact is that Amos has read Alex only too well. Sometimes it takes an exceptional person like Amos to state the truth. Someone else in his place might have apologized to Alex, but not Amos. Amos believes Alex has no reason to be mad at him. "There's nothing to be ashamed of" ("Paradigm Shift").

Amos believes there's nothing to apologize for, and hence apologizing is not even an option. Even though comforting others is sometimes the more humane response, we still have to admire Amos' consistency compared to which even well-meaning people can appear as hypocrites. Amos says things and doesn't care what others feel about them. Cohen, the cameraman for Monica Stuart's documentary project of the *Roci* crew, asks, "You don't care how you come across to other people?" Amos replies with a simple and honest "No" ("Delta-V").

Another thing to admire about Amos is that he is loyal to the core. He appreciates when others are good to him or help him out. He doesn't easily trust others, but when he does he is ready to risk his life for them. And for all his difficulty in bonding with others, Amos is actually better than many of us at trusting other people. Even the ease with which Amos is happy to delegate choices to those that are better capable of making them seems remarkable in our day and age. One of the sad trademarks of our time seems to be a mistrust of experts, and the willingness to always have an opinion even on topics outside our competence, coupled with a resentment when a more competent person makes choices for us. Our society is haunted by the ego. Amos' ability to trust others without resentment or indignance is a rare virtue nowadays. Speaking to Miller about Holden, he says: "So when he says you're out, that's just how it is, because the way I figure it he's probably right. Sure as hell has a better chance of being right than I do" ("Static"). Amos doesn't need to be the one making the decisions in order to avoid feeling like a lesser person. He doesn't care about status. He only cares about doing the right thing.

Unlike almost everyone else, Amos is selfless. He has no need to satisfy his ego or assert himself, or to prove some kind of social status. What is important to Amos is that he is safe and free to do what needs doing, and that *Roci*'s crew, his family, are safe and free too. He isn't attached to big ideas or a social image. He just does what he thinks is right, and he's not afraid to put himself at risk to do it. Again, Amos is selfless. And, perhaps ironically, this means he's actually far less evil or capable of turning evil than nearly anyone else. Just let Amos be, and he will give you far less trouble than other people.

Notes

1. Paul Slovic, "'If I look at the mass I will never act': Psychic Numbing and Genocide," *Judgment and Decision Making* 2 (2007), 79–95.
2. Jonathan Glover, *Humanity: A Moral History of the Twentieth Century* (New Haven: Yale University Press, 2012). Glover calls this response "sympathy" but what he means by this is more or less the same as emotional empathy: "caring about the miseries and happiness of others, and perhaps feeling a degree of identification with them" (22).

3. R. J. R. Blair, "A Cognitive Developmental Approach to Morality: Investigating the Psychopath," *Cognition* 57 (1995), 1–29, and R. J. R. Blair, "Moral Reasoning and the Child with Psychopathic Tendencies," *Personality and Individual Differences* 22 (1997), 731–739.

4. Jim Baxter, *Moral Responsibility and the Psychopath: The Value of Others* (Cambridge: Cambridge University Press, forthcoming, 2021).

5. The emotional deficits of psychopaths mean that even when they follow moral rules successfully, they might not understand what is "moral" about them. See Carl Elliott, *The Rules of Insanity: Moral Responsibility and the Mentally Ill Offender* (Albany: State University of New York Press, 1996). Elliott describes this by comparing the psychopath to someone who knows a lot about a piece of music but is not able to feel it: "What [the psychopath] does know is what other people think is wrong. He knows what other people feel guilty about, which actions will be punished, which will be rewarded, when to lie and when to tell the truth. In fact, he often knows all these things well enough to be able to manipulate, flatter and bamboozle people with something approaching genius . . . On the other hand, the psychopath seems to lack any sort of deep engagement with morality. His knowledge seems limited to morality's most shallow and superficial features. This sort of deficiency can be difficult to describe, a bit like describing a person who is able to say in the most technically correct, clinical terms why Duke Ellington was the greatest jazz composer of the century, yet who is also clearly and unquestionably tone deaf" (77–78).

6. The central diagnostic tool for psychopathy used by clinicians and researchers is Hare's psychopathy checklist, PCL-R. It was also the tool used by Blair in his experiments. One of the central characteristics of psychopathy according to that checklist is aggressive narcissism, of which Amos has none. In fact, the only characteristic of psychopaths Amos shares is the emotional shallowness.

7. Antonio Damasio spells out the somatic marker hypothesis in his book *Descartes' Error* (London: Penguin Books, 2005).

8. Hannah Arendt, *Eichmann in Jerusalem: A Report on the Banality of Evil* (London: Penguin Books, 2006).

9. Arendt reported the trial of Eichmann who was one of the major organizers of the Holocaust during World War II. Looking to paint a psychological portrait of the sort of person that would be behind such atrocities, Arendt grimly concludes: "The trouble with Eichmann was precisely that so many were like him, and that the many were neither perverted nor sadistic, that they were, and still are, terribly and terrifyingly normal. From the viewpoint of our legal institutions and of our moral standards of judgment, this normality was much more terrifying than all the atrocities put together" (276).

8

Moral Obligation in an Anarchic World

Matthew D. Atkinson and Darin DeWitt

Think back to "Dulcinea," the pilot episode of *The Expanse*. We find the solar system in a state of uncertainty with rising tension among Earth, Mars, and the Belt. An ice trawler named the *Canterbury* picks up a may-day alert from the *Scopuli*. A search-and-rescue mission would involve a two-day delay and, as a result, the crew would forfeit their on-time bonus. They would have less time and money to spend at the casinos and brothels of Ceres, and the mission entails big risks. The *Scopuli* could be a pirate ship. With the *Canterbury*'s crew almost unanimously opposed to respond-ing to the call for help, Captain McDowell recommends that they "move on and let the good God Darwin sort it out." Survival of the fittest! Are you satisfied with this logic? Does it disturb you? What else should the *Canterbury*'s crew take into account? Navigator Ade Nygaard, the lone voice of dissent, suggests three other considerations: international law, enlightened self-interest, and moral obligations.

It's Anarchy

The *Canterbury* seems to exist in a completely anarchic environment way out in space. But that is not entirely the case. Just like ships on the high seas, the *Canterbury* is bound by norms, rules, and conventions broadly defined as international law. When Nygaard declares, "we're obligated to check it out," Captain McDowell curtly replies, "I'm well aware of the statute." The crew is dismissive of Nygaard's point of view. They perceive themselves as living in an anarchic state of nature and embrace a wild west disposition toward the world. Semantically, both Nygaard and the rest of the crew have valid points: they are in an anarchic environment and they are not.

The Expanse and Philosophy: So Far Out Into the Darkness, First Edition. Edited by Jeffery L. Nicholas.
© 2022 John Wiley & Sons, Inc. Published 2022 by John Wiley & Sons, Inc.

Anarchy is characterized by the absence of rules and order. As such, Nygaard is right to insist that the crew lives in an environment that is partially rule-governed. To ignore the mayday call, the *Canterbury*'s crew must purge their logs—rules matter enough that proactive measures are necessary for evading them. But anarchy is also characterized by the absence of a central authority. As such, the crew's perception that rules don't apply also makes sense—it's really easy to purge the ship's logs. International law, in *The Expanse* and our modern world, depends on self-enforcement. That being the case, perhaps only an unsophisticated crew would view itself as bound by international law.

So, Nygaard pivots to a new appeal: "What goes around comes around. One of these days, it's gonna be us stranded out there." This argument has two layers: enlightened self-interest and moral obligation.

Is it in a person's self-interest to do the right thing even when they can avoid doing so? Sometimes our interests will depend on others choosing to do the right thing. So maybe it really is in our self-interest to do the right thing. In fact, societies where people act as if "what goes around comes around" are societies that thrive! If you were a very selfish person and you got to pick the society you were born into, you would choose a society that imposes strong prosocial expectations and you'd do so in spite of your (hypothetically) selfish nature. Nonetheless, Nygaard's argument falls on deaf ears. The *Canterbury* exists in a world where cooperation is not the norm and the crew doesn't put much stock in karma. Can the *Canterbury*'s crew really expect to create an international culture of cooperation by risking its own neck?

It's the moral obligation layer of the "what goes around comes around" argument that ultimately drives the *Canterbury* to undertake the rescue mission. Acting XO James Holden, who initially describes himself as a "clock-puncher"—how's that for moral absolution?!—has a bout of conscience induced by Nygaard's call for philosophical reflection. "Let the good God Darwin sort it out" is not only no way to live, but it's also no way to conceive of one's own humanity. Holden ultimately resolves to do the right thing and surreptitiously logs the distress call with HQ. He comes to recognize how morality and moral obligations are implicit in his sense of self. *The Expanse* is propelled into action when Holden does what is morally right. He does so not because it will pay tangible dividends but, rather, because he would lose his own humanity if he failed to live up to his own sense of moral obligation.

As a result of Holden's action, things are about to get really hairy for our protagonists! Self-interest and moral obligation will be pitted against one another time and time again, and most of the conflict will take place in an environment with no centralized authority capable of enforcing rules. This type of context is where the rubber really meets the road as far as moral obligations are concerned. Most of the time, domestic legal systems bring self-interest and basic social obligations into line with one another. In our everyday world, the prospect of spending time in jail short circuits the need for moral reflection. Not so in the anarchic world of *The Expanse*. In this chapter, we'll use just war theory to explore the moral obligations that exist when the political order breaks down.

How Philosophy Helps Us Discover Our Values

Chrisjen Avasarala's father taught her to "never listen to what people say," but rather to "watch what they do." This idea resonates with the concept of "cheap talk" in economic game theory, which captures situations where people say one thing and do another with impunity. As a diplomat, Avasarala doesn't believe that *all* talk is cheap. Worldly and far from naïve, she locates part of her power in her command of language. In the midst of an interplanetary war she asserts, "I solve problems by talking." Avasarala helps us appreciate the true power of language: by talking about our experiences and sharing our divergent interpretations, we discover our values and learn how to get along with one another.

Philosophy helps us develop a moral language for making choices and evaluating actions. Good moral philosophers don't dictate—from atop their ivory towers—what our values should be. Instead, they study the language that ordinary people use when thinking about and describing their life experiences. They read memoirs, history, and fiction to discern the universal values and principles that have guided human thought throughout time and across civilizations. Their job is to help you recognize and be reflective about your own values. When economists say "talk is cheap," they do so with the associated assumption that participants arrive to the conversation with predetermined and fixed preferences. Moral philosophers, however, think that people discover their preferences and values through interactions with others. Sure, people can be hypocritical and deceptive, but they are also forever in search of novel perspectives and principles.

Just war theory defines the shared moral values and vocabulary that we use to scrutinize the use of force. It's a theoretical version of how ordinary people talk about war, and its insights are the result of centuries of arguing. The theory was invented by Catholic theologians in the Middle Ages. But we'll focus on Michael Walzer's formulation because he is the most prominent living philosopher working on just war theory. Walzer studies the way that people have been thoughtful and reflective about their obligations to one another in times of war. This discussion of people's moral language amidst the hell of war will help us discover what it means to be human, what obligations we have to one another, and why such obligations exist.

Walzer insists that moral talk is *not* cheap talk, even when the stakes are high. We imagine that some of you are skeptical. Certainly some characters in *The Expanse* should give us pause. Undersecretary Errinwright will seemingly stop at nothing to achieve an "all-out war" with Mars. In the pages that follow, we'll lay out Walzer's case for why our moral vocabulary matters, in spite of our world containing its fair share of Errinwrights.

In studying moral language throughout history, Walzer distills universal moral principles that have enduringly shaped and constrained human behavior. Just war theory captures the subset of moral principles that human societies apply to war. Walzer contends that the most powerful political leaders feel constrained by these principles: "the rulers of this world embraced the theory, and did not fight a single war without describing it, or hiring intellectuals to describe it, as a war for peace and justice."[1] We see this in *The Expanse*. While Errinwright is eager for "all-out war," it takes two seasons of lying and scheming before he convinces Secretary General Sorrento-Gillis that a war against Mars could be justified as a war for peace. And when the Secretary General does act, he disingenuously manipulates the words of Reverend Volovodov. This helps illustrate the idea that moral language shapes human behavior even when we don't live up to its high ideals.

Perhaps you're still skeptical. If so, you're probably of the view that "all is fair in love and war." That view makes intuitive sense to lots of people. But think about *The Expanse*. Its most aggressive characters face constant pushback from others and their own sensibilities. The vast majority of the political and military leaders in the show firmly reject the notion that anything goes when it comes to war. If anything goes, then Errinwright and Admiral Nguyễn could wage war without murdering Minister Korshunov and Admiral Souther. In this sense, *The Expanse* is a fair representation of reality. Political leaders, military generals, and soldiers understand that timeless universal norms define their moral obligations when it comes to initiating an aggressive action—that is, when to fight—and behaving appropriately during war—how to fight.

When to Fight?

Is war ever justified? We have three general answers which we can place on a continuum. On one extreme, we have the pacifists, who believe that war is never justified; on the other extreme, we have the utilitarians, who believe that if one's goals are just, whatever steps one takes to advance those goals are also justified. In practice, goals and justifications are easy to come by and, as a result, the use of force is easy to defend. In "Here There Be Dragons," Holden exemplifies this "ends justify the means" logic when he tells Amos: "The protomolecule turned an asteroid into a missile. If we can prevent it from doing something worse, I don't mind bashing some asshole's head in." In between the two extremes, we have the just war theorists.

Just war theorists reject the "ends justify the means" rationale as an insufficient limitation on war making. Unlike pacifists, just war theorists accept that political leaders sometimes find it necessary to wage war. Indeed, war and wartime conduct can be defensible. But leaders must treat war as a last resort, even if exhausting all political options implies great risk. For example, after the battle at Ganymede Station, UN Undersecretary Errinwright pushes for a military response, warning: "We lost Ganymede, definitively. When losers seek peace, they look even weaker." In contrast, Deputy Undersecretary Avasarala recognizes the prudence of diplomacy in spite of the risks, and proposes inviting Mars to a peace summit. In the end, the decision to "talk instead of shoot" wins out when Secretary General Sorrento-Gillis puts his political reputation on the line to win support for the peace conference from the Security Council. Just war theorists would approve of the Secretary General's decision.

When is a war just? A state's decision to go to war is just when two conditions are met. One: You've been attacked or you're facing imminent threat to your sovereign territory. Two: You've exhausted all diplomatic mechanisms. In outlining these conditions, just war theorists affirm the authoritative role that nation-states play in organizing international politics.

The idea that international society is organized by nation-states dates back to the Treaty of Westphalia in 1648. The core principle of the nation-state system is that nation-states have an obligation to respect one another's sovereignty. This principle is premised on the doctrine that political communities are entitled to self-determination. In other words, the territory where a political community resides belongs to the members of that political community and their government is entitled to sovereign political authority within that territory. In theory, a system premised on self-determination depends on defining geographical boundaries and territorial sovereignty. Once we agree to this basic framework, it follows that attacks on a nation-state's territory are acts of aggression that undermine a political community's right to self-determination. The nation-state system severely restricts war, and that's why it was put in place way back in 1648.

A few political philosophers reject the nation-state system. For instance, Walzer notes that Marx "had no commitment to the existing political order, nor to the territorial integrity or political sovereignty of established states. The violation of these 'rights' raised no moral problem for him; he did not seek the punishment of aggressors."[2] Many Belter insurgents would surely agree with Marx. But the history of international society demonstrates that nations seek to uphold the rights of territorial integrity and political sovereignty. It's an appreciation of this consensus that leads Fred Johnson to argue that Belters must come together and unify under a single flag before they have any hope of earning the respect of Earth and Mars.

When war breaks out, it means that someone has committed the act of aggression. Our impulse is to ask: Who started it? For instance, at the

Earth–Mars Peace Summit, Sergeant Draper takes the blame for the Ganymede incident: "We mistook a training exercise as an active engagement and opened fire without orders. As commander of the fire team the responsibility is mine." UNN Admiral Nguyễn labels Draper the aggressor and holds her responsible for all the death and destruction that follow: "The battle on the surface is what precipitated the battle in orbit. That's what devastated Ganymede Station. That's on you, too." Of course, the devil is in the details. The complexities that surround the road to war make it difficult to parcel out blame. In fact, the attempt to parcel out blame is a key plot line that drives *The Expanse*.

While aggression is a crime, self-defense is not. The use of force is justified if it is a response to an attack on your political or territorial sovereignty. When Corporal Sa'id asks, "may we shoot the soy beans, sir?" Lieutenant Sutton responds, "only if they shoot first." Yet much of *The Expanse* is about perceived acts of aggression that are less clear cut than who shot first. In "Fight or Flight," Undersecretary Errinwright advocates an attack on the Mars' first-strike capabilities because, five years from now, they "will have the strength to impose their will on the system, to shut Earth off from the resources of the Belt," and "at that point, [Earth] may as well be their colony." Errinwright perceives Mars' efforts to expand its military capabilities as an act of aggression. He fears that Earth will be forced to forfeit its political independence if it stands down and waits for an overt military attack. What does just war theory have to say about Errinwright's predicament? Can a state act in self-defense *before* the first attack arrives? It depends. Walzer argues that states can justly use force in response to *imminent* threats to sovereignty if "doing anything other than fighting, greatly magnifies the risk."[3] But Errinwright is impatient and distrustful. He has no concrete evidence about Mars' intention to strike. His hasty push for war is unjust in the absence of a more diligent and sincere effort at diplomacy.

How to Fight?

Walzer contends that "even in hell, it is possible to be more or less humane, to fight with or without restraint."[4] To the extent that war is humane, it's because the use of force is bound by shared norms and conventions that outline what soldiers should or should not do. Is it crazy to think that enemy soldiers might adhere to humanitarian norms? No. The American military's own research suggests that the killing impulse is rare. Walzer, who digs deeply into soldier memoirs and military history, finds that soldiers are compassionate, not sociopathic fighting machines. Amos is a perfect illustration. At first glance, he appears to be an automaton who reflexively follows orders. It's hard not to agree with Miller's assessment of

Amos as a "trigger-happy whack job." But our evaluation changes as we observe Amos reflect on his actions. On Ganymede, Roma refuses to help Prax find his daughter. Amos reacts by ruthlessly beating Roma until he changes his mind. When a horrified Prax calls Amos a "homicidal maniac," Amos' retort of "I didn't kill him" clearly outlines his moral boundaries. But the incident sticks with Amos and he thinks deeply about his free will and moral culpability, telling Naomi Nagata: "I've been trying to make choices on my own lately, and I can't seem to make the right ones."

Walzer accounts for this compassionate behavior by arguing that soldiers, through reflection, come to recognize the basic moral obligations that humans have toward one another. He discerns five philosophical principles that govern our judgments about "how to fight"—all of which suggest that, deep down, we don't really believe the old canard that "all's fair in love and war."

The first "how to fight" principle: War involves combat among combatants. Whenever war occurs, civilians die. The American military euphemistically labels these deaths "collateral damage." But, in a war fought justly, civilians can never be military targets because they retain their human rights. Throughout history, soldiers and military leaders have recognized an obligation to protect civilians. Holden displays this moral sensibility. When his crew kills four members of Jules-Pierre Mao's staff on Io, Holden surveys the carnage and notes that the bodies "don't look like soldiers." But Prax Meng argues that their victims are, in fact, combatants: "They shot at us. They made the choice." Prax is right that guns and uniforms have long helped soldiers make the civilian–combatant distinction.

Everyone agrees to the principle of noncombatant immunity. However, in just war theory, the military is obligated to take positive efforts to limit collateral damage when legitimate military targets are attacked. At the planning stage, this means selecting a strategy that places civilians outside of the battle zone, even if that puts the lives of soldiers at greater risk. On Eros, we witness Captain Holden and his team take great risks to help as many innocent bystanders as they could. When Alex Kamal is troubled that they didn't save more people, Amos reminds him: "If we'd have went back for strays, we'd end up dead, like them." Just war theory doesn't condemn you to a suicide mission. But it does expect soldiers to do as much as they can just short of that. The crew of the *Rocinante* does exactly that, ramping up to a 15-g burn to keep a visual on Eros and prevent a collision with Earth that could result in 20 million casualties.

The second "how to fight" principle: When a soldier surrenders, they become a civilian again. Their captors owe their lives the same deference they accord ordinary civilians. When Holden finds three wounded Martian Marines on the *Kittur Chennamma*, he brings them to the *Roci* as POWs, or prisoners of war. The Martians are offered room, board, and medical attention, until they pick up their guns! Though the principle that surrendering soldiers become civilians is widely accepted, its application is fraught. For example, while President George W. Bush spoke often of protecting the lives of innocent women and children, he was much less defensive of the rights of POWs and led an administration that authorized their torture. Just war theory insists that leaders, like Bush, have obligations to POWs because soldiers on all sides are more innocent than we might initially assume.

When civilians become soldiers, they shed some of their rights—for instance, soldiers are legitimate targets in war. But they retain some of their pre-war innocence because of their restricted agency. Soldiers are coerced into war through force, patriotism, or poverty. *The Expanse* pushes us to question our own independence and moral culpability with reflections like the one offered by Joe Miller: "You don't choose anything. You're born into it." As Walzer discusses, such reflection is common among soldiers. Throughout time, soldiers have come to recognize that their counterparts in the opposing military were mostly thrust into combat by circumstances not of their own choosing. This helps foster an understanding that all soldiers should be treated equally.

Fred Johnson illustrates just war theory's claim of soldier innocence and shows that it even applies to volunteer armies. In "Doors & Corners," Johnson recruits Belter fighters to avenge Eros by offering "top hazard pay and first dibs on new equipment contracts." When the mission begins, Johnson frets about "sending people to their deaths." Seeking to quell his concern, Second-in-Command Camina Drummer rationalizes: "everybody here is a volunteer." But Johnson knows better: "That was the old trick. Getting them to believe that it was their own idea." Whatever cause they are fighting for, most soldiers are recruited through coercive means. Part of that coercion is getting them to believe "it was their own idea." The only way for soldiers to opt out is through the act of surrendering and, in doing so, they deserve humane treatment.

The third "how to fight" principle: Political leaders and military officers—not soldiers—bear primary responsibility for how the war is fought. Politicians declare war. Officers devise military strategies. Soldiers do what they are told.

Soldiers are morally culpable for actions they can control—for example, willfully abusing POWs. But soldiers cannot be held responsible for waging an unjust war or for their military's unjust conduct. We can observe the difference in moral responsibility between officers and soldiers by comparing Holden and Amos. After putting his crew's life at risk in the pursuit of Eros, Holden tells Naomi: "I don't want to be the one who says who lives and who dies." But Naomi tells Holden that he doesn't have much choice: "Whether you like it or not, you are the captain of this ship." Amos simultaneously confirms the great moral responsibility of an officer and the restricted agency of ordinary soldiers: He thanks Holden for "always trying to do the right thing" and remarks that "it was nice not having to worry about being on the right team."

Amos raises a fascinating dilemma: If you are fighting an unjust war, do you have an obligation to defect? Walzer says that ordinary soldiers have no such obligation. In the fog of war, patriotic emotions engulf the citizenry and ordinary soldiers cannot be expected to recognize the injustice of their side. Political leaders and officers, however, with their greater responsibility over the conduct of war, have an obligation to be reflective and defect if a war is unjust. Walzer contends that officers who serve an aggressor commit a crime if they remain in office and stay silent. This helps explain why Colonel Fred Johnson defects from the UN. He does so when he learns that UNN command failed to inform him that the ten thousand Belters of Anderson Station had surrendered, and recovered their civilian status, before Johnson's ship opened fire.

The fourth "how to fight" principle: When a state acts in self-defense and responds to the use of force, the pain it inflicts should be proportionate to the harm suffered. Without this principle of warfare, the scale of death and destruction would quickly spiral out of control. The logic of proportionality is broadly accepted, even by practitioners of *realpolitik* like Henry Kissinger. After Mars destroys Phoebe Station, Undersecretary Errinwright invokes proportionality to justify his proposed counterattack on Deimos. "A base for a base. I don't know how we can get much more proportional than that." Note that Errinwright, a war hawk, doesn't suggest blowing up Mars itself. That would be out of proportion! Instead, he proposes the destruction of the smallest Martian moon, where personnel are limited to seventeen people associated with a Deep Radar Station. More dovish leaders, like Admiral Souther, insist on greater caution and restraint—for instance, a trade embargo that would hamper the Martian terraforming project. But hawks and doves agree that whenever force is employed, it must be employed within the constraints of proportionality.

The fifth and final "how to fight" principle: Inhumane actions cannot be justified by "ends justify means" logic. Walzer insists that moral evaluations of wartime conduct must be rooted in a doctrine of human rights, not utilitarianism. In the utilitarian framework, an action is morally defensible if it does more overall good than harm. Walzer, however, rejects utilitarianism because of its history of being used and abused for selfish purposes. In theory, utilitarian systems can and should incorporate concern for universal human rights. Mitigating suffering worldwide can be an integral part of the utilitarian calculus. However, in practice, when military officers employ utilitarian modes of thinking, the result tends to be a narrow focus on the speed and scope of victory. And they use these goals to help justify human rights violations. For Walzer, choosing to kill, say, 300,000 civilians today "in order to avoid the deaths of an unknown but probably larger number of civilians and soldiers is surely a fantastic, godlike, frightening, and horrendous act."[5] Holden, rather uncharacteristically, echoes utilitarian logic on Ganymede. When Naomi questions the role that the crew of the *Rocinante* played in Santichai's death on board of the *Weeping Somnambulist*, Holden remarks: "If we do what we came here to do, I'll figure out a way to live with it." In just war theory, it's not enough to take actions that will advance a just cause—to "do what we came here to do." Moral behavior requires actions that respect human rights and our common moral notions—to do the right things for the right reasons.

What Promotes Moral Behavior?

Just war theory is premised on the idea that humans have converged around basic values regarding the sanctity of human life and liberty which inform our basic notions of what is right. At first glance, this seems like a bold premise that couldn't possibly be true. But we have observed that soldier interactions, in the real world and *The Expanse*, are often consistent with the premise!

The Expanse warns us that dramatic changes in technology and social organization will soon test humanity's mettle—imminent threats of nuclear warfare and bioengineering and the population of natural environments not conducive to human flourishing. Nonetheless, *The Expanse* is generally optimistic in its portrayal of basic human decency, as is consistent with just war theory.

Both *The Expanse* and just war theory remind us that human decency depends on actively reflecting on who we are and what obligations our sense of humanity entails. *The Expanse* highlights how changes in our environment can hinder such reflection. In witnessing Holden grapple with the challenges he confronts, we can imagine how difficult it must be to preserve one's moral sensibilities in outer space where life is governed by social isolation, sleeping pills, and artificial replications of Earth's environment. But even in these seemingly impossible circumstances, Holden is not ready to let Darwin decide.

Notes

1. Michael Walzer, *Arguing About War* (New Haven: Yale University Press, 2011), 4.
2. Michael Walzer, *Just and Unjust Wars* (New York: Basic Books, 2015), 64.
3. Ibid., 81.
4. Ibid., 33.
5. Ibid., 261.

9

Terrorism and the Churn

Trip McCrossin

"You're an OPA terrorist," United Nations Secretary General Chrisjen Avasarala accuses her prisoner, who's being subjected to gravity torture, in the series premiere. "You were carrying contraband stealth technology," she continues, demanding, "what was it for?" "I'm just a citizen of the Belt," he answers in the later, less torturous portion of his interrogation, "I work for the future of my people, as you do for yours." "Earth has created a race of exiles out in space who have no homes to return to," he states, and asks, "should this go unanswered?" Clearly this is a rhetorical question, but he'll say nothing more, even when threatened with "places far worse than this."

Also clear, while Avasarala is resolute in her opposition to the prisoner's politics, as he is to hers, she radiates nonetheless a degree of sympathy, as he does to her. "I imagine there is a mother somewhere," she continues, "who'd love to see her boy again." "I understand," he replies, "we all have our duty." Her response in turn is one of palpable sadness and resignation, wiping her hands one against the other, a bit more thoroughly than would seem to be called for by her recent snacking, as if she does indeed suffer from "dirty hands."

Avasarala can't yet foresee the larger plan of which the contraband is to be part. Still, she has an inkling. "The cold war is over," she ponders, "this is something different," and as if to complete a call-and-response, in Season 5, UN Admiral Felix Delgado rushes in to report to Avasarala that a "second rock just hit Earth." "At least now they know it's an attack," he adds on cue, evoking familiar testimony by witnesses of the second plane striking the World Trade Center on September 11, 2001. The remainder of the season is a 9-11 allegory to be sure, but also a provocative rumination on terrorism generally.

The Expanse and Philosophy: So Far Out Into the Darkness, First Edition. Edited by Jeffery L. Nicholas.
© 2022 John Wiley & Sons, Inc. Published 2022 by John Wiley & Sons, Inc.

Killing and Making Free

In the immediate aftermath of 9-11, Michael Walzer, notable theorist of warfare, reminded us that while terrorism is complex, it's not inscrutable. He breaks it down into five distinct conditions, each reflected in *The Expanse*'s storyline.[1]

First, terrorism is a *deliberate harm*. "It wasn't a rogue asteroid strike," Avasarala bellows, "it was an attack."

Second, it is deliberate harm *perpetrated against innocent civilians*. "You murdered millions," Naomi berates Marco, "innocent people."

Third, such victims are not only innocent, but as individuals, *selected at random* within a political or otherwise ideological cohort. "One hit would have been a triumph," Marco rejoices, "two proved our tactical brilliance, but after three, the Inners will never perceive us as weak again!"

Fourth, it's the hope that such a trio of conditions *produces an intended "but for the grace of the angels go we" terror in the cohort's survivors.* "High population density in the affected areas makes estimates difficult," a news outlet reports as Camina Drummer and her crew listen, "but it appears that initial fatalities will be in the range of one million to two million. The impacts have wreaked havoc on power, transportation, and desalinization infrastructures far beyond the immediate blast zones, and with Earth's aid resources already stretched to their limit, the worst is almost certainly yet to come."

Finally, it's the related hope that such widely felt terror *produces an intended political effect*, where typically this is to motivate the government that represents the cohort to alter its oppressive policies or practices. Here we need look no further than Marco's strikingly eloquent broadcast claiming responsibility for the attacks on Earth and Mars, as now the "commander of the Free Navy, the military arm and voice of the outer planets."

"I freed our people," Marco responds to Naomi's accusation about killing millions, making clear that notwithstanding the death toll, what was sought was a political effect, "return[ing] the dignity to the Belt that the Inners denied us for generations." "Th[e] attack was retribution for generations of atrocities committed by the Inners against innocent Belters," yes, as he opens his broadcast, but again, the intended effect is that "no longer will Belters be persecuted and subjected to the savagery and inhumanity that the Inners have been poisoning our species with." "With the opening of the alien gates," he continues, more eloquently still, "we are at a crossroads in human history," an occasion for "the society and culture of the Belt [to] begin again and remake humanity without the corruption, greed, and hatred that the inner planets could not transcend," into "a new, *better* form, a more *human* form." "The future of humanity is ours," he concludes, reinforcing that the intent of the attack wasn't punitive, but emancipatory: "Today and for evermore, we are free."

Implicit in the above characterization is the idea that terrorism involves a wider variety of parties than the two conventionally cited, the terrorist and their victims. A third party is the government that represents the victims, responsible for the ostensibly oppressive policies and practices the terrorist strives to undermine—the terrorist's *opponent*, if you will. In this case, this third party includes the United Nations, representing both Earth and Luna, and the Martian Congressional Republic. Finally, a fourth party is the oppressed people the terrorist acts on behalf of—the terrorist's *beneficiaries*, if you will. In this case, as per Marco's broadcast, "Citizens of the Belt, beratnas."

Recognizing this four-party characterization makes clear that the terrorist faces a sort of dilemma. Terrorists don't harm their victims because they hate them, though in fact they may. Terrorism isn't a "hate crime." Rather, they do so because their victims *as* victims have instrumental value; they serve as motivation for the terrorist's opponent to alter the policies linked to their beneficiaries' oppression. The oppression is palpable, widespread, and longstanding, they believe, and so must be addressed. (Echoes of Avasarala's prisoner's rhetorical question here: "Should this go unanswered?") In the absence of other means that the terrorist deems as effective, terrorism appears to them a last resort. (And here, echoes of Naomi's opposition to Marco: "There are other ways to protect Belters.")

The terrorist could, however, as Walzer counters, choose nonviolent movement-building instead. But it takes time, lots of time, and as it unfolds, the suffering of the terrorist's would-be beneficiaries continues, the relief of which is, we reasonably assume, the terrorist's motivation in the first place. The terrorist is, in effect, betwixt and between.

On the one hand, there's the prospect of being more like a terrorist and less like a movement-builder, creating victims imbued with instrumental political value on behalf of their beneficiaries. In the process, they fail to act justly toward the victims, for the sake of acting compassionately toward the beneficiaries. On the other hand, there's the prospect of being more like a movement-builder and less like a terrorist, refraining from unjustly creating instrumentally useful victims on behalf of their beneficiaries, and fomenting instead nonviolent popular resistance, accepting in the process that they relieve far more slowly their beneficiaries' suffering. In this, they may avoid acting unjustly toward their would-be victims, but at the same time fail to act compassionately toward their beneficiaries.[2] Hence the dilemma.

What's the would-be terrorist to do, in other words, when faced with two sets of innocents—their victims and their beneficiaries—and a choice in their regard—being a terrorist or being a movement-builder—the former appearing to be compassionate (toward beneficiaries) and unjust (toward victims), while the latter uncompassionate (toward beneficiaries) and just (toward victims)? By the same token, what's their would-be opponent to do, when faced with the prospect of the terrorist making the former choice, and so with the same two sets of innocents—the terrorist's victims and their beneficiaries—and a related choice in their regard. The choice: whether, in addition to safeguarding the prospective victims, generally speaking, to do so by acting compassionately toward the terrorist's beneficiaries, in order to relieve the terrorist of their choice.

Needless to say, the choice is more difficult, logistically and emotionally, when what's at issue is the prospect of the terrorist continuing to make the terroristic choice, but the choice is fundamentally the same nonetheless. Just as needlessly said, historically, it's rarely, if ever the choice that's made, and in this the opponent is in no small way morally culpable. The terrorist is so in any case, yes, even if their culpability is mitigated by their compassionate motivation. But to fail to act compassionately, and, in so doing, lead others to act unjustly for the sake of acting compassionately, is a sordid thing indeed.

The development of *The Expanse*'s terrorism storyline gives us hope that our future may be less sordid than our past.

People Like Us

"Why are you here?" Clarissa asks Amos, who has come to visit her in prison. He's been moved to do so by reminiscing about his surrogate mother, Lydia, who's recently passed away. "People like us," he responds, channeling language that in his reminiscence we witness Lydia offer him as a boy: "the things we do, it's not just on us. This world is messed up, and it can mess you up. I was lucky. I had somebody to help me." "Did you come here to help me?" Clarissa asks in turn, incredulously, and when he admits, "I guess I did," she's as adamant as she is despairing. "You can't," she insists. "No one can. Not every stain comes out."

As a result of the attack, however, Amos is indeed able to help Clarissa, to orchestrate for her a chance to redeem herself. On the lam, then, the two of them, on their way to Baltimore, he has occasion to return to Lydia's example, imparting to Clarissa a central idea that she embodied, which is that "there're ways that you can lead a good life, without being a good person."

"Float to the top or sink to the bottom, everything in the middle's the churn." A lesson Lydia taught Amos as a boy, which has been a guiding principle for him ever since, in his attempt to "lead a good life, without [needing to be] a good person." It's also an apt description of the morally complex landscape he inhabits, that we all do. On one extreme, those who've sunk to the bottom would likely include, for example, Jules-Pierre Mao and UN Undersecretary Errinwright. On the other extreme, those who've floated to, or at least hovered near the top would just as likely include, for example, Naomi and Holden. The churn, considerably more populated, is where Clarissa and Amos reside. It's not a static business, however, but rather an ongoing struggle. Amos has risen closer to the top, for example, guided by Naomi's moral compass, and more recently Holden's. In their absence, however, there's risk of slippage, as occurs on the road with Clarissa to Baltimore.

Their circumstances dire, Amos reverts to the more morally precarious ways of his youth, but comes eventually to realize, with Clarissa's help, that a moral lethargy is taking hold. "I'm afraid all the time," she confesses, reflecting back on her vengefully murderous pursuit of Holden, "of the things I did, how right it felt when I was doing them, how certain I was." She turns then to what's just transpired. Amos had concocted a plan, convinced that Clarissa "would've died on the road" otherwise, and also, more banally, because they "needed supplies," which she ultimately completes when it's Amos' life that's at risk.

"Why did we come here?" she asks, echoing what she'd asked Amos in prison. "We went out of our way to murder someone and take his stuff just 'cause we needed it," she continues, which, invoking Lydia, just isn't "the kind of thing good people do, not even bad people trying to live like good ones." "Yeah," he responds, clearly troubled, fearful even, "Holden never would've approved a move like that," concluding, "I need to get back to my crew." And as they develop and carry out a plan to make this happen, she continues to buck him up morally, earning her a berth on the *Roci* ultimately, and the opportunity to redeem herself, in much the same way Naomi did.

To be subject to the churn is not just to aspire to float to the top, but to be fearful of sinking to the bottom, as Clarissa is in this instance, or to be susceptible to being frightened by others to this effect, as Amos is in turn. What allows for this is what they have that Marco lacks.

In Marco's case, the incapacity is epitomized by his description of the attacks on Earth, as Naomi watches the horror unfold in newsfeeds, as "everything we ever dreamed of." If he *has* "freed our people," then this *is* the stuff of dreams, but *not* to have "murdered millions" in the process. As Hannah Arendt (1906–1975) famously wrote of the Nazi war criminal Adolf Eichmann, the "longer one listened to him, the more obvious it became that his inability to [communicate meaningfully] was closely connected with an inability to think, namely, to think from the standpoint of somebody else."[3]

So understood, Marco provides a welcome clarification of the terrorist's dilemma. It's not a dilemma for him, that is, because his victims are not, *for him*, morally considerable. The choice he faces, however, which Belters face more generally, is one nonetheless, because, regardless of his incapacity, they *are* morally considerable. The fear and reconsideration that Clarissa helps Amos to achieve, getting him to float closer to the top again, toward moral redemption without exoneration, eludes Marco ultimately, as he and the *Pella* are disintegrated by the protomolecule near the end of the sixth novel, *Babylon's Ashes*, just as Admiral Sauveterre and the *Barkeith* are as Season 5 concludes. Even so, while we can't help but regret his redemptionless demise, we've witnessed the opposite in Amos, and so can imagine it for others, which rejiggers the overall moral landscape. Not for nothing is it called *the churn*.

A Crossroads in Human History

Avasarala, for example, having not managed to thwart the attack in the way she was attempting, faces her own moment of fear and reconsideration, and ultimate redemption. "The OPA demands legitimacy through violence," we recall her shamelessly challenging her prisoner in Season 1, "because [you] haven't earned it any other way." By Season 5, however, in the wake of the attack, we find her far more humbly pleading to Delgado, "I've learned to listen."

And she continues to do just this. By the end of *Babylon's Ashes*, that is, the war has ended with an assist from the protomolecule, disintegrating not just the *Pella*, but the Free Navy generally, leaving her to ponder what peace will look like. "I have a proposal," she announces finally, to a congregation of Inner and Belter representatives, "about the architecture by which we try to unfuck ourselves," which is, of all things, a political and economic "union" of Inners and Belters. And what is this if not acting compassionately toward one's opponent's beneficiaries, so as to ward off an(other) attack. Were Marco still alive to witness this, it's not hard to imagine him musing aloud, maybe a little sarcastically, "no longer will Belters be persecuted and subjected to the savagery and inhumanity that the Inners have been poisoning our species with [*after all*]."

All of this, how can it not lend in retrospect a broader and more hopeful tenor to her "*this* is how we win" moment, toward the end of Season 5—broader and more hopeful for twenty-fourth-century humanity, and, if we're listening, for humanity already in the twenty-first.[4]

Notes

1. Michael Walzer, "Five Questions About Terrorism," *Dissent* 49 (2002); reprinted, with minor alterations, in Walzer, *Arguing About War* (New Haven and London: Yale University Press, 2004).
2. The proposal here regarding compassion is related to, but nonetheless distinct from, Robert McNamara's regarding empathy in his book, *In Retrospect: The Tragedy and Lessons of Vietnam* (New York: New York Times Books/Random House, 1995), and more explicitly in his and Errol Morris' film, *The Fog of War: Eleven Lessons from the Life of Robert S. McNamara* (Sony Pictures Classics, 2003): that we find a way to empathize with our enemy. "We must try

to put ourselves inside their skin and look at us through their eyes," he tells us in the latter, "just to understand the thoughts that lie behind their decisions and their actions," a methodology he extends explicitly to terrorism in a written addendum to the film when it went to disc in 2004.

3. Hannah Arendt, *Eichmann in Jerusalem: A Report on the Banality of Evil* (New York: Viking Press, 1963), 49. The longer essay of which this is part has as its broader context the one that's also Arendt's, which is the problem of evil.

4. I'm grateful to generations of folks in my Current Moral and Social Issues class, with whom I've developed in conversation the perspective included here, admittedly idiosyncratic, on the moral, political, and historical dimensions of terrorism and counterterrorism, which is rendered in more detail in work in preparation, tentatively entitled "The Ghost of McNamara." I'm grateful as well to Azeem Chaudry, an early contributor to the above conversation, for his steadfast friendship since, and his infectious enthusiasm for *The Expanse* in particular. Naturally, none of the above are responsible for what I've done with their insights and encouragement. Finally, I'm additionally grateful to the current volume's editor for patience and assistance far above and beyond the call.

Third Orbit
REMEMBER THE CANT!

10

The Inners Must Die

Marco Inaros and the Righteousness of Anti-Colonial Violence

Sid Simpson

The story of *The Expanse* is inseparable from the Inners' oppression of the Belters. In the opening scenes of the series, a resident of Ceres addresses his comrades: "We Belters toil and suffer, without hope and without end. And for what? One day, Mars will use its might to wrest control of Ceres from Earth, and Earth will go to war to take it back. It's all the same to us. No matter who controls Ceres, our home, to them, we will always be slaves" ("Dulcinea"). Indeed, the Belters continue to toil and suffer for the next five seasons. The Inners deny their political claims, rights, and even humanity, all while extracting the Belt's bountiful resources. The examples are endless: Protogen's use of Eros as a human petri dish for the protomolecule, Murtry and his RCE goons attempting to swindle the Belter settlers on Ilus out of their land and lithium, and UN Secretary General Avasarala's dedicated black site for subjecting Belters to gravity torture, just to name a few. The hatred that the Inners have for the Belters and the violence that accompanies it are so commonplace that they feel almost normal.

But a century of oppression didn't go unanswered. The Ring opens, the tables turn, and the Belt seizes the reins of power in Season 5. After successfully hitting Earth with three stealth-coated rocks, Free Navy Commander Marco Inaros proclaims to the entire Sol System, "This attack was retribution for generations of atrocities committed by the Inners against innocent Belters. No longer will Belters be persecuted and subjected to the savagery and inhumanity that the Inners have been poisoning our species with" ("Gaugamela"). The Inners, of course, see in Marco an unforgivable monster.

For us viewers, however, the situation is more ambiguous. After all, we've seen first-hand the suffering of the Belters at the hands of the Inners. We felt the sting, for example, when we learned that Fred Johnson killed thousands of innocent Belters on Anderson Station simply because UNN Command wanted to send a message: "Defy us, we wipe you out" ("Doors

The Expanse and Philosophy: So Far Out Into the Darkness, First Edition. Edited by Jeffery L. Nicholas.
© 2022 John Wiley & Sons, Inc. Published 2022 by John Wiley & Sons, Inc.

& Corners"). While the atrocities that Marco mentioned really did happen, and countless Belter souls really were lost to the greed and hatred of the Inners, we are left wondering, is such brazen retribution justified?

Is violence the way?

Colonization

Before we confront this question head-on, we need more context on the relationship between the Inners and the Belt. Specifically, we need more insight into the *colonial* relationship between them.

Colonization is writ large onto our understanding of space. The first frames of the show explain that "In the 23rd century, humans have colonized the solar system" ("Dulcinea"). Likewise, Mars is a former colony of the Earth; the UN and Mars send colony ships through the Ring to the (new) "new world." Finally, the first words out of Solomon Epstein's mouth when he discovers a more fuel-efficient drive are, "Mars would be able to move outward. Mine the asteroids. Colonize the Belt" ("Paradigm Shift"). What's more, the language of the show reflects the language of reality. In our world we're already envisioning establishing a colony on Mars in the coming decades, Epstein drive or not.

Colonization, however, isn't just a synonym for exploration and settlement. Historically it's intertwined with resource extraction, dehumanization, and genocide. Christopher Columbus, whose name is invoked by Avasarala as she ponders the dangers beyond the Ring gates ("New Terra"), makes this connection in the letters he wrote in 1493 back to the Spanish Crown, describing his "discovery" of the Greater Antilles. Columbus marvels at the natural beauty of the islands, practically salivating over the raw natural resources: clean streams, many harbors, lots of gold and silver. At the same time, he describes the people who live there—how timid, trusting, and loving they are.

What happens next is hardly a surprise, but the 1542 account of Spanish Dominican friar Bartolomé de las Casas leaves nothing to the imagination. He writes that in the 49 years he had lived in Hispaniola, the population of 3 million indigenous people shrunk to a mere 200, whereas on Puerto Rico, Cuba, and Jamaica the entire indigenous population disappeared altogether. De las Casas blames Spanish greed for the countless islands that lay newly desolate, writing that "the Spaniards have shown not the slightest consideration for these people, treating them not as brute animals—indeed, I would to God they had done and had shown them the consideration they afford their animals—so much as piles of dung in the middle of the road."[1]

It turns out that the intertwinement of resource extraction and dehumanization that animated the colonization of the New World on Earth doesn't simply disappear in space. The Belters' resources are violently pillaged by the Inners: "Ceres was once covered in ice. Enough water for

1,000 generations. Until Earth and Mars stripped it away for themselves. . .
They built their solar system on our backs, spilled the blood of a million of
our brothers. But in their eyes, we're not even human anymore"
("Dulcinea"). Anderson Dawes puts the Inners' extractive greed clearly:
"Earthers get to walk outside into the light, breathe pure air, look up at a
blue sky, and see something that gives them hope. And what do they do?
They look past that light. . . Past that blue sky. . . They see the stars, and
they think, 'mine'" ("Back to the Butcher"). It should be no surprise, then,
that news coverage calls the riots in Ceres' Medina District after the
destruction of the *Canterbury* "a wave of anti-colonial outrage" ("Back to
the Butcher").

The issue isn't merely the violence and extraction—though those elements of colonialism are indeed horrid beyond belief. It's also the profound dehumanization of the Belters that structures their relationship to
the Inners. In the wake of the crisis on Eros, the Belters know exactly why
they were chosen for experimentation and why they receive no aid: Dawes
shouts to his beratnas: "Earthers, Martians, they see us as their posses-
sions. Animals to test their new weapons on" ("The Seventh Man"), while
Miller tells Holden that "they picked Eros to test their weapon on because
they knew nobody would give a shit about 100,000 Belters" ("Safe"). The
Inners even have a slur for the Belters: "skinnies," a reference to the bodily
frailness that Belters develop during a life of zero-G. Of course, these various elements of colonialism reinforce each other: it is easier to rob and
murder those whom you see as subhuman; one has incentive to dehumanize those who have valuable resources for the taking.

The Wretched of the Belt

Frantz Fanon (1925–1961), the Martinican political philosopher whose
writings on colonialism and anti-colonial revolution inspired radical political leaders like Malcolm X, Che Guevara, Kwame Ture, and Steve Biko, is
particularly helpful here. In his book *Black Skin, White Masks*, Fanon
argues that colonialism proceeds by establishing an ontological division
between the colonizers and colonized. That is, it defines the colonizers as
"truly" human and their culture as "real" culture, while regarding the colonized as a degradation—or even negation—of these gold standards.
Writing in the context of colonial Algeria, Fanon sees this division organized around the color line: "Black and White represent the two poles of this
world, poles in perpetual conflict: a genuinely Manichaean notion of the
world. There, we've said it—Black or White, that is the question."[2] In the
eyes of the white European, the Black man isn't even a man. For Fanon,
this traps the colonized in a vicious cycle of trying to earn recognition as a
human from the Europeans in various ways—perhaps through gaining the

love of a white partner or becoming an expert in European culture. At the same time, they don't realize that their subjection isn't a consequence of how "well" they act, but rather of the fact that Europeans don't see them as people in the first place.

This ontological inequality also structures the relationship between the Inners and the Belt. Because Belters are not afforded the same recognition that Inners reserve for each other, they are dismissed wholesale as terrorists, worked in the mines until they die of cadmium vapors ("Back to the Butcher"), and exploited so much that the average lifespan on a station like Ceres (68) is only half of what it is on Earth (123) ("CQB"). In other words, to the Inners the Belters are less than people and can be treated as such. This is why when OPA Commander Klaes Ashford offers the spin gravity of the *Behemoth* to those harmed when the speed limit inside the Ring gate suddenly drops, a Martian private smirks, "Bunch of skinnies saving us. This place keeps getting more and more fucked up" ("Fallen World"). Apparently, the prospect of Belters acting with the compassion the Inners expect of each other is more shocking than the protomolecule's ability to change the laws of physics. One Belter on Ceres sums it up simply: "the Inners hate us down to our brittle bones" ("Remember the Cant").

As Fanon helps us to see, colonialism depends on exploiting this ontological division. At the same time that the colonizers speak of universal peace and humanity, they treat the colonized as if they were subhuman. Recall the various peace treaties supposedly in place between the Inners and the Belt during their century of suffering. The Belters are no idiots; they know that the Inners see an unbridgeable gap between them. Miller shares this wisdom with Diogo. "You don't choose anything. You're born into it, man. One side or the other" ("Static"). What's worse, the Belt already knows exactly what that division is for. When Drummer's crew contemplates joining Marco, Serge says, "you think the Earthers are going to care whose side we say we're on? They will kill every Belter they find." Oksana immediately adds, "They always have" ("Tribes").

The Limits of Peace

Emphasizing the colonial relationship between the Inners and the Belt gives us insight into why attempts to forge a peaceful alliance between Earth, Mars, and the Belt fail time and time again.

Unsurprisingly, what passes for peace depends on who's defining it. When Avasarala is torturing a Belter for information at the beginning of the series, she demands that he tell her how he got his hands on stealth technology that could "destroy the balance in the system." The Belter, Heikki Sobong, understands that the Belt does not fit into Earth's considerations: "You mean the balance between Earth and Mars. Either way, it's a lousy deal for the Belters" ("The Big Empty"). This fundamental lack of recognition recurs throughout *The Expanse*, yet factions of the Belt continue to fall for promises the Inners never intend to keep. Fred Johnson is perhaps the best exemplar of this tragedy. After having been duped by the UNN Command, he nevertheless believes that a peace between the Inners and the Belt can be forged; he's "been the oppressor, and I know his mind" ("Critical Mass"). The irony was that he didn't. That same disdain for Belter life that alienated him in the first place never abated no matter how many truces or peace agreements were formed. Marco, however, understands the stakes perfectly. When Drummer mentions the truce to Ashford within earshot, Marco simply replies: "That means nothing to them" ("Retrograde").

When Inners like Avasarala accuse Marco of "starting" a war, that means that they don't consider the ongoing oppression of the Belt an act of aggression in itself. Because Earth and Mars see Belters as subhuman, withholding vital resources like air and water from them is acceptable under a "peace" treaty, as is their constant exploitation. Colonial violence doesn't appear as violence to the colonizer because they're the ones doing it. In this way, the promise of "peace" with the Inners is an illusion: it's simply the status quo, in which the Belt agrees to nonviolence while it suffers, and the Inners continue their extraction undeterred. Fanon, deeply aware of the way that the colonial division deems the colonizers human and the colonized subhuman, already identifies in *The Wretched of the Earth* the tendency for nonviolence to be a tactic in service of the oppressor. He calls it a type of "hypnotherapy,"[3] a distraction that makes room for the ongoing violence of colonization and holds the colonized to a standard that their oppressors have no interest in meeting. The worst thing that the colonized can do, then, is play the games of peace and nonviolence.

Marco Inaros identifies this point in particular, while his OPA comrades flounder. Moments away from being spaced, Marco saves his own life in front of a tribunal of OPA faction leaders by emphasizing that this reality won't change, even with the Rings opened. "The Rings did not change the Inners. There are systems enough for everyone, they say. Riches for all. That has always been true. The Belt has always been rich, and our wealth has always been taken from us." Drummer stammers about the agreement they hold with the Inners to keep Medina Station, but Marco cuts her off: "After all their broken promises, what makes you think they will honor them now? Their hearts haven't changed" ("Retrograde").

No peace treaties or even the emergence of alien technologies will stop the lying, extraction, and dehumanization—in short, the colonial relationship—the Inners have with the Belt.

Peace with the Inners would require them to recognize the humanity of the Belters, which they cannot face if they continue to rely on the Belt's labor and resources. Worse still, no peace could answer for the past. After the *Sojourner* was attacked, Ashford understood: "It sends a message: that peace cannot change a century of anger overnight. . . and that there are Belters who still know how to hate" ("Jetsam").

A Cleansing Violence

With the prospect of peace proving to be a mirage, it's finally time to turn our attention toward violence. Prior to Marco's attack, the OPA is in an understandably tight spot. Just because you don't trust the Inners to redress the ills they've done to you doesn't necessarily mean you think violence is your best bet. Ashford, for example, is circumspect: "[Marco's] brave, yes, very brave, but also very naïve because he believes that violence is the only way to get what he feels is his due. . . Violence is indiscriminate. If you use it as a tool, it will do more than just kill your enemies. Sometimes it will kill the ones you love most" ("Cibola Burn"). Drummer, however, saw an element of truth in Marco's words: "The Mormon pictures in my office always made me laugh, celebrating the pride of the Inners, a history of coveting another's homeland and killing to take it. I believed in Fred's vision for an independent Belt, but now that we're free, we're painting those same pictures, murdering innocent people, our own people, in exchange for peace with the Inners" ("The One-Eyed Man"). When it becomes clear that "peace" comes at the cost of perpetuating Belter deaths, other options are required.

Let's set aside until later the question of Marco's personal failings—his manipulative relationship to Filip and Naomi, his narcissism and egotistical urge to take sole responsibility for the efforts of the entire Free Navy, and so on—and think about violence as such in this colonial context. It's not clear that we can dismiss his violent strategizing as an outgrowth of his megalomania; what would we then say about the myriad Belters who assembled behind him? Aren't their pain, anger, and grievances warranted?

Once again, Fanon's writing on the Algerian revolution clarifies the meaning of violence in the context of decolonization. "Decolonization is always a violent event. . . In its bare reality, decolonization reeks of red-hot cannonballs and bloody knives."[4] It's not for nothing, then, that when Marco takes control of the Rings at the end of Season 5 he whispers to Filip, "You must always have a knife in the darkness" ("Nemesis Games"). Fanon contends that anti-colonial violence is no mere reactionary emotional response or glorification of violence for the sake of violence. Instead, it attacks not only the oppressors' physical bodies but, more importantly, the ontology of colonialism itself. The colonial logics of extraction, violence, and dehumanization are shattered when the colonized pick up their knives to fight back. In these conflicts "the colonized subject thus discovers that his life, his breathing and his heartbeats are the same as the colonist's. He discovers that the skin of a colonist is not worth more than the 'native's.' In other words, his world receives a fundamental jolt."[5] Striking back at the colonizers reasserts the humanity of those who have been routinely and efficiently exploited: "At the individual level, violence is a cleansing force. It rids the colonized of their inferiority complex, of their passive and despairing attitude. It emboldens them and restores their self-confidence."[6]

It's telling that when Marco addresses the Free Navy after the attacks, the Inners' perception of the Belt is his focus: "One hit. . . would have been a triumph! Two proved our tactical brilliance. But after three, the Inners will never perceive us as weak again!" ("Gaugamela"). The point of the attacks was not to revel in the blood of the oppressor, but to destroy the colonial system as a whole. Marco even claims that Earth and Mars have a right to exist—they must just stay within their respective atmospheres. The attacks are more about ending the persecution of the Belt than the Inner lives that are lost.

The violence of the Inners is fundamentally different from the anti-colonial violence of the Belters. The violence of the Inners normalizes the colonial relationship between them, causing tragedies like Eros to be nothing more than a news story during prime time and the murder of thousands of innocent Belters on Anderson Station a "message." Because the violence of the Inners—the boot on the Belt's neck—and the dehumanization that make it possible are baked into their relationship with the Belt, they fail to even see their hypocrisy in demanding nonviolence from those they exploit. Anti-colonial violence, on the other hand, strikes out directly at this double standard: the ontological categories of colonialism that keep the colonized from being fully recognized as humans. In the colonial context, the usual insistence that violence is never the answer (the "official" position of the Inners and a sentiment to which various members of the OPA are sympathetic) effectively accepts the terms of the oppressors: that a century of exploitation and murder can coexist with a peace treaty, while righteous self-assertion cannot. If we instead understand the Belt's attack as transcending mere bloodthirst and demolishing the unquestioned colonial system that denies their very humanity, the case for anti-colonial violence becomes much more compelling.

A More Human Future

However, neither Inaros, nor Fanon stop here. If an attack on the oppressors destroys the ontological foundations of colonialism, what it means to be a free, flourishing human is up for redefinition. As Fanon writes, decolonization is a kind of *tabula rasa*, it "infuses a new rhythm, specific to a new generation of men, with a new language and a new humanity. Decolonization is truly the creation of new men. But such a creation cannot be attributed to a supernatural power: the 'thing' colonized becomes a man through the very process of liberation."[7] What Fanon called a "new humanism" could arise once the fundamentally divided world under colonialism was destroyed. The choice, it seems, is between two mutually exclusive paths: one in which the extraction, violence, and dehumanization of colonialism are never overcome, and another in which that system is exploded and left behind. Marco deftly identifies this crossroads in his address to the Sol System: "Already, we are seeing how easy it would be to carry on legacies of exploitation, injustice, prejudice, and oppression into the new worlds, but there is a better path. Under the protection of the Free Navy, the society and culture of the Belt will begin again and remake humanity without the corruption, greed, and hatred that the inner planets could not transcend. We will take what is ours by right, yes, but more than that, we will lead the Belt to a new, better form, a more human form" ("Gaugamela"). As Fanon helps us to understand, decolonization isn't about reversing the polarity of power by simply switching the oppressor with the oppressed; it's about breaking down the colonial division altogether and allowing the formerly oppressed to define for themselves who they are.

Marco's vision of the future, in which Earth and Mars keep to their planets and a self-determining Belt can finally live free of persecution, is juxtaposed against Avasarala's vision of peace in Luna Station. As the *Roci* crew and various high-ranking Inner officials laugh and drink champagne together, Avasarala toasts: "I want you all to take a good look around. This is what Marco Inaros hates. This is what he is afraid of. Why he tried so hard to destroy you and your ship. All we have to do now is turn every Belter, Martian, and Earther into this. This is how we win" ("Nemesis Games"). While superficially heartwarming, the "let's just all be friends" impulse fails in the same way that each prior peace treaty failed: it doesn't take the Belters' grievances seriously because it doesn't see Belters as people deserving of respect in the first place. Marco unified the disparate OPA factions not because friendship is scary, but because the grievances he spoke to were real—a connection that doesn't seem to occur to the Inners. Indeed, it took five seasons for Avasarala to come to the conclusion that doing violence to innocent Belters would radicalize them: "right now everyone who loved someone on Pallas is feeling what I feel. For every partisan we killed, we made ten more" ("Winnipesaukee"). However, she never took the obvious next step of connecting that revelation to the Belters' prior century of suffering. For the Belters, then, righteous anti-colonial violence that reestablishes their humanity and curtails the conditions of their domination isn't only their last option; it's the most just one.

We do, of course, have to deal with Marco the man. It seems clear that we can distinguish between his profound personal failings and his political visions. Marco might be a manipulative, sociopathic, and all-around abhorrent person, but it doesn't necessarily follow that his political claims with regard to decolonization are wrong. As Fanon demonstrates, one need not be an egotistical narcissist to want to destroy colonialism by any means possible, even if that means violence. A related, but distinct, concern is whether or not we should consider Marco's political speeches to be sincere. In other words, even if we do believe that anti-colonial violence is justified because it makes possible a more humane future, do we necessarily believe that Marco actually wants that? If an indefensible person is insincere about the defensible politics that he holds, how does that change things? We as viewers are led to at least suspect this possibility, given the show's emphasis on Marco's considerable interpersonal failings. The hard and potentially unsettling answer is that it simply may not matter in the end. Regardless of whether or not Marco intends to follow through with helping the Belt achieve a better, more human form, the alternative stays the same: "peace" as the Inners understand it, which gives Earth and Mars' colonial tendencies a free pass and guarantees continued exploitation of the Belt. Even if we take the most cynical view and say that Marco is driven entirely by his ego rather than genuine love for his fellow Belters, the Belt still has everything to gain from asserting itself in a way that ends its exploitation.

Fanon knew that decolonization was necessarily a bloody event, and the same logic ultimately applies in *The Expanse*: Belters will either continue to die in darkness, or Inners' blood must be spilled in a gamble for a freer future for humanity. At the end of the day, those in the Belt simply want the humanity that they've been denied for a century. If the only way to take it is by force, so be it.

In Marco's words, "Citizens of the Belt, beratnas, rise up now in joy and glorious resolve. This day is ours. Tomorrow is ours. The future of humanity is ours. Today and forevermore. . . we are free!" ("Gaugamela").

Notes

1. Bartolomé de las Casas, *A Short Account of the Destruction of the Indies* (London: Penguin Books, 1992 [1552]), 13.
2. Frantz Fanon, *Black Skin, White Masks* (New York: Grove Press, 2008 [1952]), 27.
3. Frantz Fanon, *The Wretched of the Earth* (New York: Grove Press, 2004 [1963]), 28.
4. Ibid., 1–3.
5. Ibid., 10.
6. Ibid., 51.
7. Ibid., 2.

11

Being Beltalowda
Patriotism and Nationalism in *The Expanse*

Caleb McGee Husmann and Elizabeth Kusko

"Beltalowda!"

It is a made-up word from a made-up language for a made-up nation. When viewers of *The Expanse* first hear the collective noun in "Dulcinea" it is borderline nonsense, a foreign sound unintelligibly shouted by skinny rabble-rousers with too little body fat and too many tattoos. Little does the audience know that over the course of six seasons, *The Expanse* will develop "Beltalowda" into one of the most meaningful and complex linguistic inventions fiction has seen. It is a word with the catchiness of Anthony Burgess's "droogies" and the profundity of Joseph Heller's "Catch-22." Beltalowda is a word that both unites and divides; a word that inspires and frightens. Most importantly, it is a word that reminds us of one clear and uncomfortable truth: loving one's nation is a tricky business.

While the debate around the appropriate way to love one's nation extends back to at least the Hellenistic period, much of the contemporary discourse on the topic can be traced to George Orwell's 1945 essay, *Notes on Nationalism*. In this work, Orwell draws a distinction between the concepts of patriotism and nationalism, two terms synonymous with love of nation, and two terms that, up until that point, had been used almost interchangeably. This distinction, although not the main focus of Orwell's essay, effectively laid the groundwork for much of the discussion on the topic ever since then. So, it is not surprising that *The Expanse*, a work of fiction, dramatizes the issue. Indeed, the past, present, and future of the Belt is in many ways *the* central storyline of the series. How the nation should be loved and how it should be led is a constant point of deliberation amongst Belters in general, and the Outer Planets Alliance (OPA) in particular. Yes, *The Expanse* is a sprawling space opera about saving the universe from an alien lifeform; at its core, though, it is a study in what it means to love one's nation the right way.

It is an exploration of what it means to be Beltalowda.

The Expanse and Philosophy: So Far Out Into the Darkness, First Edition. Edited by Jeffery L. Nicholas.
© 2022 John Wiley & Sons, Inc. Published 2022 by John Wiley & Sons, Inc.

Patriotism and Nationalism According to Orwell

By 'nationalism' I mean first of all the habit of assuming that human beings can be classified like insects and that whole blocks of millions or tens of millions of people can be confidently labelled 'good' or 'bad'. But secondly— and this is much more important—I mean the habit of identifying oneself with a single nation or other unit, placing it beyond good and evil and rec- ognizing no other duty than that of advancing its interests. *Nationalism is not to be confused with patriotism* . . . By 'patriotism' I mean devotion to a particular place and a particular way of life, which one believes to be the best in the world but has no wish to force on other people. Patriotism is of its nature defensive, both militarily and culturally. Nationalism, on the other hand, is inseparable from the desire for power. The abiding purpose of every nationalist is to secure more power and more prestige, *not* for himself but for the nation or other unit in which he has chosen to sink his own individuality.[1]

In the above passage George Orwell succinctly delineates between the atti- tudes of patriotism and nationalism. Patriotism involves being proud of one's nation but not blind to its shortcomings. It involves an affinity for a culture but not a zealous obsession in forcing others to adopt it. It involves sticking up for one's nation when it is unduly attacked, but also acknowl- edging when it can do better and then helping it along that path. In con- trast, nationalism is about unquestioning allegiance, forceful proselytizing, and a rapacious desire for ever greater influence over others. According to Orwell, nationalist thought is dominated by three principal characteristics: obsession, instability, and an indifference to reality.[2]

Obsession, the first of Orwell's principal characteristics of nationalism, is self-explanatory. Nationalists are fixated on their unit and furthering its cause whatever that may be. They revel in their allegiance and bristle at any critique. Such behavior is repeatedly evident in *The Expanse* from UN Undersecretary Errinwright's "Earth must come first" mentality, to Admiral Sauveterre and Lieutenant Babbage's "one mind, one cause" vision for future Martian settlements, to every Belter that labels another Belter that they deem insufficiently zealous a *welwala*.

The second characteristic, instability, is less intuitive. Orwell is not refer- ring to the instability of the nation, but rather the instability of individual nationalists.[3] He is talking about the fact that many people with intense nationalist attitudes can, and have, transferred their loyalty. Yes, some nationalists were born into the unit to which they are loyal and remain in that unit forever; other nationalists, however, were born into units that are different from the ones to which they are loyal. Furthermore, some nation- alists have been born into one unit, become nationalists for another, then completed an about-face and rejoined their original unit, or even a new third unit, the intensity of their attitude never waning in the process. Such behavior, although contradictory in many ways, is remarkably consistent in one way: the type of thinking taking place. As Orwell says, "What remains constant in the nationalist is his own state of mind: the object of his feelings is changeable, and may be imaginary."[4] Examples of this kind of instability abound in *The Expanse* and are particularly prominent amongst the ranks of the OPA, with Fred Johnson and Julie Mao serving as the most prominent examples.

The last of Orwell's principal characteristics of nationalism, indifference to reality, is much like the first in that it is largely self-explanatory. Quite simply, nationalists are blind to facts that go against their unit in any way. Furthermore, they neither feel nor perceive any inconsistency when their unit engages in a behavior for which they have stridently criticized others. Thus, "Actions are held to be good or bad, not on their own merits but according to who does them."[5] This principle is one which many loyalists, but especially Filip, maintain with respect to Marco Inaros, one which Naomi, Filip's mother, tries to open his eyes to.

In light of Orwell's account of patriotism and nationalism, it becomes clear that the two attitudes are on constant display throughout *The Expanse*. We see them in the heated arguments between Martian Marines, in the wildly disparate views of Earth's Security Council members, in the cynical interactions of diplomats; the list goes on and on. That said, these competing schools of thought clearly come to blows most frequently and most intensely amongst the people of the Belt. Indeed, when it comes to fiery debates over how to love one's nation and how to treat other nations, the Inners have nothing on the Outers.

Drummer the Patriot, Marco the Nationalist

Anderson Dawes, Joe Miller, Naomi Nagata, Klaes Ashford, Fred Johnson, Julie Mao, Cyn, Diogo, Karal, Filip, Oksana, the Black Sky faction, the Golden Bough, the Voltaire Collective, all of these people, all of these groups, are either native Belters, members of the OPA, or both. Each of them can claim Beltalowda status, and each of them have their own distinct view of what that status means and what actions that status demands. Of course, addressing each of these character's perspectives individually is a monumental task well beyond the scope of this chapter. To get a good view of the contrasting attitudes, let's turn our attention to two of the broadcast series' most compelling characters: Camina Drummer and Marco Inaros.

Camina Drummer is a proud Belter. Thin, fit, and unapologetically tattooed, her physical stature reflects the harsh environment of the Belt. As she screams out commands to the Beltalowda while captaining Medina Station or the *Dewalt* ship, Drummer's native language unites her with fellow Outers and renders her distinct from the Inners. Whether she is working alongside native-born Belters such as Anderson Dawes or Klaes

Ashford, or whether she is working for the Earth-born Fred Johnson, Drummer is unfailing in her commitment to and advocacy for the Belt. No one can question that Camina Drummer loves and is loyal to her home. But importantly, Drummer never allows her love or loyalty to disconnect her from reality. She is a clear-eyed and enthusiastic champion of the Belt, but not a blind fanatic. Her affection is unwavering, but not unquestioning; indefatigable, but not insensible. In short, Camina Drummer is a patriot.

In contrast, Marco Inaros is a nationalist. He is a product of the same culture as Drummer, shares the same language, identifies with the same people, and has affection for the same place. The history of his people is the history of her people. The object of his love and loyalty is the object of her love and loyalty. Yet, the way he expresses that love and loyalty is wildly different from the way that she does. Marco is not a clear-eyed champion; he is a blind fanatic. He is both unwavering and unquestioning, indefatigable and insensible.

As one marches point by point through Orwell's work on patriotism and nationalism, it becomes increasingly apparent that Drummer and Inaros are nearly perfect representations of each concept.

Offensive Versus Defensive Attitudes

According to Orwell, the foremost difference between patriotism and nationalism is the distinction between defensive and offensive attitudes, which is demonstrated in the different approaches of Drummer and Inaros.[6] Drummer believes in the Belter way of life. She seems to believe that way of life is, as Orwell says, "the best in the world."[7] However, she never pushes it upon others. Throughout the series Drummer repeatedly demonstrates a willingness to defend what belongs to her nation and her culture, but she never attempts to force other nations and cultures into submission. Take for instance Drummer's initial meeting with the *Rocinante* and its crew. Although she originally means to meet them with guns, by the end of that same episode, she is cooperating with Earthers and Martians in a raid on Thoth Station, and by the next episode, announces in reference to repairs on the *Rocinante*, "don't worry, we're going to treat her like one of our own" ("Doors & Corners").

Drummer's evolution in thought and attitude toward a group of Inners is indicative not only of her determination to defend the Belt, but also of her willingness to work collegially with others once they have shown that they mean her nation no harm. Similarly, when giving her epic speech onboard the *Behemoth* ship in "Intransigence," she demonstrates her immense pride and belief in the people of the Belt, but her tone is always defensive in attitude. She repeatedly argues that the Beltalowda belong, and that they have as much right to explore the Rings as the Inners, but she never asserts that they have an exclusive claim on the Rings, nor that the Inners must adopt the Belter way of life.

In contrast, Marco Inaros is always on the offense. In his first appearance in "Retrograde" he talks his way out of a death sentence by speaking about spreading the power of the Belt. It is not enough to be guarded in diplomatic efforts with other nations; there must be no diplomatic efforts with other nations. It is not enough to have an equal share of the Rings; he must have control of the Rings. It is not enough to send a clear message with a tactical strike against Earth; he must carry out a massacre against Earth. Marco's love of his nation is infused with an insatiable thirst for more power; that is how a nationalist loves his nation.

Obsession

According to Orwell, "as nearly as possible, no nationalist ever thinks, talks, or writes about anything except the superiority of his own power unit."[8] Furthermore, they cannot "conceal their allegiance," or endure even "the smallest slur" upon their nation.[9] In a word, they are obsessed. Once again, this principal characteristic of nationalism applies perfectly to Marco Inaros and not to Camina Drummer.

When we are introduced to Camina, we learn that she is second in command of Tycho Station behind Fred Johnson ("Doors & Corners"). Although Fred Johnson is an ardent Belter advocate and an OPA sympathizer, he is also an Earth-born, former United Nations Marine who previously murdered countless civilian Belters at Anderson Station. The simple fact that Drummer can work with and respect someone who was born into another nation, and once fought for another nation, serves as a testament to the fact that she is not obsessed.

Juxtaposing Drummer's interaction with Fred to that of others, such as Marco Inaros, Anderson Dawes, and various OPA, makes this point more compelling. Yes, they cooperate with Fred when it is convenient, but their embrace is always skeptical and half-hearted. In the end it is no surprise when Johnson ultimately dies as a result of an Inaros plot ("Gaugamela"). Indeed, it had been evident for over a season that Marco would not allow an Inner, no matter how sympathetic to the cause, to play a major role in his uprising. His infamous speech claiming credit for the terrorist attack on Earth testifies to this actuality. No nationalist who refers to people from other nations as a different "species" will allow his nation to be led, or even co-led, by someone they still perceive to be part of a rival unit.

In contrast, Drummer has not only spent years working with and for Fred Johnson, she is also loyal to him, an Earther. When, for instance in "Pyre," Tycho Station is raided by Anderson Dawes' OPA faction, the leader of that attack demands, with gun in hand, that Drummer provide missile codes and join their cause. She declines, stating, "I work for Fred." That declaration of fealty results in the OPA leader shooting Drummer. As she is escorted to safety by Earthers and Martians, Drummer shoots the Belters who invaded her station, threatened her crew and her boss, and shot her for taking a contrarian stance to the OPA. Drummer does not adjudicate based only on the label of Earther, Martian, or Belter. Rather, she judges and ultimately decides upon an individual based on their actions, befriending "enemy" Earthers and Martians and assassinating her own Belter people when their behavior justifies her doing so. This aspect of Drummer's character is fundamental to her belief system. It is so fundamental that she goes against Marco, Karal, and other Belter radicals by opening fire on their ships in order to save her "Earther friends" on the *Rocinante* ("Nemesis Games").

Evidence of Marco's obsession and Drummer's lack thereof is also on display in their differing treatment of Naomi Nagata. Naomi is a Belter who loves her home, but also a Belter who doesn't shy away from critiquing her nation when appropriate, nor from working with people of other nations when they demonstrate good faith, nor from identifying people from other nations as part of her family. Such behavior ultimately results in Drummer heaping praise and affection on Naomi, calling her the smartest person she ever knew ("Winnipesaukee"). Contrariwise, that same behavior results in Marco imprisoning, tormenting, and disowning her ("Oyedeng"). The fact that Naomi is the mother of his child does not matter, the sin of being a *welwala* is unforgivable. Marco's behavior is obsession at its peak. It is also an excellent example of his indifference to reality.

Indifference to Reality

Orwell notes that, "All nationalists have the power of not seeing resemblances between similar sets of facts."[10] Marco exhibits this inability to recognize resemblances whenever he interacts with Naomi Nagata. In some ways it seems as though Marco and Naomi's son, Filip, was created for the sole purpose of showing the audience how nationalism can divorce people from objective truth. From the moment Filip stuns Naomi and takes her captive in "Mother," until the moment she leaps out into space in "Hard Vacuum," Naomi and Marco are constantly trying to persuade their son to see the world their way. Marco uses emotional manipulation and nationalist-style brainwashing. Inaros seems aware that he is emotionally manipulating his son, but he doesn't seem aware that he is brainwashing him. All indicators suggest that Marco sincerely believes the nationalist version of reality he is preaching. True, one could argue that he is a narcissist only allegiant to himself, but this viewpoint ignores the fact that the nation and the individual are indistinguishable for Marco, just as they are indistinguishable for all nationalists. Nationalism requires one to sink one's individuality into the unit, and Marco makes it clear from the start that he has done precisely that. Indeed, within thirty minutes of his first appearance Marco says, "All I did, I did for all Belters," and the audience believes him because he believes it himself ("Retrograde"). Thus, even if one accepts that Marco's primary motivation is Marco himself, that doesn't preclude him from being a nationalist. Instead, it is only further proof of his indifference to reality on behalf of the unit, an indifference to reality that is also evident in his belief that theft, terrorism, and genocide are acceptable so long as his nation is the one carrying them out.

In contrast, Naomi constantly encourages her son to heed reality. She tells him that his nationalist actions are objectively wrong. The fact that they were carried out on behalf of the Belt makes no difference. Killing millions of civilians is bad no matter who those civilians are. Inner, Outer, it does not matter. Furthermore, Naomi always takes great pains to tell the whole story, not just the portion of the story that is convenient to her narrative. When Filip says proudly to her, "I just read some accounts of what you did inside the Ring. You saved a lot of Belta lives" ("Oyedeng"), Naomi goes out of her way to say, "It was not just me alone. It was all of us together. Despite what your father may have told you." Even in a moment when Naomi is being praised by her son, a son whose approval she desperately wants, she still refuses to deny reality; she refuses to give an inch to nationalism.

Naomi's steadfast rejection of Marco's approach makes it easy to see why the patriotic Drummer holds her in such high regard. Drummer has taken similarly principled stands against the hypocrisy of Marco's nationalism. She will not even concede minor distortions of reality intended to alleviate her own people's consciences. When Bertold, a member of her crew, attempts to make himself feel better by asserting that the ins and outs of their day-to-day are unchanged under Marco's rule, and that it does not matter that the ship they are currently salvaging is filled with dead members of an OPA faction who Marco killed for voting against him, Drummer immediately sets her underling straight. "We're not salvagers," she says, correcting his word choice ("Hard Vacuum"). "We're scavengers. Marco kills those who defy him, and we pick the bodies clean." A nationalist could never have uttered this sharp retort, an uncompromising condemnation of one's own unit.

Against Love of Nation

So what is the big takeaway? Is it as simple as patriotism is good and nationalism is bad? Throughout the first few seasons of *The Expanse* it seemed like this was indeed the point being made. Sure, the show was offering up a nuanced and richly layered portrayal of each concept, but at its core, it was sticking to this fairly conventional message. Then, as Season 4 concludes and Season 5 unfolds, something interesting starts to happen: the patriots start losing.

At first, the nationalists' wins are relatively small. Marco gets a favorable judgment from the tribunal; he persuades various fringe OPA factions to his cause; and he gets away with stealing from the Inners. Such successes are substantive, but none of them make it seem as though the nationalist attitude will win out over the patriotism of leaders such as Drummer and Ashford and Johnson, at least not at first. By Season 5, however, the situation looks different. The patriots' minor losses have snowballed into cataclysmic defeats. Marco and his fellow nationalists have risen to power. They have become the leaders of the Belt both in force and in spirit, and they have done so via outrageously aggressive nationalist tactics. Furthermore, as one looks back at their rise to power, it seems as if that rise was inevitable, as if the patriots never really stood a chance. One explanation for this stands out: nationalists can always one up patriots.

Certain similarities run through all of the most compelling speeches given by various members of the OPA. Whether delivered by a patriot or a nationalist, all of the inspirational and moving words spoken to the Beltalowda draw on the same spirit, the same emotions, shared experiences and affections, and because of this shared message, the patriots are destined to lose. Patriots can never go as far as nationalists, because they have the same fuel but half as many tools. In short, patriots can only play defense. Nationalists can play defense and offense, and that makes their job infinitely easier and their cause more appealing. No one wants to play defense all the time. People want to play both sides of the ball, or they want to play offense all the time. Only nationalism can offer them those options, and as a result, nationalism will always win.

The Expanse's final word on the matter is that nationalism is bad, but patriotism is also bad because it inevitably loses to nationalism. So, neither Camina Drummer nor Marco Inaros has the correct attitude toward Beltalowda, because there should be no Beltalowda, just as there should be no Earther or Martian. *The Expanse* does not want a universe divided into nations, because such a universe is destined to stay divided. Instead, it wants a cosmopolitan universe, a universe where shared humanity takes precedence over all other loyalties. In the Season 5 finale, UN Secretary General Chrisjen Avasarala says, "I want you all to take a good look around. This is what Marco Inaros hates. This is what he is afraid of, why he tried so hard to destroy you and your ship. All you have to do now is turn every Belter, Martian, and Earther into this. This is how we win" ("Nemesis Games").

In other words, the answer has been there all along. It is neither patriotism nor nationalism. Instead, it is the cosmopolitanism of the *Rocinante*.

Notes

1. George Orwell, *Notes on Nationalism* (London: Penguin Modern Classics, 2018), 1–2. See also Martha C. Nussbaum, *For Love of Country?* (Boston: Beacon Press, 2002), and Igor Primoratz and Aleksandar Pavkovic, eds., *Patriotism: Philosophical and Political Perspectives* (Burlington: Ashgate Publishing, 2007).
2. Orwell, *Notes on Nationalism*, 9–18.
3. Ibid., 11.
4. Ibid., 12.
5. Ibid., 13.
6. Ibid., 2.
7. Ibid.
8. Ibid., 9.
9. Ibid.
10. Ibid., 13.

12

Anarchy in the OPA
Sovereignty, Capitalism, and Bare Life

Lisa Wenger Bro

"Jim, there's something you should know," Ade Nygaard tells James Holden over the com. Then there's a blinding flash of light as the water-crawler *Canterbury* disintegrates on torpedo impact. Off ship investigating a distress call, Holden and his small crew watch helplessly as Martian torpedoes score a direct hit in *The Expanse* pilot "Dulcinea." Nothing is left; no one lives. But, will anyone really care? The *Canterbury* was home to all those who didn't fit anywhere else, whose lives were deemed less valuable, for one reason or another, and who now worked a menial job hauling chunks of ice across the Belt to replenish water supplies. *The Expanse*'s world is one of hierarchies and oppression—what do a few more Belter deaths matter to the Inners? Yet, Holden refuses to let the deaths go unnoticed and unpunished; he broadcasts Mars' alleged senseless destruction of the *Canterbury* and its lives, demanding justice. Holden's cry stirs up long-smoldering problems tied to sovereignty, capitalism's corruptive influence on sovereign power, and the biopolitical, which is fitting, because at the heart of *The Expanse* lie questions about just who has power, who profits, and whose life holds value.

"Every Breath You Take"

The episode: "Back to the Butcher." The scene: Anderson Station. The situation: All the children have been diagnosed with "hypoxic brain injury due to low oxygen." Marama Brown, holding his daughter Kira, pleads with the faceless oppressors: "The company is refusing us medical assistance, and they're denying the problem even exists." Behind Brown, lighting murkily illuminates dejected Belters trying to calm the cries of their children. *Leviathan Wakes*, the novel, tells us that the Inners placed such high surcharges on necessities that "5 percent of Belters buying their air from

The Expanse and Philosophy: So Far Out Into the Darkness, First Edition. Edited by Jeffery L. Nicholas.
© 2022 John Wiley & Sons, Inc. Published 2022 by John Wiley & Sons, Inc.

Anderson were living bottle to mouth, so just under fifty thousand Belters
might have to spend one day of each month not breathing."[1] Desperate, the
Belters take up arms and take over the station, but as Brown explains,
voice quavering, "We're not violent people. . . We just wanted to be heard
for the sake of our children."

Taking place 11 years before the events in *Leviathan Wakes*, the story
from Anderson Station sets up issues related to sovereign authority and
biopolitics that will complicate the entire series, while also setting a precedent for later events. First, we see the way that contemporary sovereignty
blurs and shifts. Just who is in charge of Anderson Station? Who has the
authority over both the station and people who live there? One of the
problems related to contemporary sovereignty is that it's no longer static
and centralized like it was with the early monarchs or with the political
sovereign that emerged, according to Michel Foucault (1926–1984), with
the market in the sixteenth century.[2] Sovereignty is blurred and fragmented,
no longer residing within a single individual or political entity.
Contemporary philosophers Michael Hardt and Antonio Negri call this
new and global sovereign power "empire."[3] Hardt and Negri also note the
vagueness of where sovereignty is located when they say it's found in
"national and supranational organisms."[4] Just what are these organisms
that have sovereign power? The sovereign political still exists; Earth sends
both naval and marine forces to secure Anderson Station. However, capitalist interests also attain sovereign power. The sovereign power Earth
sends troops to the station, not on their own, but only at the request of
Anderson-Hyosung, the corporation running the station. The political sovereign plays a secondary role to the capitalist sovereign, taking action only
because of corporate demands. The military comprises a third component
in this fragmented sovereignty, invested with its own sovereign power
when sent to secure the station.

"Seek and Destroy"

Brown finishes his plea; a flash of light illuminates the station; a loud
explosion follows. Screams echo through the cramped room. Everything
goes dark. The view shifts outside the station where Brown, still clutching
his daughter, floats through the cold darkness. The camera pans to hundreds of Belter bodies drifting through space. A voice speaks through a
military channel: "Anderson Station is secure. All terrorists have been
subdued."

All are dead—not just those who rebelled, but also innocent civilians.
Brown initially reached out to the corporate sovereign, but Anderson-
Hyosung refused to listen, acknowledge any problems (or culpability), or
assist in any way. With the military fast approaching, Brown's now broad-
casting out to the political sovereign as he desperately tries to save his

people. In fact, the Belter rebels surrender, and Earth accepts that surrender. Yet, sovereignty is fragmented and decentralized. Word doesn't reach the military.

The Anderson Station massacre highlights problems with both sovereignty's fragmentation and biopolitics. Sovereign entities have power over and determine the value of human life. According to contemporary Italian philosopher Giorgio Agamben, sovereignty recognizes two different types of life. The first type of life Agamben calls *bios*, which is the politically invested life, the citizen granted rights and protections through birth into a sovereign nation. The second type is what he calls *zoē*, or bare life, the life that simply exists. Bare life is life that is outside law (outlaw) and politics; life that has no rights and no value. Bare life is, Agamben says, the life that the sovereign "is permitted to kill without committing homicide."[5] The massacre proves the Belters are bare life. The spectacle of lifeless Belter bodies floating in space demonstrates that certain lives—that Belter lives—are of less value and are expendable. The sovereign can kill them without committing murder because they don't belong to the sovereign realm.

"I Fought the Law"

How does a sovereign determine the value of a human life? Adolphus Murtry, head of the Royal Charter Energy (RCE) corp's security force, stalks through the darkness across the Ilus/New Terra camp in "Jetsam." A small group of Belters call out to him. Murtry stops, expression stony as he surveys the group of "squatters," the Belters who don't belong on the RCE-claimed planet, New Terra. Coop, one of the Belter leaders, tells Murtry,

> Belters, we built Ganymede. We turned it from a ball of ice into a garden. You fucking Inners, you come and wreck it all. And when we need to flee, do the Inners help us? No. They turn us from every port like we a disease. . . So we come here. . . we built this. We make something again. . . And here come the fucking Inners who take it all away again.

Murtry challenges Coop. The Belters blew up an RCE ship landing pad, killing 23 Inners. Coop, insinuating more violence and deaths, says, "Careful, Earther. The day ain't over yet." Murtry calmly turns around, pulls his gun, and fires twice, claiming, "That was a threat." Blood splatters the housing station behind Coop as the unarmed corpse crumples to the ground.

What makes life bare, expendable, of no value? Early on, Murtry echoes the ideology of his corporate employers while traveling to New Terra.

Despite the fact that the Belters had nowhere to go after the alien proto-molecule decimated their previous home, Murtry calls them "squatters" and "illegals." This idea of the Belter refugees as illegal positions them as bare life. They are not a part of the sovereign realm, not afforded the same rights as birthed citizens; they exist outside the realm. Excluded from the realm, their claims to the planet are dismissed. The RCE also has an Earth-granted charter backing them up. After the landing pad explosion that injures and kills dozens of incoming Inner settlers, the Belters are not just illegals, but also terrorists. Outside the law and outside the sovereign realm, nothing protects their lives from sovereign retaliation.

Murtry isn't following a new idea; he's following the same logic that led to the massacre at Anderson Station.

Belters try to eliminate Inner oppression, try to secure their own futures, but inevitably death and destruction occur in their struggles as they come up against the immobility of Inner policy and prejudice. Belters are viewed, at best, as criminals and thugs, and at worst as terrorists. Even Ceres police detective Joe Miller says the Belter political organization, the Outer Planets Alliance (OPA), is "beloved by the people it helped and feared by the ones who got in its way. Part social movement, part wannabe nation, and part terrorist network, it totally lacked an institutional conscience."[6] Across all strata of Belter population—from ordinary citizen to political representa-tive to police—the same, as Miller calls it, "moral flexibility" applies. No one outside the Belt cares about their lives and living situation, so the Belter mentality is do whatever it takes. It doesn't matter if the action is right or wrong so long as the desired (and "just") outcome is achieved. At Anderson Station, the governor is accidentally killed during the uprising; at Ilus/New Terra, the landing pad explosion is detonated too late, killing Inner passengers, including the new governor. Already placed outside sov-ereign protection when they're called illegals, as terrorists and as a threat to *bios* or protected life, Belter lives lose all value.

More Inhuman than Human

Battling their way across the chaos on Eros Station, Holden and Miller stand, guns raised, as a pod comes to a stop on their floor and the doors slowly open in "Leviathan Wakes." Belters lie unmoving and moaning on the floor or feebly crawl across the pod, while a bright blue light spreads through their veins. There is little "human" life left in the pod; all are infected with the alien protomolecule that reshapes their bodies as it kills them. In the novel, those who stagger out are vomit zombies, "their eyes glassy. . . [movements] listless, driven, automatic. Like rabid dogs whose minds had already been given over to their disease."[7] Watching the bodies in horror, Holden has a realization:

HOLDEN: They're spreading it deliberately.

MILLER: It's an experiment—the whole goddamn station. . . Watch a hundred thousand people die. Just like bugs in a dish. That's why they picked Eros. They don't consider these people human.

A million and a half Belters on Eros Station turned into a corporate experiment, deliberately infected with the alien protomolecule, herded into chambers, and then exposed to radiation. All those deaths just to see what would happen and to determine if and how the protomolecule's powers could be harnessed.

Miller's words expose the second rationale seen in *The Expanse* for categorizing Belters as bare life—they are Other, a being so different from the Inners that the Inners question whether the Belters are even human anymore, whether they've evolved into some new, alien species. With their lanky frames (stretched from life in low gravity), their Creole language, and their strange customs, Belters appear inhuman to Inners. As a result, Inners place Belters into what Agamben calls a "state of exception," excluding Belters from sovereign citizenship, and, therefore, from rights guaranteed those born and raised on Earth and Mars. Agamben and Foucault, among other philosophers, note that the processes of dehumanizing and Othering have long been used to exclude people and even to justify genocide. Agamben says Hitler, for instance, first stripped Jews of German citizenship because excluding the Jewish people from the sovereign realm stripped them of all legal and political rights and reduced them to bare life. Mirroring the use of gas chambers on the Jewish people, Protogen forces the Belters into radiation chambers, highlighting how easily such atrocities can occur when prejudice and fear reign. Miller makes this Belter–Jewish connection, and Holden expresses disbelief that Inners see Belters as inhuman or that such a view could lead to genocide. Miller tells Holden, "People have been getting tossed into ovens for less than that ever since they invented ovens."[8]

"Sunday, Bloody vunday"

The Earth-based Anderson-Hyosung corporation that runs Anderson Station refuses to provide the essentials—sufficient air and water, much less the basics of safety and healthcare—so the Belters take up arms and strike. For that, they are massacred. Belter refugees head through a Ring Gate and find Ilus; RCE finds New Terra. Who cares that it's the same planet the Belter refugees landed on? RCE has a charter proving ownership and a corporate security force to secure capitalist interests. The Belters again revolt; they are again gunned down. Mao-Kwikowski wants to harness the power of the protomolecule but needs test subjects to conduct experiments on. An entire station holding millions of Belter lives is eradicated. Millions of Belter lives are exchanged for the pursuit of profits and power.

Over and over, Belter life is reduced to bare life. They are exploited and then exterminated when their "usefulness" runs its course. What we often see in these reductions of Belters to bare life is the way that capitalism corrupts—both other sovereign entities *and* as a sovereign. *The Expanse* illustrates ideas echoed from Karl Marx (1818–1883) to Hardt and Negri—that capitalism will always seek the highest "surplus-value" (prof-its), that it will always seek to expand in order to attain more profits, and it will exploit the lower class/laborers in order to do so.[9] As Hardt and Negri say, "left to its own devices, capital would never abandon a regime of profit. In other words, capitalism undergoes systemic transformation only when it is forced to and when its current regime is no longer tena-ble."[10] What Hardt and Negri mean is that capitalism, when left unchecked or when allowed too much power, will take any means necessary, no mat-ter how wrong or exploitive, to keep amassing more profits.

In *The Expanse*, the problems with the uncontrolled capitalist sovereign and the influence of capitalism on other sovereign entities are stark. Adding in the aspect of biopolitics, a people considered inferior like the Belters, makes these problems even more stark. First, the reduction of Belters to bare life paves the way for the exploitation of the people. Ceres OPA leader Anderson Dawes tells Miller,

> The inner planets look on us as their labor force. They tax us. They direct what we do. They enforce their laws and ignore ours in the name of stabil-ity. In the last year, they've doubled the tariffs to Titania. . . They've blocked any Belter freighters from taking Europa contracts. They charge us twice as much to dock at Ganymede. The science station on Phoebe? We aren't even allowed to orbit it. There isn't a Belter in the place. Whatever they do there, we won't find out until they sell the technology back to us, ten years from now.[11]

From the corporate sovereigns like Anderson-Hyosung and RCE to the political and neocolonial sovereigns of Earth and Mars, time and again profits and property prove more valuable than Belter life. At best, Belters provide cheap labor. As "bare life," Belters work harder, earn less, live in poverty, and have no voice or rights. When Belters resist their role as cheap labor by attempting to attain certain rights and benefits that should be common for all people, then they are no longer useful. When they go further in resisting injustice by refusing to work, sabotaging equipment, or taking over a station, they threaten profits and property. No longer producing, and too costly for the sovereign, they become expendable.

"Where Eagles Dare"

If Anderson Station shows the precedent—that the sovereign can kill a few thousand Belters who interfere with capitalist enterprises—then Eros Station stands as the culminating proof that Belter life is forfeit to capitalist pursuits. In "Static," lead Protogen scientist Antony Dresden claims, "A million and a half people is small potatoes," speaking of the Belters killed on Eros.[12] Echoing Dresden, Jules-Pierre Mao, head of Mao-Kwikowski Mercantile and the money behind Protogen's experiment on Eros, believes the lives of a few million Belters mean little when "the control of this technology will represent the base of all political and economic power from now on."[13] Or as Dresden says in "Doors & Corners," "If we master it [the protomolecule]. . . we become our own gods." *The Expanse* shows how capitalism warps those at the top. For people like Mao and Dresden, money equates to power and control; it makes them believe they are superior, are "gods."

Suddenly, a bullet pierces Dresden's forehead, blood and brains spattering the wall behind him. Miller lowers his gun, walks up to the body, and fires two more shots at the man responsible for overseeing the release of the protomolecule on Eros. Later, Miller tells Johnson, "I know that you know that Dresden was gonna get away with it." In *Leviathan Wakes*, Miller also tells a furious Holden, "He was untouchable, and he knew it. Too much money. Too much power."[14]

Warning about capitalist sovereignty, the philosopher Rosa Luxemburg (1871–1919) writes about the inevitable corruption "where the sovereign will of the individual capitalist is the highest law."[15] Luxemburg mirrors Miller's words—too much money and too much power lead to a capitalist sovereign that, when unchecked, becomes untouchable and corrupts or destroys everything that interferes with the one goal: the joint expansion of profits and power. The capitalist sovereign's quest for profits and power also means the strengthening of class stratification. Those with money and power—like Mao and Dresden—make the rules, rules that benefit themselves, and they couldn't care less about all those "below" them who suffer.

For unchecked corporate sovereigns, profit and power take precedence over people. The profit and power need not be threatened as they seemingly were with Anderson Station and Ilus/New Terra. With Protogen and the protomolecule experiment, Mao looks toward possibilities—toward a variable that *could* increase both wealth and power. Millions of lives hold less value than a *potential* profit. Mao is the capitalist sovereign at its worst—unchecked, uncontrolled, and monstrous. He has no compassion and no humanity; everything he desires comes at the expense of others, and he's fine with that fact.

"3's and 7's"

The Expanse shows not only how the capitalist sovereign's drive for profits and power stratifies class and oppresses, but also how that stratification and oppression creates instability and fear, leading to the rise of "superheroes" who promise their people the world.

First, Murtry, furious about the losses suffered during the Belter-rigged landing pad explosion, declares martial law on Ilus/New Terra. He tells the Belters, "I have given my people 'shoot first' authorization. They may, if they feel threatened, utilize lethal force to defuse the threat."[16] With Earth over a year and a half away, he knows no one can challenge his authority.

Second, Marco Inaros, leader of the Belter Free Navy, takes over the Ring System, a system of protomolecule-built gates leading to other solar systems. Inaros announces a victory for the Belt and pledges that the Free Navy will protect the Belters "against the historical and established crimes of economy and violence they have suffered at the gun barrels of Earth and Mars."[17] This victory both establishes the Belt's independence and sovereignty and prohibits inner migration. Inner migration had left the Belters, whose bodies can't handle the full g (gravity) of planetary life, with no prospects for survival.

Third, Winston Duarte, High Consul of the Laconian Empire and former admiral of the Martian Congressional Republic Navy, promises those who follow him a utopian world where he will "bring order to humanity's chaos. . . [B]ring the peace that would last forever. The end of all wars."[18] Duarte believes humanity is on the brink of collapse. So, he recruits likeminded followers willing to abandon the continually warring and deeply flawed inhabitants of the Sol System and start over in another world.

Murtry, Inaros, and Duarte represent the rise of a new sovereign power that plays on the fears and instability that capitalism creates. Each man offers a "glorious" plan for aiding and securing the fearful population. Or, in other words, each man serves up an ideology that offers people hope. Murtry will protect all RCE people from Belter terrorism. Inaros will free and aid all Belters whose lives are forfeit if Earthers and Martians abandon the Sol System, Belters whose lives, as Inaros says, "don't mean shit to inners."[19] And with the grandest plans of all, Duarte will bring world peace. These ideologies alleviate fears, offer hope, and provide a sense of security missing before.

Through each of these men, *The Expanse* shows the power of ideology *and* how individuals can attain sovereign power through the use of ideology. Contemporary philosopher Terry Eagleton states that ruling ideologies must "engage significantly with the wants and desires that people already have. . . must furnish some solid motivations for effective action."[20] Considering the way Murtry, Inaros, and Duarte promise their people salvation while preying on their fears and desires, it's easy to see, as Eagleton says, how ideology "persuades men and women to mistake each other from time to time for gods or vermin."[21]

"Personal Jesus"

"Wei, I'm comin' for your boss. Don't be there when I do," Amos Burton, Holden's backup on New Terra and the *Rocinante*'s mechanic, warns the woman he's involved with, RCE security employee Chandra Wei, in "Saeculum." Murtry wants Wei to kill Amos; Amos wants to save Holden. Wei knows her options, but her devotion to Murtry wins out. Wei stands her ground. She dies, still believing in, as Amos puts it, "the story Murtry sold you."

A longtime member of Inaros' crew, Cyn forces a choice on Naomi Nagata, the *Rocinante*'s Executive Officer and his old friend. Cyn believes Inaros has brought the Belt "the promised land. Belt standing up. You know how it was before. You remember running thin because we couldn't get enough oxygen. Breaking bones because the meds got taxed too much."[22] Cyn tells Naomi she should join the Free Navy because of all the good both Inaros and the Free Navy will do for Belters, starting with stealing from the Inners. When she tries to escape Inaros, Cyn tries to stop her—it's her life or his. "We travel so far, vide—uns the promised land. And we go all of us together. Tu y mé y alles."[23] Like Wei, Cyn dies, still clinging to the belief in the "promised land" Inaros will provide.

Santiago Singh continually sings Duarte's praises and is validated when Duarte's High Admiral, Anton Trejo, calls the Laconian captain a "true believer," giving Singh a position as governor in the soon-to-be-invaded Sol System.[24] He hopes "I can give my daughter the version of humanity that the high consul has planned. . . A galactic society of peace and prosperity and cooperation is the best legacy I can imagine for her."[25] But when Singh fails to control the Belt-run Medina Station, he ends up pleading for his life to one of his own men. "But I was loyal. . . I've *obeyed*."[26] He dies after listening to Overstreet, the officer in charge of his execution, say, "I believe what I'm told to believe."[27]

Wei, Cyn, and Singh all show the blind and absolute devotion that ideology can inspire. Both Wei and Cyn stay the course, even when they know their lives are on the line. Amos even warns Wei that if she doesn't get out of the way, "I'm going through you." Singh, though, realizes too late that he bought a complete load when he hears Overstreet spouting back Singh's own words. *The Expanse* shows how ideology—especially for authoritarian and totalitarian power seekers like Murtry, Inaros, and Duarte—inspires. German American philosopher Hannah Arendt (1906–1975) provides insight; authoritarian power requires "total, unrestricted, unconditional, and unalterable loyalty of the individual member."[28] For all three followers, the till death part comes quickly.

These characters illustrate not just the blind adoration and devotion given to power, but also how power is gained. Each gives their respective leader power—power to make the right choices, power to protect them and create the laws that do so, power over them. Foucault says power isn't "something that's acquired, seized, or shared. . . Power comes from below."[29] *The Expanse* shows, then, how individuals gain not just power, but sovereign power. Murtry, Inaros, and Duarte, thanks to the faith and devotion they garner, are given power over their people's lives—power to determine which lives are worthy and which bare, which lives can be sacrificed for the greater good without committing murder.

"I Want to Conquer the World"

"We're all just walking in the footsteps of history. The ancient frontier—all those post offices and railroads and jails cost thousands of lives to build. And this is no different. I am the kind of man the frontier needs," Murtry spits out in "Saeculum," pausing his threatening advance toward Holden. Murtry is the great frontiersman, forging a new world out of the lives of those who follow him. In *Cibola Burn*, he tells Holden, "I came to conquer a new world. This is how you do that. . . I have no illusion about what it will take to carve out a place in this new frontier. It will take sacrifices, and it will take blood, and things we wouldn't do back where everything's regulated and controlled."[30]

Inaros revels: "Fire and metal and blood. It was like joy. Like music. . . This was battle. This was glory and victory and power." He ignores all of his own ships and people lost in the battle.[31] His victory is all that matters. Again, what he can win is all that matters when he strips Ceres Station of all resources, supplies, and ships and abandons the six million Belter inhabitants as Earth's forces close in. But, "maybe a million and a half would escape before the enemy arrived. The ones that remained would be in a shell of stone and titanium hardly more capable of sustaining life than the original asteroid had been."[32]

"The best governments in history have been kings and emperors. . . A philosopher-king can manage great things in his lifetime. And his grandchildren can squander it. . . If you want to create a lasting, stable, social order. . . only one person can ever be immortal," Duarte says as he's injected with the protomolecule.[33] Duarte believes the protomolecule will grant him the immortality he "needs" to secure his realm's stability. Or, in other words, to secure his absolute power. Duarte's "vision" is law, and as Trejo tells the people of the Sol System after the Laconian invasion, "to those who intend to defy this new government and try to deny humanity its bright future, I say this: You will be eradicated without hesitation or mercy."[34]

The Expanse shows how easily sovereignty can shift, in this case moving from the corrupt capitalist sovereign to the corrupt authoritarian and totalitarian sovereigns. Furthermore, we see how each form of sovereign power preys on the people for power and profit. In other words, the series shows the ways that, when given too much faith, when not reined in, and when given too much power, the natural tendency for sovereign entities is toward corruption and self-gain at the expense of the people. The sovereign can shift, as well, from the decentralized and multiple sovereign powers split among the political, capitalist, and military from earlier in the series to the rise of a single, centralized, sovereign power—the monstrous individual sovereigns later in the series. This shift demonstrates something frequently ignored in our decentralized and globalized world; the fact that a single, centralized sovereign power could rise again—even in a democracy.

Men like Murtry, Inaros, and Duarte, then, show us several things about sovereign power. First, they show how easily political sovereignty can be abused and corrupted. Second, they show how easily men can be corrupted. Each man starts with promising his people the world; each ends up a power-hungry monster who cares for nothing but his own gains. What happened in between? Why the sovereign's shift from savior to oppressor? The problem, which *The Expanse* and many philosophers point out, is that the threat of corruption, and with it the potential for oppression, is attached to all liberal governments or democracies. Foucault cautions that

[l]iberalism must produce freedom, but this very act entails the establishment of limitations, controls, forms of coercion, and obligations relying on threats, etcetera. . . That is to say liberalism, the liberal art of government, is forced to determine the precise extent to which and up to what point individual interests. . . constitute a danger for the interest of all.[35]

In other words, the danger is threefold: (a) to secure freedom, freedom must be limited; (b) the more security is needed, the more freedom is taken away; and (c) at some point corruption will seep in, and the abuse of power begins. Consequently, what begins as a liberal government aimed at helping the people can turn into an authoritarian or totalitarian regime where nothing matters but the sovereign's own agenda. Furthermore, instability and fear frequently precipitate the rise of the dictatorial sovereign with the population readily giving power to the one who promises security. This factor is seen not only with *The Expanse*'s Murtry, Inaros, and Duarte, but also in the rise of real-world dictators like Hitler, Mussolini, and Stalin. Promises of protection and security, however, quickly turn to oppression and genocide in the sovereign's quest for power.

The examples of all three men also show the way that sovereign power gives them absolute power over all life—the ability to reduce all life to bare life. They can even turn the lives of the very people they are supposed to protect into bare life. Amos flat out tells Murtry he's a "killer. . . You've got a nifty excuse and the shiny badge to make you seem right, but that's not what this is about. You got off on smoking that guy in front of everyone. You can't wait to do it again."[36] Speaking of Inaros' "grandiosity," Rosenfeld Guoliang, a member of Inaros' inner circle, says, "He's slaughtered billions of people and remade the shape of human civilization. No one can do something on that scale and see themselves as fully human anymore. He may be a god or he may be a devil, but he can't stomach the idea of being just an unreasonably pretty man who stumbled into the right combination of charisma and opportunity."[37] Finally, Holden forefronts Duarte's monstrosity:

> Duarte was a thoughtful, educated, civilized man and a murderer. He was charming and funny and a little melancholy and, as far as Holden could tell, completely unaware of his own monstrous ambition. Like a religious fanatic, the man really believed that everything he'd done was justified by his goal in doing it. Even when it was the push for his own personal immortality. . . Duarte managed to cast it as a necessary burden for the good of the species.[38]

Adored, raised up, and empowered by the people after feeding them promises for a better world and for better lives, once they are invested with sovereign power, nothing matters but each man's own agenda. All life becomes bare under Murtry's, Inaros', and Duarte's "rule"—sacrificed to build a glorious civilization, executed for disobedience, and left to die when their leader decides his life is more important.

The Expanse warns its audience about the dangers of capitalism's sovereign power. It explores the way capitalism is a naturally corrupt sovereign when left unchecked. It also looks at the way capitalism can corrupt other sovereign powers—from the political to the military. The sovereign is supposed to look out for its people, protecting and securing them, but what we see in *The Expanse* is the way, when given free rein, sovereign powers instead look after their own interests, exploiting those outside their realms for gains. This tendency toward self-interest above all else is particularly evident in the way Belters are oppressed and exploited for labor. Yet, the sovereigns all have ready justifications for that oppression—the Belters are alien, inhuman, Other, lesser, inferior. No matter the justification, the end result is that Belters are reduced to bare lives, viewed as expendable, and even exterminated when they interfere with profits, or as in this case with Mao-Kwikowski, when their deaths can help grow profits.

On the other hand, the measures taken to correct the capitalist injustices end up tilting sovereignty from one extreme to another. Individuals rise to power on promises of salvation and security, much like what occurred with the rise of Stalin and Hitler, of centralized regimes like Nazism and communism, in the early twentieth century. These individuals will fix the instability, insecurity, exploitation, and oppression; they provide ideologies of change and inspire their followers' devotion, gaining both trust and power from these followers who expect the changes promised. But, as *The Expanse* shows, corruption once again enters sovereignty. Promises of freedom and security for the people quickly shift into the leader's individual quest for power. Rather than a glorious utopia, authoritarian and totalitarian realms unfold where violence is the new law, no one is safe from exploitation, and all life becomes bare life.

Notes

1. James S. A. Corey, *Leviathan Wakes* (New York: Orbit, 2011), 96.
2. Michel Foucault, *The Birth of Biopolitics: Lectures at the Collège de France, 1978–79*, trans. Graham Burchill, ed. Michel Senellart (New York: Palgrave Macmillan, 2008).
3. Michael Hardt and Antonio Negri, *Empire* (Cambridge, MA: Harvard University Press, 2000).
4. Ibid., xii.
5. Giorgio Agamben, *Homo Sacer: Sovereign Power and Bare Life*, trans. Daniel Heller (Stanford: Stanford University Press, 1995), 53.
6. *Leviathan Wakes*, 21–22.
7. Ibid., 298.
8. Ibid., 370.
9. Karl Marx, *Capital: A Critique of Political Economy, Vol. 2: The Process of Circulation of Capital*, trans. Ernest Untermann, ed. Frederick Engels (Chicago: Charles H. Kerr & Co., 1910).
10. Hardt and Negri, *Empire*, 268.
11. *Leviathan Wakes*, 108.
12. Ibid., 417.
13. Ibid., 345.
14. Ibid., 437.
15. Rosa Luxemburg, *The Accumulation of Capital*, trans. Agnes Schwarzchild (London: Routledge Classics, 2003), 17.
16. James S. A. Corey, *Cibola Burn* (New York: Orbit, 2014), 114, 121.
17. James S. A. Corey, *Nemesis Games* (New York: Orbit, 2015), 390.
18. James S. A. Corey, *Persepolis Rising* (New York: Orbit, 2017), 398.
19. *Nemesis Games*, 224.
20. Terry Eagleton, *Ideology: An Introduction* (London: Verso, 1991), 14, 15.
21. Ibid., xiii.
22. *Nemesis Games*, 264.
23. Ibid., 424.
24. *Persepolis Rising*, 92.
25. Ibid.
26. Ibid., 519.
27. Ibid., 520.

28. Hannah Arendt, *Totalitarianism: Part Three of the Origins of Totalitarianism* (San Diego: Harcourt Brace Jovanovich, 1968), 21.
29. Michel Foucault, A *History of Sexuality, Vol. 1: An Introduction*, trans. Robert Hurley (New York: Pantheon Books, 1978), 94.
30. *Cibola Burn*, 536.
31. James S. A. Corey, *Babylon's Ashes* (New York: Orbit, 2016), 417–418.
32. Ibid., 147.
33. *Persepolis Rising*, 11.
34. Ibid., 137.
35. Foucault, *The Birth of Biopolitics*, 64, 65.
36. *Cibola Burn*, 115.
37. *Babylon's Ashes*, 82–83.
38. James S. A. Corey, *Tiamat's Wrath* (New York: Orbit, 2019), 252–253.

13

"Can't We Try Something Else?" Is James Holden a Hero?

Jeffery L. Nicholas

The Ring Gates are open, doors leading to 1,300 possible worlds. Belters, Martians, and Earthers are primed for travel. And already, people are disputing land. So, Chrisjen Avasarala, UN Secretary General, calls on James Holden to go to Ilus/New Terra as her envoy.

We have to wonder why, because her instructions to him are quite . . . Avasarala-worthy: "Don't put your dick in it. It's fucked enough already" ("New Terra").

In *Cibola Burn*, she's even clearer about her feelings regarding Holden. "Everybody hates him equally, so we can argue he's impartial . . . He's a fucking awful choice for a diplomatic mission, so it makes him perfect."[1]

And why is Holden perfect? We learn later, in the book not the TV series, that it's because Avasarala "trusted Holden. Not to do anything I told him to. I'm not an idiot. But I thought he would be himself."

Bobbie Draper asked, "Himself, how?"

"[Fred] Johnson and I sent Holden to mediate because he was the perfect person to show what a clusterfuck it was out there. How ugly it would be. I was expecting press releases every time someone sneezed. The man starts wars all the fucking time, only this time, when I needed a little conflict? Now he's the fucking peacemaker."[2]

Johnson and Avasarala see Holden as a nuisance, a pawn they can manipulate. Perhaps naming the ship the *Rocinante* convinces them that he's too much of a romantic idealist to be anything but a pawn or a nuisance.

It does seem odd that Holden doesn't send press releases. When Adolphus (name implications anyone?) Murtry shoots the Belter leader Coop in cold blood, wouldn't you expect Holden to broadcast the travesty to the world—Mars dominating the Belt, shooting for no reason? I mean, he kicks Joe Miller off the *Rocinante* for the same reason. Are we to expect

The Expanse and Philosophy: So Far Out Into the Darkness, First Edition. Edited by Jeffery L. Nicholas.
© 2022 John Wiley & Sons, Inc. Published 2022 by John Wiley & Sons, Inc.

that Holden has learned something in the meantime . . . all that time to think as he travels between asteroids, planets, and the Ring Gate? All that Investigator-Miller in his head chattering.

In the TV series, Miller is the stop-cap which keeps Holden occupied so he doesn't have time to send constant broadcasts out to the world. In the books, it might be Johnson, who doesn't care what Avasarala's plans are as much as he does his own concerns.

"You get them talking, and you keep them talking. And you do what you always do, you maintain absolute transparency. This is one time secrets won't help anyone. Should be right up your alley."[3]

Yet, Johnson's words aren't enough either. Discussing whether to take the job or not with the rest of the crew, Holden is noncommittal. He likes a lot of the possibilities, including the possibility of being a hero . . . the ones that help establish interstellar law out beyond the Ring Gates. Yet, he's wise enough now to know that way lies a trap. What he wants isn't so much to be the hero as to help. Naomi tells him that they will go because, if they don't, he'll be mad at himself for not helping.

It's actually Miller who convinces Holden not to play into Avasarala's and Johnson's hands. Miller says to him, "Your pals Avasarala and Johnson have handed you the bloody knife and you think it's because they trust you." Holden replies that he hates Miller, "mostly because I hate every-thing you say, but you're not always wrong."[4]

When we think about Holden helping others, why he's always in the midst of things, it's helpful to think about what distinguishes Holden from other characters in the series and what makes him unique—that he grew up on a farm.

Filling Our Ears with Wax and Our Brains with Electromagnetic Waves

Dr. Antony Dresden was the mind behind the Eros incident that killed a hundred thousand Belters and the man who claimed it was hardly a round-ing error given what the protomolecule experiments promised. When he's giving his speech to convince Johnson and Holden to cut a deal with him, to let him go, he justifies his murder of innocent Belters by proclaiming the advantages the protomolecule will give them. Naomi wonders how Dresden convinced his science team to enact these deaths, to watch them.

"We modified our science team to remove ethical restraints."

Dresden admits that they created high-functioning sociopaths out of the entire science team, which presumably includes himself. Transcranial mag-netic stimulation involves the use of drugs and electromagnetic forces to alter the brain, resulting in a loss of empathy. He could feel no empathy for the people he experimented on. No member of the science team could.

Transcranial magnetic stimulation doesn't involve any cutting as far as we can tell, but it follows a long line of surgical procedures by which men have sought to control nature. The "dream of millennia," according to Max Horkheimer and Theodor Adorno, founders of critical theory, is a boundless domination of nature which "turn[s] the cosmos into an endless hunting ground." In fact, "it shaped the idea of man in a male society."[5] Horkheimer and Adorno reinterpret the story of Odysseus in a way which might give us insight into Dresden and Mao.

Odysseus, as you may recall, was a hero of the Trojan War who encountered many obstacles, including the Sirens, on his voyage home. The Sirens, who lived on an island in the Mediterranean, sang beautiful songs and were themselves beautiful to behold. Sailors would jump ship to find their way to the Sirens, only to be captured and enslaved by them. Odysseus knows the legends, but he wants to hear the siren song. So, he has his men tie him to the mast of his ship so that he cannot escape. Then he has them fill their ears with wax so that they cannot be lured away by the siren song. Thus, by dominating his own nature and manipulating the nature of his men, Odysseus is able to hear the siren call without being subject to it, without becoming a slave. In doing so, however, he has separated his actions from his desires. He has become a slave of a different kind, one unable to even acknowledge his own desires.

Like Odysseus' sailors, Dresden has manipulated his nature, severing the ties between himself and the rest of humanity. He does it for knowledge, power, both, or maybe just for money. It doesn't matter. What matters is that the guy responsible for Eros, Antony Dresden, is a monster of his own making, one descended from a long line of monsters.

No Nature, No Nurture

Dr. Strickland likewise lacks empathy for his patients, and this brings him into conflict with Jules-Pierre Mao, who, on seeing the children on Io, wants to stop the protomolecule experiments. "We're torturing children," Mao says ("IFF"). Yet, Strickland is able to convince him to carry on with the project. When the men view Katoa, they realize he is able to communicate with the protomolecule as it develops on Venus. This provides an opportunity to control. Mao approves a restart of the experiment.

Mao is an interesting character here. He's already sacrificed his favorite daughter to the protomolecule. Akin to Dresden and Strickland, Mao wants to dominate nature, though he wishes to be like Odysseus, severing himself from his desires while yet hearing the siren song, rather than like the sailors who must plug their ears with hot wax. Mao hears Julie's cries. As Dresden shows him video of Julie's protomolecule encrusted body, Mao turns from the camera and wipes a single tear from his eye. Then he tells

Dresden that "we got lucky" and instructs him to continue with the project. Only a man tied to the mast of his ship could call the death of his daughter, a sacrifice to his scientific project, lucky.

Does he mourn his daughter's death? Yes. When Undersecretary Errinwright bemoans possible sacrifice on his part in their joint protomolecule project, Mao tells him, "don't talk to me about sacrifice." Mao sounds like Dresden, "Sadavir, you're witnessing a discovery that could rewrite the story of humankind." He then sets down some flowers at "Julie's spot," a tree in the vast yard. After praising Julie, he says, "even losing her was worth it. She's a sacred part of it now" ("Safe"). It's not clear what Mao could mean by "sacred." His mansion and its environs are pictured against the background of a massive and, the audience knows, over-crowded city. Where billions are jammed together, Mao's family enjoys enough room for perhaps a hundred people to live, more open air and space than a Belter could ever imagine. Yet, the loss of Julie was "worth it."

What was worth it?

Francis Bacon, the father of modern science, was like Odysseus before him. He believed that men must control nature, enslave it, dissect it. His utopian novel, *New Atlantis*, had to be a model for Dresden. In it, scientists, who are the lords over society, take nature and make it more fecund by cutting plants and animals apart and splicing them back together as different creatures. Bacon would be on the front lines with Dr. Strickland splicing the protomolecule into Belter children, to make it do what he wanted. The feminist Marxist Maria Mies tells us that Bacon wanted to unify knowledge with material power. "Many of the technological inventions were in fact related to warfare and conquest . . . Violence, therefore, was the key word and the key method by which the New Man established his domination over women and nature."[6]

Mao's ultimate goal was profit through warfare. The *Canterbury* was sacrificed to start a fake war between Earth and Mars as a cover for Dresden's experiment. Yet, Dresden's justification references Genghis Khan, warfare as a way forward for humanity. The violence of Eros is the key method. Similarly, Strickland seeks to make a weapon from his experiments, and it is weaponry that Mao wants to sell to Earth and Mars, or whoever the highest bidder is.

Mao has been dishonest with us. Julie's death wasn't worth it; it was necessary for the process to even begin.

Of Mother Born

Horkheimer and Adorno, on the one hand, and feminists like Mies, on the other, link the domination of nature to the domination of women and race. "Man must act and strive," Horkheimer and Adorno write. Woman embodies biological functions and, as such, signifies nature. If domination of nature is the dream of men in a male society, that dream sees women as weaker and smaller. Woman's weakness "invites violence" because the difference between her and man was one she could not overcome.[7]

Bacon interpreted nature as a woman, adopting language from the witch trials to describe the scientific method. He writes, "But likewise for the further disclosing of the secrets of nature. Neither ought a man to make scruple of entering and penetrating into these holes and corners, when the inquisition of truth is his whole objective."[8] Is it any wonder that, in his big argument with Julie, Mao says, "I'm not going to allow any daughter of mine to go whoring around the Belt" ("Intransigence"). For Mao, Julie might as well be a witch. She has aligned herself with the Belters against his violent method, against the domination of nature which will lead to conquest. As such, she can only be a whore because she has betrayed him.

The control that Mao, Dresden, and Strickland seek has its roots in the earliest stages of human civilization. Mies reports that men, on their own, do not generate significant means of subsistence. Hunting is less productive of calories and proteins than gathering and even simple forms of agriculture. Women were the true producers of early human societies. Men had to learn to be productive through controlling nature, by castrating it. Early pastoralists discovered that, by castrating the bulls in a herd, they could select out the weaker animals and select for the stronger ones. This gave them coercive control over sexual reproduction in animals, which served as a prelude to controlling the reproduction of women. What they cannot control must be a whore or a witch.

Thus, we come to the great hero, Marco Inaros. Like the early pastoralists, after Marco learns to castrate the bulls of his herd, he learns to control the reproductive powers of women. When Naomi won't follow his lead, won't treat him like the great man he is, Marco takes her child from her, not once but twice. The first time, he takes the child from her physically, enlisting Naomi's friend, Cyn, to make sure that Naomi does not know where Filip is. Naomi almost walks out an airlock then. And when Marco tries to kill her friends, her new family, she does walk out an airlock, Cyn dying behind her as he tries to stop her. Then, Marco tells Filip, "She left us. She left us both. Again" ("Winnipesaukee").

Naomi's actions can only be seen as a betrayal for Marco. Inaros is more of a narcissist than a sociopath, but still unable to recognize anyone else's pain. "He's a great man. Great men, they're not like you or me," Rosenfeld tells Filip.[9] Jules-Pierre Mao was a great man too, so says Dr. Strickland. Yet, Marco is able to take that act and turn it into a knife, cutting once more the umbilical cord between mother and child. Naomi didn't leave to save her friends. She didn't leave because Marco is a monster. She "left us"—Marco and Filip, her son.

Marco has castrated the love between Filip and his mother by forcibly separating the mother from the child, once physically, once with lies. His goal is conquest through any means, including the deaths of millions—or billions. In her absence, Marco described her as too weak for what needed doing. Naomi signifies nature—the creative, generative element of nature. Not only does she bear a son for Marco, but she bears a code, one that Marco uses for his own means to kill thousands without her knowledge. Filip's pain is a lever by which Marco can control Filip. In *Babylon's Ashes*, Book 6 of the series, Marco again and again manipulates Filip's emotions, blaming Filip for his own mistakes and taking credit for Filip's successes. The end of Season 5 foreshadows this manipulation as his crew chants Marco's name and Filip lives vicariously, for the moment, in Marco's glory.

Tilting at Windmills

Mother Elise explains James Holden to Avasarala. Each of his eight parents is a genetic part of Holden. They raised him with the expectation that he would grow up and farm the land they held in common. They gave him an impossible dream. So, before his eighteenth birthday, while they were out fixing gates, she told him to run and get as far away as he could. We know that, just because he ran, doesn't mean he gave up the belief that he had to protect the land, the farm. Why did he end up on an ice hauler after the Navy? It was a different form of farming, bringing something necessary to life back to people who needed it to live.

I would suggest that the reason Avasarala thinks she can control Holden is the exact reason she can't. She thinks she understands his hero complex and that she can manipulate him by putting him in impossible situations where she can nudge him to get the results she wants. But Holden comes from a different world where conquest isn't the goal. The goal, rather, is life.

On Maria Mies' reading, early women gatherers and farmers saw themselves as "necessarily responsible" for caring for the needs of the children and the clan. This necessity arose from their bodies as nurturers and defined their relations to the earth. It was something they cooperated with in order to "let grow and to make grow."[10] I imagine here that the Holden farmstead is different from the centuries of farming under modern science and capitalism. Modern science and capitalism seek to control, to dominate nature, to twist it to human will. The Holden family must be different, a utopian venture in a dystopian world. It is, for that reason, a world Avasarala cannot understand. Avasarala belongs in a world where a card game can involve running to a tree or using a close family friend as a means to discover Martian secrets. Holden's cannot, which is why Naomi's secretly giving the protomolecule to Johnson is so problematic for Holden.

Holden doesn't broadcast every little thing about Ilus because he wants the Belters there to have a say in what happens. He wants to let grow, preferably a peace between Belters and Earthers, similar to the peace that Belter, Martian, and Earthers enjoy on the *Rocinante*. It is also the reason that he doesn't want to accept the leadership position at the end of *Babylon's Ashes*. Holden is the exact opposite of Dresden, Strickland, Mao, and Marco. And that's what Naomi loves about him.

I honestly don't know what James S. A. Corey intended for us to think about Holden. *The Expanse* is dark science fiction whose references are to a war of all against all (Thomas Hobbes' *Leviathan*), to the massacre of American Indians, and to a dark intelligence that maybe intended the ultimate domination of nature. And one of their protagonists is a guy who thinks he's a knight tilting at windmills. He's clearly not always right. He should not have kicked Miller off the *Rocinante* for shooting Dresden. But we see growth there as well. Only Miller and Naomi see Dresden as the racist he is, see the domination of nature in the scientific experiment of Eros, see it as racism. Race is "a regression. To nature as mere violence, to the hidebound particularism . . . is the self-assertion of the bourgeois individual, integrated into the barbaric collective."[11] Mao, Dresden, Strickland are all bourgeois individuals seeking conquest. Dresden admits as much when he compares himself to Khan, one of the original barbarians.

Later, though, Holden warns one of his crew not to use the slur "skinny" and grows angry with one of his fathers for using the racial slur. Even if it takes time for Holden to open his eyes to the sexism and racism of the bourgeois individual, he never plugged his ears or tied himself to the mast—saved just barely by the explosion of the *Canterbury*. Even then, though, he wants for the Belters what he wants for himself, what he learned farming—for everyone to grow, to speak for themselves.

To make their desires known.

Perhaps the question for us is whether Holden is really a relic of a foregone world we can no longer inhabit, or a prophecy of a possible world to come. Or maybe just a hope for what we can be if we just listen to one another without trying to dominate.

Notes

1. James S. A. Corey, *Cibola Burn* (London: Orbit, 2014), 45.
2. Ibid., 578.
3. Ibid., 47.
4. Ibid., 146.
5. Max Horkheimer and Theodor Adorno, *Dialectic of Enlightenment* (Palo Alto, CA: Stanford University Press, 2007), 206.
6. Carolyn Merchant, *The Death of Nature* (San Francisco: HarperOne, 1990), 88.
7. Horkheimer and Adorno, *Dialectic of Enlightenment*, 206.
8. Merchant, *The Death of Nature*, 168.

9. James S. A. Corey, *Babylon's Ashes* (London: Orbit, 2017), 178.
10. Maria Mies, *Patriarchy and Accumulation on a World Scale* (London: Zed Books, 2014), 55.
11. Horkheimer and Adorno, *Dialectic of Enlightenment*, 138.

Fourth Orbit
THEY STILL DREAM

14

"We had a garden and we paved it"

The Expanse and the Philosophy of the Anthropocene

Diletta De Cristofaro

Captain Martens, of the MCRN *Scirocco*, had warned Gunnery Sergeant Bobbie Draper about a "dirty" ocean, whose "stench [is] like the recycling vat" ("The Weeping Somnambulist"). Arriving on Earth, however, Bobbie is curious. She wants to see the natural features of the planet that she hopes terraforming will one day bring to Mars. As she walks through a drainage tunnel, a contemplative soundtrack interspersed with the sound of waves accompanies her ("Cascade"). For nearly two minutes, the camera alternates between shots of Bobbie's dark silhouette against the overexposed body of water at sunset and closeups of her lit-up face, full of a longing that seems at once hopeful and mournful as she scans the unfamiliar landscape. During these two minutes, the viewer never sees the water clearly. Only when the camera zooms out do we realize that Bobbie hasn't been contemplating the beauty of natural wonders. Instead, she's been pondering the awful ocean Captain Martens had warned her about.

Sadly, *The Expanse*'s ocean is the lifeless and polluted ocean forecast by the United Nations' Intergovernmental Panel on Climate Change (IPCC).[1] This ocean's rising levels clearly threaten New York, as the drainage tunnel Bobbie comes through is part of a system of defensive walls that protect the city from the water. The scene reminds us of the words of Franklin DeGraaf, Earth's ambassador to Mars: "We [Earthers] had a garden and we paved it" ("Remember the Cant").

The Anthropocene

The disastrous impact of human activities on the Earth characterizes our age. In 2000, Paul Crutzen, atmospheric chemist and Nobel laureate, popularized the term "Anthropocene" to name this age. Literally meaning

The Expanse and Philosophy: So Far Out Into the Darkness, First Edition. Edited by Jeffery L. Nicholas.
© 2022 John Wiley & Sons, Inc. Published 2022 by John Wiley & Sons, Inc.

the "recent age of the human" (from the Greek *anthropos*, "human," and *-cene*, "new" or "recent"), the Anthropocene marks the shift from the Holocene to a proposed new geological epoch in which humankind is understood as a geological force in its own right.[2] As of 2021, the Anthropocene still hasn't been formally recognized as the current geological epoch. Yet the term has become a buzzword, indicating a widespread realization of the human potential to alter our planet and shape its future.

The Anthropocene is marked by anthropogenic climate change—climate change caused by human activity—and what this might entail for all life forms, including the human species. As a dire 2018 report by the IPCC outlines, it's vital to limit the global temperature increase at 1.5°C above pre-industrial levels. This limit would require drastic changes and might constitute an impossible feat, as we're on track for at least 3–4°C of warming by the end of the century.[3] Without that limit, the "recent age of the human" might turn out to be short; in fact, it might spell the end, not only of many species, but also the human one.

In *The Expanse*, humankind has survived climate change thanks to technological solutions aimed at stabilizing the climate and managing the risks of global warming. These solutions include the colonization of the Sol System. These days, an environmentalist slogan tells us that the Earth must be preserved at all costs as "there is no Planet B." But in *The Expanse* humankind found its Planet B, Mars, as well as some asteroids and satellites. Though climate change is no longer an existential threat to humanity in the twenty-third century, legacies of the Anthropocene, material and ideological, continue to inform *The Expanse*'s world.

On the one hand, Bobbie's encounter with the ocean exemplifies the show's strong sense of loss over a natural world that humanity has taken for granted and irreparably compromised on Earth—paved, as DeGraaf puts it—before trying to recreate it, for the most part unsuccessfully, on Mars and the Belt. Images of gardens, at once objects of mourning and of desire and hope, recur in *The Expanse*, symbolizing the Anthropocene as an epoch where human activities destroy and remake entire ecosystems.

On the other hand, the Anthropocene is not just a scientific problem but an ethical one, as our values and how we interact with the rest of nature and other human beings produce these stresses. *The Expanse* depicts humanity as having failed to learn the Anthropocene's lessons, and hence repeating the mistakes made on Earth across the Sol System and beyond. So, what does the show tell us about the worldviews, ethics, and values underlying the current ecological crisis and its potential futures?

The Cascade

Let's jump on the *Rocinante* for an Epstein drive-powered tour of *The Expanse*'s advanced Anthropocene, where humankind is a force shaping not just the Earth, but the Sol System and beyond. Let's start with the episode in which Bobbie sees the ocean for the first time, because "Cascade" perfectly encapsulates the centrality of the Anthropocene to *The Expanse* and the show's core message about the present environmental crisis.

The episode's title alludes to the collapse of Ganymede. The station is the breadbasket of the Belt, a garden-like ecosystem artificially developed—"a ball of ice [turned] into a garden" ("Jetsam")—as part of humankind's technological solutions to the Anthropocene. Surveying the wreckage caused by the Ganymede incident, Dr. Prax Meng explains the concept that gives "Cascade" its name. The use of distilled water in Ganymede's hydroponic cultures, rather than the mineral solution needed for the long-term stability of this artificial ecosystem, is about to trigger a series of cascading catastrophic failures that are hard to predict and model, but that effectively entail that "the station's dead already. They just don't know it yet." The collapse of its ecosystem means famine and dispossession for a large number of people, not only on Ganymede, but throughout the Outer Planets. This event turns the Belters into climate refugees overnight.

Bobbie's encounter with a lifeless and polluted ocean and the prediction of Ganymede's cascade combine to drive home *The Expanse*'s warning about our Anthropocene. Thanks to human actions that don't take the long view, Earth's garden is dangerously close to being paved once and for all by an irreversible cascade of interlinked environmental catastrophes that have already begun to displace people. And it will only get worse.[4]

What's more, *The Expanse* suggests that relying on space colonization as a technological solution to the existential threats to humanity posed by the Anthropocene is also short-sighted. Space colonization doesn't address anthropocentrism, the problematic worldview that underlies the epoch. Anthropocentrism is the belief that humans are the most important entities in the universe and that our interests matter above anything else. The view also includes a stratified understanding of what we value as fully human and, therefore, worth protecting from environmental and other risks.

The Anthropocentrism of the Anthropocene

The concept of the Anthropocene is important for framing how our activities are endangering the survival of humans and numerous other species. Already, scientists talk of a sixth mass extinction underway.[5] Nevertheless, the concept of the Anthropocene has issues, and anthropocentrism is one of them.

As contemporary philosopher Brian G. Henning writes, it's clear that climate change and the related environmental crisis are the "result of an anthropocentric worldview and narrative that have for millennia sanctioned human dominion over a world denuded of all (intrinsic) value."[6]

This worldview functions by separating the human from, and elevating it above, the rest of nature. *The Expanse* depicts a future in which the anthropocentric worldview remains the pillar of human relationships with the rest of nature long after the damages of our activities have become apparent in paving Earth's garden.

When Avasarala joins Bobbie at the shore, she asks, "Is [the ocean] everything you thought it would be?" Bobbie evades the question—it's obvious the ocean isn't what she expected—and instead emphasizes that Earthers "take it for granted" ("Cascade"), echoing Captain Martens' words in the previous episode ("The Weeping Somnambulist"). The same accusation of a careless anthropocentric attitude toward the natural world—a misguided confidence in human superiority and separation from the rest of nature—can be found in an exchange between Holden and Lieutenant K. Lopez of the MCRN *Donnager*. Earthers, Lopez tells Holden, are "short-sighted and selfish," since they "care so little" for the bountiful nature the universe had once bestowed upon them ("CQB"). Some Earthers do care, like Holden's family, who brought him up to think that "the land needed him" in an example of a symbiotic, rather than anthropocentric, relationship with the rest of nature. But even these people face "a fight [they] could never win" ("Windmills"), given that anthropocentrism is the prevailing worldview. Despite Lopez and Bobbie's holier-than-thou attitude, Martians aren't exactly immune from anthropocentrism, as we'll see.

Henning points out that "rather than challenging the narrative of human dominance and control over every aspect of nature, the Anthropocene discourse effectively enshrines it in seemingly neutral, objective language."[7] Climate policy documents (including the IPCC's) reflect this judgment. As contemporary philosopher Katie McShane emphasizes, often such documents fall into the anthropocentric trap by suggesting that the need to protect the environment derives, first and foremost, from the need to protect human interests.[8] After all, in its very name, which foregrounds the human (*anthropos*), the Anthropocene reproduces the anthropocentric worldview that generated the prospect of climate breakdown in the first place.

In leaving anthropocentrism unchallenged, the concept of the Anthropocene treats environmental issues not as something that requires a paradigm shift in our worldviews, but as something "to be 'managed' through the application of ever more aggressive forms of technology, geoengineering the very climate if necessary."[9] This management approach thus paradoxically amounts to proposing anthropocentric solutions to issues caused by anthropocentrism itself. Because these management solutions are technological, Henning calls the Anthropocene a "Technozoic era," whose aim is to extend human dominion not only on Earth but out into space thanks to technological developments.[10] Illustrating Henning's point, *The Expanse*'s humankind manages anthropogenic problems on

Earth by colonizing the Sol System and, once the Ring System is opened, what lies beyond it.

The Issue with Wanting to "Turn a lifeless rock into a garden"

Henning warns us that a Technozoic response to the Anthropocene isn't viable in the long term. Instead, we risk bringing to other planets a flawed environmental ethics that "places virtually no moral limits to human exploitation of the Earth, our solar system, and beyond."[11] *The Expanse* is a case in point. After paving Earth's garden, humankind doesn't learn to recognize that, whether on Earth or in space, we're intertwined with the rest of nature and aren't its masters. Rather, *The Expanse*'s humanity simply exports its anthropocentric mentality to its Planet Bs and, with it, practices that are profoundly damaging to the environment.

Throughout the show, humans use technology to dominate the nonhuman. Take, for instance, the Martian geoengineering dream of turning "a lifeless rock into a garden" ("Remember the Cant"). This dream assumes that remaking an entire planetary system is morally justifiable. Because Mars is devoid of life, its empty expanses should be put to good use by serving the interests of life—specifically, human life. Or, consider UN Secretary General Nancy Gao's decision to fully open the Ring System "for exploration and colonization" ("Cibola Burn"). Gao makes this decision even though the first colonizing mission to Ilus ended up, thanks to Holden's interaction with alien technology, endangering the settlers' lives and profoundly altering the planet in the space of a single day. The devastating tsunami Holden inadvertently unleashes on Ilus acts as a powerful metaphor for the unintended consequences of human activities on Earth, especially given the role that rising sea levels will play in our Anthropocene future. Or take the unfettered exploitation of the Belt's resources, an exploitation that conveniently ignores that these resources are finite. As an OPA activist explains, "Ceres was once covered in ice. Enough water for 1,000 generations. Until Earth and Mars stripped it away for themselves." Water is now scarce and, for Belters, "more precious than gold" ("Dulcinea"). Even Protogen's research on the protomolecule rests on the principle of human dominion: "If we master it, we can apply it" ("Doors & Corners"). This plan, of course, backfires, making tangible the risks of exporting our anthropocentrism to other planets.

All in all, *The Expanse*'s future illustrates Henning's thesis that a Technozoic response to the Anthropocene's existential threats through space colonization would repeat anthropocentric environmental mistakes made on Earth. As humankind continues to work on making space colonization a reality—think SpaceX, for instance—*The Expanse* demonstrates that developing a different kind of environmental ethics is imperative.

This new environmental ethics should be profoundly non-anthropocentric. Contemporary philosopher Keekok Lee argues that in order to be "capable of defending other planets against human control and domination," this ethics should be based on "inanimate Nature as a locus of intrinsic value."[12] Condemning anthropocentric arrogant mastery, Lee identifies awe and humility, such as those that Bobbie exhibits when seeing the ocean for the first time, as the ideal foundations of our relationship with the rest of nature, on Earth and beyond. After all, the reality of the Anthropocene is that, through anthropogenic climate change, we might cause our own extinction but the Earth itself would find a new and different equilibrium. We need to recognize that nature—and not only Earth's garden but also the lifeless rocks found in space—has intrinsic value. Therefore, our goal shouldn't be to alter nature relentlessly to serve human interests. We'd do better to follow Miller's advice here: "stars are better off without us" ("Godspeed").

"We're all in this together." "That is a story"

Another issue with the concept of the Anthropocene is that it's based upon the notion of a homogeneous humanity—the *anthropos* giving the epoch its name—that is in this predicament together. Anderson Dawes' words to Holden remind us to question the "story" that "we're all in this together" ("The Seventh Man").

The truth is that stark inequalities characterize the climate crisis. Climate and environmental justice therefore seeks to remedy these injustices. On the one hand, we're living through the unintended consequences of centuries of human activities, in particular the burning of fossil fuels. What we do in this century to mitigate, or not, climate change will determine what kind of Earth future generations will inhabit or whether they have a habitable Earth at all. Thus, the principle of intergenerational justice holds that each generation should act to ensure that future generations don't have a standard of living worse than their own.[13]

The lack of fundamental change in national and international policies, however, suggests a much darker reality. Science fiction author Kim Stanley Robinson observes, "We don't care enough about those future people, our descendants, who will have to fix, or just survive on, the planet we're now wrecking . . . [W]e're creating problems that they'll be unable to solve. You can't fix extinctions, or ocean acidification, or melted permafrost."[14] This intergenerational injustice shapes *The Expanse*'s advanced Anthropocene. The image of Earth's paved garden captures how humanity will have to live with the environmental devastation we're now producing. As

"Cascade" shows, Robinson is right: you just can't fix something like ocean acidification.

Moreover, the Anthropocene involves an unjust distribution of responsibilities and vulnerabilities. Contemporary philosopher Henry Shue writes,

> the largest cumulative emissions have come from the nations which were the early industrializers and which thereby gained great wealth from the energy consumption that produced their damaging emissions, while the nations which will, under business as usual, suffer most from the climate change driven by those emissions will be the poorer countries that have not fully industrialized (and have emitted very little). This is primarily because these less industrialized nations control less wealth that can readily be used for coping with the effects of climate change as it occurs.[15]

Philosophers like Shue have produced models that seek to distribute the burdens of the climate crisis and its mitigation equitably. Yet the reality of the Anthropocene is that the populations that are the least responsible for the origins of climate change—the Global South—are already bearing the brunt of climate change and its extreme weather events. Even within the wealthier countries of the Global North, poor communities and people of color are the most exposed to environmental risks.[16]

The world of *The Expanse* reflects the distributive injustice in our world's environmental risks. Most scenes on Earth take place in the homes and offices of the UN elite. Yet, their lush gardens, airy houses, and high-tech glass aesthetics are a far cry from the glimpses we get of what lies just beyond the compounds of the rich. "Cascade" is again crucial, as it offers one of these glimpses.

On her way to the ocean, Bobbie walks through the slum outside the UN's gates. Ironically, soon after an ad calls citizens to "register today for a better tomorrow," we see poor people, many ill or intoxicated, who have no such prospects. Bobbie strikes up a conversation with Nico, and we're introduced to further aspects of the wretched life of Earth's poor: children exposed to radiation from a power plant and people forced to drink sewer water. Notwithstanding all its Technozoic advancements, *The Expanse*'s Earth has failed to address the fact that the poor and often non-white communities shoulder the majority of environmental burdens and toxicities.

In our world, the uneven distribution of the vulnerabilities of the climate crisis is the legacy of colonial racist hierarchies. Colonizers saw natives as part of the realm of nature—to be mastered and exploited alongside their lands. As contemporary philosopher Kyle P. Whyte emphasizes, the challenges of the supposedly new epoch of the Anthropocene are ones that colonized peoples have already faced.[17] For the populations of the Global South, Indigenous communities, and people of color, twenty-first-century climate and environmental injustices are often a continuation of the violence of the colonial era.

The Anthropocene's core worldview is an anthropocentric belief in the importance of protecting human interests above those of the rest of nature. But it's also true that the epoch is defined by the reality that not all human interests are seen as equally worthy of protection. We humans aren't in the Anthropocene together. Some of us are more affected by it than others. "That is a story" indeed, dear Dawes.

"Earthers, Martians—they see us as their possessions, animals"

The section title above is a quote from Dawes in "The Seventh Man." His words draw attention to the uneven power dynamic between Inners and Belters that we see playing out throughout *The Expanse*. In the Belters, indeed, we find the clearest articulation of the hierarchical understating of the human at the heart of the Anthropocene and of the links between this epoch and colonialism.

As Henning notes, those who are working on making space colonization a reality appear to be willfully ignoring how colonialism brought about immense devastation on our planet, including, as Whyte underlines, environmental devastation.[18] Characters in *The Expanse* use images from the colonial era to understand the protomolecule's existential threat. For instance, upon seeing what seems to be an impossible sight—the protomolecule-hybrid—Holden tells Alex: "When the European tall-ships first arrived on the American continent, the natives couldn't see them. The sight was so completely outside of their experience, they just couldn't compute." Alex responds: "Those natives all got wiped out in the end, didn't they? If that thing out there really is some sort of human-protocrap hybrid, then we're yesterday's model. Obsolete" ("The Monster and the Rocket"). Pondering the colonization of what lies beyond the Ring System, Avasarala observes that "When Columbus arrived, at least he knew what was waving at him was human" ("New Terra"). These moments indicate that *The Expanse*'s humankind is worried about the prospect of being colonized and annihilated by an alien species. Yet, it's evident that human colonization of the Sol System has already replicated the violence of old colonial patterns.

The exploitation of the Belt's resources—both natural and human—is a form of colonialism grounded in the belief that Belters aren't, in fact, fully human. As an OPA activist explains, "to them, we will always be slaves. That's all we are to the Earthers and Dusters. They built their solar system on our backs, spilled the blood of a million of our brothers. But in their eyes, we're not even human anymore" ("Dulcinea"). Eros is chosen for the protomolecule experiment because Belters are viewed as "animals to test their [Inners] new weapons on" ("The Seventh Man"). For the same reason, Belters are victims of environmental injustices, from the exposure of Anderson Station's children to the health hazards of living in a low-oxygen environment ("Back to the Butcher"), to the refugees created by the collapse of Ganymede. Indeed, as a "race of exiles in space" ("The Big Empty"), all Belters are de facto climate refugees produced by the Anthropocene on Earth.

The Expanse's humanity, therefore, ends up exporting to its Planet Bs not only the Anthropocene's anthropocentrism, but also its environmental injustices and stratified understanding of what we value as fully human. Failing to address these worldviews in an ethical paradigm shift repeats the mistakes made on Earth's garden.

"Doing nothing is just as bad as doing the wrong thing"

Where does *The Expanse* leave us in relation to the challenges of this epoch? Holden firmly holds on to the possibility of justice, even in the face of atrocities like the genocide on Eros ("Safe"). As Alex explains, the *Roci*'s philosophy is that "You can talk all day long about, you know, looking out for yourself, minding your own business, just trying to survive. It all boils down to an excuse and that excuse ain't worth a good goddamn thing when the world is burning down around you. Doing nothing is just as bad as doing the wrong thing" ("Doors & Corners").

When the world is quite literally burning down around us due to climate change—think the Australian bushfires emergency—the *Roci*'s crew remind us of the importance of the fight for environmental justice and for a different ethics in our relationships with the rest of nature.

What is at stake is nothing less than the possibility of a future.

Notes

1. IPCC, "Special Report on the Ocean and Cryosphere in a Changing Climate," 2019, https://www.ipcc.ch/srocc/.
2. Simon L. Lewis and Mark A. Maslin, *The Human Planet: How We Created the Anthropocene* (London: Pelican, 2018).
3. IPCC, "Global Warming of 1.5°C," 2018, at https://www.ipcc.ch/sr15/.
4. For an analysis that shows how Earth might be "approaching a global cascade of tipping points that [will] le[a]d to a new, less habitable, 'hothouse' climate state," see Timothy M. Lenton et al., "Climate Tipping Points—Too Risky to Bet Against," *Nature*, November 27, 2019, https://www.nature.com/articles/

d41586-019-03595-0#ref-CR1. It is estimated that, by 2050, there could be up to 1 billion people forced to migrate due to environmental degradation (desertification, ocean acidification, erosion), rising temperatures and sea levels, as well as sudden onset disasters such as storms and floods. See International Organization for Migration (IOM), "IOM Outlook on Migration, Environment and Climate Change," 2014, at https://environmentalmigration. iom.int/iom-outlook-migration-environment-and-climate-change-1.

5. That animals are rarely featured in *The Expanse*—and not only in space, where they would have problems adapting to different gravity conditions, but, crucially, on Earth—might, in this sense, be an allusion to the Anthropocene as an age of mass extinctions.

6. Brian G. Henning, "From the Anthropocene to the Ecozoic: Philosophy and Global Climate Change," *Midwest Studies in Philosophy* 40 (2016), 284–295, 288.

7. Ibid.

8. Katie McShane, "Anthropocentrism in Climate Ethics and Policy," *Midwest Studies in Philosophy* 40 (2016), 189–204.

9. Henning, "From the Anthropocene to the Ecozoic," 288.

10. Ibid., 290.

11. Ibid., 291.

12. Keekok Lee, "Awe and Humility: Intrinsic Value in Nature. Beyond an Earthbound Environmental Ethics," *Royal Institute of Philosophy Supplements* 36 (1994), 92. It is interesting to note that Lee develops her non-Earthbound environmental ethics by thinking through the project of terraforming Mars.

13. Simon Caney, "Justice and Posterity," in *Climate Justice: Integrating Economics and Philosophy*, ed. Ravi Kanbur and Henry Shue (Oxford: Oxford University Press, 2018), 157–174.

14. Kim Stanley Robinson, "The Coronavirus is Rewriting our Imaginations," *The New Yorker*, May 1, 2020, https://www.newyorker.com/culture/annals-of-inquiry/the-coronavirus-and-our-future.

15. Henry Shue, *Climate Justice: Vulnerability and Protection* (Oxford: Oxford University Press, 2014), 5.

16. On the effects of climate change on the Global South, see, for instance, Christian Parenti, *Climate Change and the New Geography of Violence* (New York: Bold Type, 2011). In terms of the uneven distribution of environmental risks in the Global North, consider the case of Hurricane Katrina and its disproportionate impact on the black community: Gary Rivlin, "White New Orleans Has Recovered from Hurricane Katrina. Black New Orleans Has Not," *The Nation*, August 29, 2016, https://www.thenation.com/article/archive/white-new-orleans-has-recovered-from-hurricane-katrina-black-new-orleans-has-not/.

17. Kyle P. Whyte, "Indigenous Science (Fiction) for the Anthropocene: Ancestral Dystopias and Fantasies of Climate Change Crises," *Environment and Planning E: Nature and Space* 1 (2018), 224–242.

18. Henning, "From the Anthropocene to the Ecozoic," 290; Whyte, "Indigenous Science (Fiction) for the Anthropocene."

15

We Can Be Gods
Remorseless Logic or Shared Humanity

Max Gemeinhardt

DRESDEN: If we master it, we can apply it.
HOLDEN: Apply it to what?
DRESDEN: To everything. We become our own gods. Imagine human beings able to live in hard vacuum without a suit or under the crushing atmosphere of a gas giant. Or able to hibernate long enough to travel to the stars. ("Doors & Corners")

Dresden gives his lines unironically to those surrounding him on Thoth Station. They've come there specifically to capture him and stop his experiment, an experiment that led to thousands being turned into vomit zombies and sacrificed to science on Eros. Dresden defends his actions from two distinct viewpoints. The first is the modern model of science, according to which knowledge results from experimentation and allows us to control the world. The second is the utilitarian justification of science. If scientific progress benefits more people than it hurts, it is morally permissible. In Dresden's case, the deaths of those on Eros as part of "The Project" amount to, as he puts it, "hardly a rounding error." When weighed against all humanity, the only logical choice was obvious.

"I wonder what that rain tastes like?"

Science aims to understand reality through experimentation, inference, and deduction. The overall goal is to increase the totality of human knowledge. Of course, how we define knowledge, truth, and the nature of reality impacts our arguments about the ethics of science. And those answers can also lead down strange paths.

René Descartes (1596–1650) famously reasoned that "I think, therefore I am." Simply put, because he was thinking, he must exist. Everything else,

The Expanse and Philosophy: So Far Out Into the Darkness, First Edition. Edited by Jeffery L. Nicholas.

however, could be an illusion of the senses. He could be dreaming or being deceived by a demon. Descartes' philosophy culminates in the separation of the mind from the rest of the world. Does that description sound like our long-lost detective Miller?

Consider post-Eros Miller, who appears only to Holden. Holden has no way to prove that anything he sees or knows is real. The protomolecule is like Descartes' demon; it can trick his senses into perceiving anything, like Miller—who is dead. If the protomolecule could make Holden see his lost friend, then why not the bulkhead of the *Roci*? Maybe Holden is in a padded room on Earth, hallucinating or hooked up to a virtual reality program. From Descartes' point of view, Holden can't know. All he can know is that he exists because someone—Holden—is seeing something, whether that is Miller or the bulkhead of the *Roci*.

Think about this issue from Miller's perspective. He is always asking questions and having a dialogue with himself. "I wonder what that does?" "So what do we got here?" "Reach out." "Flipping switches. . ." Miller's constant questioning and experimentation allow him to remain in existence and possibly sane. Through this experimentation, Miller interacts with the world around him. We'll follow up with this point later.

For now, let's return to Descartes and the separation of the mind from the world. Usually, the philosophy of science starts with a series of assumptions to overcome this separation and establish the universality of natural law, a principle of the scientific project. A first assumption is that things outside of us exist and that we share some part of our reality with other people who can perceive it as we do. From these perceptions, we can determine what reality is truly like and, importantly, make predictions about it. For instance, Miller can direct Holden to flip some switches and overload an alien powerplant to see what happens. In fact, Miller and Holden do some hands-on epistemology, theory of knowledge. Experimenting and interacting with the universe is a vital part of applied epistemology, leading to knowledge of the results of those interactions.

"If we master it, we can apply it"

According to Francis Bacon (1561–1626), the father of modern science, we derive knowledge not from some distant or abstract source, but instead from observation and experimentation. Bacon's approach goes beyond mere explanation. Using inductive reasoning, we are to make predictions and test them with experiments. For Bacon, observation of nature does not deliver facts; instead, facts are the result of meticulous observation and experimentation going through trial and error to arrive at conclusions that can be predictive. If we understand the mechanisms of our experiments, we should be able to replicate them, which will lead to supporting or rejecting our theories on how the universe works.

Dresden appears cut from Bacon's mold. He tells us, "I'm not interested in the cosmic fate of bacteria" ("Doors & Corners"). He does not want to merely speculate on what the protomolecule would do to humanity; he wants to know precisely what it will do. The only way to know is to expose people and find out. Dr. Cortázar agrees: "It learns, you know. It does something different every time. The more biomass you feed it, the faster it learns, the more it changes . . . We can only learn by letting it learn." Dresden and Cortázar want to experiment, make predictions, and experiment again. They have an end goal.

In short, if we study the mechanism of nature, we can command nature. As Dresden says, "If we master it, we can apply it." For Bacon, controlling nature is a way to remake the world into a new garden of Eden. He writes, "the true and lawful goal of the sciences is none other than this: that human life be endowed with new discoveries and powers."[1] Dresden echoes from the future, "We can be our own gods."

Yet, Bacon would likely disagree with Dresden about his Eros experiment. Science is more of a tool than anything else. The scientist has an ethical responsibility. In Bacon's view, the acquisition of knowledge does not coincide with exerting power. Instead, scientific knowledge is a condition for the development of civilization; therefore, knowledge must be shared. Knowledge should be used for a universal human good to build toward a better society. This view starkly contrasts many of those inhabiting the world of *The Expanse*. Those inhabitants seek to control, not only knowledge of the protomolecule, but also through that knowledge the protomolecule itself. If they're unlucky, they might create a dystopia where the extinction of humanity is a real possibility. Only once knowledge of the Ring System is shared after the initial crisis do we see any real progress toward a more peaceful and potentially utopian society. In "Congregation" and "Abaddon's Gate," various people experiment and observe, and then the knowledge is shared among the three represented powers. Momentarily, humanity is spared the worst results from the acquisition of knowledge and the control it brings.

Detecting Stealth Ships

Pragmatism is a direct response to the notion that some branches of philosophy lead to dead ends or lack practical applications. The pragmatist C. S. Peirce (1839–1914) developed ideas for logic gates that would become the basis for modern computing, and he was critical of Descartes' dualism. According to pragmatism we should think of our minds as being connected to the world at large.

Pragmatism prides itself on practical, measurable ways to arrive at answers, and Peirce held that the goal of science is unlimited inquiry. We must always leave room for the possibility that a better hypothesis may come along that will replace the current theory with something more accurate. In this way, we move toward understanding the true nature of reality. If your hypothesis cannot stand up to inquiry, or if the inquiry goes nowhere, then it is not worth pursuing until it can be reformulated in a way that yields answers.

The Protogen stealth ships provide an interesting example ("CQB"). How do the people onboard the *Donnager* know that the stealth ships are there? They base their beliefs on the fact that the sensors detect heat from the engines. The laser range finders reflect off the hull of the lead ship, but it blinds them to the other ships we suspect are there. Only when the other vessels accelerate to attack and fire their rail guns do they become as clear as the first stealth. We use the same logic to determine the existence of black holes; they have effects on the space around them.

In *The Expanse*, the protomolecule disassembles and reassembles human bodies in random and horrific ways. We see the zombification of humans infected with the protomolecule, but we don't know if these people are dead, alive, or something else entirely. A pragmatic approach would lead us to believe that, dead or alive, these beings no longer exist as humans. The response of those infected with the protomolecule and the way that they interact or affect the world around them are so different from uninfected humans that they must be something else now. The rest of the solar system concludes that they are dead because that is the most straightforward conclusion to draw from the effects of the protomolecule. Later, though, we learn through Miller's ghost that this may not be entirely correct.

The pragmatist John Dewey (1859–1952) can help us think through the ethical implications of science. A pragmatic ethical system does not explicitly allow or disallow actions. Rather, pragmatism suggests that our ethics and our ability to judge an action's morality evolve as we do. Dewey, like other pragmatists, believed we could not judge means and ends separately. Is the means by which we come to knowledge—exposing Belters to the protomolecule—distinct from the ends—learning about and mastering the protomolecule? The means alone, according to Dewey, could not provide a rational decision. Yet, the worthiness of an end is inextricably coupled with the means to achieve it and any unintended consequences.

In *The Expanse*, we don't know what information Dresden's project might have produced. We do know of one cost for that knowledge, and it was Eros. Yet, in "Doors & Corners," Fred Johnson is ready to negotiate with Dresden. For him, Dresden's science is the only way to safeguard the rest of the Belt. Eros and its consequences didn't matter. Indeed, it seems that Fred Johnson is not judging Dresden on a moral basis. The Belt's survival outweighed the cost of Eros, in Johnson's mind.

"... hardly a rounding error"

Jeremy Bentham (1748–1832) and John Stuart Mill (1806–1873) advocated the philosophy of utilitarianism, according to which we should act so as to produce the greatest good for the greatest number of people. Because unjust laws result in unhappiness, Bentham and Mill called for social and legal reforms. Their moral goal was to maximize happiness for the greatest number of people.

In theory, utilitarianism could justify any scientific project that benefits humanity by maximizing happiness. According to one line of reasoning, people can only be happy if they are alive, so maximizing happiness calls for keeping the greatest number of people alive. Dresden reasons this way. For him, it is purely a numbers game. Eros had to be sacrificed to protect the rest of humanity from the threat of the protomolecule. The cost was a mere rounding error: a few thousands sacrificed for billions.

Dresden makes a lot of sense to some people. So, we are all shocked when Miller steps up and shoots him in the head ("Doors & Corners"). Miller voices the most straightforward critique of utilitarianism when he says, "I didn't kill him because he was crazy. I killed him because he was making sense." Utilitarianism operates according to a relentless logic. The answer to whether some action is morally right or wrong is simple. Just crunch the numbers. When we weigh the lives of an individual or a group of individuals against the whole of humanity, the only logical conclusion is that the group or the individual must be sacrificed. The Eros incident illuminates the way the remorseless logic of utilitarianism can lead to dreadful results.

"What happens to us now?"

The Expanse allows us to look at different views on the moral limits of science. It also illuminates our shared humanity. Earth is ultimately saved from Eros by Miller connecting with Julie. In later episodes, Prax's love for his daughter leads the *Roci* crew to Project Caliban, thereby preventing Mars' protomolecule infection.

Indeed, the entirety of the Eros incident can be seen as the result of losing track of our shared humanity. Consider what Holden learns about Dr. Cortázar.

HOLDEN: "So someone waves a magnet at the right side on my head, and suddenly I can watch 100,000 people die in agony and not give a shit?"

DOCTOR: "Well, he's not a homicidal maniac; he just no longer has the capacity to consider any life other than his own meaningful." ("Static")

The technology that erased the empathy of Cortázar and others likely was not developed with that purpose. Transcranial magnetic stimulation is a real technology that may treat certain brain disorders. The application in *The Expanse*, while theoretical, may not be outside the realm of possibility, though. So we need to think carefully. One of the lessons from *The Expanse* is that when we lose sight of our shared humanity terrible things tend to happen—Eros, Project Caliban, the Earth/Mars War. To resolve these issues we need an ethical system that relies on an individual's empathy to make moral decisions. Holden seems to embody such empathy, much to the frustration of everyone else. When that is taken away or ignored, it results in disaster. *The Expanse* suggests that when we lose sight of our humanity, even if the goal is to save humanity, we make the wrong decisions.

Though the goal of science is to expand our knowledge, we must recognize that the path we choose matters. Do we want a path that is based solely on the greatest good for the greatest number? Or do we want a path of mutual respect for a shared humanity?

Note

1. Francis Bacon, *The New Organon* (1620), https://www.aub.edu.lb/fas/cvsp/documents/the-new-organon-francis-bacon.pdf.

16

Gunnery Sergeant Draper and the Martian Congressional Republic's Vision for Mars

James S. J. Schwartz

"You know what I love most about Mars?" Franklin DeGraaf asks Chrisjen Avasarala. "They still dream. We gave up. They're an entire culture dedicated to a common goal, working together as one to turn a lifeless rock into a garden. We had a garden and we paved it" ("Remember the Cant"). We only see Mars from Earth's perspective in the first season of *The Expanse*, but Season 2 changes that by introducing Gunnery Sergeant Bobbie Draper, a Martian Congressional Republic Navy (MCRN) marine. Mars as seen by Martians resembles our Mars: ruddy, rocky, dusty, inhospitable, and cold. When we first encounter Draper, she activates a terrain-overlaying simulation of Mariner Valley as it will be 100 years into the planet's terraforming project. The dull browns and reds in front of her recede into vibrant blues and greens. The intimidating, unsaturated sky above transforms into an inviting blue with white clouds. A desiccated crater basin becomes a placid lake. Abundant plant life exists in harmony with a thriving city.

With determination as well as awareness that she may not live to see the dream become reality, Draper says, "Someday."

This easy-to-miss, seconds-long moment encapsulates the hopes and dreams of the people of the Mars Congressional Republic (MCR), at least prior to the dramatic events of the fifth season. Many on Earth today share these hopes and dreams. Throughout the arc of Draper's story, however, from her days as an eager marine to her later and uncertain relationship with the Martian government, we discover many reasons why we might question the worthiness of the MCR's societal projects, or at least the ways it chooses to implement them.

The Expanse and Philosophy: So Far Out Into the Darkness, First Edition. Edited by Jeffery L. Nicholas.
© 2022 John Wiley & Sons, Inc. Published 2022 by John Wiley & Sons, Inc.

Revolutionary Revelations

Consider when MCRN Lieutenant Lopez aboard the *Donnager* interrogates James Holden for his role in the destruction of the ice hauler *Canterbury* ("CQB"). This scene gives us an early window into how the people of the MCR view their closest neighbors in the Sol System.

LOPEZ: When you spend your whole life living under a dome, even the idea of an ocean seems impossible to imagine. I could never understand your people. Why, when the universe has bestowed so much upon you, do you seem to care so little for it?

HOLDEN: Wrecking things is what Earthers do best. Martians too, by the look of your ship.

LOPEZ: We are nothing like you. The only thing Earthers care about is government handouts. Free food, free water, free drugs so you can forget the aimless lives you lead. You're short-sighted. And selfish. And it will destroy you. Earth is over, Mr. Holden. My only hope is that we can bring Mars to life before you destroy that too.

The "Martian exceptionalism" of the MCR is on full display, with Lopez as its mouthpiece. He has absolute confidence in the superiority of the Martian way of life. Non-Martians are inferior, free-riders, who have no vision for the future, and who ought to be grateful to Mars for the security, jobs, and stability provided by the omnipresent Martian navy. To the audience, however, Lopez—and with him the MCR—appears belligerent, arrogant, and ignorant. How could a society built upon scientific and technological advancement produce such close-minded people?

The philosopher Alasdair MacIntyre can help us unravel where Lopez has gone astray—and ultimately, how Draper is able to see past her home planet's culture of arrogance and ignorance.[1] According to MacIntyre, determining whether your ideals and your beliefs are the best ones for you to hold, to act upon, and to ask others to hold and act upon is no simple task. It requires assembling a considerable amount of "self-knowledge." Self-knowledge is knowledge of how you as an individual are situated in the wider social and political world. This situated self-knowledge requires an awareness of the political and social currents that shape your experiences of the world. The pursuit of self-knowledge is, ultimately, an attempt to uncover the true origin and history of your beliefs. The danger for those not on the path to self-knowledge is that they have surrendered their agency; they are no longer in control of their beliefs, and consequently, their desires and actions are no longer their own. Those who attain self-knowledge can, to the greatest extent possible, claim that their beliefs are based on reason and evidence as opposed to being imposed by political or cultural forces.

Fortunately for us, *The Expanse* is as much of a political thriller as it is a space opera, and it borrows heavily from familiar examples—from science fiction as well as real life—of political upheaval, rebellion, conflict, and nation-building. Consequently, the series provides ample opportunities to observe and reflect on the forces that shape the beliefs and actions of its characters, including Draper.

Within the realm of science fiction, *The Expanse* is a spiritual successor to *Babylon 5*, *Star Trek: Deep Space 9*, and *Dune*, in which protagonists struggle to confront, reform, or dismantle institutions that have become indifferent or even hostile to the people they were designed to help. Meanwhile, *The Expanse*'s attention to detail and its brutal honesty about the dangers of living and working in space are reminiscent of novels such as Allen Steele's *Orbital Decay* and Stephen Baxter's *Proxima*. While these comparisons are worthy of further development, none is as interesting as the comparison between the MCR and the real-life United States.

Prior to the events of *The Expanse*, the MCR began life as a colony under the control of Earth, later waging a successful war of independence against its terrestrial sovereign. In the years since, Mars sought to demonstrate its technological and military superiority. It became home to the best scientists of the Sol System, as well as its most advanced navy, the MCRN. Even though Mars is a small "nation" compared to Earth, it amassed comparable political and military power. Mars' relationship to Earth is, in this sense, a direct parallel to the United States' relationship with the British Empire during the twilight of British naval supremacy (that is, in the time leading up to World Wars I and II). We even see these "superpowers" frequently sparring over control of their version of the "Global South": the Belters and the Outers.

These parallels suggest that the political and cultural forces shaping the lives of citizens of the MCR are deeply similar to the forces shaping the lives of ordinary Americans. In fact, the MCR's culture is modeled after American attitudes about personal responsibility, America's role on the world stage, and, of course, America's vision for space exploration. MCRN Captain Theresa Yao brags about "cleansing the Belt of pirates," a thinly veiled slight against America's treatment of "enemy combatants" in its "war on terror" ("CQB"). Draper's squad jokes about Mars' terraforming machinery being owned by a single wealthy family, an allusion to the increasing inequalities of wealth and opportunity in the US and across the world ("Safe"). In numerous episodes, Martians insult the "takers" on Earth for being ungrateful, lazy, and for living life waiting for handouts, analogues of the "victim-blaming" attitudes many Americans have regarding the poor, and especially immigrants and refugees.

These examples and others like them reveal a Martian version of the American exceptionalism taught to American schoolchildren. For Martians, glory is only possible through the hard work of conquering the Martian frontier and supporting Mars' terraforming project. Achieving greatness as a "nation" requires technological and military domination over others. Citizens of Mariner Valley even have Texan accents and listen to the kind of country music that would have been suitable for saving the Earth from the Martians of *Mars Attacks!*

The MCR, therefore, represents a distinctively American interpretation of space exploration. For this reason, examining American attitudes about space exploration can help us understand the culture of the MCR, as well as Draper's unplanned quest for self-knowledge. For the same reason, examining the culture of the MCR can help those of us living today better understand the forces that shape American attitudes toward space exploration—and to finally decide for ourselves whether these attitudes are worth keeping around.

Nothing New in Orbit of the Sun

What is striking about the culture of the MCR is how naturally it flows from contemporary visions of space exploration, especially those from the *Apollo* era forward. In contrast to popular memory, the *Apollo* lunar landings did not occur because of America's interests in lunar geology or due to a spirit of exploration. Rather, the fundamental objective of *Apollo* was rooted in American exceptionalism, national security, and the need to accumulate prestige in the "Space Race" against the Soviet Union.[2]

As an example of how political forces drove America's space program, consider the speech that many Americans mistakenly believe was responsible for instigating the space race, President John F. Kennedy's 1961 "Address at Rice University on the Nation's Space Effort."

> Those who came before us made certain that this country rode the first waves of the industrial revolutions, the first waves of modern invention, and the first wave of nuclear power, and this generation does not intend to founder in the backwash of the coming age of space. We mean to be a part of it—we mean to lead it. For the eyes of the world now look into space, to the moon and to the planets beyond, and we have vowed that we shall not see it governed by a hostile flag of conquest, but by a banner of freedom and peace . . . the vows of this Nation can only be fulfilled if we in this Nation are first, and, therefore, we intend to be first.

For President Kennedy, it is not enough that humanity ventures into space; America ("we") must take the lead each step along the way.[3] The ideas presented in Kennedy's speech continue to shape American attitudes toward space exploration. This enduring American space exceptionalism is no different from the "Martian exceptionalism" we see throughout *The Expanse*—through the MCR's insistence on "leading" or being in control (of the Belt, the shipping lanes, the protomolecule)—again, at least prior to the dramatic events of the fifth season.

The connections run deeper. Specific elements of the MCR culture echo contemporary American attitudes about Mars. For example, in the "Founding Declaration" of the Mars Society (one of the better-known space advocacy organizations in the US), we see Mars settlement presented as an opportunity to find superior ways of living. "The settling of the Martian New World is an opportunity for a noble experiment in which humanity has another chance to shed old baggage and begin the world anew; carrying forward as much of the best of our heritage as possible and leaving the worst behind. Such chances do not come often, and are not to be disdained lightly."[4] We should not be surprised to discover that people living in societies which teach them that "others" are "the worst," who are to be left behind, will often come to unjustly disdain other societies and their peoples. *The Expanse* illuminates this attitude in the myriad ways the MCR disdains and seeks to subjugate Earth and the Belt.[5]

For somewhat more specific examples, let's consider the "Statement of Philosophy" of the National Space Society, another well-known space advocacy organization in the US. It holds that space is the key to providing

> the human species with a new "frontier" for exploration and adventure, and to thought and expression, culture and art, and modes of government. The opening of "the New World" to western civilization brought about an unprecedented 500-year period of growth and experimentation in science, technology, literature, music, art, recreation, and government (including the development and gradual acceptance of democracy). The presence of a frontier led to the development of the "open society" founded on the principles of individual rights and freedoms. Many of these rights and freedoms are being placed under increasingly stringent limitations as human population grows and humanity moves towards a "closed society," where eventually everyone eats the same, speaks the same, and dresses the same.[6]

The culture of the MCR results from a long-term affirmation of these ideas. Citizens of the MCR view themselves as belonging to the sole "open" or advanced democracy; they view Earth, the Belt, and the OPA as authoritarian backwater nations.

Back in our world, Dr. Robert Zubrin, one of the founders of the Mars Society, has offered specific reasons why Martian culture will be exceptional.

Its future will depend critically upon the progress of science and technology . . . [T]he "Martian ingenuity" born in a culture that puts the utmost premium on intelligence, practical education, and the determination required to make real contributions will make much more than its fair share of the scientific and technological breakthroughs, which will dramatically advance the human condition in the twenty-first century.[7]

Before the opening of the Ring Gates, the Mars of *The Expanse* is the living embodiment of these ambitions. The MCR's commitment to terra-forming Mars demonstrates that its future depends "upon the progress of science and technology." Its unparalleled terraforming and military technologies were "born in a culture that puts the utmost premium on intelligence, practical education, and the determination to make real contributions" to the MCR.

Now that we have some "self-knowledge," that is, now that we have identified the prevailing social and political currents that shape our attitudes about space exploration and Mars settlement, we face a reconciliation. How can we square our contemporary views about space exploration with our disapproval of a fictional future society (the MCR) that is rooted in the same ideals? Can we appropriately admire Draper's heroic transformation without rejecting the founding principles of the institutions she came to feel compelled to rebel against?

Philosophy on the Martian Frontier

With a Sol System either at war or ever at the brink of war, *The Expanse* does not paint a hopeful future for humanity. Nor does it shy away from the harsh realities of living in space. The Belt and the OPA have unsteady access to life's basic necessities (air, water, medicine). Whereas *Star Trek* portrays a largely harmonious future in which humanity has "learned its lessons" before venturing into space, *The Expanse* depicts a future where we have failed entirely to learn how to coexist with one another peacefully. Conflict and provincialism reign, human equality and wellbeing are scarce luxuries, and self-knowledge is in short supply.

The Expanse is here to warn us about trouble above the horizon.

Just as a home built on a faulty foundation becomes more and more difficult to maintain as time progresses, a project, culture, or society built on a faulty vision becomes more and more difficult to sustain as time progresses. Philosophers are students of the possible, caring not only about the world as it is, but as it could be, and as it should be. Science fiction provides windows into possible futures so that we can more vividly entertain questions about the future. The two together can help us avoid setting out unwittingly on dangerous and unwise paths.

The indifference to human life on display in *The Expanse* does not come about through accident, nor through necessity. It results from choices made by those in power concerning how to arrange and govern space societies and concerning whose needs will receive priority and whose will be ignored. If we do not like the way our beliefs about space exploration look in the mirror after we have been blessed (or cursed) by this self-knowledge, then the best way forward is to consider alternative possibilities, ideals, or visions for space exploration.

Am I exaggerating how influential ideals and visions can be? Dr. Patricia Limerick, a renowned historian of the American West, highlights the importance of a founding vision in her criticism of Americans' propensity for speaking about space exploration as the "conquering of the space frontier." Limerick describes an intellectual version of the aphorism that when all you have is a hammer, everything looks like a nail. "The metaphors and comparisons and analogies that a group chooses do in fact carry a lot of meaning and can indeed control actual behavior. The metaphor you choose guides your decisions—it makes some alternatives seem logical and necessary, while it makes other alternatives nearly invisible."[8] Her concerns about faulty or inappropriate metaphors have important precursors in philosophy.

For instance, Rudolf Carnap's (1891–1970) notion of a conceptual framework holds that our understanding of the world is always filtered by the languages and concepts available to us. Meanwhile, Thomas Kuhn's (1922–1996) ideas about the incommensurability of scientific theories holds that different scientific theories offer distinct lenses through which we can interpret and understand the world. Persons adopting differing frameworks, or differing scientific theories, can have fundamental and oftentimes irreconcilable disagreements about the structure of the world. The same is true of metaphors. Well-chosen metaphors, like conceptual frameworks and scientific theories, can help us in our quest for self-knowledge by opening our eyes to more of the world around us. When poorly chosen, however, they can shield us from important truths and possibilities. For instance, it was not until Einstein's ideas about the structure of spacetime overtook Newton's that we discovered it was impossible to accelerate ordinary matter to the speed of light.

How does the "space frontier" metaphor championed by space enthusiasts and the MCR fare?

Limerick, who takes issue with the idea that America has a destiny that lies in space, warns that if you "[c]ommit yourself to a destiny" then "you are handing over your free will; you are volunteering for compulsion; you are doing things because you must do them, not because you have reflected, pondered, and chosen to do them."[9] America, in its failure to reflect on its use of the space frontier metaphor, shields itself from any awareness of its past mistakes. MacIntyre might describe this as a critical failure to accumulate self-knowledge. Either way, the result is the same. In failing to acknowledge its past mistakes it becomes impossible for America to learn from its past mistakes. And since America is accustomed to promoting space as a frontier that needs to be conquered, we should not be surprised to find Americans who think that their country has a right to defend its interests in space, by force, if necessary.

Dr. Linda Billings, a consultant to NASA's Astrobiology Program and to its Planetary Defense Coordination Office, expresses this worry, writing that "NASA and its partners in space should be vigilant in their efforts to avoid repeating past mistakes. Exploration for aiding and abetting conquest and exploitation will not build a sound foundation for humanity's future in space. Initiatives intended to conquer and exploit, to fence off bits and pieces of the Solar System . . . are not worthy of public funding."[10] The MCR, steeped in the same metaphors of conquest, continues to repeat the mistakes of the past.

Fortunately for the people living in the universe of *The Expanse*, Draper is exposed to exactly the right people and circumstances that help her grow out of her formative but defective ideals.

For those of us not so lucky, we have philosophy. Philosophy teaches us to see alternative possibilities, such as alternative ways to understand the purpose and value of space exploration. Perhaps we could value cooperative projects (like the International Space Station) over competitive projects (like the first Moon landings). Perhaps we could prioritize finding ways to make living in space enjoyable rather than barely sustainable. Perhaps we could create systems of governing space that prioritize human wellbeing over the accumulation of wealth and power. And perhaps it was wrong in the first place to suppose that we could escape our problems by going into space.[11]

Though these suggestions will be familiar to *Star Trek* enthusiasts, they are often rejected as utopian or unrealistic by the more dogmatic proponents of space exploration. But the suggestions raised in the previous paragraph would not require nonexistent or impossibly expensive technologies. The reason why these suggestions are so often dismissed is that they do not line up with the ways we are used to talking about space exploration; they are not in line with the "space frontier" metaphor. We are too used to talking about space as a place that will provide us with limitless energy and resources. We are too used to talking about space as a place where we will finally learn how to govern ourselves properly. We are not used to talking about space as a place of malnutrition and confinement. We are not used to talking about space as a place ripe for corruption and tyranny.

The Expanse makes clear that we should not take it on faith that our institutions and our leaders will always make humanitarian choices, in space or elsewhere. Most importantly, *The Expanse* teaches us about the need to be vigilant in seeking out additional information, especially information that might call into question some of our most closely held beliefs. One of the greatest virtues on display among the protagonists is their unrelenting willingness to update their beliefs when faced with new evidence. In Draper's case, we see her yearning for a better understanding of the world and her place in it through her unwillingness to fire first as UNN troops are advancing toward the Martian line on Ganymede. We see it in her violation of an order to bear false witness during the sensitive negotiations between Earth and Mars following the Ganymede incident. We see it in her decision to defect from Mars and to work for UN Deputy Undersecretary Crisjen Avasarala. We see it in her uncompromising desire to protect and listen to Holden despite her fellow marines' desires to execute him following his capture at the Ring Station. We see it in her unwillingness to believe Martian propaganda as she tries to resume an ordinary life on Mars. And we see it in her effective use of analytical skills when helping rescue Naomi Nagata following Naomi's harrowing escape from Marco Inaros. Draper draws strength and earns redemption precisely because she is on a quest for self-knowledge and recognizes that she will only ever have a partial understanding of the universe around her.

This ever-present need to be aware of one's surroundings, to ask questions, and to reexamine one's beliefs and their origins, is a core philosophical teaching. We will never overcome the need to ask ourselves if we are doing the right things, for the right reasons, at the right times, and in the right ways. While the focus of this chapter has been on Draper and the MCR, it could just as easily have been on James Holden, Naomi Nagata, Alex Kamal, Crisjen Avasarala, Camina Drummer, Amos Burton, Joe Miller, Fred Johnson, Lucia Mazur, or even Clarissa Mao. Each either earns their redemption or becomes a better person by remaining open always to the possibility that additional information could completely upend everything they believe or have been fighting for.

Unfortunately, what we see in the case of the MCR is a society that never seeks any self-knowledge and that never pauses to reconsider the wisdom of its overarching vision and the means by which it imposes that vision on the Sol System. It is a future that we may create if we do not pause to reconsider the role of space exploration in our societies. If we are not careful, any progress we make in spaceflight technology may not produce the societal progress promised by space advocates. That is the lesson of Martian alliance with Marco Inaros and the move to Laconia.

It's Life in the Solar System, Jim, But Not as We Know It

The Expanse presents space as beautiful but terrifying; as providing great opportunities for human expansion but even greater opportunities for human suffering. In this regard it offers one of the most grounded, gritty, and realistic depictions of what living in space will be like, where hardship will always be one step ahead of us. The rosy, secure societies we are accustomed to seeing in *Star Trek* may be in our future, but, if so, that future is a long way away. It is far more likely that if we venture into space our future will resemble what we see in *The Expanse*. *The Expanse* is at its most powerful when it provides answers to the question, what if we proceed in the exploration of space without self-knowledge—that is, without ever reexamining our basic assumptions about the purpose and value of spaceflight? If we think that it is not the best future to work toward, then we should start by questioning whether popular visions of space exploration, including the contemporary precursors of the MCR's vision for Mars, are the right visions for us. Philosophy stands ready to help.[12]

Notes

1. Alasdair MacIntyre, "The Recovery of Moral Agency?" in *The Best Christian Writing 2000*, ed. Joseph Wilson (San Francisco, CA: HarperCollins, 2000), 111–136.
2. Because of this, many analysts now claim that the US is in a new space race, this time with China.
3. This is just one example among countless others. For an excellent political history of the space age, see either Walter McDougall, *The Heavens and the Earth: A Political History of the Space Age* (New York: Basic Books, 1985) or Howard McCurdy, *Space and the American Imagination*, 2nd edition (Baltimore: Johns Hopkins University Press, 2011).
4. https://www.marssociety.org/founding-declaration/.
5. Of this, Earthers and Beltalowda are equally guilty.
6. https://space.nss.org/nss-statement-of-philosophy/.
7. Robert Zubrin, *The Case for Mars: The Plan to Settle the Red Planet and Why We Must* (New York: Touchstone Books, 1997), 301.
8. Patricia Limerick, "Imagined Frontiers: Westward Expansion and the Future of the Space Program," in *Space Policy Alternatives*, ed. Radford Byerly (Boulder, CO: Westview Press, 1992), 250.
9. Ibid., 256.
10. Linda Billings, "Frontier Days in Space: Are They Over?" *Space* Policy 13 (1997), 189.
11. For my own position on what is important about space exploration, see James S. J. Schwartz, *The Value of Science in Space Exploration* (New York: Oxford University Press, 2020).
12. I thank Jeffery Nicholas, Neal Allen, Ben Ragan, and Carmen van Ommen for commenting on earlier versions of this chapter.

Fifth Orbit
TILTING AT WINDMILLS

17

How to Be a Hero
Hannah Arendt and Naomi Nagata on Making and Doing Politics

Tiago Cerqueira Lazier

The protomolecule is about to overtake Ganymede, killing everyone on the surface. Naomi manages to buy herself and Amos a ticket to safety by offering to fix Melissa's freighter. She also wants to rescue the Belters stranded in the same station; but there's a problem. While the vessel can fit 300 people, the air is only enough for 52 plus the crew. Outside the ship, more than one hundred Belters are scared and angry—getting angrier by the minute. Melissa and Amos reason that if they open the door and try to explain the situation, people will tear each other and the crew apart by trying to make sure they get in. So, it's better not to risk it and live to help other people another day, right?

Naomi disagrees. She manages to get out of the ship alone, risking a fight with Amos. Outside, she faces the scared crowd, explains the problem and proposes her solution. Risking her life to speak with them, she convinces the Belters to allow the youngest to be saved. Choosing to act and creating an alternative where none seemed to exist, Naomi escapes as a hero.

However, it's easy to imagine another scenario in which Naomi failed to convince the people of her plan and ended up dead, no longer able to play a part in the important mission ahead of her. In that case, would we think differently about what she did? Should we?

Escaping the Monster of Ganymede

The philosopher Hannah Arendt (1906–1975) distinguishes between making and doing politics.[1] To make politics is to behave strategically like one is playing a chess game, in hopes of being able to control the results. To do politics is to speak and communicate with others for the benefit of taking part in the construction of a common world that one cannot control.

The Expanse and Philosophy: So Far Out Into the Darkness, First Edition. Edited by Jeffery L. Nicholas.

In our set-up, Melissa, a relief worker, and Amos exemplify the behavior typical of politics as making. They measured their odds of surviving an attempt to rescue some of those people stranded in the station against what they could accomplish if they survived. We might be tempted to believe that, when push comes to shove, they were only concerned with their survival. Their fear of dying or their desire to live overwhelmed any other consideration. Yet, this narrowing of our characters' interests seems unfair.

It also evades the more interesting political dilemma.

Their assessment seemed reasonable. The odds were stacked against them if they tried to help the Belters. By contrast, if they ensured their own survival, they would probably have the chance—Melissa as a humanitarian worker and Amos as a member of the crew of the *Rocinante*—of saving many more people in the future. So, choosing a course of action that would likely lead to everyone dying could hardly be considered a superior decision.

But then comes Naomi. In that moment, nothing was more important to her than the chance to speak with her fellow human beings and try to create a common understanding with them, in that situation of despair. Her action, taking the chance of going outside and speaking publicly, is a prime example of politics as doing.

Naomi wanted to achieve a specific result: to save as many people as possible. However, her action could not be justified as a means to an end. Otherwise, she would have to answer: does acting now really maximize the number of lives saved in the long run? This question of strategic calculations is a matter of politics as making.

To properly understand Naomi's behavior, we need to look not at the results she was hoping for, but at what she was doing. We cannot really say that she was risking her life in order to save more people, but we can say that she was willing to put her life on the line in order to talk with the people there.

By going outside, Naomi was affirming, above everything else, our capacity to see and to be seen as human beings, as we try to shape a world that is suitable to us as unique, expressive (political) beings. Her ship was ready for departure. Naomi was locked inside, resigned, but still able to see their singular faces—a teenage girl, a couple, a mother. They were more than just numbers; she was more than a calculator. Naomi decided to act, to address them politically. She had to make herself seen just as much as she was seeing them. Nothing more was needed to justify her acting; nothing less was worth her while. As Arendt might put it, doing politics—the seeing and being seen—is its own justification.[2]

And just like that, the girl, the couple, the mother, and so many others, all managed throughout those brief moments to live together. Each had to face the situation from a different perspective. They had different memories, were burdened by different sorrows and elevated by different joys.

Yet, they each found a way to arrive at a common ground. They framed the situation in a way that allowed them to meet. The mother said goodbye to her child, the boyfriend to his girlfriend. Together, they avoided unnecessary death.

Perhaps Melissa and Amos miscalculated the odds; perhaps the odds could be changed if people just began challenging them. In any case, Naomi decided to act and affirmed a possibility that had become real in herself, the possibility of putting the world—that which we share as unique, political beings—above mere survival. Precisely because of the direness of the situation, precisely because Melissa and Amos had such good reasons not to help those people, Naomi came to a different conclusion: now was the right time for her to act.

Waddling Between Making and Doing Politics

Naomi's example is powerful and heroic, but we should be careful not to mistake her lesson. She is not teaching us to be blind to the consequences of our actions, to live a life of purity guided by abstract principles.

Violence is bad, reprehensible, and against abstract principles. Yet, Naomi twice resorted to violence. Twice she suspended doing politics, as she gave up trying to convince others by the raw appeal of "the living deed and the spoken word."[3] Instead, Naomi opted to get her hands dirty by making politics. On both occasions, her calculated use of physical force was instrumental to her success.

The first time Naomi employed physical strength to acquire strategic advantage was just after deciding to break ranks and expose herself both politically and physically by going outside. She would make sure not to endanger the people inside the ship by closing the door behind her, but Amos, out of concern, grabbed her arms and tried to restrain her. Naomi did not think twice, quickly stabbing Amos with an injection of instantaneous sedative, knocking him out.

Naomi knew that to do politics later, she would have to make politics first.

Yet it's also true that standing up was already doing politics.[4] The people outside could not have known that she had to fight Amos to leave the ship. But the example of her courage and care in exposing herself, which we as spectators had the benefit of watching in full, was fundamental in ensuring her credibility and inspiring the Belters to calm down in that desperate situation.

The second time Naomi employed or, rather, assented to the use of violence was when she enlisted the help of a big and strong Belter, Champa, to organize the people and allow them to save the youngest among them.

Champa came to play a necessary role, akin to Naomi's, taking the baton that Naomi offered him. The other Belters feared Champa due to his physical strength, but also respected him for his ability to talk with and inspire them. Inspire them he did. He was after all just one guy. His physical force alone would not be enough to control a multitude of people trying to get in. Still, he had to get violent a few times. He knocked out a guy who was keen on assaulting Naomi, and he threateningly postured his body before the door to discourage trespassing by the few who might not be ready to accept the resolution of saving the youngest.

Naomi did not protest Champa's use or threat of violence. She wanted to talk with the people outside, to reason with them, to address them as unique, political beings, and she was willing to die for it. But she never once said that, no matter what, they were not allowed to resort to making politics.

Despite our examples, making politics is not all about violence. Making politics refers to any attempt to gain strategic advantage by changing incentives, rather than trying to convince people by the power of deed and word. Better strategizing and leveraging our voices and gestures is already making politics. More importantly, the examples of Naomi and Champa are not abstract justifications of violence. Rather, they remind us that politics cannot be done in the abstract.

Deontological ethics strives for purity and cannot abide a world without definitive abstract rules.[5] By contrast, politics is motivated by a love of the world and of being part of it.[6] Consequently, politics sometimes requires us not just to behave strategically, but to do so in a way that would be wrong in the abstract though right in practice.

Be Mindful Not to Trip Over Your Own Foot

Naomi goes back and forth between doing and making politics, as though politics were some kind of dance. You do it, you make it, and you try not to trip over your own foot. The tricky part is that no ultimate model exists for us to follow. The conditions are always changing, the terrain is moving under our feet, and we must decide anew what to do every time.

Despair not. We can still establish a basic guideline, one often forgotten though easily summarized. Making politics has its place, but it cannot replace or substitute for doing politics. It should not become, as in consequentialism, the metric for judging ethical behavior.[7]

Naomi's example doesn't imply that we shouldn't calculate the risks associated with the courses of action available to us and never behave strategically. She was wary, however, of a second type of risk that arises when trying to manage risks. Though easier to ignore, especially if the situation becomes complicated, we should not overlook this second type of risk.

Naomi understood that our behavior informs our character. Like every other person, her identity as a human being—her capacities, sensibilities, and experiences—was being molded by each individual action in the fight against the protomolecule. In her words: "every shitty thing we do makes the next one that much easier, doesn't it?" ("Cascade").

Getting up from her chair with the ship ready to leave, Naomi knew that later would be too late. If they did not begin practicing a world in which they could live together, its possibility would dwindle. If, due to the urgency of the problems they faced, they kept postponing doing politics, then their very acting would make it impossible for a meaningful world to exist.

This is Naomi's and Arendt's point: as we go about our daily lives, we should be mindful of the risk that, by trying to manage the risks and control the results, we may be left with little of worth, both in ourselves and in our societies.

Naomi's problem was not that she was failing some sort of universal rule and making herself impure; rather, she was losing her balance. She was relying too much on making politics, and this was destroying the possibility of her being seen and seeing others as unique, expressive beings—capable of creating and enduring a world that we may enjoy together.

Neither Naomi nor Arendt can tell us how to behave in any specific situation. In the abstract, beyond our specific personal and societal context, no right answers exist. However, if we want to inhabit a world that gives meaning to our humanity, ultimately, the only thing for us to do is to leave our weapons at the door of our ship. Like Naomi, we must bravely enter the square where people meet, saying, "I am here, unarmed; I see you; please listen to me."

Naomi did not believe the people outside the ship were better than most. Rather, she acted as she did because she acknowledged that they were as imperfect as she was. Naomi could see them in their complexity. She wanted to share a world with them, and she believed they might want the same.

Naomi could not have known that she would be successful or that she would be remembered as an example, that essays, such as this one, would be written about her.[8] She knew, however, that it was up to her to make this world actual by "the living deed and the spoken word."[9] Her very acting had ensured it was true.

Somewhere Beyond Inaros and Holden

Naomi's previous partner, Inaros, and current one, Holden, symbolize her relationship with politics and her search for a better way.

Inaros' origin story is similar to Naomi's. Born in the Belt and oppressed as a Belter by the larger powers of the system, the young Inaros finds in this situation a good cause for which to fight. Naomi, still a young woman, meets him at Ceres Station and falls in love. They have a child together, and they both do and make politics together. Their love and political partnership, however, will not last. Naomi will break personally and politically with him after his decision to destroy a transport ship, killing all people on board.

Inaros serves as an illustration of how damning it can be to neglect doing politics. His life embodies Naomi's fear when she says that "every shitty thing we do makes the next one that much easier." He actually begins playing a different game of power and control, precisely what we should expect to happen whenever politics is reduced to making.[10]

We can sympathize with the young Inaros, his cause, and the difficulties of trying to balance making and doing politics under such unfavorable circumstances. However, once Naomi breaks with him, his motivation becomes clear. It is no longer to fight oppression and injustice but to defeat his opponents, to come out on top as the best strategist and manipulator. Years later he will attempt to destroy Earth, to bring about chaos and war, in spite of there being a clear opportunity, which had been welcomed by so many leaders of the Belt, to set anew their relationship with Earth and Mars. This same logic is prefigured in how he dealt with Naomi. He considers her a traitor and enemy who should be destroyed, defamed, and denied the right of seeing her infant son.

Holden's origin story contrasts with Inaros'. Born on Earth into a rich family co-op, he joins the United Nations Navy but is discharged after refusing to follow an order to destroy a ship that could be trafficking people. Critical of both Earth's and Mars' making of politics, he does not take up the cause politically. Rather, he decides to move to the Belt, far away from everything, taking a job as an executive officer on an ice hauler. We first meet him as the guy who always tries to do the right thing, perhaps without duly considering other risks involved.

As the series develops, Holden gives the impression that he is too focused on his righteousness. This focus explains why he felt the urge to run away; hiding is the only alternative for a true idealist.[11] It's the only way to keep pure.

Forced by circumstances to once again deal with the politics of Earth, Mars, and the Belt, Holden had not learned how to do politics. As a result, in the first five seasons, he is caught up in the logic of making politics. His situation is not easy, and sometimes he seems pushed into taking the role of the guy who alone knows how to deal with everything. Still, this comes too naturally to Holden's idealistic personality.

Naomi will be the one to actually show us how to act as a hero in Arendt's definition, how to escape the reduction of politics by giving up rather than seeking control.

Naomi risks her life to share information with the Belters, to talk with them instead of trying to make it alone. In doing so, she manages to give meaning to their mission and to find what the crew of the *Rocinante* had been searching for all along: a better way to live together. That these scenes do not work as a grand conclusion for the series or the season is fitting, for the doing of politics is not an end. Doing politics is a beginning that will keep on being challenged to recreate anew a world that it cannot control.

Naomi will have to keep trying to regain her footing, not necessarily because she is doing something wrong, but because the conditions are changing. Her lesson, however, stands.

The Burden of the End of the World

One final point remains for us to consider. We have seen that we need to balance the risk of relying too much on making politics with the risk of doing politics. Let's say that the risk of trying to do politics is the destruction of the entire human species by the protomolecule. Wouldn't this give Holden, or whoever else, a whole lot of room to behave strategically as long as he has a fairly good chance of destroying this threat?

You would think so.

Consider this catch, however. People who believe they can get results by behaving strategically tend to underestimate the uncertainty of the situation and overestimate their strategic capabilities. This happens repeatedly throughout *The Expanse*.

As outcasts and pariahs, who had explicitly rejected the politics of their time, Holden and his crew were uniquely positioned to make room for doing politics. However, they often overestimate their ability to defeat uncertainty.

In the beginning, we are right there with Holden; just do it, man. It sucks that you might have to allow yourself not to be so perfect after all, but, I mean, you can destroy this protomolecule before it gets into the wrong hands and save humanity. Just do it, and we can get on with our lives.

Holden does not fail. He achieves his objective every time; yet, somehow, the protomolecule lives on. At some point, should we not just be humbler about the whole ordeal? Perhaps our framing of the situation has been wrong all along?

The protomolecule is a great example of how uncertainty works. If you try to eliminate it, you just ended up creating more. This is true physically, as quantum mechanics has showed us that it is impossible to actually catch a particle. We can either know its place or its velocity but cannot know both.

It's true politically.

The idea that a smart guy should be able to spare people from the troubles of uncertainty by preemptively ruling over all has been with us at least since Plato (428–348 BCE). As Arendt tells us, Plato, after witnessing the citizens of democratic Athens execute Socrates, proposed that a smart philosopher like him should govern as king.[12] But taking political responsibility away from people just creates new political risks and problems.

The strategic attempt by Holden and the crew of the *Rocinante* to destroy uncertainty, as represented by the protomolecule, turned out to be a bad replacement for transparency, dialogue, and sharing responsibility. The crew's attempt to beat the protomolecule and everyone else to the punch, taking on as much responsibility as they could, ended up playing into a game of secrets, nefarious interests, and lack of accountability.

So, what is the lesson? Rather than trying to outmaneuver uncertainty, we can increase our societies' resilience by doing politics, funding a meta-phorical political savings account that enables us to deal constructively with a reality we cannot control. Because uncertainties are here to stay, we need heroes like Naomi, who are brave enough to talk with people, to share the power and the burden, to speak aloud even though they do not know if people will listen to them.

Together, it's up to us to cultivate, nurture, and grow a culture where we can bind ourselves to others, for the benefit of being seen and seeing others as unique, political beings.

Notes

1. Hannah Arendt, *The Human Condition* (Chicago: University of Chicago Press, 1998 [1958]).
2. Ibid., 175–247.
3. Ibid., 206.
4. Ibid., 192–199.
5. Max Weber, *Politics as a Vocation*, in *The Vocation Lectures: Science as a Vocation, Politics as a Vocation*, trans. Rodney Livingstone, ed. David S. Owen and Tracy B. Strong (Indianapolis: Hackett Publishing Company, 2004).
6. Hannah Arendt, *The Promise of Politics*, ed. Jerome Kohn (New York: Schocken Books, 2007), 201–204.
7. Weber, *Politics as a Vocation*.
8. Hannah Arendt, *Lectures on Kant's Political Philosophy*, ed. Ronald Beiner (Chicago: University of Chicago Press, 1992).
9. Arendt, *The Human Condition*, 206.
10. According to Arendt, politics gets captured by this logic whenever someone—usually a man—takes on the role of the all-knowing "patriarchy" (ibid., 220–230).
11. Hannah Arendt, *The Jewish Writings*, ed. Jerome Kohn and Ron H. Feldman (New York: Schocken Books, 2008), 275–298.
12. Arendt, *The Human Condition*, 12, 37, 220–230.

18

The Lives of Naomi Nagata
Intersectionality and the Impossible Choices of Resistance

Guilel Treiber

James Holden, second in command on the *Canterbury*, just watched it explode while on an away mission. He demands Alex, his pilot, to pursue the unknown stealth ship that torpedoed their old lives into the nothingness of space. Holden grows furious with Alex's hesitant reaction. "What's wrong with you? I gave you an order." The engineer Amos calmly replies, "You think rank matters now?" When Holden decides to proceed nonetheless, Naomi breaks the chain of command and takes control of the *Knight*: "we're not going anywhere," she concludes. Later in the same episode, Amos confirms what the viewer suspected. Holden is not really in charge, not yet at least. As they repair the shuttle's broken antenna, he says to Holden, "as far as I'm concerned, she's [Naomi] the cap now." By the end of the episode, even Holden refers to Naomi as sir. Indeed, Naomi clarifies that the four other survivors do not support Holden's video blaming the MCRN for the *Canterbury* explosion. She states wryly, "You do not speak for us." This tension remains throughout the first season of *The Expanse*, ending only with Holden and Miller's tormented return from the hell that Eros has become. Naomi relinquishes her implicit claim for captainship, telling a wounded Holden, "Being in charge is a shit job."

Then how come Naomi isn't the captain of the *Rocinante*? She is more experienced and reasonable than Holden, less impulsive, and not tangled up in a savior complex. Throughout Holden's psychological disintegration following Eros, Naomi is more emotionally stable and reliable. Yet, Naomi's refusal to take command of the *Rocinante* follows not from some implicit bias, but from the universe and storylines of *The Expanse*. Naomi knows she cannot make choices for others. She sees herself, rather, as the resistant who always resisted, remaining faithful to herself.

The Expanse and Philosophy: So Far Out Into the Darkness, First Edition. Edited by Jeffery L. Nicholas.
© 2022 John Wiley & Sons, Inc. Published 2022 by John Wiley & Sons, Inc.

Intersectionality and Betrayal

Let's face it, Naomi Nagata is repeatedly presented as a traitor. She betrays the Belt for Holden, and then Holden for Fred Johnson. She betrays Marco Inaros, only to betray her son, Filip. Naomi even betrays Amos' blind trust in her leadership. Why is that so? Why do Naomi's decisions feel, at times, incoherent? The answer has to do with her identity. Naomi is both the only Belter and the only woman among the *Rocinante*'s crew, and this intersection begins to explain her reluctance to lead. The intersection of race and gender generates specific forms of oppression from which arise possible forms of resistance. In *Nemesis Games*, we read about Naomi's different identities: "It felt like there were many versions of her—the captive, the collaborator, the mother reunited, the mother who went away—and all of them spoke differently. She didn't know which was her real self. If any of them. Probably, it was all."[1]

These different identities give coherence to Naomi's seemingly incoherent acts. She gives the protomolecule to Fred Johnson, not to betray Holden, but to fulfill her commitment to the Belt. She crosses Inaros because it is one way to resist the constraints of her gender. She leaves Filip, not only because she refuses to participate in the murder of innocents for a political agenda, but also to escape Inaros' control of her through her motherhood. Naomi exemplifies the impossible choices that an individual shaped by intersecting systems of oppression has to make to resist them and remain faithful to herself.

The legal scholar Kimberlé Crenshaw coined the term "intersectionality" in 1989 to capture the specific ways in which racism, gender discrimination, and economic inequality shape Black American women's lives. Nowadays, we commonly use the term to describe a set of theories trying to address a recurring gap in feminist theorizing. The end of the twentieth century saw some feminists argue that feminism had failed to address the issues that women of marginalized backgrounds face. Such women, be they black, indigenous, or queer, confront multiple, intersecting systems of oppression in addition to those related to gender.

The actions of individuals who stand at the intersection of such systems of oppression may not seem coherent to an outside observer. Imagine an LGBTQ+ Palestinian living today under the Israeli occupation of the West Bank. As a sexual minority in a traditionalist society, this woman faces exclusion, violence, and the constant threat of death. She may find herself taking refuge in Tel Aviv, a gay haven, but also the financial and cultural capital of the oppressors. She thus betrays the Palestinian liberation struggle and, at the same time, may never be fully included in the LGBTQ+ community in Israel because she is Palestinian. She will continuously face a combination of racism, discrimination, and homophobia both in the community she left (which she identifies with as well) and the community in which she can live her sexuality (which she may learn to love). Hence, not just her wellbeing, but her very survival depends on navigating constantly fluctuating forms of domination and resistance.

Naomi's story highlights the intersections of race, class, and gender, and it clarifies the cost of resistance. Indeed, her every act of resistance seems to betray someone she loves. Naomi is a Belter woman who comes to reject the OPA wing's violent struggle, even if it means losing her son. Later, she sides with an Earther against that same wing. Facing an impossible choice again, she decides to side with the Belt even if the price is losing her teammates and partner's trust. In Naomi's life we see the impossible ethical and political choices an individual shaped by multiple, and sometimes contradicting, systems of oppression must make almost daily. She is a striking representation of the contradictory decisions that individuals make when profoundly shaped by the intersection of race, gender, and class as they navigate their lives. Individuals like Naomi fight both the oppressor and the resistance at once.

Belter Lives Matter?

In the second season episode "Static," Holden and Naomi argue about Miller, who executed Dresden, the mind behind the protomolecule event on Eros. Holden acts as though Miller shot an unarmed man. Naomi, however, sides with Miller. Dresden was not just a bystander, she argues, but a mass murderer, responsible for the loss of a hundred thousand lives in the name of some monstrous version of science. Naomi finds it frustrating that Holden misunderstands Miller's action as an act of revenge. Holden wanted to strike a deal "with a man who casually murdered countless Belters, a man who was a threat to all human life." Miller, though, cared about "all of us," meaning Belters: "that is why Miller shot him." According to Naomi, Miller has as much right to execute Dresden as Holden had to try to save him.

Indeed, both the Eros and Ganymede incidents testify that in the Sol System of *The Expanse*, Belter lives matter less. Some Belters are disposable. Whether in *Caliban's War* or the second season of the television series, the *Weeping Somnambulist* is a striking example. The *Weeping Somnambulist* is a relief ship boarded by Holden and crew in disguise. In the book, the ship lands on Ganymede where Belters are starving while Inner corporations are still sending food to other stations throughout the Sol System. In the television series, the ship is first attacked by criminals trying to hijack it and then shot at by MCRN ships besieging Ganymede, despite carrying 55 refugees on board.

Similarities exist between the situation of Belters and marginalized minorities in our world history, such as Jews in Europe, Palestinians in Israel, or African Americans in the US. However, Belters are not just a different race, a working class, a nation under occupation, or refugees without proper citizenship. They are all of these combined. Different systems of oppression shape them as a collective.

It is a mistake to consider Belters a homogenized group. They divide themselves into different political factions, ethnic origins, and dialects. They also live in a variety of habitats. If anything, what unites them is their long-term existence in low gravity, resulting in different physical traits compared with Inners, such as a thinner and taller frame and a frail bone structure. A crucial unifying factor is precisely the fact that most, if not all, Belters when confronted with an Inner on an individual or organizational level will face some types of discrimination. Their response takes the forms of different kinds of resistance: poaching, gang criminality, the moderate and hard-core factions of the OPA, and eventually, the semi-organized, paramilitary Free Navy. Like Naomi (and perhaps even Miller or Prax), many Belters try to find an individual route between all these conflicting loyalties.

In some cases, such as the events on Anderson Station, the *Weeping Somnambulist* incident, or Eros' purposeful infection, Belters' lives are not counted as fully human. Even those who side with Belters (as Holden does) tend to forget some of them, specifically those occupying the lowest echelons of society, such as the inhabitants of Eros. Another striking example is the series of events following the UN and the Royal Charter Energy's dispute with the Ganymede colonists who have settled Ilus IV. The colonial undertones of the situation are evident. Elvi Okoye's chapter begins with a reminder of the European colonization of the Americas. Okoye, an exobiologist, is one of the scientists on board the *Edward Israel*. The writers set the stage for understanding Okoye, the others on the vessel, and their mission, with the violent colonization of the Americas.

> Centuries before, Europeans had invaded the plague-emptied shell of the Americas, climbing onboard wooden ships with vast canvas sails and the skills of sailors to take them from the lands they knew to what they called the New World. [. . .] Eighteen months ago, Elvi Okoye left Ceres station under contract to Royal Charter Energy. [. . .] The age of adventure has come again, and the old warrior had returned, sword newly sharpened and armor shining after tarnished years.[2]

The passage, brilliantly written, leaves the reader to sort out the analogy. Are the writers of *The Expanse* highlighting the return of an age of adventure and wonder? Or, more likely, are they suggesting that the Belters on Ilus are like those remnants of the Americas' indigenous population facing the superior might of Europe and centuries of enslavement and murder? The Earthers treat the Belters as indigenous populations, imposing on them laws and regulations they do not recognize as legitimate. The oppression does not arise just from the *Edward Israel*'s security chief Adolphus Murtry. His rigid position on ownership and charter rights leads to outright killing. If he were not as rigid, though, the RCE and the UN would have taken control of Ilus as planned, renaming it Terra Nova. The Belters still would have found themselves under the occupation of Earth. The UN had already ignored their claims to the planet; they would have treated them as outsiders, a subjugated population to be ignored or exterminated.

The concept of intersectionality illuminates the ways Belters are subjected to different forms of oppression and discrimination not just as individuals, but as a collectivity. The Belters on Ilus are simultaneously another race and an oppressed working class. Intersectionality refuses to reduce their condition to a single defining type, and instead calls for a more sophisticated analysis of their situation.

Knuckles and the *Augustín Gamarra*

Naomi identifies as a Belter, a group subjected to different and, at times, conflicting forms of oppression; she is also a woman, a group that has faced, and continues to face, other forms of oppression.

Nemesis Games deepens our understanding of Naomi (and the *Rocinante*'s crewmembers') motivations and backgrounds. Her past relations, specifically her relationship with Marco Inaros, set the plot and move it forward. A full picture of Naomi's previous life opens for us, revealing the risks and sacrifices necessary for her escape. Gender becomes a focal point in her struggles. When she chooses to refuse the collective struggle of the Belt, she has to sacrifice her femininity, her motherhood, and her love. Guilt and regret are two psychological mechanisms of submission and control commonly directed against women or sexual minorities, including Naomi. Being a woman in the twenty-fourth century is too much like it is in our times; the Belt specifically seems to have remained mostly a man's world.

The television series introduces Naomi's background story much earlier than the books. The second season of the series ends with Holden discovering Naomi's betrayal. The crew of the *Rocinante* came to possess samples of the protomolecule. They agreed to destroy the samples. Naomi, however, wanting to level the playing field between Earth, Mars, and the Belt, gives them to Fred Johnson. Naomi's betrayal cast a shadow over the relations on board the ship. After a few tense episodes where the viewer is unsure whether Naomi will leave the ship or not, in "Triple Point" she finally explains her action to Holden:

> Jim, I know you feel like I betrayed you. [. . .] I want you to understand why I did it. You know, I used to run with the OPA. I was with someone; he was a romantic, an idealist. A fighter. He always believed what he was doing was right. [. . .] I had a child with him. A baby boy. Filip. The man I loved took

him away because I refused to do what he wanted. I was desperate, wrecked. And then finally, I shut it all off and I signed to the *Canterbury* to disappear.

Naomi does not tell Holden about her suicide attempt or her role in the destruction of the *Augustín Gamarra*. But she does tell her story to Lucia, one of Ganymede's refugees on Ilus, a full season later, in Episode 5 of the fourth season aptly titled "Oppressor":

The first one we tried was the *Augustín Gamarra*. [. . .] It was the one that blew up in the docks at Luna, because the man I loved, the father of my child, used the code to overload the reactor. We killed 516 people and he wanted to do it again. [. . .] I chose not to see what kind of man my lover was until it was too late. Then when I told him I'd never help him again, it was the last time he let me see my little boy. I almost walked out an airlock. Being dead seemed better.

Nemesis Games reveals even more about her past as an unwilling terrorist of sorts. The book tells the story of her abusive relationship with Inaros, her failed suicide attempt when she thought she had no way to evade his control, and the abandonment of her son, Filip, when the options were down to having a dead or a gone mother. Unlike other "bad men" she grew up around, Inaros "never hit her, never forced himself on her, never threatened to shoot her or throw her out an airlock or pour acid in her eyes."[3] As though she needed to feel grateful for that, Inaros wanted in return to have complete control over her body and mind. A manipulative, abusive partner, he made her believe "she was the one being unreasonable, irrational."[4] Like a caged animal, the old Naomi, who joined a collective political struggle, would have put on fear or weakness to avoid Inaros' wrath.

The intersection of Naomi's gender and identity as a Belter causes great suffering, leading her to attempt taking her own life. In the end, she leaves, trying to vanish onboard an anonymous ice freighter. Her conflicting motivations concerning what happened to the *Augustín Gamarra* highlight the contradictory demands certain systems of oppression require and the impossibility of resisting them. Being a Belter, she wants to participate in the struggle toward the liberation of the Belt. However, Inaros' leadership and plans cause her to resist. Being a loving mother, she wants to remain with her child, a child she wants to protect from the violence of the struggle for liberation. To remain with her child, she must go on killing innocents. In the end, her choice is reduced to killing herself or leaving.

Years later, in *Nemesis Games* and in Season 5, she confronts her son, who played an active part in the destruction of Earth and the genocidal murder of more than 250 million people. "The only right you have with anyone in life," she explains, "is the right to walk away."[5] Whether walking away means killing oneself or abandoning all, it is clear that Naomi thought, at the time, that only this possibility existed when confronting intersecting systems of oppression for the first time.

The television series suggests a different way to walk away, however. The crew aboard the *Rocinante* consists of Inners with whom she has deep, meaningful relationships of love and friendship. Her relationships with the crew provide a way to rejoin the struggle for Belters' dignity and freedom. After Holden hears Naomi's confession and asks why she did not tell him her story, she says:

> I don't know. I just couldn't. But then Eros happened, and Ganymede, seeing all those Belters suffering and you cared so much. It made it hard for me to stay numb. I imagined Filip amongst them. It woke me up. I'm not sorry I gave the protomolecule to the Belt, but I'm sorry for the way I did it.

For the series' writers, Naomi's way back to the struggle (though a different one) and to a more serene relation to motherhood goes through finding a new family.

The fifth season of *The Expanse* revolves, like the *Nemesis Games* book, around Naomi's betrayals, specifically those of her past coming to haunt her. To some extent Cyn, Marco, Filip or even Karal all feel they have been betrayed by Naomi in the past and understand her departure as such. However, the fifth season of the series shows clearly that once Naomi's side has been definitively chosen, i.e., her "family" onboard the *Rocinante*, she stops feeling guilty for leaving Marco and Filip years before. In "Tribes," when Filip comes to confront her after she attempts to kill Marco, this becomes evident to the spectators as well as to Filip and, perhaps, even to Naomi herself. When Filip tells her, "You deserve to die for what you did," he unknowingly reveals to her that she saved the *Rocinante* and Holden. Naomi answers, relieved, "I can tell my people are all right." Filip, angered, replies, "Your people. . . You don't even think of our family as your own anymore." Naomi indeed, content and calm, answers, "I guess I don't." In Episode 7, "Oyedeng," when Marco wants her to express shame for her departure 16 years earlier, she assumes her actions perhaps for the first time and states the "relief" she felt for leaving him outweighed the pain of leaving Filip. As she states later in the same episode, when losing Filip, she thought she lost her life. Leaving was the only way to reclaim it, to resist the conditions she was forced to face. Indeed, once she accepts during the chapter her fidelity to her new, unorthodox "family," this fidelity transcends all previous loyalties, old friendships, and even the relation of a mother to her son.

Perhaps we can apply Naomi's solution in our world. Perhaps we can resist intersecting forms of oppression by creating new bonds of solidarity that are not limited by gender, race, or socioeconomic status. The Naomi of the *Roci* constructs new alliances that succeed in bridging the gaps she couldn't bridge on her own. These bridges enable her to renew the energies needed to struggle for both her home and her son. Though she wonders for a moment if she is only "a pet Belter"[6] on the *Rocinante*, she does not fall into the same mind games as her younger self. She sees Inaros for what he is, "a monster,"[7] "an egomaniac and a sadist."[8] Her friends on the *Rocinante* are not like that. Her bonds with them represent hopeful resistance.

Notes

1. James S. A. Corey, *Nemesis Games* (New York: Orbit Books, 2015), 268.
2. James S. A. Corey, *Cibola Burns* (New York: Orbit Books, 2014), ch. 2.
3. *Nemesis Games*, 363.
4. Ibid.
5. Ibid., 270. See Episode 7, Season 5 for a similar dialogue with Filip. Here Naomi states, "But walking away was the only choice I had left. . . Walking away is the only choice anyone ever has."
6. *Nemesis Games*, 265.
7. Ibid., 269.
8. Ibid., 368.

19

Risky Tradeoffs in
The Expanse

Claire Field and Stefano Lo Re

Chrisjen Avasarala faces a difficult choice when deciding whether to nuke the *Sojourner*: waiting to identify the vessel could put the Earth's entire defense system at risk, but an immediate strike could mean attacking an innocent civilian ship. Avasarala's choice is a moral one; it is concerned with doing the right thing. Although often difficult to make, moral choices are made easier by their focus on one type of value, moral value.

Sometimes, however, we must choose between radically different types of values—values that are not even in the same ballpark. In addition to moral values, there are aesthetic values, prudential values, epistemic values, scientific values, and others. How should we go about making a decision when competing, but apparently incommensurable values are at stake? *The Expanse* doesn't provide an easy answer to this vexing question, but considering conflicts of values on the show can help us reason about tough choices in real life.

Epistemic Value vs. Moral Value: Evil Scientists

Jules-Pierre Mao, for example, must decide whether the protomolecule research justifies risking the lives of the children he met on Io. Is the risk worth it? Jules-Pierre Mao's interest in protomolecule research is motivated primarily by power and wealth. Insofar as his self-interest leads him to disregard the suffering inflicted on his human guinea pigs, he is an evil character. The scientists involved in his projects appear unconcerned with the moral consequences of protomolecule research. Instead, they seem to be driven exclusively by epistemic values—such as knowledge and understanding.

Antony Dresden's hubristic aspiration is captured in an exchange between him, Jim Holden, Fred Johnson, and Joe Miller in "Doors & Corners." Dresden claims that by mastering the protomolecule we will be

The Expanse and Philosophy: So Far Out Into the Darkness, First Edition. Edited by Jeffery L. Nicholas.
© 2022 John Wiley & Sons, Inc. Published 2022 by John Wiley & Sons, Inc.

able to "apply it to everything" and "become our own gods." When Holden asks him, "And that justifies all of this?" meaning incidents like Eros, Dresden exclaims, "Of course it does!" For Dresden, the loss of life on Eros is worth the sacrifice for a chance at mastering the protomolecule. This fits with his pursuit of knowledge as an epistemic value. Dresden, we know, went a long way to overcome what he perceived as limitations to scientific research: after all, he underwent transcranial magnetic hyperstimulation, as all Protogen researchers did, in order to see human lives as expendable in the name of scientific progress.

Lawrence Strickland did not have to undergo transcranial magnetic hyperstimulation in order to show a complete disregard for the life of human children—for example, the deception and lack of consent involved in experimentation for Project Caliban. This alone would make him morally worse than Dresden. He understands the moral reasons that are sufficient to quit the project, yet he chooses to live in denial. Not only that, his awareness of the morally abhorrent nature of his research only leads him to attempt to shield Jules-Pierre Mao from the horrible consequences of the experiment. He is concerned not with the atrocities he is committing, but with the fact that they might lead his sponsor to shut down the project. In fact, even Mao has a moment of moral remorse, though only after he forms a bond with Mei and sees the horrible consequences of the experiment with his own eyes. When that happens, an unfazed Strickland tells him, "I'm sorry that you had to see that." And when Strickland tries to convince him not to stop the project, Mao reveals to him what he knew all along: "we're torturing children" ("Assured Destruction").

Aesthetic Value vs. Moral Value: Mad Scientists, Awestruck Reverends

Unlike Dresden, Paolo Cortázar does not exactly volunteer for transcranial magnetic hyperstimulation. However, once he undergoes the treatment he decides to remain under the effects of the mind-altering drugs permanently, and he no longer has qualms about extreme human experimentation. In "Static," when confronted by Holden, Johnson, and Amos about the Eros incident, Cortázar shows no concern for human suffering or for Dresden's death. With his mind focused solely on the protomolecule research, he asks, "What about the project?" "Are you taking up the project?" Nor does he understand why anyone would want to develop a vaccine. His exchange with Amos later in the same episode reveals how obsessive fascination with the protomolecule has replaced any sensitivity to even the most basic moral values. Julie Mao was not "dead," but "beautiful," even "becoming." When Holden describes the state of the protomolecule on the *Anubis*, Cortázar is deeply upset. But his upset is like the reaction one might have to the potential death of an extraordinary or irreplaceable specimen, or to the extinction of a species. In fact, whereas Dresden's interest in the protomolecule is pragmatic and transhumanistic in nature—aimed at overcoming our limitations—Cortázar's curiosity is a child-like wonder, verging on the aesthetic. At the end of Season 5 we see a happier, enthusiastic Cortázar on Laconia speaking of "beautiful results" ("Nemesis Games"). More than a scientist, Cortázar seems like a minister devoted to a natural god.

Anna Volovodov, though not wholly innocent, is markedly different from Cortázar. Her curiosity about the Ring, fed by her discussions with Kolvoord ("It Reaches Out"), leads her to ask Tilly to help her stay aboard the *Thomas Prince* ("Intransigence"). Anna struggles to understand this desire to remain. First, she tells Tilly, "It's the only miracle that's happened in my lifetime. And it's not a miracle–miracle, but . . . it changes everything, and to be so close and then just turn away? It seems wrong." However, pushed to reveal her real motivation, Anna eventually agrees with Tilly's words: "You want to indulge in a selfish desire to be a part of something amazing." Previously, Anna willingly sacrificed her own prudential interests in order to do the right thing when she decided to stay at the UN instead of going back to her family. But things are different on the *Thomas Prince*. Nono reminds Anna, "First, it was a few weeks away to write a speech at the UN, now it's months at the edge of the solar system?" ("Delta-V"). Nono's tone upsets Anna, perhaps precisely because it reveals to Anna that her main motivation to be on the ship was never moral (providing pastoral support), but rather the aesthetic desire to experience the sublime.

Anna could have made a morally better decision, as her curiosity about the Ring leads her to neglect her family. But maybe her decision was not wrong. Perhaps it is sometimes okay to prioritize aesthetic value or self-interested pursuits. However, the desire to understand, or even just to witness the mystery of the Ring, leads Anna to ignore Jordaan Nemeroff's repeated calls for help, resulting in his suicide ("Dandelion Sky"). She thus fails at her chosen purpose in life—helping others in need. However we decide to consider competing values, Anna's case is problematic.

Epistemic Value vs. Prudential Value: Intrepid Scientists

Sometimes, the quest for scientific progress demands that we go to extremes, taking great risks to advance our understanding beyond its current limits. The political arrangement of *The Expanse*—in particular, colonization of the Belt—is made possible only by the speed of the Epstein drive and the death of its inventor. Sometimes, scientific progress conflicts with the prudential value of self-preservation. Dr. Iturbi and Colonel Janus exemplify this conflict in their attitude toward the protomolecule. Iturbi complains that Janus "lacks imagination" and "can only conceive of the world in terms of things he's already seen" ("Paradigm Shift"). This attitude, as Avasarala points out in the same episode, is a useful skill for talking to politicians. However, it is likely to be far less useful when it comes to understanding an alien substance that defies the known laws of physics. It is Iturbi who is more willing to leave his comfort zone to confront the uncertainty of things we have not already seen. He eventually convinces Janus to further investigate the mystery with him, although this means becoming an experiment themselves as the protomolecule takes apart the *Arboghast* and its crew in order to understand more about human beings ("Caliban's War").

To sacrifice everything for the sake of knowledge in this way requires a truly scientific mindset. From the beginning, Holden lacks any such interest in the purely epistemic value of knowledge for the sake of knowledge. Although he is granted special access to the mysteries of the protomolecule, he would much prefer not to be in such a position: he does not appear to value his privileged status. The conflict between the prudential and the epistemic plays out again when Dr. Elvi Okoye chastises him for not appreciating his direct line of communication to the protomolecule. In "A Shot in the Dark," she tells Holden: "You make it sound like a burden. . . You are being given knowledge and answers that humans have only dreamt about." When he complains, "I've also been given horrific nightmares and visions of death I can never unsee," Okoye replies, "To me, that sounds like an acceptable tradeoff. I have traveled billions of kilometers to be the first exobiologist to study the most basic forms of extraterrestrial life, and you, on the other hand, are the only person in human history with a direct line of communication to an advanced alien species, and you're annoyed?. . . Any scientist would kill to change places with you. I know I would." Okoye would happily exchange Holden's nightmares for the blessing that he insists on seeing as a curse.

Conflicts Between Values

How should we understand the conflicts between the incommensurable values that we have mentioned—prudential, moral, epistemic, and aesthetic?

One way to understand the conflicts is as dilemmas. Dilemmas are situations where whatever we do, we do something wrong. For example: what would you do if you had to kill either your father or your mother, otherwise both your parents would die? This relatively straightforward case exemplifies an intra-domain moral dilemma: either decision would ultimately be morally wrong, even if you have reasons pulling you in either direction. Building on this, we can understand inter-domain conflicts in the same way. Consider an example in which moral value and aesthetic value conflict: suppose you had to kill your parents in order to save the last existing copy of *The Expanse* book series. Killing your parents would be morally wrong, but destroying *The Expanse* would be aesthetically wrong. Whichever option you choose, you are doing something wrong: it's a lose–lose situation.

A second way of understanding conflicts between values is to see them as situations in which it doesn't really matter whether you prioritize moral, prudential, epistemic, or aesthetic value. Perhaps these are situations in which individuals are free to decide for themselves, in accordance with their own idiosyncrasies. Just as it doesn't really matter whether you choose chocolate or strawberry ice cream for dessert, perhaps it doesn't really matter whether you choose moral value over epistemic value. The James Holdens of the world would choose a life without nightmares, the Elvi Okoyes would kill for them. Perhaps both are equally permissible choices, based on the individual's unique preferences.

There is a third way to understand conflicts between values. Perhaps there is a definite right answer about what we should do. For example: you should not kill your parents, because they are more important than *The Expanse*. Perhaps moral value is always more important than aesthetic value. Or, perhaps we would need much more aesthetic value to outweigh the wrongness of killing your parents: not just *The Expanse*, but the Mona Lisa and the rest of the contents of the Louvre too. Importantly, making the right choice does not guarantee freedom from a lingering sense of regret about the choice that you didn't make. You wouldn't feel good about killing your parents no matter how clearly you reasoned about the values involved in the decision.

We now have three ways of understanding value conflicts: as situations in which every option is forbidden, situations in which every option is permissible, or situations in which some options are obligatory and some options are forbidden. According to the first two options, the conflicts are not resolvable, and you can't do much more than decide whether to be pessimistic or optimistic about your predicament. Pessimists will think that these situations are dilemmas, and the human condition is fraught with choices in which everything we do is wrong. Optimists will think that it doesn't really matter what we choose. Both of these answers are frustrating because they don't help us decide what to do when values conflict. However, if some options are right and others are wrong, then the conflicts are resolvable, and making the right choice is important.

So, how should we do this?

One answer is that we can rank values in terms of their importance. Of course, people will disagree about rankings. Oscar Wilde (1854–1900) was committed to aesthetic value over everything else! You, by contrast, might be committed to moral value over everything else. If moral value is always more important than epistemic value, then the decision whether to conduct purely theoretical scientific research by torturing children is an easy one: never do it. Perhaps even sending the *Arboghast* to explore the protomolecule crater is morally wrong: that money could have been spent supporting Earth's many destitute citizens. But, this would mean that we always have to sacrifice the opportunity to gain significant scientific knowledge if it conflicts with even the smallest amount of moral value. Even the most significant scientific breakthrough would not be justifiable if it meant, say, failing to return a library book, or breaking a promise to meet a friend for lunch, or stepping on someone's toes. Moreover, the idea that we can rank values suggests that they share a common currency—a sort of overarching or "meta" value that we can use to adjudicate conflicts between them. After all, how could we say that, for example, epistemic value is in any sense "better" or "worse" than moral value if there was no way to measure them against each other?

The idea that all these different kinds of value can be traded with a common currency is tempting. But contra Keats, beauty is not truth; and it certainly isn't goodness, as Tolstoy says. Epistemic, moral, prudential, and aesthetic values are very different.

Comparing all the radically different human values is worse than comparing apples and oranges. Apples and oranges, at least, are both kinds of fruit. We can compare how they taste, or how well they go with a particular meal. To push the analogy further: while it is fine to like apples more than oranges, it is less obviously fine to like beauty more than truth, or truth more than goodness. In some contexts it might be appropriate to prioritize one rather than another—truth in the laboratory, beauty in the art studio. Well-rounded humans value each to the appropriate degree and in the appropriate way.

Perhaps, then, we should be pluralists about value. We should simply accept that our lives involve many incommensurable values, and which value takes precedence depends on the situation. Epistemic value is important when doing scientific research, but moral value is important when governing. Although pluralism respects the specific nature of each sphere, it offers little practical guidance on how to resolve specific conflicts between values. How can we even begin to think of weighing values against each other if they all use different scales?

Risky Tradeoffs

There is a further difficulty. When deciding whether to prioritize, say, moral or epistemic value, we cannot know exactly how things will turn out. If we are unsure about which kind of value is important, then we are taking a risk that we are getting it wrong. This puts us in a different kind of predicament—even if we get it right, we are being reckless!

For example, if I think that a particular situation is one where epistemic value is the most important consideration, then I would think that risking life and limb is justified. However, what if I am uncertain about this? This is likely: cases of this sort are complex, and often it is difficult to work out which kind of value is more important. If I am uncertain, then I am taking a risk that my sacrifice of one kind of value in pursuit of another is correct. I am risking doing something wrong. Such action displays a kind of recklessness: someone who ignores the pull of moral value at the expense of other kinds of value is reckless about moral value. They display a culpable indifference to it.

This makes tradeoffs between values difficult: even if the risk pays off, a residue remains—taking a decision to prioritize one kind of value demands sacrificing other kinds of value. Of course, no such residue appears if we are certain about how the values line up. But, certainty is no good without good reason to be certain. Cortázar and Dresden are certain that their research into the protomolecule justifies all the moral costs, or perhaps that the moral costs are negligible. Either way, their certainty is suspicious—it does not seem to be based on good reasons. In the end, certainty might be a risk as well.

Perhaps the lesson to take from all this is that avoiding risk is impossible. Sometimes, like Holden on Tycho station ("Churn"), we must go through life pushing buttons as we find them, accepting the risks that come, and hoping we manage to make the right choice when the time comes.

Sixth Orbit
RIDING THE *ROCI*

20

The Long Dark Night of The Hat

The Metaphysical Fate of Detective Josephus Miller and His Headwear

S. W. Sondheimer

Fedora in hand, Josephus Miller, Star Helix detective and cheddar thief, pulls off one more run-around the rules. The dead, so the rules say, must appear to the living wearing whatever it was they died in. But when Miller pops in on an unsuspecting Jim Holden, his Eros vac suit is nowhere to be seen.

An anomaly, to be certain. And one that has implications for the state of Miller's soul.

For if clothes make the man, then style is an integral part of him, and the ability to adopt someone's signature look implies there is something of *them* in *you*. If the protomolecule-constructed Investigator can choose Miller's civilian clothes over his ghostly ones, then it must logically contain a part of him. If Miller is dead, only one part of him could be left.

His soul.

But is it even possible for the Investigator to possess some or all of Joe Miller's soul? Does the soul exist? If it does, does it survive death? Can it be absorbed by another entity?

The Investigator, as constructed by the protomolecule to interface with Holden, looked like Miller. It sounded like Miller. It (usually) acted like Miller. But was anything of Miller actually animating the construct, or was it nothing more than an elaborate facsimile, programmed with Miller's code insofar as the protomolecule understood it? Has there been any conservation of Miller's metaphysical mass or was his Miller-ness lost to the universe when Eros crashed into Venus?

Does the Investigator have a right to don the hat?

In this corner, we have the Platonists, believers in the born-again, avatars of the afterlife, evincers of the eternal ever after!

In the far corner, you'll see the Aristotelians, denizens of the demise, lords of this life, proponents of the final passage!

The Expanse and Philosophy: So Far Out Into the Darkness, First Edition. Edited by Jeffery L. Nicholas.
© 2022 John Wiley & Sons, Inc. Published 2022 by John Wiley & Sons, Inc.

Hemlock and Haberdashery:
Plato and Socrates

We begin in ancient Greece where men were men and the women were, for the most part, half-baked, embryonic beings incapable of generating a coherent thought unless helped along by a guardian with dangly bits. Those men with their dangly bits believed something ineffable animated the body, allowing them to philosophize and to reach beyond the meatsack into the great beyond. That was, of course, the soul.

Plato (428–348 BCE) had a great deal to say about the nature and function of the soul, much of it inspired by Socrates' (469–399 BCE) death by hemlock. According to Plato, the body and soul are two separate entities. In fact, the body is a hindrance to the soul in its pursuit of knowledge. When the body dies, the soul experiences what modern "sage" Gwyneth Paltrow refers to as a "conscious uncoupling," becoming purified in the process. What happens to this soul? Plato suggests that if souls exist in life, they must necessarily exist in death as the two states mirror one another. If they exist in death, they must travel to some place to await reincarnation, because, if they have lived and died, they must live again (I don't make the philosophy, I just untangle it) lest existence run out of souls to animate humans and animals.

Fervor and Fedoras: Aristotle

Where Plato had an opinion, Aristotle (384–322 BCE) was unable to resist making his own known, which, in the matter of the soul, runs counter to that of his teacher.

The soul, Aristotle hypothesized, is a sort of non-corporeal nervous system that directs sensory perception, movement, and thought, a great blob of *form* that animates a *matter*, entirely useless without a vessel to fill. In direct opposition to Plato and Socrates, Aristotle believed the physical and metaphysical comprised an integrated system, and, therefore, the soul could not exist separate from a body. Life after death was not possible in his philosophy; without soul to enliven it, matter was just so much proto-molecule skulking around the guts of the *Rocinante* waiting for the Investigator to come along and turn it into a hat. The soul died with the body and that was that; the end of existence without so much as a peek at what was behind the curtain guarding the mysteries of the universe. A life lived and all for what little insight you gained while slogging your way through the drama and blood and suffering on this here ball of dirt.

Bummer.

Spiritual Guts: Aquinas

Medieval theologian, and later saint, Thomas Aquinas (1225–1274), really, *really* tried to tint the stained-glass windows rose by combining the Platonic and Aristotelian philosophies on the nature of our spiritual guts. Or maybe he was just trying to one hundred percent hedge every possible "what if?" in case the god of which his undoubtedly heavy bible spoke was actually the ancient and pissed-off deity that smote the Amalekites and forced his Chosen People to wander in the desert for forty years after what was really, in the grand scheme, an *itty-bitty* infraction.

In the end, however, Thomas leaned much more heavily on Aristotle than he did on Plato when formulating his own theory of post-demise, body–soul logistics. The soul could survive death in an incorruptible and immaterial form. Sounds Platonic, I know, but hear me out: it could do that, but that soul would have limited functionality until it was reunited with its original host body via resurrection. Thus, for Thomas, eternal life was only an option provided one found existence as a zombie acceptable. Just kidding. But no one, nor any soul, was going anywhere until the Second Coming, and even then, true existence was predicated on reintegration with not simply *a* body but the soul's *original* vessel.

The Grudge Match: Philosophy vs. The Protomolecule

And there's the bell!

What is the Investigator? Is it a program, lines of code fused with electronic echoes of a dead man? Or is it a construct inhabited by Josephus Miller's soul? What's the difference?

Does it matter?

Of course it matters!

It matters because only the being known as Josephus Miller gets to wear the hat Miller stole from his childhood friend, "Semi" Sematimba. If the Investigator has nothing of Joe Miller in him other than stray electrical patters, lines of random code, then he is no Miller and must, therefore, relinquish said accessory, and *identity*, forthwith.

And what is it that ultimately determines a being's identity, at least according to philosophers and theologians?

The soul.

It stands to reason, then, and to logic, that the Investigator, to have a right to Miller's identity, and thus his haberdashery, must have at least a *part* of his soul.

So. Does it? Is the Investigator in possession of even the most *minute* fraction of Josephus Miller's essential self? His inherent Millerness?

If it is, our philosophical tag team will find it.

Gentlemen, do your worst. Or best. Depending on which answer our readers are hoping for. . .

We know the Investigator doesn't have a physical body. We know because he appears to Jim Holden and speaks only to Holden even when other people are present in the same confined space (such as Holden's quarters or the bridge of the *Roci*). We think at first that the construct might be a hallucination caused by brain damage from Holden's time in the protomolecule's historical matrix or residual guilt related to Miller's death. As the story progresses, however, the Investigator starts to give Holden information about how the protomolecule's creators' tech is responding to the ways which humans are fucking with it in real time; information Holden wouldn't, and couldn't, have received from the matrix. It also has a goal: to reach the phenomenon below the surface of Ilus, a phenomenon Holden isn't, at the beginning of their journey, aware exists.

As hallucinations come from one's own mind, they cannot, by definition, know things the person creating them doesn't, which defines the Investigator as an entity *independent* of Holden.

That does not, however, mean it is who it appears to be.

Holden remains the only living being who can see and hear the Investigator in its Miller form throughout *The Expanse* Season 4, which suggests that, while independent, it isn't a *physical* being and that has implications for the nature of the force animating it. If, per Plato, the conservation of Miller's soul were necessary for the continuation of the human race and awaiting resurrection in a new body, it would, by necessity, resist being combined with a non-corporeal entity, for to do so would be counter to the soul's purpose. And if conserving part of Miller's mass, as it were, is a prerequisite for *being* Miller, and thus having the right to wear the hat, the Investigator's lack of physical form disqualifies it as a proper vessel. That on both the *Roci* and Ilus the Investigator is subject to glitches during which it ripples visually, alternates between rigid and colloquial speech patterns, repeats rote stories and truly interacts further proves that it has neither a stable personality nor a stable form, especially since, when it does reappear after such episodes, it is consistently as an idealized, rigid Miller-puppet rather than the slouchy, surly, unpredictable Joe Miller that Holden, and the rest of us, know so well.

And the Investigator takes one on the chin from Plato!

But Aristotle comes in with a left hook!

If Joe Miller's body died when Eros crashed into Venus or before that from exposure to the protomolecule, and if Plato was wrong (of course Plato was wrong, for gods' sakes, he was wrong about everything, I'm *Aristotle*, fools), then his soul hasn't simply drifted off to await the next round on the wagon wheel. No, no, it too is deceased! Dead as Diogo's uncle (too soon?). Inert before the blue goo even thought to create the Investigator. Like the useful if inept sensory processing system once used by Miller's body to observe *it*, the protomolecule had watched Miller: it watched him search for Julie on Eros, meet up with the *Roci*'s crew. It watched him mourn her loss and observed him while he and Holden fought to survive. It learned his mannerisms as he integrated with Naomi, Alex, and Amos and it saw his compassion when he found Julie once more at the end. Saw, but didn't *understand*. Copied, hijacked, reused but didn't *comprehend*. And so the Investigator's shell was capable of tasting the rain or hearing the voices on Eros, but no matter how full the emperor's bag of tricks, no matter how decent his wardrobe, the ghost in the shell had no animus.

Round one to the philosophers!

The protomolecule is on the ropes, folks, but this fight isn't over yet. Oh, it's escaped the philosophers, gotten behind them! Wow, what a hit! Plato is looking a little unsteady but it's too early to count anyone out. Let's see how they counter.

Let's say, for the sake of argument, that the Investigator does have Miller's soul. That Thomas Aquinas was right (gah, typing that actually hurt me physically) and the soul survives physical death in a reduced state and floats around doing . . . stuff . . . while it waits for the Second Coming and reunion with the body. While it's waiting, the body comes to irreparable harm; zombie apocalypse, walking dead, double tap, burn the corpse kind of harm (may as well stick with the theme).

Oooh, gut punch. Thomas is on the mat.

But he's up! An exception has been made! The Power That Is has decided, in this one case, for whatever reason (my Talmud teacher liked, "He's God, he can do what he wants." I dropped that class. And synagogue. And religious Judaism. I mean, honestly) to allow for the substitution of a metal . . . amalgamation. The Investigator is in the bowels of an ancient structure on Ilus, staring down the eye or mouth or . . . some other weird orifice created by the protomolecule creators . . . and if no one closes it, a lot of people are going to die. Whether or not some of them deserve it (ahem, Murtry), is another matter entirely. What would Joe Miller do?

Joe Miller would sacrifice himself to save everyone. We know this because he's already done it. Holden believes the Investigator is Miller, has Miller's soul even if that's not the word he uses, because he sees this tendency toward self-sacrifice, among others, appear at intervals in his interactions with the Investigator. But are they real? Is demonstrating these traits a conscious decision the Investigator is making or is it part of the proto-programming? Part of the phantoms and echoes the protomolecule absorbed from Miller as it studied him?

The Investigator starts the cascade of disasters in Ilus. That cascade traps two warring factions in a small, underground space in the middle of a medical emergency, low on supplies and at the mercy of deadly fauna. Joe Miller certainly had the capacity to be an epic dick, but would he have allowed any of that to happen had he been in control of the Investigator?

Resounding no.

Would he have brought Holden, who trusted him, who counted him a friend, who mourned his loss, anywhere near the portal?

No.

Would he have allowed Elvi, who was completely innocent in the whole debacle, who had risked her own life to save others the same way Joe Miller had when he was still alive, to end up in the middle of his final battle?

Absolutely not.

Does the Investigator save the day in the end?

He does but barely, the protomolecule yeeting him out of his disaster form only halfway to his destination. And the manner in which the Investigator saves the Ilus contingent is almost identical to the way Miller saves humanity when he diverts Eros; throwing himself on a grenade and hoping it works. The method doesn't take independent thought the second time around because it's already been done.

The Investigator is down.

The soul of Josephus Miller is at rest.

The philosophers claim the hat.

The Investigator Must, Therefore, Relinquish the Hat

Ultimately, the existence of the soul and an afterlife are matters of faith. We can, as individuals, choose to believe in them or not. It's interesting to consider whether seeing more of the universe, what's through the Ring Gates, as it were, will make humanity more or less invested in the divine, whether a growing understanding of the great machine's workings will give us a thirst for discovery or a need for comfort.

Insofar as the Investigator and its right to the hat are concerned, the general consensus, whether from the Platonic or Aristotelian side of the divide, is that Joe Miller's soul may be awaiting reincarnation into a different human body, gone back to its creator, or may be as deceased as his body, but it ain't part of what makes the Investigator tick. Regardless of the specific philosophy, Western thought seems to agree that the Investigator might have access to echoes of Miller and perhaps even to some of his memories, but not to his essence, not to his soul. And as that fedora he stole from Simi was so important to Detective Josephus Miller's fundamental *Millerness*, and to keeping the rain off his head, we demand the Investigator relinquish it forthwith or a party will be sent to recover it by any means necessary.

If we can find it. On the other side of that portal.

Or whatever the Hell that thing was.

Possibly actual Hell.

But that's another chapter altogether.

21

Between Worlds
The Multiplicitous Subjectivity of Naomi Nagata

Eric Chelstrom

Once upon a time there had been a Belter girl named Naomi Nagata, and now there was a woman. Even though the difference between the two had been created a day, an hour, a minute at a time, the Venn diagram of the two almost didn't overlap. What could be cut away, she'd cut years ago. What remained did so in spite of her efforts. For the most part, she could work around them.[1]

In *The Expanse*, Naomi Nagata, the *Roci*'s XO and engineering marvel, is a person caught between worlds, someone torn in multiple directions by the social situations she finds herself immersed in. Throughout the series, she embodies *multiplicitous subjectivity*. The basic idea of multiplicitous subjectivity is that each of us can experience being multiple selves at once, depending on the varied, overlapping contexts one finds oneself in. To say the self is multiplicitous is to argue that there is not just one thing that is one's "true self," but to acknowledge that who we are shifts and adapts to the various, sometimes overlapping social contexts we find ourselves in.

Directly or indirectly, our histories affect who each of us is. The interconnectedness of my history with others means that as the world and people around me change, I change. Because the people around me affect the context I find myself in, in different contexts I might be a different person. Holden, for example, doesn't act with the same vulnerability in the world outside the *Roci* as he does with its crew or his family. Further, the way people or society in general think of various groups affects their possibilities, often undermining questions of self-worth and limiting possibilities through biases. If the dominant parts of society systematically refused to recognize you and people like you as a person, you could be subjected to mistreatment like the Belters.

The Expanse and Philosophy: So Far Out Into the Darkness, First Edition. Edited by Jeffery L. Nicholas.
© 2022 John Wiley & Sons, Inc. Published 2022 by John Wiley & Sons, Inc.

Self and World

If you were one born in the Belt, you would have a fragile skeleton, extended body with limited muscle mass, and you might experience the gravity we take for granted on Earth as a painful kind of torture.[2] Most of us recognize that, born in different circumstances, we'd be different people. We'd hold different beliefs, have different attitudes, have different bodies even. Yet, sometimes our imaginations are too limited to capture how radical these differences might be and what they would mean for who we are.

In *Nemesis Games* Naomi Nagata experiences the kind of inner conflict of the self that can occur in moving between worlds. She is tricked into helping her estranged son Filip and abducted by Marco Inaros and a radical faction of the OPA. Marco's crew still see Naomi as if "she was the girl she'd been, like they could all ignore the years and the differences, fold her back in as though she'd never gone away."[3] They believe she's forgotten who she really is, having betrayed her Belter values by crewing with Inners and falling in love with one. For Naomi's part, she is frightened by how easily she was able to slip back into being part of Marco's world, how easy she found it to blend back into a life she knows to be wrong. It unsettles her because it feels "as if she'd never been anyone else. Hiding her fear and her outrage slipped back on so easily, it was as if she'd never stopped. It made her wonder whether perhaps she hadn't."[4]

Naomi's possible relationship to the OPA is first exposed during interrogations on the MCRN *Donnager* ("Remember the Cant"). The first season confirms some connection to the OPA as Naomi reads OPA markings to navigate the service tunnels to escape Eros Station, but the viewer remains unclear about what that connection is ("Leviathan Wakes"). Naomi tries to avoid confronting her past during an exchange with Holden on Tycho Station, telling him she signed on to the *Cant* to avoid having conversations about her past ("Salvage"). We can gather that Naomi still understood the world she'd been involuntarily returned to, even if she simultaneously knew that world to be corrupt and no longer identified herself as a willing participant in it.

Tragically, Filip can't see past the world in which he's been raised, a world in which mass violence is justified, if not demanded for the sake of the Belt. He takes immense pride in participating in the mass murder of a quarter billion people. Naomi's rebuke of Filip is an attempt to open other worlds to him. She struggles to not be the person who was part of Marco's world, even if she can act the role with unnerving ease precisely because it is still part of who she is. At the same time, Naomi lives as *part of* that world and as *apart from* that world.

Contemporary philosopher Mariana Ortega could be describing Naomi, or any of us, when she writes, "We are multiple, both belonging to the herd and not belonging to it; we are the product of history and circumstances but also of our own making, not in the sense of a fully autonomous subject but of a multiplicitous self who is constantly and critically negotiating our given and chosen identities."[5] Naomi is a prime example of multiplicitous subjectivity, a self who is caught between her identities. Subjectivity means being a subject, instead of an object, one who has experiences and is capable of acting. A rock has no experiences; it is just an object in the world. A human is also an object in the world, but a human has experiences and makes choices. A human is a conscious being, a subject. To call subjectivity multiplicitous means that the subject can be, not just uniformly singular, but multidimensional. The multiplicitous subject can have conflicting experiences of the same thing in the same moment. Avasarala, for instance, has to navigate different experiences of the Eros incident while attempting to expose the Errinwright–Mao conspiracy. She both has to see things as one unaware of the conspiracy and see them as someone aware of the conspiracy and subject of her own conspiracy in order to survive and gather evidence to expose the conspiracy ("Leviathan Wakes").

Worlds and World Travel

Belters consistently point out that they do not receive full recognition from Inners. People living lives of subjugation must often move between worlds, including worlds where they aren't recognized as full subjects. Along these lines, Ortega discusses the plight of the subject who finds herself between worlds, who is a member of multiple worlds at the same time. "A multiplicitous subject may have a set of norms and practices from different cultures that are not consistent with each other; consequently, she may experience contradictions and feel fragmented."[6] Reverend Doctor Anna Volovodov has this kind of disorienting experience when arriving in her quarters on the UNN *Thomas Prince*. "Anna felt a brief moment of vertigo as the two different Annas she'd been reacted to the space in three different ways."[7] She was both an Earther and a European. Her room on the ship was monstrous for the navy, but claustrophobic for an Earther, and ordinary for a European.

The term "world" can mean different locations and different places, such as Mars and Ganymede Station, but it can also refer to shared sets of background meanings that help organize and sustain how we live and act together. At times, Naomi finds herself caught between the worlds of the Belter, which she consistently marks out as home, and the worlds of the Inners where Belters are treated poorly. Consider that in "Delta-V" Naomi leaves the *Roci* to serve on the *Behemoth* because "it's the Belt's time," only later to return to the *Roci*. Later still, she faces Murtry's anti-Belter bigotry on Ilus-IV; her status as part of a UN authorized mission under Avasarala's order makes no difference to him. At the same time, Belters on Ilus-IV view her ties with the UN as suspect ("New Terra").

Worlds in the social sense are open to change. They result from our collective action; we form and establish them together. Ortega observes, "not only are humans dependent on their context, but context itself is dependent on us."[8] Context helps inform how we interpret the world, but it is our interpretations, especially shared ones, that establish contexts. As such, no context is permanently fixed for all time. For example, Naomi notes the shifting of context throughout *Caliban's War* in which she confronts Holden and Amos, pointing out how they've become quicker to engage in preemptory acts of violence.

Just as one can travel between Earth and Mars, "one can 'travel' between these [social] 'worlds.'" Unlike places such as Earth and Mars, with worlds in the social sense, "one can inhabit more than one of these 'worlds' at the very same time."[9] Inhabiting multiple worlds simultaneously is a common part of the experiences of those subjugated or living at the margins of society. They have their own communal norms, whereby they affirm identities for themselves; but they also have to navigate the world of the dominant culture in which they face backlash for asserting themselves or defending themselves against aggressions. The contemporary philosopher Ofelia Schutte provides some insight.

> From a cultural standpoint as well as a psychoanalytical one, I have become a split subject. When I act as "myself" (in my reflexive sense of self, the "me" that includes and grows out of my early Cuban upbringing), my Anglo-American sociocultural environment will often mark me as "other." When, alternatively, I discursively perform the speaking position expected of a subject of the dominant culture, I am recognized as a real agent in the real world.[10]

In Schutte's case, Cuban identity doesn't go away because she plays into the dominant culture's norms in order to be recognized. Her feeling of being compromised, of working against herself, is there.[11] In Naomi's case, she finds herself split internally, caught between being a crewmate on the *Roci* and being a Belter, navigating also the factions throughout the Belt. Clearly, factional identities affect Belter identity, such as when Drummer sides with the factions against Ashford in letting Marco Inaros live ("Retrograde"). When Ashford joins the OPAS *Behemoth*, he keeps pressing Drummer on the importance of symbols of the Belt's unity—OPA uniforms, the *Behemoth*, not spacing the dealer selling pixie dust to the crew. This is important for the sake of unifying the nascent idea of a Belter nation, but also so the Inners see the Belt as united ("Delta-V").

Internal conflict illuminates the multiple worlds Naomi inhabits. Ashford asks Naomi who she thinks the Belt should be, listing the worlds she inhabited: "radical, betrayed, hid with the Inners, big hero" ("Delta-V"). Note how Ashford frames Naomi's time on the *Roci* in terms of hiding, something Naomi can both understand as a Belter and disagree with as a member of the *Roci*'s family. Here we may think of W. E. B. Du Bois' (1868–1963) famous discussion of the experience of double consciousness. Du Bois writes,

> It is a peculiar sensation, this double-consciousness, this sense of always looking at one's self through the eyes of others, of measuring one's soul by the tape of a world that looks on in amused contempt and pity. One ever feels his two-ness—an American, a Negro; two souls, two worlds, two unreconciled strivings; two warring ideals in one dark body, whose dogged strength alone keeps it from being torn asunder.[12]

Two-ness refers to two overlapping experiences of meaning that often don't agree with one another in the moment.[13] Much as Du Bois can see something the way a white world does while also seeing it as a black person, Naomi sees herself both as the Belt does and as the crew of the *Rocinante* does. Indeed, as Naomi illustrates, multiplicitous subjectivity acknowledges the possibility of more than two simultaneous meanings in experience.

Between Worlds and Borderlands

The multiplicitous self might experience multiple incompatible things at once.[14] Consider what happens after Miller kills Dresden, the Protogen scientist behind the Eros incident. Holden believes Miller murdered Dresden in cold blood. Naomi, on the other hand, experiences the killing in two ways: on the one hand, the way her captain and romantic partner views it, and on the other, as a fellow Belter, Miller, sees it. Speaking of Dresden, she says, "He was a monster with power, access, and allies who would have paid any price to keep his science project going. . . And I'm telling you as a Belter, Miller wasn't wrong."[15] She doesn't just interpret it in two ways as an intellectual exercise like a philosopher or therapist. Rather, she experiences it in its two-ness. She sees Dresden's death both as a Belter and as a crewmember onboard a ship where Inner interpretations dominate. Her experience is a direct result of the worlds she finds herself in and the dominant norms of those worlds. Likewise, in the streaming series, Naomi simultaneously knows that she should destroy the protomolecule and that she should give it to Fred Johnson ("Paradigm Shift").

In *Nemesis Games* we learn more about Naomi's past. She was young when she fell for Marco, and their relationship was one of manipulation, abuse, and gaslighting. Not long after Filip is born, Marco returns gloating about their shared "success" in getting "even for Terryon Lock" by having executed code Naomi had written on the *Gamarra*, killing its entire crew.[16]

Marco had people bring Naomi engineering problems to solve while recovering from Filip's difficult birthing. While in relative isolation, "she did them from goodwill and the need to do something intellectually challenging."[17] Naomi's discovery of her unintended and unknown contribution to mass murder shatters her naïveté. At the same time, she can be both proud of a clever bit of coding and horrified at how it was used. Either way she's unable to feel at home in the world shared with Marco and the radical factions of the OPA.

In framing spaces of meaning, the establishment of borders between worlds creates borderlands. Those who fail to conform to a given world's normative expectations often find themselves there. As Gloria Anzaldúa writes, "The prohibited and forbidden are its inhabitants. *Los atravesados* live here: the squint-eyed, the perverse, the queer, the troublesome, the mongrel, the mulato, the half-breed, the half dead; in short, those who cross over, pass over, or go through the confines of the 'normal.'"[18] Those who straddle borders are those denied an ability to be at home as themselves in the world. The inability to fit, figuratively or literally, to be marked out as deviant or alien, as other, impacts who someone is, how one understands herself and those around her, and is grounded in an experience of unease which permeates her engagements with the world.

If anyone knows what it means to inhabit a borderland, Belters do, living within and beyond the border between the inner and outer solar system. Discriminated against by Inners and subjected to economic exploitation, Belters are marked out by their distinctively multilinguistic creole and by the way their bodies have features exaggerated by living in low gravity.

In *Leviathan Wakes*, Miller and Naomi discuss with the rest of the crew of the *Roci* (all Inners) why someone might release the protomolecule on Eros Station, using over a million Belters as a science experiment. Naomi tells her crewmates, who've worked in the Belt awhile, they "still don't get us [Belters]. . . Not really. No one who grew up with free air ever will. And that's why they [Protogen] can kill a million and a half of us to figure out what their bug really does."[19] As the crew protest, Miller points out that Belters practically have their own language. He explains how his Earther ex-partner, Havelock, may have been smart and lived on Ceres Station a few years, but he lacked the knowledge of what it's like to be from the Belt. Havelock never lived as a Belter, never had formative experiences of being a Belter in a world indifferent to Belters. Living in the Belt doesn't make him a Belter. Miller insists that Inners see Belters as not "really human anymore" because of the changes to Belter bodies in low-g environments.[20]

Borders between social locations mark who is "in" and who is "out." Importantly, borders are enforced. Those in positions of social power, with privilege, enforce the borders to maintain their often-unjust power. Those without power also reinforce borders sometimes when they're socialized into thinking they should act a certain way. People with social privilege and power can be at ease or at home in the world. The subjugated or oppressed, however, always have to review their understanding and compliance with dominant norms, especially as those norms shift between worlds. Naomi effortlessly moves within most Belter contexts, but she has to think about her actions when abducted by Marco's crew, or while she's figuring out how to navigate meeting Holden's parents who are not just Earthers, but also a genetic collective of eight parents.

The feeling of not being at ease in the world is not always a bad thing.[21] If I'm too at ease, I'm not thinking, not reflecting on the things I'm doing and whether or not I should be doing them. In a society in which racist norms of acting are part of everyday life, one would simply replicate those norms uncritically. In a world in which slurs like "skinnies" and "dusters" are normalized, one might utter those slurs as a matter of course even though one should not feel at ease about using such language. Those actions are reinforced by one's shared history with others, that "we" speak this way and "we" accept it as within the norm to do so. As Ortega notes, "Even though all of us are multiplicitous selves, our experiences are greatly affected by relations of power influencing the construction, understanding, and regulation of our various social identities."[22]

One and Multitudes

Despite multiplicity, the self is still one in the sense that experience is always experienced by someone. "I" am the subject of my experiences, singular or multiply layered.[23] Just because each of us has one stream of experience doesn't mean that all of the experiences happening at one time in that stream are also singular. Instead, one might experience the same event in more than one way simultaneously. So, even if Naomi is one person, Naomi is not one-dimensional as a person. Rather, she is multiple, complex, and capable of experiencing multiple, possibly conflicting meanings at one time. Naomi's worlds and related sense of self may not ever fully play nice with one another, but that's okay. All of it is who Naomi is, no one part any more who Naomi is than any another.

Notes

1. James S. A. Corey, *Nemesis Games* (New York: Orbit Books, 2015), 93.
2. See especially the world-building opening episodes of *The Expanse*, "Dulcinea" and "The Big Empty." Watch especially the scenes in "Dulcinea" first where Miller and Havelock discuss differences in Belter physiology, then the scene of Avasarala's gravity torture of an OPA agent.
3. *Nemesis Games*, 219.
4. Ibid.

5. Mariana Ortega, "Multiplicity, Inbetweenness, and the Question of Assimilation," *Southern Journal of Philosophy* 46 (2008), 78.
6. Ibid., 73.
7. James S. A. Corey, *Abaddon's Gate* (New York: Orbit Books, 2013), 84. See "It Reaches Out," Season 3, Episode 8.
8. Mariana Ortega, "'New Mestizas,' 'World'-Travelers,' and '*Dasein*': Phenomenology and the Multi-Voiced, Multi-Cultural Self," *Hypatia* 16 (2001), 7.
9. María Lugones, "Playfulness, 'World'-Travelling, and Loving Perception," *Hypatia* 2 (1987), 10–11.
10. Ofelia Schutte, "Cultural Alterity: Cross-Cultural Communication and Feminist Theory in North–South Contexts," *Hypatia* 13 (1998), 60.
11. Consider here the various videos online of some US citizens demanding of Spanish speakers, and speakers of other foreign languages, that they "speak English" or "speak American" *because* they are in "America." The US as a country has no official language, even if its current dominant cultural norm generally favors English speaking. Schutte's point is that a similar demand to speak or hold oneself a certain way is prevalent even in less overtly confrontational cases.
12. W. E. B. Du Bois, *The Souls of Black Folk* (New York: Dover, 1994), 2.
13. An elaboration of this point in phenomenological philosophy is famously made by Frantz Fanon in *Black Skin, White Masks* (New York: Grove Press, 2008), ch. 5.
14. Mariana Ortega, *In-Between: Latina Feminist Phenomenology, Multiplicity, and the Self* (Albany: State University of New York Press, 2016), 59.
15. James S. A. Corey, *Leviathan Wakes* (New York: Orbit Books, 2011), 480. In the television series, these events take place in Season 2, Episodes 2–3.
16. *Nemesis Games*, 153.
17. Ibid., 151.
18. Gloria Anzaldúa, *Borderlands/La Frontera: The New Mestiza* (San Francisco: Aunt Lute Books, 1987), 3.
19. *Leviathan Wakes*, 390.
20. Ibid., 62.
21. Ortega, *In-Between*, 62.
22. Ibid., 71.
23. Ibid., 46.

22

Language Games in *The Expanse*
If a Lion Could *Showxa*, We Would Not *Pochuye* Him

Andrew Magrath

"If a lion could talk, we would not understand him." So wrote Ludwig Wittgenstein (1889–1951).[1] In *The Expanse*, the major powers do a great deal of talking, but don't have a great deal of understanding. When Belters ask if someone comprehends, they might use one of two phrases: *sasa ke?* or *pochuye ke?* In Belter Creole, these mean "Do you know what I'm saying?" and "Do you understand?" respectively. At first pass, little seems to differ between these two phrases and the underlying concepts of knowing versus understanding. Yet, the difference between knowing and understanding is the reason why the Inners can never seem to fully interpret, sympathize with, or perceive the world as the Belters do (and vice versa).

Within the novels, the people of Earth, Luna, and Mars (the Inners) are portrayed as sharing the same language. While the people of the Belt are able to understand and speak the solar system standard language, they also have their own wildly divergent creole that many Inners cannot understand. Belter Creole is a kaleidoscope of various languages that captures the diaspora of settlements and cultural isolation of the Belt. Without a Polaris such as Earth's history or Mars' mission of terraforming, the Belt is more a loosely organized collection of city-states than a culturally unified whole, and the language beautifully reflects the contradictions, slapdash, and intersectional nature of the Belt. Yet, this language difference also leads to the incomprehensibility of the Belt to an outsider. This incomprehensibility turns out to be a problem because the other most salient feature of the relationship between Inners and Belters is that they are locked in a generational conflict, a conflict that culminates in Earth's devastation at the hands of radicalized Belters.

Is this linguistic inability to understand each other at the root of the escalating conflict? One can easily imagine how a lack of communication

The Expanse and Philosophy: So Far Out Into the Darkness, First Edition. Edited by Jeffery L. Nicholas.
© 2022 John Wiley & Sons, Inc. Published 2022 by John Wiley & Sons, Inc.

leads to a lack of understanding, which leads to an empathy gap or a dehumanizing of the other side, which finally leads to open conflict. Maybe what is really needed between Belters and Inners is a shared understanding from which to negotiate.

The Expanse seems to reject this solution. The Inners could know what Belters are saying. They could take the time to translate Belter Creole into their language. Additionally, Belters know what Inners are saying—the two groups have a shared language—and could negotiate using the common tongue. Yet, neither side seems to understand the other because they lack the context that gives rise to understanding. The disagreement between Inners and Belters is not solely linguistic. The conflict is contextual, and Wittgenstein's lion may give us a deeper understanding of why.

Use–Mention Distinction

Before we begin, we need to make a philosophical distinction. Discussing language can be surprisingly difficult, because the only way to discuss language is with language and that peculiar arrangement can lead to some outright strangeness.

Imagine the following scene. The crew of the *Rocinante* enter a bar on Earth's moon. The barkeep takes one look at Naomi and tells her, "We don't serve skinnies here." Alex might respond, "It is not polite to call a lady a skinny." In this example, we would condemn the bartender for calling Naomi a slur, that is to say, the barkeep used the term, 'skinny.' We likely do not have the same negative response to Alex. Yet, he too said the hurtful word aloud. The difference is that Alex is mentioning the term, not using it. He is pointing out that a word is hurtful, not using it to hurt. While in both instances someone has said a potentially harmful word, in one case, the person was using the word, and in the other a person was mentioning it.

We often discuss what words mean, but at times, we also want to discuss a word itself. Within philosophy, when a person uses a word, they are invoking its meaning. In most of our communications, we are using words. More often than not, when we say a word, we are attempting to convey the meaning of that word within a shared understanding of the language. On the other hand, to mention a word is to talk about the word itself. In these instances, the word is not being used—we are not saying the word because of its meaning. When we mention a word, the word is being brought up, talked about, or some aspect of the word itself is being discussed. We call this distinction of invoking a word's meaning versus talking about a word itself the use–mention distinction.

This philosophically important point, by the way, becomes moot if Alex never got to say anything because Amos jumped the bar and punched the barkeep in the face.

Consider another example. "Mars has four letters." This sentence mentions the word 'Mars.' The sentence is not trying to convey information about the red planet. It is pointing out a fact about the word itself. On the other hand, the sentence, "The Laconians originated on Mars," uses the word 'Mars.' We are being given a fact about the planet and its history. As basic as the use–mention distinction may appear, keeping it straight as we talk about language is necessary. To help do so, philosophers have developed a way of notating the use–mention distinction. When we mention a word, we place it in single quotes to indicate that we are not intending to think about what the word means but rather talk about it as a bit of linguistic stuff—a word. We can, thus, properly rewrite my examples of mentioning words above:

It is not polite to call a lady a 'skinny.'
'Mars' has four letters.

Much better!
From here on out, let's keep the use–mention distinction in mind.

Wittgenstein

Wittgenstein and Fred Johnson would have seen something in each other.

Eccentric, reclusive, and hot-tempered, Ludwig Wittgenstein is a key philosopher in the examination of language and meaning. Wittgenstein was born in 1889 to wealthy Austrian parents. His philosophical studies centered around how to express meaning and why conveying meaning so often breaks down. He grew convinced that many philosophical problems were at their root linguistic problems. If one could understand how language worked, one could solve philosophy. In his youth, he believed he had done just that and retired from the field.

Yet, Wittgenstein returned to philosophy later in life. One of the things that makes Wittgenstein such a fascinating philosopher is how drastically his thinking changed over time. His later works, some of the most important published posthumously, are highly critical of his earlier thoughts. Wittgenstein began his career arguing that meaning comes from a word's ability to create pictures in the minds of others, but he ended his career arguing that context is where meaning can be found.

The Picture Book Model of Language

In Wittgenstein's earlier writings he articulates the picture book model of language (although Wittgenstein used the example of a museum).[2] Language's job seems to be to convey meaning to help others understand the thoughts of the speaker. We'll use the word 'speaker' to mean more broadly someone using language in any form. Language can be written, spoken, signed, and so forth, but it is convention to refer to any language user as a 'speaker.' This convention does not imply that only audible language is legitimate. All language (be it spoken, signed, written, read, or communicated by some other means) is legitimate. All forms of language attempt the same thing: to convey meaning. Wittgenstein's early work is novel in that he asserts that we see the world largely as pictures in our mind's eye; most of our thoughts are pictures. The job of language is to transmit these pictures from one mind to another.

Suppose you wanted to learn Belter Creole. If language is about linking pictures to words, the best way to do that is with picture books. Imagine a massive picture book containing every word in Belter Creole along with its meaning as a picture. Looking through the book, you come to a page with a picture of a flat-sided, rectangular container. As a speaker of English, you call this object a 'box,' but in our Belter Creole picture book, you see the word 'boite' written. You know from experience that every time you say 'box' to a speaker of English, they get a mental picture of a flat-sided, rectangular container. Now you are confident that every time you say the word 'boite' to a speaker of Belter Creole, they also will get a mental picture of a similarly flat-sided, rectangular container. Thus, 'box' and 'boite' are synonyms (albeit in different languages) because they create the same mental picture. The revelation that 'box' and 'boite' are the same because they create the same mental picture is particularly important because, if words do not convey the same mental image, they are not the same. This is why the words 'Clarissa Mao' and 'Melba Koh' are synonyms, but the words 'Clarissa Mao' and 'Julie Mao' are not. Under the picture book model of language, to learn a language is just to learn the words used to represent these pictures.

This idea seems reasonable. We often teach children language using this technique. Parents hold up a ball and repeat 'ball' over and over until the child associates the image of the ball with the word. If the picture book model of language is how language works, either Belters need to speak the common language, or the Inners need to actually learn Belter Creole.

Not so fast!

Imagine a character introduced early in *The Expanse* who consistently refers to the *Rocinante* as the 'MCRN *Tachi*' or simply '*Tachi*.' That would provide insight into the character's thinking without needing a single line of exposition about the character. From this one line, we likely gather that the character does not view Holden and company's claim on the ship to be valid and that the character likely sees the ship as the legal property of the Martian navy. We can begin to form theories about the character: they are likely an Inner because Belters by and large subscribe to the salvage rights that Holden is claiming; the character may harbor sympathies to Mars; and so forth. Maybe our assumptions are correct or maybe they are wrong, but just one word gave the reader a great deal of information about how this character sees the world.

We may be tempted to believe that the words '*Rocinante*' and 'MCRN *Tachi*' mean the same thing because they both create the same mental picture—the ship that the primary protagonists of *The Expanse* live and work in—and that if we were communicating, we could use these words interchangeably. In practice, however, the words are not interchangeable. The difference in meaning is enough to change the way we understand what is being said. Holden would not tolerate someone calling his ship the '*Tachi*.' The Martian navy did not tolerate someone calling the ship the '*Rocinante*.' Even though both words refer to the same object and create the same mental picture, the different words reveal different attitudes about that object.

This is a serious challenge to the picture book model of language. The model asserts that if the words all name the same object and create the same mental pictures, they are equivalent: 'box' is equivalent to 'boite,' 'Martian' is equivalent to 'tumang,' and so on. Yet, in practice, '*Tachi*' and '*Rocinante*' are not synonyms. If an MCRN commander calls that ship '*Tachi*,' but Holden calls the ship '*Rocinante*,' the two do not really understand each other. They both have the same mental picture and understand that the word used by the other refers to that picture, but they do not agree. It seems that these words, despite naming the same object, do not actually mean the same thing. What the picture book model of language fails to account for is context, and, according to Wittgenstein's later work, context is where meaning really resides.

The Language Game Model of Language

Wittgenstein rejected his earlier belief in the picture book model of language in part because he came to believe that language does more than just pass pictures back and forth.

In later writings, Wittgenstein argues that language works much like a game, relying on contextual rules and actions to guide and form meaning.[3] Just because Wittgenstein describes language as games does not mean that he believes it to be trivial or frivolous. Games are serious business to Wittgenstein. "To imagine a [game] means to imagine a form of life."[4] We will call this theory of language, the language game model of language.

Think of this scene. Even as the solar system is seemingly falling apart, Naomi tells a distraught Holden that, "It's going to be okay." Her language is doing something, but it probably is not trying to shove some image of a solar system doing okay into Holden's mind. Naomi is comforting Holden. Her language is meant to convey a feeling, not a series of pictures. A distraught Holden may respond by listing off all of the terrible things happening at that moment, all of the unknown threats gathering around them, all the people they have lost, and on through the list of horrible things that have befallen the crew. Yet, she is not playing that game. Her words are not meant to be taken as a geopolitical statement of fact. She is not playing the "it is factually the case that the entire universe will be okay" language game. She is playing the "reassurance" language game. She is playing the "loving partner and friend" language game. She is doing something very different with language than what the picture book model of language can describe.

Wittgenstein picks games as his model for how language works because games are so incredibly varied. In some games the lowest score wins, others the highest. Some games involve cards, others physical movement, others are electronic. Games can be communal or solitary. Games can be easy or difficult. Games can be competitive or cooperative or some combination of both. Games are incredibly diverse, dynamic, and have a wide range of rules. Yet, those rules apply only to that specific game. If someone were playing baseball and suddenly dealt a three of clubs, we would be perplexed. The rules of baseball do not work that way. Yet, if one were playing blackjack, one would expect to be dealt a card because that is a rule within the context of the ruleset for blackjack. All games, including language games, have contexts where certain actions make sense and certain actions do not.

Imagine that Dr. Elvi Okoye is in her lab dissecting a specimen. She might turn to her assistant and say, "Scalpel." This is not a grammatical sentence; yet, the assistant understands the context of this situation and the language game being played. The rules of the language game are, Okoye names instruments that she would like handed to her and the assistant hands them over. Okoye might next say, "Gene sequencer," and the assistant will give her that tool. If Okoye asks for a bone saw, but the assistant hands her toothpaste, the rules of the game are no longer being properly followed and meaning has collapsed. Like the shortstop being dealt a card in the middle of a baseball game, something went wrong here.

People achieve meaning when all sides play the same language game.

Imagine further that Dr. Okoye and her assistant are attending a Laconian state dinner. During cocktails, Okoye makes a joke, saying to her assistant, "Crab cake," and the assistant hands her a crab cake. Okoye keeps the joke going, "Champagne" and the assistant grabs a flute and dutifully places it in Okoye's hand as if they were still within the context of the lab. Understanding why this is a joke relies upon understanding the context of the pair's relationship and the language games they play. We expect the assistant to fetch tools for Okoye while they are in the lab. The language used at the party is a joke because they are playing this laboratory language game in a silly situation. Parties do not normally go this way. Playing this language game here is absurd; in the absurdity lies the humor.

Yet, without the understanding of language games, this situation may not appear as a joke to an outsider. If you had no knowledge of who Okoye or the assistant were, or how they interact within their normal workdays, it might appear that Dr. Okoye is throwing the weight of her position around in a distasteful manner, making some poor lab assistant fetch her hors d'oeuvres. Put differently, the joke only registers as a joke if we are in on the language games being played. Despite the facts that Okoye used a language we speak, used words we know the definitions of, and was in a situation we generally understand, all the heavy lifting of understanding the interaction was done by the language game—the context.

The picture book model of language fails to truly capture the rich and diverse abilities of language. It is stark and barren, failing to account for language's playfulness, complexity, subtlety, and ability to comfort or harm. Wittgenstein came to believe that the language game model of language is able to better provide an account of the full diversity of language's roles and what it can do. Importantly, the model shows that language can be as varied as games with just as many ways to play, ways to win, and ways to interact.

The language game model of language also better explains why Belters and the Inners seem doomed to fail to communicate.

The Language Games the Solar System Plays

Let's circle back to the distinction between the two initial questions in Belter Creole: *sasa ke?* and *pochuye ke?* The ability of language games to convey meaning lies in the distinction between knowing what is being said versus understanding what is being said. Wittgenstein's saying that "If a lion could talk, we would not understand him"[5] is about *sasa* versus *pochuye*, knowing versus understanding. Wittgenstein is imagining a lion that can speak the language that you speak. To hear the lion talk, you would recognize every word, be able to define every word. You would know the language; but you would not understand the lion. To understand the lion requires knowledge of the context, but that context is utterly alien. Even speaking your language, the lion would have such a different worldview stemming from such a vastly dissimilar experience of life and value system that it would be incomprehensible.

For example, among lions when an upstart male ousts a dominant male from the pride, the usurper male will often kill all of the cubs of the previously dominant male. The loss of the young cubs causes the females of the pride to reenter estrus, allowing the usurper the chance to reproduce. If a male lion were to explain this practice to us humans, we would certainly know what he is talking about. However, if that male lion were to extol the action's virtue, explain in detail the excitement of killing the cubs and thrill of the rewards, we could not understand the lion. We know what actions and outcomes the lion is talking about, but we cannot understand the joy it feels or why the lion sees the murder of children as virtuous. It is not that we fail to know what the lion is describing; it is that we cannot understand the context of what is being described. We can *sasa* the lion, but we cannot *pochuye* him. Put in Wittgensteinian terms, the lion and humans are not playing the same language game.

The major players in *The Expanse* inhabit this state of affairs. They know what each other is saying. When Belters say they are oppressed, Mars and Earth know what those words mean (so long as it is said in the solar system standard language), but they cannot understand what is being said. They are not privy to the lived experience of the Belt. They can know but not understand. Similarly, the Belt looks upon the Inners as a unified oppressor, unable to understand fractures between Mars and Earth or within these societies. The Belt can know that Earth and Mars are different entities but cannot understand them as anything but a monolithic oppressor. Earth and Mars too cannot see beyond the context that they exist within. In *The Expanse*, everyone is always playing a different language game, and very little meaning can come from the situation.

One of the small but demonstrative examples of the different language games the major powers play concerns beliefs surrounding Earth's universal basic assistance, or 'Basic' for short. Despite being far from a utopian system, Avasarala often argues for the necessity of Basic and seemingly takes a degree of pride in maintaining such a comprehensive welfare state. Most characters from Earth seem to view the program favorably or neutrally. While most characters from Earth may not want to be on Basic, they do not express disdain for the program itself.

In contrast, the Martians, as seen through Bobby's attitudes, view Basic as a reward for laziness. During Bobby's trip to meet Avasarala for the first time, she expresses scorn for the program. The Martian worldview is tied so completely to accomplishing the terraforming of the planet that the idea that individuals in a society would not have jobs or contribute is antithetical to the project of Mars. In a different contrast, Belters see Basic as a sign of lavishness. Marco Inaros radicalizes others by manipulating perceptions of the supposed opulence of Earth—including Basic. From the Belt's perspective, the abundance of Earth is a direct result of the imperial role Earth has played in the Belt's development: stripping supplies and keeping Belters in relative poverty so that resources could be pushed down the gravity well. Judging Basic, as an expression of Earth's supposed opulence, as a moral evil is easy.

In each instance, the various sides may be able to understand why the other views Basic the way they do, but they likely cannot have a deeper experience of understanding. They cannot see eye-to-eye (-to-eye) because they are all caught up in the language games they are playing. Where Earth plays the language game of post-scarcity superpower and Mars plays the language game of driven upstart, the Belt plays the language game of liberation.

Unfortunately for all concerned, these language games are incompatible.

After the Free Navy's devastating attack on Earth, Holden's family meet Naomi in person for the first time. They played the language games of love, support, and meeting the romantic partner of their child very well. Yet, before Holden and crew set off again, a member of Holden's family refers to Belters by the slur 'skinnies.' In that moment, Holden is caught between two worlds, two language games. He can both know and understand his family's anger: Earth is dying, and the person responsible was a Belter. Yet, he also loves a Belter, has worked with and deeply respects Belters. By gaining a context that his parents do not have, Holden, at least to some degree, is able to play both language games at once. He can understand both the righteous anger of the language games played by Earth and the pained horror and victimization of being painted by a single brush language game so much of the Belt plays. He cannot explain any of this to his parents, however. In this instance, he is a lion, and they would not understand him even if he tried to speak.

These two examples are pretty low-level: an economic policy and an ethnic slur used casually. Yet, even at this basic, foundational level of communication, understanding has fallen apart. If Earth, Mars, and the Belt cannot understand each other on even the small things, then how can meaning take root at the grand political level of the solar system? The colonized can use the language of the colonizers, but the colonized will never have the frame of reference required to actually speak to the colonizers. Likewise, the colonizers may try to speak to the colonized, but they can never understand the context of the colonized. Despite differences in language, the world of *The Expanse* is one where the sides know what each other is saying. Unfortunately, though, it is also one where the sides do not understand each other. They are playing different language games.

Some of them are even playing the language game of genocide.

It is interesting here to note that the Sol System does eventually come to play the same language game, but it takes the upending of most previous language games, the opening of the Ring System and everything that follows. Easy access to planets rich with resources lead to abandoning zero and low-G environments, which results in the Belt's language games of survival no longer needing to be played. The Laconian subjugation of the Sol System means Earth's cultural dominance language game can no longer be played. Thousands of habitable worlds mean the language game of the Martian terraforming project is no longer being played at its generational scale.

We can also see this language game shift at the personal level. Bobby finds the Laconians both familiar and foreign. She often recognizes

Martian language games in Laconian society, but from her perspective, these Martian language games have been twisted. At both the geopolitical and personal levels, as the language games played by the Laconians diverge from the language games played by their Martian lineage, the gulf in understanding between the two grows. Similarly, as Duarte, High Consul of the Laconian Empire, becomes more and more whatever it is he is becoming, he is likewise rendered more and more inscrutable as he starts to play language games that no other human has ever (nor can ever) play.

On the Other Side of the Ring: A Difficult Consequence

Philosophy encourages us to circle back around and look at any position we advocate for to see if that position might also have flaws or create new (possibly more vexing!) problems. If you are now convinced that the language game model of language is how it all works, well, this view has some consequences that might have to be addressed.

One of my favorite science-fiction series remains next generation-era *Star Trek*. The optimism in all three series set within that timeframe can be incredibly comforting, and I find myself returning to the series again and again. Perhaps the biggest reason why is because next generation-era *Star Trek* argues that if we can know each other's languages, we can understand one another, and, through that understanding, we can build a better future for all parties. *Star Trek*'s utopianism can be supremely comforting, particularly to someone interested in philosophy. It imagines a world where problems can be solved through discussion, applying reason, compassion, and a willingness to see issues through multiple perspectives. Unfortunately, if meaning is found in context and language games, it seems this kind of utopian view is hopelessly and woefully naïve. Without a shared context of experience, history, and culture, it seems impossible to believe species could find sufficient context to communicate and play the same language game. We would all be lions to each other. To think that we might traverse the unfathomable distances between stars, find other advanced civilizations, and never understand them is an existential kind of tragic. It also might be fatal.

The Expanse offers two alien species, the Ring Builders and the Unknown Aggressors. Throughout the series, humans attempt to understand them but fail. If the language game model is correct, then it seems understanding will always be out of reach. Wittgenstein's lion cannot be understood because the context of our worlds, our language games, is so different.

Despite the fact that lions and humans have much in common—mammals, live on Earth, and so forth—we still could not find enough common ground to really understand each other. Within *The Expanse*, Inners and Belters have even more in common—same species, common languages, shared histories, and so forth; yet, even that is not enough to create the shared context required for them to play the same language games. Even with all of these shared contexts, a shared meaning could not take root without the radical upending of the way the solar system had existed for hundreds of years. If humanity could not create a successful series of language games even among humans, how can it possibly hope to create a context where it understands the truly alien?

The Unknown Aggressors do not seem to inhabit the same physical universe as humanity, making it hard to believe that even the austere offerings of the picture book model of language could produce a shared understanding. How can you teach an alien our word for tree when even the atoms making up the tree do not exist within the same physical reality as the aliens? Without even a physical reality to share, the real horror of the Unknown Aggressors is not their unfathomable power, but that they are truly unknowable.

In both the starkness of his early works and vibrancy of his later works, Wittgenstein focuses on the need of human beings to communicate and desire to communicate clearly. To be understood and to understand others is, for Wittgenstein, a deeply ingrained human drive. It comes as no surprise, then, that the end of our examination of meaning and of language produces melancholy. We did all of this work just to realize that, even if we all shared the same language, we could never really understand Belters or Ring Builders and certainly not Unknown Aggressors. In the world of *The Expanse*, humanity may be exterminated wholesale by the Unknown Aggressors and even if the Aggressors explained their actions to us in a human language, humanity (and the readers) would never be able to understand why the Aggressors did it. It is not a particularly happy end to this examination, but, given the harshness of the world presented in *The Expanse*, it is perhaps a fitting one.

The Expanse shows that the type of understanding required to have a life well lived does not often arise at the geopolitical scale, but through the small, personal relations we develop along the way. We may never understand the machinations of Mars, but we understand where Bobby and Alex are coming from. Earth's politics is all wheels within wheels, but we know what Holden, Amos, and Clarissa mean when they speak. The Belt is a loose collection of languages, cultures, and locations that barely make sense even to itself, but Naomi is understandable. Maybe all we can really hope for is that we are understood by and understand those closest to us.

Maybe that is enough.

Notes

1. Ludwig Wittgenstein, *Philosophical Investigations*, 4th edition, trans. G. E. M. Anscombe, P. M. S. Hacker, and Joachim Schulte (Oxford: Wiley Blackwell, 2009), §327.
2. See Ludwig Wittgenstein, *Tractatus Logico-Philosophicus*, trans. C. K. Ogden (Edinburgh: Kegan Paul, Trench, Trubner & Co., 1922).
3. Wittgenstein, *Philosophical Investigations*.
4. Ibid., §19.
5. Ibid., §327.

Appendix:
The Expanse Episodes List

Season 1

Episode 1: "Dulcinea"
Episode 2: "The Big Empty"
Episode 3: "Remember the Cant"
Episode 4: "CQB"
Episode 5: "Back to the Butcher"
Episode 6: "Rock Bottom"
Episode 7: "Windmills"
Episode 8: "Salvage"
Episode 9: "Critical Mass"
Episode 10: "Leviathan Wakes"

Season 2

Episode 1: "Safe"
Episode 2: "Doors & Corners"
Episode 3: "Static"
Episode 4: "Godspeed"
Episode 5: "Home"
Episode 6: "Paradigm Shift"
Episode 7: "The Seventh Man"
Episode 8: "Pyre"
Episode 9: "The Weeping Somnambulist"
Episode 10: "Cascade"
Episode 11: "Here There Be Dragons"
Episode 12: "The Monster and the Rocket"
Episode 13: "Caliban's War"

The Expanse and Philosophy: So Far Out Into the Darkness, First Edition. Edited by Jeffery L. Nicholas.
© 2022 John Wiley & Sons, Inc. Published 2022 by John Wiley & Sons, Inc.

Season 3

Episode 1: "Fight or Flight"
Episode 2: "IFF"
Episode 3: "Assured Destruction"
Episode 4: "Reload"
Episode 5: "Triple Point"
Episode 6: "Immolation"
Episode 7: "Delta-V"
Episode 8: "It Reaches Out"
Episode 9: "Intransigence"
Episode 10: "Dandelion Sky"
Episode 11: "Fallen World"
Episode 12: "Congregation"
Episode 13: "Abaddon's Gate"

Season 4

Episode 1: "New Terra"
Episode 2: "Jetsam"
Episode 3: "Subduction"
Episode 4: "Retrograde"
Episode 5: "Oppressor"
Episode 6: "Displacement"
Episode 7: "A Shot In The Dark"
Episode 8: "The One-Eyed Man"
Episode 9: "Saeculum"
Episode 10: "Cibola Burn"

Season 5

Episode 1: "Exodus"
Episode 2: "Churn"
Episode 3: "Mother"
Episode 4: "Gaugamela"
Episode 5: "Down and Out"
Episode 6: "Tribes"
Episode 7: "Oyedeng"
Episode 8: "Hard Vacuum"
Episode 9: "Winnipesaukee"
Episode 10: "Nemesis Games"

Index

Episodes are shown in inverted commas

The Expanse and Philosophy: So Far Out Into the Darkness, First Edition. Edited by Jeffery L. Nicholas.
© 2022 John Wiley & Sons, Inc. Published 2022 by John Wiley & Sons, Inc.